TOMORROW'S
RAINBOW

Previous books by Sara Hylton,
author of *Tomorrow's Rainbow*:

The Hills Are Eternal
The Whispering Glade
The Talisman of Set
The Crimson Falcon
Jacintha
Caprice

TOMORROW'S RAINBOW

Sara Hylton

St. Martin's Press
New York

Library of Congress Cataloging-in-Publication Data

Hylton, Sara.
      Tomorrow's rainbow / by Sara Hylton.
         p.   cm.
   ISBN 0-312-01523-2
   I. Title.
PR6058.Y63T6 1988
823'.914—dc19
                                                    87-27479
                                                      CIP

First published in Great Britain by Century Hutchinson Ltd.

First U.S. Edition

10 9 8 7 6 5 4 3 2 1

I dedicate this book to Nancy, my Canadian friend, in memory of the happy time we spent in Egypt, and the most wonderful holiday we enjoyed in Canada

> Now is the only time you own
> Decide now what you will,
> Place faith not in tomorrow
> For the clock may then be still

from the wall of a Coptic church in Old Cairo

TOMORROW'S RAINBOW

Chapter 1

They overwhelmed our tiny living room, sitting like three black crows as they lectured my gentle grieving mother on how she should manage the rest of her life. They were Grandmother Cassidy and the Widows Murphy and Malone, all three clad in deepest mourning although why they had attired themselves in such a parody of grief I shall never know since Grandmother had hated my father and the two neighbours had regarded him as a man of little consequence.

There had surely never been a funeral in Dunfanaghy to rival that of my father and yet most of those people who thronged the streets and the tiny churchyard scarcely knew him in life, and those who did had had little to say on his behalf. The priest extolled his virtues, calling him a hero, a man of God who had not been afraid to lay down his own life in order to save another, but these high-flown phrases meant little to me as I stood clutching my brother Terrence's hand and listening to my mother's quiet sobbing as she cradled my sister Eileen in her arms.

I was thirteen years old and I had never been to a funeral before, not even Grandfather Cassidy's, because my father had insisted that children had no place at funerals, that life would punish them soon enough. Now when I looked round at faces familiar and unfamiliar I could not believe that never again would I walk with my father through the soft summer rain, listening to his stories of chivalry and enchantment, or sit with him on Horn Head watching the seabirds wheeling gracefully above the waves, their voices echoing mournfully across the lofty cliffs of Croaghnammady.

Father had filled my childhood with poetry and the

1

knowledge he had learned from books, largely self-taught. While the other men fished the streams and thronged the race tracks my father pored over his books, but it was true he had never been known to keep a job for longer than a few months.

He had only been in his last employment at the Wilcox stables for just over three weeks when he was killed stopping a runaway horse carrying Major Wilcox's young daughter, and suddenly Michael O'Donovan was a hero and my mother was a widow and we were his fatherless children.

I stole a swift glance at my grandmother's impassive face under her Sunday-best black hat and I remembered all the harsh words she had said about him. How she had held up her own two sons as shining examples when compared to my father's shiftlessness; and my mother's tears after Grandmother had left us, so that I wished savagely that she would never set foot in our cottage again. Grandmother Cassidy lived in the big red-brick house at the top of the rise while we lived in a two-up and two-down cottage on the straggling street that led downhill to the shore.

To say that my mother had been a disappointment to her was an understatement. Her eldest son, Uncle Shamus, had emigrated to America when he was just twenty and from his letters home he appeared to be doing very well. Uncle Turlough lived in England and was employed in one of the cotton mills in Lancashire, with his own house, two daughters and a good Catholic girl for a wife. My mother on the other hand had married the village ne'er do well, handsome, charming Michael O'Donovan who was neither a good Catholic, a steady worker nor a good provider.

Those gathered round the graveside were throwing handfuls of soil on to the coffin. They fell with dull thuds into the open grave and I cowered back, hating the hollow sound, then we were leaving the graveside to walk back along the paths, and the crowd parted to make way for us. The women were wiping their eyes with their aprons, the men were raising their hats and as we reached the gates a smartly dressed man stepped forward and took my

2

mother's hand. I recognized him as Major Wilcox because he had been the one to visit our cottage to break the news of my father's death.

'This is a sad business, Mrs O'Donovan,' he said grimly. 'Please don't hesitate to come to me for help should it be needed.'

'Thank you sir,' my mother said softly, 'we shall manage.'

'I have taken care of the funeral expenses. If it had not been for your husband it would be my little girl they would be burying today.'

For a brief moment he let his hand rest on my head, then shaking his head sadly he turned away.

I was hoping my grandmother would not return to the cottage with us but I soon realized that she intended to come, as well as the two widows. Mother rushed about making tea and I helped to fill plates with home-baked scones and fruit loaf, then we sat in miserable silence watching the three black-clad figures making short work of the humble repast.

Grandmother looked round the room and sniffed disdainfully.

'How soon can you be packed and out o' this place?' she demanded.

'Packed!' my mother echoed, stupefied.

'Certainly I mean packed. There's no way you can keep this cottage on without a man's wages comin' in. I'll be payin' Peter O'Grady a week's rent, he'll not have the gall to ask for a penny more,' my grandmother snapped.

'But this is our home, these are our own things around us. Michael would never have wanted me to leave the cottage.'

'Michael O'Donovan didn't think about ye or the children when he flung himself after that runaway horse, did he? You'll have to be practical Mary, your man's gone and there'll be no money comin' in. That lass'll be leavin school any time an' there's plenty to do in a house the size o' mine. I don't suppose she's given any thought to what she wants to do with her loife.'

Before she could say another word I interrupted.

3

'Mother, you know what Father always said, that we'd go to the city and there'd be work in plenty.'

'Hold your tongue, girl,' Grandmother snapped irritably. 'Your father was a romantic dreamer with his head in the clouds. I'll not have you fillin' your mother's head with such foolishness. The city indeed, and him without a penny to his name and changin' his jobs as often as he changed his socks.'

'Mother, please,' my mother murmured, 'not in front of the children.'

'You'll 'ave trouble with that one or my name's not Janie Cassidy. She's loike her father, it's the other two that's loike yourself. Why she even looks like him, the other two are Cassidys fer sure.'

It is true that I was like my father. I was small for my age and thin whereas my father had been a big man, tall and broad shouldered, but I had his dark red hair and clear blue eyes, and my mouth was generous, with that same whimsical curve to it. Both my brother and sister were dark like the Cassidys, with large brown eyes, and Terrence spoke only when he was spoken to and had none of my independent spirit.

'I'll be sendin' Alice down tonight to help you pack your bags, and I'll let O'Grady call round with his handcart to bring them up to the house, he owes me a favour or two.'

'But Mother, we can't leave tonight, I need time to sort things out, besides there's the furniture to see to and the household linen.'

'I wants none of your furniture. My house is furnished from top to bottom, there'll be no room for any of this.'

'But these are our things, Mother, we can't leave them here.'

'You can sell them, you'll not be gettin' much for them but you'll be glad of the money. Some of the neighbours might take a few things off your hands and the rest can go to Cavanagh's. Old Mrs Cavanagh'll give you very little but like I said the money'll come in handy.'

I ran to my mother's side, pleading with her to stay, not to sell our things or leave the cottage, but Grandmother

4

Cassidy took my shoulder in a grip of iron and pulled me away.

'Make yourself useful, girl,' she commanded, 'and stop interfering in things you know nothing about. You can't afford to stay here and you're a lucky girl to be offered a home with me, just when I thought I'd got all mi children off mi hands, even when I've always had misgivings about the mess our Mary's made of her life.'

'Do as your grandmother asks, Kathleen,' Mother said anxiously, and to save the peace I collected the cups and saucers and carried them into the little kitchen at the back of the parlour.

I could hear their voices through the open doorway and I clenched my teeth in anger.

How could I bear to live in my grandmother's dark old house surrounded by ponderous furniture, with old Alice cackling like a demented thing as she went about her work and Mother tearful and miserable?

The two widows were adding their advice, and I could hear them sorting out our furniture, both of them anxious to get their hands on it even if Grandmother had proclaimed it worthless.

'That little sideboard'll do nicely for our Maeve,' Widow Malone was saying, 'and her gitting married in November. They've got a little cottage about this size, it'll go very nicely agin' the far wall.'

'An I'd like yer bookcase, Mary. Oi'll pay ye for it if it's not too expensive, but mi grandson's taken to books, clever he is, he'll be glad of it one day. Will you be partin' with any of Michael's books?'

'Oh Mrs Malone, I can't part with Michael's books. Kathleen reads a lot, her father would haved liked her to have them.'

'I'll not have her lazing about with her head stuck into a lot of books,' Grandmother interrupted. 'There's plenty to be done in a house that size and old Alice is getting past the heavy work. Besides it's all good training for when she's older and like as not married. A good hard-working wife is what a man wants, not a girl with her head filled with rubbish from books.'

I couldn't bear to hear any more. Snatching my coat from a nail in the kitchen I escaped out of the back door and ran sobbing along the street. I was crying for my father, for the ending of the old, and the beginning of the new which held little promise of happiness for any of us.

Without caring where I was going I took the old familiar pathway that led towards Horn Head, and it was there sitting on a familiar crag that I poured out my grief and anger to the wheeling gulls and the tossing sea. I shivered a little, pulling my coat closer round me. The rays of the setting sun slanted through clouds darkened by rain, and for the first time I could feel it on my face as well as the taste of salt on my lips. Expectantly I looked out across the sea and then I saw it, the beginning of a rainbow.

A long time ago I had sat with my father on Horn Head watching a rainbow dying in the sky and I had wept bitter tears at its passing.

With his arm around my shoulders Father had said, 'Don't you be cryin' after rainbows, Katie, there'll be another tomorrow, if not here somewhere else. Sure and there's always a rainbow if you knows where to look for it.'

I had looked many times for a rainbow but until this moment I had never found one, and as it sprang into beautiful colourful life I watched it with the rain on my face and the wind in my hair. It was as though my father had sent a message of hope into my shattered life.

Chapter 2

The six months we spent in my grandmother's house are a recurring nightmare. I hated the kitchen. It smelled permanently of carbolic, which Alice used to scrub the table top and the flagged floor, and I hated the dustsheets which were kept on the chairs in the parlour except for Sunday afternoons when Father McGinty called to pay his respects.

My bedroom was cold and cheerless and I was not allowed to bring my friend Mary McAuley into the house because Grandmother said her folk were little better than tinkers. It is true they were as poor as church mice but her father earned a pittance working on the land and he had nine children to support. Freckle-faced Mary was the youngest, with a mop of carroty curls on her pert little head. She was almost a year older than me but she was considerably smaller and painfully thin.

I was not allowed to read because Grandmother said I must learn to cook and sew and clean the house. Father's books were packed away in a suitcase and stored in the loft. I complained bitterly to Mr Moran, our schoolteacher, but he was as frightened of my grandmother as I was and refused to take any part in the argument.

'Do as your grandmother says,' he admonished me, 'she's giving you a good home and aims to make a good woman out of you. Books can come later.'

Three weeks after we went to Grandmother's house she got rid of Alice, Alice who had worked her fingers to the bone for her for nigh on thirty years, giving the excuse that the old woman was senile, disobedient and slipshod. No amount of pleading on Alice's part moved her stony heart one jot. Alice departed, carrying her few possessions in an old carpet bag and Mary told me she was living in an old shepherd's shack which was no longer in use.

I was appalled by the shack. There was a dirt floor and no lighting, though a local farmer had been good enough to set down straw for her to sleep on. A peat fire burned on a stone hearth in the corner and she insisted on making tea for me in a cooking pot which seemed to be her only cooking utensil. The tea was strong and nauseous but I made myself drink it so as not to offend her.

I shivered in the biting wind that found its way in through the cracks but she seemed unaware of it in her old navy-blue serge coat, which she had worn for as long as I could remember.

'It's cold you are, lassy,' she mumbled, 'yer shouldn't 'ave come up here on sich a cold day.'

'How can you bear to live in this place Alice? You'll catch your death of cold. How I hate my grandmother for making you leave her.'

'Ay well, herself's not come to the end of 'er loife yet, she'll be paid out for what she's done to old Alice, make no mistake.'

'Why don't you go to see Father McGinty? He'll find you a better place than this.'

She cackled lewdly. 'Not he, and he as frightened of Janie Cassidy as the rest of 'em. Doesn't he sit all Sunday afternoon in her parlour while she plies 'im with whiskey, what'd happen to his Sunday afternoons if he spoke out for me then?'

'But why, after all these years, Alice?'

'Well hasn't she got a young 'un now to do the rough work, an one she doesn't 'ave to give a brass farthin' to.'

'A young one?' I echoed stupidly.

She cackled again. 'Sure, an' who's bin cleaning the front step and polishin' the pans? Next news it'll be the kitchen floor an the privy.'

I stared at her in horror and she leered at me slyly.

'Who better than yer own granddaughter, especially one yer givin' a home to? Janie Cassidy never did anythin' for anybody unless it came back to her threefold. She'll turn ye

8

into a skivvy 'afore ye knows what it's all about, mark my words.'

Alice was right. My hands were sore from contact with raw carbolic, and all the time my grandmother stood over me finding fault with the way I scrubbed and the amount of soap I was using.

That night I complained to my mother but she only looked at me sorrowfully.

'We mustn't complain, Kathleen. Your father didn't leave any money and the bit we got for our furniture will soon be gone. Our Terrence needs new shoes for his feet and you're fast growing out of your Sunday-best coat.'

'Does that mean we shall always have to live in Grandmother's house, then?'

'No,' she whispered, and pulling me into the larder where she thought we wouldn't be overheard, she said, 'I've written to mi brothers. Neither of them got on with your grandmother, and I've asked them to help us.'

My face brightened. 'Will they, do you think?'

'I hope so. Mi brother Shamus was a darlin' man and we were always close. I'm not so sure about Turlough, and him with an English wife and two children.'

For the next few days my hopes flew high and then as Alice had predicted I was scrubbing the kitchen floor and the outside privy.

Winter stretched before us and the strong winds blew in from the sea. There was no more talk of replacing my Sunday-best coat, which was too short in the sleeve although the hem was long enough to be let down.

Mary McAuley went to work at the fish docks and I saw her seldom. When I suggested looking for work Grandmother said it wasn't fitting that Janie Cassidy's granddaughter should work anywhere but at home, and there was plenty to do there.

At the beginning of December they found Alice dead in her miserable shack. Grandmother and the rest of us went dutifully to her funeral, which Alice's meagre savings in an insurance fund paid for. She had once confided to me that she was paying twopence a week and had done so since she was little more than a girl.

'There'll be enough to bury me, Katie, it'll not cost your grandmother a penny,' she had said.

I wept for Alice, for the misery of her end and the poverty of her life. She had spent most of it working for my grandmother who, I doubt, even shed a tear.

We spent a miserable Christmas as I had expected, although we were allowed to sit in the parlour on Christmas night. Grandmother bought presents for us of the useful variety, aprons and thick woollen stockings, stout shoes for Terrence and a shapeless cardigan for my pretty mother who was fast becoming plain and pinched.

From my twopence a week spending money I had saved sufficient to buy sweets for my brother and sister, and a bottle of cheap perfume for my mother. I had knitted a woollen tea cosy for Grandmother.

I was glad when Christmas was over. Every day I looked forward more and more to letters from my uncles, and I watched the postman pass by our door with the utmost despair.

The letters' arrival within days of each other sparked off the worst row of all. My grandmother accused Mother of going behind her back, and worse still of the utmost ingratitude, for which God would no doubt punish her in due course. She enlisted the aid of Father McGinty, who agreed that Grandmother did not deserve such treatment – she should have been consulted before Mother wrote off to her brothers for aid.

Mother took the criticism with bowed head and tears, but inwardly I rejoiced when the contents of their letters were made known to me.

Uncle Shamus offered us a home in America even though life was not easy for him, but Uncle Turlough said he could only offer a home to one of us, preferably me as I was old enough to work. Life in Lancashire was hard; the cotton industry was undergoing a bad time after many years of prosperity.

Once Grandmother had got over her initial anger she began to make the arrangements for us. Mother and the

10

two younger children would go to Uncle Shamus and I would go to England. Needless to say the mere idea of being separated was unthinkable, but there was no arguing with her. And with every day that passed I realized she would have her way.

'It'll only be for a short while, Kathleen,' Mother said unhappily. 'There'll be work for you in England and when we've got enough money together you'll come out to us in America.'

'But it might be years!' I cried helplessly.

'Oh no, darlin', it won't be years. One day quite soon we'll be sendin' for you, Uncle Shamus will see to that.'

I didn't believe a word of it. Mother should be fighting to keep us together, but she was listening to her mother and Father McGinty and the two widows, who all thought emigrating to America would be the making of Terrence and Eileen.

They seemed quite unconcerned about my fate but that did not surprise me considering the two youngest were Cassidys and I was the O'Donovan.

It was finally decided that Mother and the two little ones would sail to America from Dublin the second week in February while I would sail from Belfast to Liverpool at the end of January.

Two weeks before I was due to sail Father McGinty arrived at the house looking well pleased with himself and with the news that one of his flock, a certain Liam Clancy, was sailing on the same boat and had promised to look out for me.

I knew Liam Clancy from school. He was about two years older than me, a tall gangling boy with a shock of straw-coloured hair. According to the Widow Murphy he was going to England to live with his Aunt Mary and Uncle Joel who had a builder's business somewhere in the north of England.

'They've no children of their own,' she confided to us, 'so it's falling on his feet he is. You're a lucky girl that Liam's promised to look after you, Kathleen. If you've got your head screwed on right you'll be keepin' in touch wi' Liam

11

Clancy.'

I glared at her balefully. I had no intention of keeping in touch with Liam, the sooner I saved enough money to get me to America the better I was going to like it, but I said nothing of this ambition in front of my grandmother.

Chapter 3

I had spent the first thirteen years of my life in County Donegal and the furthest I had travelled had been to Gweedore and Inisfree Bay. I was a child of the sea and the sky and the wild beauty of Donegal but I was also a survivor and not all the tears I shed at parting from my mother and the children prevented me absorbing the excitement of that train journey from Donegal to Belfast.

I sat in a corner seat of the third-class compartment, opposite Liam Clancy, watching him munch his way through a huge package of sandwiches washed down by several bottles of fizzy lemonade.

I was making a supreme effort not to appear tearful so that Liam would not think me a cry-baby, but I was missing my mother and the children something terrible. It seemed incredible that they were going to the other side of the world and I would not see them grow up or ever again join in their games. In later years when I thought about this day I realized that even then I believed our parting was final in spite of Mother's promises to the contrary.

I was attired in my Sunday-best coat, whose sleeves had been lengthened by tweed of an entirely different colour, and wearing a woollen tam o'shanter sporting an enormous pom-pom.

There were black woollen gloves on my hands to match my black woollen stockings and sturdy lace-up boots on my feet, and in an old straw bag on the rack was everything else I possessed: clean underwear, my night attire, a skirt and several woollen jumpers and three of my father's books which I had retrieved from the attic. They were *Uncle Tom's Cabin*, *Pride and Prejudice*, and a selection of Irish poems. I would dearly have liked to bring more but I doubted if I could have carried the larger volumes.

Liam Clancy was not in the least pleased to have had me thrust upon him and this was evident from his sulky face and desultory conversation. I was relieved when he went off to sleep soon after we left Londonderry and I didn't have to rack my brains in order to find something to talk about.

It was late afternoon when we reached Belfast and I had to run to keep up with his long strides as we made our way towards the harbour. I wanted to stand and look at the lights and the great buildings, but all the time he was urging me on, telling me we had no time to lose, and eventually out of sheer exasperation he took my bag and carried it with his own.

The icy wind from the harbour shot through my coat, tearing at my hair so that I had to cling on to my hat for fear of it being swept away. Icy sleet pelted from dark leaden skies, and slithering and sliding through icy puddles, we came at last to the boat. It loomed above me like some dark monster straining against his chains.

It was a packed boat and I wondered miserably what all those people were doing travelling to Liverpool on such a January night. There was not a single seat left inside and, gritting his teeth, Liam said we would have to resign ourselves to spending the voyage on deck. I had the feeling that he blamed me for this, that if I had only run a little harder we would by this time have found somewhere warm.

In spite of the cold I stood at the ship's rail watching the lights from the Irish shore diminish in the distance, then I realized I should have hung back because it looked as though I would have to spend the entire voyage hanging on to the rail.

I shall never forget that voyage as the ship slunk and slithered, deluged by rain and mountainous waves, tossing like a cork on a sea that every second threatened to engulf us and with all those around me seasick and groaning.

I found myself wondering if it was a relief for those lost at sea to give themselves up to the deep. I felt so ill I wanted to die. The voyage seemed to go on for ever and when the lights of Liverpool Bay came at last into view we stared at them stupidly, not realising that this was indeed land and not a mirage conjured from our deep despair.

My coat was heavy and damp and I felt chilled to the marrow. My teeth were chattering and though I had survived the voyage I could not see how I was going to escape pneumonia. I found myself being swept along by the crowd that had surged forward to look at the shore, then I struggled through, looking for Liam. The last I had seen of him was cowering against a bulkhead, his face a strange shade of green, and I came across him slouched on the deck exactly where I had left him.

For one awful moment I thought he was dead and I started to shake him, calling, 'Liam, Liam we're here, you can see the lights.'

He opened his eyes and stared at me, at first unseeing and then, as he realized that he was still alive he scrambled painfully to his feet. What he saw seemed to give him sudden reassurance.

'Oi thought we were done for, Oi thought we'd nivver get out of it aloive.'

'Were you very ill, Liam? I was fine until they started bein' sick all around me and then I wished I was dead.'

He groaned miserably. 'Where's your bag, then?'

'I left it with you, right here where I left you.'

We hunted for it, stepping over inert forms lying on the deck, but my miserable little bag had gone and I looked at Liam in dismay.

'Oh Liam,' I cried tearfully, 'that's all I had in the world, now I've not even a change o' dry clothin', and mi father's books were in that bag.'

'We'd best find a ship's officer an' tell him what's happened,' he said, and by shoving and pushing we eventually made our way to a staircase leading to a lower deck. An officer was standing near the rail directing operations but the crowd around him was dense, and we earned ourselves scowls and harsh words as we thrust through them. The officer looked down at me sternly, saying, 'Hold on a bit, little 'un, you'll get off in due time, the ship hasn't docked yet.'

Tearfully I explained my loss to him and in some exasperation he said, 'If they'll thieve a bag off a chit of a girl in a storm like that they'll thieve anythin'. Stand besides me and keep your eyes on everybody getting off the boat. Tell me if you spots your bag.'

The pushing and jostling to be the first off the boat went on around us but I kept my eyes upon the luggage people were carrying. There were straw bags in plenty but I saw none held together by that distinctive red string which had decorated mine.

Liam watched with ill-disguised annoyance – it was my fault that he was having to wait. From his height he was able to see much further than I, and suddenly he cried, 'There he is, that's your bag, Katie!'

Sure enough a small weasel-faced man with a small boy was attempting to edge through the crowd, hiding the bag as best he could between himself and the child.

The officer stepped forward and placed his hand on the man's shoulder. 'I'd like you to come with me, Sir,' he said sternly. 'And I'll want you two to come with us,' he said to us.

The man wriggled and protested but to no avail, he was frogmarched along the deck and Liam and I followed as best we could.

We were taken into a small office where another officer sat at a desk. Matters were explained to him while the man continued to express his innocence and I was aware of Liam's glowering face and air of resigned disgust.

'What makes you so sure this bag is yours, Miss?' the new officer asked.

'The red string round it, Sir. Mi mother tied it up herself, she said I'd be sure to recognize it if it went missin'.'

'What was in the bag?'

With a blushing face I gave him the details of my underwear and the titles of my father's books, then he commanded the man to open the bag.

They were my things sure enough. Liam helped me to fasten the bag together again and we were allowed to depart, leaving the man and the boy in the office. I felt sorry for the child.

By the time we reached the gangway there were only a few stragglers left and once again Liam's long strides left me struggling and panting behind.

He turned round, exasperation evident on his sulky face. 'Mi uncle'll be thinkin' oi've missed the boat, and them comin' all the way down from Middlefield to meet me.'

'Then you'd best go on and leave me. I can't keep up when you walk so fast.'

He stood hesitantly, looking back at me, and in a voice choked with tears I cried, 'Go on, I can find my own way. I don't need you to wait. Go find yer uncle.'

I had given him the opportunity he was looking for. I was an ungrateful brat. Hadn't he helped me to find my luggage and gone down to the officer's office with me? Now I was telling him to go off and leave me as though I had nothing to be grateful for.

'Well, I'll probably be seein' you one o' these days, Katie, Oi'll look out for you.'

He escaped, hurrying with those great strides, and I stared after him, angry and tearful. I hated Liam Clancy and my grandmother. I even hated Father McGinty who had been responsible for thrusting us together. Then with something like my old humour I squared my shoulders and marched at my own speed along the quay.

I emerged from the jumble of buildings that lined the harbour into the bright lights of the city and stood in amazement, gawping. A train rumbled above me and I stared after it in dismay – I had never seen an overhead train before. Then I was caught up in the excitement of being in a large port with the tall Royal Liver Building staring straight at me and the trams screeching along the tracks and the hotch-potch of traffic – noisy motor cars side by side with horse-drawn traffic, and people hurrying from the boat towards waiting carriages and relatives.

If Liam's relatives had turned up to meet him there was now no sign of them and I took Uncle Turlough's letter out of my purse to consult his instructions. I was to take a conveyance from the harbour to the railway station and get the last train to Manchester where there would be somebody to meet me. We were to stay in Manchester that night and the following morning we would travel north to Marsdale.

The taxis were dearer than the carriages but I paid the extra money because I was assured the taxi would be quicker and I sat back in the dark interior hugging my straw bag, looking out at the shops and offices and hurrying crowds. I wondered where they were all going and what sort of homes they lived in. Back in Donegal we had pictured every English family to be rich but some of these people looked far from rich, shuffling along the pavements in poor, thin clothing.

Now and again I did see a motor car filled with more opulently dressed people, but they were few and far between and I concluded that wealthy English families would not be on the streets of Liverpool on such a night. More likely they would be sitting down to eat dinner off gold plate in their own beautiful houses – which only goes to prove that I had a lot to learn.

The boat had been late because of the storm, and I caught the last train to Manchester by the skin of my teeth, flinging myself in the last coach as the train started to move.

The other four in the compartment stared at me curiously, and I realized I must look a sight, for I had had no time to smarten myself up since leaving the boat. A man stood up to put my bag on the shelf, then I settled down in a corner seat with a swift smile at my companions.

'Bin travelling far?' A woman sitting opposite asked curiously.

'From County Donegal in Ireland.'

'Ireland is it,' said the man who had lifted up my luggage. 'And what brings you to this country then?'

'I am going to live with my uncle and his wife in Marsdale.'

'Have yer got work ter go to?'

'I don't know. It's the first time I've been out of Ireland.'

'Ah well, it's nice to hear the old talk and a voice that's got a lilt to it.'

'You mean you're Irish?'

'Sure an' oi come from County Mayo though oi've not bin home for nigh on fifteen years. Oi've got an old mother there an' brothers and sisters and one o' these days oi'll be goin' back to see them, that's when oi've made mi fortune.'

I laughed. I'd heard it all before from those who expected to make their fortunes in England and America and would only return to see their kinfolk when they had done so.

'Have you no family in Donegal then?' he asked me curiously.

'I have a grandmother but the rest of my kin will be livin' in America.'

'America is it. An what are ye aimin' to do in Marsdale besides live with your aunt and uncle?'

'I expect I'll know soon enough. Mi uncle'll be meeting the train.'

'Do ye think you'll like Marsdale?' he persisted.

'I don't know anything about it. Have you bin there?'

'That oi have. It's one o' the Lancashire cotton towns, lots o' big mills and a forest o' mill chimneys but there's some pretty country round about. You could be living i' worse places.'

'Does everybody work in the mills?'

'Most of 'em does. Some wealthy families owns five or six mills, some owns just one. Thi says i' Yorkshire that wheer there's muck there's brass, an' there's bin plenty o' brass i' Marsdale.'

It was another man who was talking to me now and with an entirely different way of speaking, broader and coarser, entirely without the Irish lilt I was accustomed to.

'Do you live in Marsdale?' I asked him.

'No. I lives in the next town in't valley, it's noan as posh as Marsdale but A were born theer an' I reckon I'll die theer.'

The woman sitting opposite held out a paper bag containing an assortment of sweets, and I took one gratefully, aware for the first time that my stomach felt empty. The last time I had eaten was on the train into Belfast, when I made short work of the sandwiches my mother had packed for me.

Almost as though the woman knew, she said, 'When did yer last 'ave a bite ter eat, luv?'

'On the train from my home to Belfast.'

'Keep the toffees, luv. They'll 'elp til yer con get someat to eat.'

I thanked her for her kindness and she smiled sadly.

'I've got a lass about your age dyin' o' consumption. She's in a sanatorium up i' the Pennines, that's wheer we're goin', mi 'usband an' me. We goes once a month to see 'er, it's so expensive yer see, all the way fro' Liverpool, but she looks forward to our visits, we wouldn't like ter disappoint 'er.'

'I am sorry. Will she get better soon?'

Her face clouded over and her lips began to tremble, then in a choked voice she said, 'They don't 'old out much 'ope, but we 'as ter keep prayin' an' askin' for miracles.'

She leaned back in her seat, her face pensive.

'You'll not be gettin' to Marsdale tonoight,' the Irishman said.

'I know, I think my uncle has arranged for us to stay in Manchester.'

He nodded, keeping his eyes on me until I felt embarrassed. There was little to see outside the window. Now and again I caught sight of a street lamp or a sheet of water but we seemed to be travelling through open country and when I turned away I was relieved to see that he was sitting with his head buried in a newspaper.

I suddenly felt very weary, and I let my head fall back against the seat. The next thing I remember is being gently shaken by the woman sitting opposite.

'We're comin' into Manchester now, luv, ye'd best get yer things together.'

Her husband lifted down my bag and placed it on the seat beside me and I stood up to look in the dingy mirror. As I had imagined my hair was an untidy mess, so I hunted in my bag for a comb. But there were so many tangles in my hair the comb had little success.

'Yer'll feel better when ye've 'ad a good night's sleep,' the woman said, and then we were slowly pulling into the station and stepping down from the train.

'Oi'll carry yer bag,' the Irishman said, 'I've no luggage of mi own.'

I set off beside him and once again I had to run to keep up with long strides. Then to my utmost dismay I saw Liam in the company of an elderly couple striding out in front of us, little more than a coach distance away.

They reached the barrier before me and I saw them being greeted by my uncle, and I bit my lip in frustration. I thanked my companion for carrying my bag and then found myself being embraced by my uncle and introduced to Liam's aunt and uncle.

'My but you've grown,' Uncle Turlough said. 'It's a little tot you were the last time I saw you. Did you know Liam was travelling on this train then?'

'I travelled with him on the boat, Uncle, and on the train into Belfast.'

'Did you indeed, well that would be nice for ye both. I've got rooms for us quite close to the station. You'll be glad to get out o' those wet things and into a warm bed.'

Much to my chagrin Liam and his relatives were booked into the same lodging house and we walked together out of the station.

'I'm glad you found your uncle waitin' for you, Liam. He didn't think you'd missed the boat then?'

He had the grace to blush and I was glad that I had embarrassed him.

The lodging house was a dark dismal building round the corner from the station, three storeys high with a tiled hall dimly lit by a single gas jet. We were met by a stout woman wearing curling pins and a floral apron which was none too clean. The house felt cold and smelt vaguely of cabbage and burnt food but she did not ask if any of us would like something to eat. Instead we were bustled upstairs and shown our rooms.

My room was dark, chill and narrow. I watched the woman drawing flimsy curtains across the window. Then she said, 'Breakfast is at eight sharp,' and was gone.

21

I sat on the skimpy bed, shivering with cold. My coat was still damp, and the bedclothes too felt cold. I couldn't prevent the tears that rolled slowly down my cheeks. I was missing my mother and Terrence and Eileen, and I hated this cold dark city which left me yearning miserably for the keen fresh wind that blew from the sea over the wild beauty of Donegal.

I had never been a girl long out of countenance however, so I took off my damp clothing and changed into a woollen jumper and skirt, and hung my coat on the single hook behind the door in the vain hope that by morning it would have dried out.

I lay on top of the bed in my clothing with the single blanket tucked around me, not daring to crawl in between those cold sheets. I vowed there and then that nothing was going to defeat me. I was going to prosper and survive. I was going to show Grandmother Cassidy and all those like her that Katie O'Donovan had the will and the spirit to overcome anything that fate might choose to throw at her, and one day I would be somebody in this strange new world.

Chapter 4

The next thing I remember was a bell ringing loudly outside my room and a woman's voice calling that breakfast would be ready in a quarter of an hour.

My toilet was a hurried affair but I was glad I had kept my clothes on, even though my skirt was more creased than usual. The hunger pains in my stomach were so acute I wondered if I would be able to eat at all.

There was porridge and thick wedges of bread and margarine, but more than anything I was glad of the hot rich tea.

Liam appeared with dark circles under his eyes and a hang-dog expression but I greeted him cheerfully and in no time at all his relatives and my uncle were talking about the old days, leaving us to get on with our breakfast.

I bit my lip with vexation when my uncle said to Liam, 'Oi'll be givin' you mi address in Marsdale, and then when you've settled in no doubt you'll be callin' to see us.'

Liam's Uncle Joel pocketed the address with the remark that he didn't get into Marsdale often.

'Then Liam must come out to see us, you'd be very welcome, lad,' my uncle replied generously.

'What sort o' work are you in then? There's not a lot outside cotton in Marsdale.'

'No, that's what I'm in, overlooker at one o' the mills there.'

'Good job is it?'

'Not bad, the wife's a weaver in the same mill but how long it's goin' to last oi can't be sure. Cotton's not doin' as well as it did when oi came over here.'

'No, that's what I've heard. I'm a builder miself and folks'll always be wantin' houses and repairs to them. If

23

Liam here applies himself there'll be a nice little business there for him one day.'

My uncle nodded. 'Well, don't forget to come out to see us, Liam, it'll be nice for Katie to see a friendly face from the old country.'

Liam promised nothing and I wished my uncle would drop the idea. I didn't want to see Liam Clancy in Marsdale, he reminded me too much of things I wanted to forget, like Grandmother Cassidy, Father McGinty and those Sunday afternoons when we had sat in the kitchen listening to their voices and the clink of glasses from the parlour.

It was a dismal journey for the first few miles on the way to Marsdale. We passed through a series of small towns each with its quota of tall chimneys surrounded by wild moorland, but at last the countryside became prettier and I sat forward so as not to miss a single thing.

The people entering and leaving the train were buttoned up warmly against the morning chill but they seemed very much like the people back home. I listened eagerly to their speech which was very different, indeed some of it I could not understand and I felt sure they in turn would have a great deal of trouble understanding me. Still, Uncle Turlough seemed to have survived reasonably well, although he had lost some of the lilt in his voice.

'Have we far to go?' I asked eagerly.

'Three more stations and we're there. You'll recognize Marsdale when ye sees the castle on the hill. Sure and it's an old ruin now and they've built a park around it, but from the train it looks real grand.'

'It's getting hillier all the time.'

'Well yes, this is Pennine country. I knows most of 'em by name and in the summer it's noice to go walkin' over the fells. Marsdale itself is built between two hills so it nestles in the valley with Tremayne Hill on one side an Evening Hill on the other.'

'Evening Hill. That's a pretty name.'

'It is indeed but it's just a fell with nothin' much on it except a few homesteads. Now Tremayne Hill's different. All the gentry and the wealthy millowners live on Tremayne Hill. They don't amount to much if they don't 'ave a house on it, but the finest one o' the lot is Sir Joshua Tremayne's house right at the top. It were the first to be built on it and all the others have gone up much later.'

'Why don't they build on Evening Hill?'

'The farmers own the land there for their sheep and cattle but Sir Joshua's bin a philanthropist, he owns most o' Marsdale and he built the library and the art gallery and he had that park laid out surrounding the castle. You'll see a statue to him in the main square, baronet he is, and there's not a thing goes on around Marsdale but what he and Lady Dorothy don't have a hand in.'

'Do they own mills in Marsdale too?'

'No, but they say he's a big shareholder in most of 'em. Lots o' fingers he has in a great many pies, but if you're ever walkin' on Tremayne Hill an' he drives past you or walks his dog in the same direction he's never against passin' the time o' day. Gentleman he is, and that's more than can be said for some of 'em.'

'I suppose it's a very beautiful house he lives in?'

'Indeed it is, and next Sunday the girls'll take you walkin' up there and you can see it for yourself.'

'Don't they mind mi comin' to live with you, Uncle Turlough?'

'It's not so much that they mind, Katie, but the house is small and there's not much room. They'll come to terms and although Martha's got a sharp tongue in her head her heart's in the right place.'

His words were not encouraging but I tried not to let them worry me as we made our way out of the station into the main square of Mardsale. The first thing he pointed out was Sir Joshua's statue standing on a dais surrounded by stone urns which, my uncle explained, were filled with plants in the summer time. On one side of the square stood the parish church, a stone building with a tall pointing spire, and directly across from it was the largest hotel in

Marsdale. There were several fine shops and a new police station.

'What is that?' I asked, pointing to an ornamental tower immediately behind the square.

He chuckled. 'That, Katie, is Lampton's Folly. He was an eccentric old chap who fancied himself another Sir Joshua. He had a bit o' money so he thought he'd build somethin' for the town to remember him by, but his money ran out and all he finished was the tower. The council have let it stand and there's a staircase to the top so that you can climb it and look out all over Marsdale and the surroundin' countryside.'

'So it's just a tower,' I mused softly. 'I wonder why Sir Joshua didn't finish it as part of a building.'

'Nay, Katie, the Tremaynes don't go in for finishing work they haven't started, but they do say he kept old Mr Lampton out of the workhouse and paid for his funeral.'

'Do we have far to walk?'

'Not far, but we're goin' to take a cab. Oi'll get him to drop us at the end of the street so Martha doesn't see us arrivin' in style. She'd have somethin' to say about that, and no mistake.'

Aunt Martha was beginning to loom a formidable figure in my imagination and I had visions of another Grandmother Cassidy.

Uncle Turlough hailed the solitary cab standing in the station yard and soon we were clattering along the main street. I could see now how the little town nestled in the valley between the two gentle hills, surrounded by Pennine hills which were far loftier and wilder. My uncle pointed out the big houses on Tremayne Hill but it was Evening Hill that I thought to be much prettier, possibly because its only adornments were grazing sheep and a small wood. He pointed out the various mill chimneys, giving me the names of the mills – Woodstock and Nile, Langley and Gresham – then told me a little of the millowners who employed most of the town's workforce.

'Do we have far to go?' I asked curiously, for we were driving along narrow streets now that we had left the town centre, and from Grandmother Cassidy's stories of his affluence I had always imagined Uncle Turlough living in some degree of magnificence.

'We're almost there, Katie. See, that little street with the shop on the corner. We'll leave the cab there.'

I stared in amazement at the neat little street. The road was cobbled and the houses came right on to the pavement, without front gardens. It is true that door knockers were polished and clean lace curtains hung at most of the windows, but there was no magnificence such as Grandmother Cassidy had been throwing at my father for years.

I kept my thoughts to myself as we walked down the street, then the door of the fifth house down the street opened suddenly and a woman stood on the doorstep. It was my first sight of Aunt Martha, a buxom, dark-haired woman wearing a floral apron but no welcoming smile.

'Hallo, luv,' Uncle Turlough called out, and for the first time I realized how his Irish brogue had given way to the Lancashire dialect, and hoped mine would not go the same way. But there was no time to speculate further because we had reached the house and Aunt Martha was looking me over and I was holding out a tentative hand, saying, 'Hello, Aunt Martha, I'm Katie O'Donovan.'

She took my hand, then opening the door wider she said, 'Come along in, I expect yer'd like some tea.'

The front parlour shone with polish and there was a bright fire in the grate. It was obvious from the hand-embroidered chair-back covers on the two easy chairs set before the fire and the snowy tablecloth spread over the table that Aunt Martha was very houseproud.

There was no indication that this was a house belonging to rich people; it was a comfortable cottage lovingly tended, with everything in its place and everything paid for.

Apart from that first word she had said nothing more to me and it was left to Uncle Turlough to help me off with my coat while she busied herself making tea and buttering bread.

'You'll be having a cup of tea before you looks at your bedroom, Katie. We've only two bedrooms, so you'll have to share with the girls. I hope you won't mind that.'

'No of course not. Will they?'

'They'll do as they're told,' Aunt Martha said firmly.

I felt uncomfortable. I believed I had been thrust upon them by a grandmother who thought they were in a better way than they actually were, but she could only have gained this impression from my uncle's letters.

As if to corroborate this my aunt said, 'We were surprised when your mother wrote to us askin' for 'elp, life's not bin easy these last few years, what wi' four mouths to feed an' yer uncle on't dole several weeks out o' the year.'

I stared at her helplessly, and in some exasperation she snapped at him, 'I suppose yer told yer mother we were i' clover rather than admit things were 'ard fer us.'

'Sure an' if you knew mi mother you'd understand why,' he answered her. 'Come on, Katie, sit by the fire and get warm. She's had a bad crossing and that place i' Manchester were none too comfortable.'

He added more coal to the fire and Aunt Martha poured the tea into thick white cups.

'I've asked May O'Connor to see if there's anythin' at Foxland's for 'er. She's callin' in tonight to let us know,' she said, handing me a cup.

Aunt Martha appeared to want very little of my company. She was bustling about in the kitchen and we could hear pans clattering, and occasionally she muttered to herself.

'You mustn't be mindin' Martha,' Uncle Turlough whispered, 'you'll be findin' out for yourself, she's a rare good woman. She's gettin' a meal ready for when the girls get 'ome fro' school.'

I nodded. Mixing the Irish and the Lancashire came so easily to him now, and I couldn't help thinking that Grandmother Cassidy wouldn't be too pleased with her younger son if she could hear him now.

I was curious about my two cousins and I didn't have long to wait. Just after four o'clock the front door was unceremoniously flung open and two girls came laughing into the house.

The smaller of the two ran immediately to her father and flung her arms around his neck, while the other stood tentatively near the door, eyeing me suspiciously.

'Come an' meet your cousin Kathleen,' Uncle Turlough said, beckoning the older girl. 'This is Frances, but we calls her Fanny, and the young 'un 'ere is Lucy. Girls, this is yer cousin Kathleen, but like as not she'll ask yer to call her Katie. Yer father allus called yer Katie, didn't he, lass?'

'Yes Uncle, always. He was the only one that did.'

I smiled at the two girls but they watched me with wide-eyed wonder, offering no word of greeting. The older girl was tall and thin, with dark hair which fell in great waves on to her shoulders, her eyes as blue as a summer sky. She had a typical Irish beauty, the same sort of colouring as my mother, while the younger girl was a roly-poly, short and plump, with pale blonde hair, eyes which were less stormy, and dimples round her mouth.

'Well, 'ave yer nothin' to say to yer cousin Katie, then?' he chided them.

Their greeting was perfunctory, then Frances went to sit at the table with her head buried in a comic and the younger sister continued to sit on her father's knee.

He smiled at me over her head. 'Don't worry about 'em, Katie, it's all very new to them, 'avin' you here, they'll soon adjust.'

The older girl got up from the table and flounced into the kitchen where I could hear her talking to her mother. I felt sure they were discussing me.

Lucy stared at me unashamedly, then said, 'Jeannie McLoughlan 'as red air, but it's not as pretty as yours.'

I smiled. This was progress indeed. 'Do you like red hair, Lucy?'

'Not much, I don't like dark hair either, I like mine.'

'That's just as well then,' I couldn't resist answering, 'since it's the colour the good God has given you.'

Uncle Turlough threw back his head and laughed. 'That's one fer you, Lucy, you're not goin' to 'ave all your own way, not with your cousin Katie and that's for sure.'

Quite unabashed she left her father's knee and came to

29

stand in front of me. 'Did you come from Ireland in a big boat like mi father did?'

'Yes, and it was a rough sea so that everybody was ill on the boat.'

'You too?' she asked hopefully.

'Me too.'

Aunt Martha bustled in, carrying hot plates held by her apron. 'Don't be droppin' them dishes,' she called out to Frances, 'yer'll need to use a pot towel if they're 'ot.'

My eyes lit up as the dishes appeared. Frances brought in a dish of boiled potatoes and my aunt returned carrying carrots and a small joint of meat which Uncle Turlough carved, handing round the plates to each of us. I had never been so hungry and the food was well cooked and the meat succulent, though there was not a great deal of it.

'We 'as a joint every Friday,' Aunt Martha explained, 'but meat's that dear it's just 'avin' ter go a bit further now you're 'ere.'

After that the meal didn't taste half so appetizing. I felt it was my fault that their rations had had to be cut down, but when the pudding arrived my spirits soared again. It was a suet pudding with tender apple filling and there was more than enough for second helpings.

I helped my aunt to clear away and wash the dishes. The kitchen was very small, with a long dark cupboard along the wall opposite the door and a stone sink and draining board under the window. The floor was flagged but there was a home-made rug on the floor. Behind the door was a row of coat pegs.

'Tomorrer's Saturday,' she said, 'and I usually goes to the market. Yer can come with me if yer likes, that'll give yer some idea o' the lie o' the land.'

'Thank you Aunt Martha, I should like that.'

'Oh well, Frances usually comes with mi but she'll be glad not to go, 'as 'er 'ead in the clouds, that one. We'll 'ave a talk tomorrer about what yer can expect ter give me for yer board an' lodging. I 'ope May O'Connor's found someat for yer at Foxland's.'

'Do you and Uncle Turlough work at Foxland's too?'

'Yer uncle does.'

'But I thought you were a weaver at the same mill?'

'I were till yesterday, I've bin played off.'

'Played off!'

'Ay, twenty of us told there's no work fer us. I 'aven't told yer uncle yet, I'll tell 'im in mi own good time. An 'e's lost two days' pay this week wi' 'avin' to meet you in Manchester.'

I felt responsible for their problems but one look at my downcast face made my aunt retort, 'Don't go lookin' like that, Katie, or yer uncle'll think A've bin talking out o' turn. We'll manage, we've managed 'afore an' we can do so again.'

I wasn't looking forward to the evening. Frances had her head buried in a book while Lucy sat at the table colouring a picture book. My uncle puffed placidly at his pipe and Aunt Martha's knitting needles clicked sharply. Occasionally we could hear the quick patter of rain on the windows but the small room was cosy and warm. I felt strangely idle with nothing to do. In Grandmother Cassidy's house there had always been mending to be done or brass to be polished, but this tiny house shone with the vigour of Martha's polishing.

Soon after seven there was a knock at the door and my aunt jumped to her feet, saying, 'This'll be May, let's 'ope she's got good news for us.'

The woman who entered the room wore a dark grey shawl and black clogs, and her face was narrow and pinched.

She was invited to sit down in front of the fire, and offered a cup of tea, but she shook her head, saying, 'I've left mi mother on 'er own, I told 'er I wouldn't be long before I were back.'

'Ow is yer mother, May?' Uncle Turlough asked.

'Not so good today, but she does 'ave 'er ups and downs. I'm 'opin' she'll be a bit better when the better weather comes round.'

'This is Turlough's niece Kathleen fro' County Donegal,' my aunt said. 'She had a bad crossin', isn't that right, Kathleen?'

'Yes Aunt, it was dreadful.'

'Well, is there likely to be anythin' for 'er at Foxland's?' my aunt asked in her direct fashion.

'We could do wi' a sweeper-up i' number three shed. A girl who doesn't mind runnin' errands and fetchin' the dinners in. The wage isn't much but it's better than nowt.'

'How much?' my aunt demanded.

'Two and sixpence.'

'Yer reet, it's not much, but she's got eyes in 'er 'ead. She can watch the weavers and pick up their trade.'

'Ay, but there might not be so many job's on't looms the way things are goin',' May began, but a warning look from my aunt silenced her.

'What do you think o' Kathleen takin' that job at Foxland's?' my aunt demanded of Uncle Turlough.

'It's a start,' was his laconic reply.

'Right, May, well I'll 'ave 'er there at seven o'clock sharp on Monday mornin', an' thanks.'

May departed and the evening resumed its tranquillity. Promptly at half-past eight Aunt Martha bustled once more into the kitchen and soon emerged with steaming cups of cocoa.

'After you've drunk that you'll get washed and go to bed,' she advised her daughters.

'But it's Saturday tomorrow,' Frances objected.

'I'm well aware it's Saturday but I want to talk to Kathleen 'ere an' I don't want you listenin' and pryin'. Now drink yer cocoa and get off to bed.'

Frances favoured me with a hostile glance and Uncle Turlough said quickly, 'I'll 'ave an early night too, Martha, I didn't get much sleep in Manchester last night.' But I knew he wanted no part in the financial arrangements my aunt wished to discuss with me.

After we had washed the cups she added another cob of coal to the fire and indicated that I should sit in my uncle's chair.

'I thowt Turlough'd make himself scarce, but we've got to talk about money, Kathleen. Ye see that, don't ye?'

'Yes, of course I do.'

'Well then. Yer'll be earnin' two and sixpence a week and I'm goin' to ask yer for two of 'em for yer board an' lodging. We tries to keep a good table an' another mouth is goin' to make a difference, but your bit'll 'elp and wi' the sixpence yer 'ave left yer can buy the few things yer want. I don't know 'ow yer fixed for clothes.'

'Not very well, I'm afraid.'

'Oh well, I does a bit o' sewin' an' I can run yer up a few cotton dresses for the summer. We'll 'ave a look on the market tomorrer. Did yer grandmother give yer any money 'afore yer left Ireland?'

'My mother gave me five shillings.'

'Well, that'll do nicely to get yerself a few pieces o' material. Why couldn't the old skinflint give yer someat?'

'Grandmother Cassidy isn't free with her money.'

'That I can believe. She never sent us a weddin' present, and in all the years the girls 'aven't 'ad as much as a brass farthin from 'er.'

'It doesn't surprise me, Aunt Martha. We lived practically on her doorstep an' she never brought us birthday presents an' only ever gave us useful things at Christmas.'

'Yer must get yerself a library ticket. It's a good library an' yer allowed two books a week. It's free so if yer likes readin' that won't take any of yer money.'

'I shall be allowed to read, Aunt Martha?'

She stared at me. 'Yer can *read*, can't yer?'

'Why yes, but Grandmother Cassidy said there were more important things for a girl to be doin' than readin' books.'

'There's four women in this 'ouse and the 'ouse is small. It won't take four of us to cook and clean and do the shoppin', so I reckon there'll be time for some pleasure. O' course yer can read, how could yer ever think I'd object?'

For the first time I felt happier about my life in my aunt's house and I resolved to be a help to her, both around the house and on market days. She had taken up her knitting again and with a brief nod she said, 'Get off to bed now,

33

Kathleen, I reckon yer tired.'

'Am I to wash in the kitchen, Aunt Martha?'

'Ay, there's boilin' water in the kettle an' you'll find towels i' the dresser drawer. If yer'll get mi yer nightie I'll be warmin' it in front o' the fire for yer.'

It was so cold in the kitchen. The wind seemed to whistle through the chinks round the door, but when my aunt eventually passed my nightdress to me it felt lovely and warm and I knew that under that brusque exterior she had a very warm heart.

'Take yer case upstairs now, Kathleen, it's the door on yer right at the back of the 'ouse. Be very quiet, I expect the girls are asleep.'

Indeed only the sound of steady breathing broke the silence but the curtains had been pulled back and moonlight lit up the room. The girls occupied the bed nearest to the wall, so the one under the window must be mine. In vain I tried to turn back the sheets. No amount of tugging on my part could dislodge them. I felt under the quilt and my hands encountered something large and lumpy. The girls had made me an apple-pie bed, and I was so weary and miserable I could have cried with frustration.

It wasn't light enough to see properly what they had done, and from the next bed I was now aware of giggling and suppressed laughter. In some anger I stormed, 'You rotten little monkeys, what a mean thing to do.'

Just then the door opened and my aunt saw me delving under the bedclothes, bringing out books and toys, dolls and any old thing the girls had found to stuff into my bed. In some exasperation she lit the gas jet and went to give them a shake.

'Get out of bed, the pair of you, and help Kathleen to put 'er bed to rights. Right welcome this is you've given 'er, and no mistake. You're the ringleader, our Fanny. Now get 'old of yer scissors and undo those stitches, an' if yer makes a 'ole in the sheet I'll let yer 'ave the back of mi 'and.'

Both girls leapt out of bed and made themselves busy putting my bed to rights, while their mother stood with arms akimbo. Only when she was satisfied that I would

34

now be able to sleep in the bed did she order them back to their own, then she turned off the gas jet and left us alone.

'I hate you, Katie O'Donovan,' Frances murmured in the darkness. 'What did you 'ave to come here for?'

I didn't answer her – how could I when I didn't rightly know myself? I cried myself to sleep that night, thinking it was a hard and dismal thing to be aware of so many people who hated you: Grandmother Cassidy and Frances, probably Liam Clancy and young Lucy too.

Chapter 5

Market day in Marsdale was a bustling affair. The stalls were set out in the main square and I marched down to it with my aunt the following morning armed with a shopping basket over my arm while she carried two oilcloth bags under her arm. We made our way first of all to the fruit and vegetable stalls.

'Don't yer be letting 'em give yer all the fruit fro' the back, Katie, keep yer eyes open an' ask for some fro' the front, an' pick yer own cabbages and cauliflowers.'

So, as she ordered I picked, until one of the stall owners said, 'Nay, Mrs Cassidy, don't yer be takin' all mi best, I 'as other customers ter serve.'

'Then shouldn't ye be pullin' all yer bad fruit out? Two bad apples I 'ad last week in only three pounds, I'm not lettin' that 'appen again.'

To my amusement other women joined in, pointing out bad fruit or bad vegetables they had had and eventually the man shrugged his shoulders and allowed us to carry on with our selecting.

As we left the stall my aunt confided, 'Yer've got to keep yer eye on that one, Kathleen. If yer lets 'im pick out your fruit 'e allus slips one or two bad 'uns among em.'

From one of the material stalls I bought a remnant of grey serge for a skirt, and from another stall a piece of pale blue and white cotton that would make a pretty blouse.

As we approached the cobbler's a carriage drew up at the large shop on the square and my aunt murmured, 'That's the Foxland carriage. They don't usually come down to the town on market days – Tuesday's when the gentry do their shoppin'.'

I stared curiously at the two women who were alighting

from the carriage. One of them was an older woman in a severe grey costume with a fox tie round her throat and a large grey hat trimmed with feathers, but it was the girl who made me gasp with admiration.

She was lovely, with silver-fair hair and a delicate pink and white face. She too was in grey, but a very soft, delicate grey. She carried a little white fur muff and there was a tie of white ermine round her throat. She wore a grey velvet hat on her exquisitely dressed hair and she picked up her long skirts daintily from the wet pavements as they swept into the shop.

'Who are they?' I asked my aunt in a whisper.

'Mrs Foxland and her daughter.'

'She's beautiful,' I murmured.

'Oh ay, they do say she's got all the young fellers just where she wants 'em, but it's my mind she's waitin' for something better than the gentry i' Marsdale.'

'Do they live on Tremayne Hill?'

'Ay, the big red-brick house halfway up. I should think she's a spoilt little madam, they've only the one child so she comes in for all the attention.'

'What's her name?'

'Lois. Lois Foxland.'

'Can't we go into the shop and take a look round, Aunt Martha?'

'Nay, there isn't time, and me with a dinner to cook. Things are expensive at Lawson's, in all mi married life I reckon I've only bin in three times. I 'aven't enough money to shop at Lawson's.'

'I only meant to look, Aunt Martha.'

'There's no use in givin' yerself high-falutin' ideas, Katie, you'd do well ter keep yer feet on the ground. You an' Miss Lois Foxland come fro' different worlds.'

As we reached the doors an attendant ushered the two women out on to the pavement, going to their carriage and opening the door for them. As they turned to look round the square, for the first time I looked into the china-blue eyes of Lois Foxland.

We watched them clatter off and my aunt said with a

37

grim smile, 'Nigh on twenty-three years I've worked for that lass's father an' yet she doesn't know me well enough to give mi the time o' day, not 'er or 'er mother.'

Over our evening meal Uncle Turlough said, 'If it's nice tomorrow, Katie, I'll take you walking up on Tremayne Hill so ye can see the fine houses and the beautiful gardens.'

My aunt sniffed her disapproval. 'What call is there to walk on Tremayne Hill? Make the lass discontented, that's what it will.'

He smiled at her vehemence. 'Your aunt doesn't think much o' the folk on the hill, Katie, but she doesn't really know any of 'em.'

'We saw Mrs Foxland and that daughter of 'ers goin' into Lawson's this mornin'. Snobs, that's what they are. At least if yer sees Lady Dorothy she'll smile and bid yer good mornin', but not them two.'

'I'm goin' to live on Tremayne Hill one day,' Frances said. 'I'm goin' to marry a man with plenty o' money and live in one o' them big houses.'

'Yer can get such ideas firmly out o' yer 'ead, our Fanny,' her mother responded crisply. Then turning to me she said, 'Did'nt A tell yer she 'ad 'er 'ead in the clouds? I'll not 'ave 'er talkin' such rubbish.'

'Oh, come now, Martha, did you never hanker after bein' somebody when you were Fanny's age?'

She didn't answer her husband, but started to collect the dishes, and I hurried to help her. 'Stay 'ere and talk to yer uncle, Kathleen. Frances can 'elp mi, she's done nowt all day.'

'But Mother, why should it always be me, why can't our Lucy somethin'?' the girl protested. But after one stern look from her mother she got to her feet with bad grace and started to remove the dishes.

'She's not a bad, lass,' my uncle said gently. 'We spoiled 'er a bit before Lucy was born, she were such a pretty little thing.'

'Is it always raining?' I complained. 'I thought it rained a lot in Ireland but it wasn't the same as this.'

'Nay, the rain in Ireland's soft and it lies on the wind that sweeps in fro' the sea in Donegal. This is different, Katie. On the other side o' them hills there the weather is colder and drier, but we lives on the wet side o' the Pennines. But it isn't always raining, Katie. You'll see how pretty it can be in the spring.'

I remained unconvinced, and Saturday night passed very much as Friday night had done, though by the time we retired I was helping Lucy with her drawing. I knew from the outset that Frances was the one I would have trouble with but I tried not to let it worry me unduly. My thoughts were centred on Monday morning and my first day of employment.

It rained steadily throughout Sunday morning but shortly after midday a pale watery sun came out and soon the flags were drying and people were passing the house in their Sunday best.

My aunt said, 'If yer wants to take Kathleen walkin', now's the time ter go 'afore it rains again.'

I donned my tweed coat and woollen tammy. The others were invited to join us but all three declined. Uncle Turlough and I set out, walking quickly with our heads down against the sharp wind that swept down from the fells and over the southern hill. As we approached it the houses got bigger and the roads wider. There were more lamps along the roads and the houses sported neat front gardens and larger windows.

'What sort of people live in these houses?' I asked curiously.

'Managers fro' the mills and tradespeople, accountants and solicitors – ye know, Katie, professional people.'

'People who earn more money than you do, Uncle Turlough?'

He laughed. 'That's about it. Mind you, Katie, there's folk i' this town who earn a lot less than me.'

'Where do they live then?'

'Oh, nearer the mills on the canal bankin'. I should keep away fro' there, Katie. There's a lot o' bitterness an' they don't take kindly to folk better off than them seein' how they live.'

'I can understand that, Uncle Turlough.'

'Ay. Well, 'ere we are then, yer can see 'ow the hill rises and curves and 'ow all the 'ouses 'ave been built so that each one 'as a view o' the valley. This long curvin' drive goes right up to the top o' the 'ill and the Tremayne House. If we walks to the top you'll be able to see the layout fro' there.'

By the time we had reached the top of the gentle slope it had started to rain again, and the clouds were sitting low on the surrounding fells. All the same I was immediately aware of the beauty of the Tremayne mansion, built from grey Pennine stone and surrounded by well-kept lawns and gardens. There was a conservatory along one side of the house and virginia creeper covered most of the front.

'The stables are at the back,' my uncle explained. 'They all rides their 'orses and most of 'em keep a couple or p'raps more, dependin' on the size o' their families.'

'I'll bet they don't ride any better than you did, Uncle Turlough.'

He threw back his head and laughed. 'You remember it, do you Katie, those races along the shore wi' the ribbons flyin' an' all the folks gathered round to do their bettin'? Ay, I could ride a good 'orse i' them days and yer right, many's the toime I rode in first to collect mi forfeit.'

We stood for a while without speaking, both thinking about Donegal and the green turf and pools of clear blue water, at the white scudding clouds and the gulls wheeling about the riders, who were cheered on by their folks. At last Uncle Turlough said sadly, 'There'll be no goin' back, Katie, not for either of us, an' it's best not to look back, only forward.'

We set off down the hill, with him pointing out the different houses.

'That's Colonel Carslake's house there in the trees. They own four mills, three i' Marsdale and one in Copplethorpe, and that house lower down belongs to the Rigbys, they 'as the Isis Mill. And there's the Foxland house, that big red-brick one on the lower slope.'

'Why isn't it built from stone like all the others?'

He chuckled. 'Trust Mrs Foxland to want somethin' different. There were a bit o' trouble from the rest of 'em when she wanted it built i' brick, an' I do 'ere tell that there's to be nothin' built on the 'ill now unless it's stone. It does stick out like a sore thumb now yer comes to think about it.'

We had almost reached the bottom of the hill when two people on horseback emerged from a side lane, a man riding a dark bay horse and a girl riding a chestnut. My uncle raised his hat respectfully and the man said, 'Afternoon, Cassidy', while the girl merely stared. I recognized her as Lois Foxland.

'That's the girl we saw in the town yesterday morning, Uncle,' I exclaimed.

'Ay, with 'er father.'

'He spoke to you, Uncle.'

'So he should, I've worked for 'im long enough.'

'I don't think Aunt Martha likes us to talk about the gentry.'

'No, an' she doesn't like Frances gettin' ideas above 'er station. We've had some bad times when trade's bin bad, Katie, but if it gets worse it's folk like that who'll suffer more than us. It's goin' to be hard for them to come down fro' their foine big houses an' their genteel way o' livin', the difference'll not be so terrible for us.'

'Is trade goin' to get worse, do you think?'

'Oh yes, it'll get worse. 'Ere we are showin' all these poor benighted heathens round our factories, showin' 'em 'ow clever we are, 'ow to build looms and weave cotton. Mark my words, Katie, i' just a few years they'll be beatin' us at our own game an we 'aven't the sense to see it.'

'But surely people like the Foxlands must know what they're doing?'

'They don't believe it could 'appen. It's complacent they are, and when it does 'appen they'll all be caught wi' their trousers down an they'll have no way o' knowing which way to turn.'

'And we'll all be out of work.'

'That's right, Katie. Wouldn't you think that these educated gentlemen with three or four sons'd know better than to put 'em all into cotton? Wouldn't ye just think they could see further than their noses?'

As we walked quickly down the rest of the hill my thoughts were very occupied.

I was not going to be like Frances and talk about my hopes for the future, although I had them in plenty. My man would not be one who worked in cotton when cotton was a dying industry. By the time I was old enough to marry and build a house I reckoned they would be building houses on Evening Hill, and mine would be the first, and right at the crest of the hill just like the Tremayne House. There would be beautiful gardens and a conservatory, there would be great trees edging the lawns and fine horses in the stables, and I would be beautiful and gracious so that the gentry would come to my musical evenings and garden parties. Then I laughed, thinking how Aunt Martha would view my fantasies.

'What's amusin' ye, Katie?' my uncle demanded.

'Just something I thought of, Uncle Turlough. We're likely to get a scoldin' for gettin' wet.'

'Ay, yer right, but with a bit o' luck tea'll be ready and we can soon dry off. It'll be an early night tonight, Katie, yer've a job to go to in the mornin'.'

That job was constantly in my mind. How was I ever going to stand working in a mill after the wild open spaces of County Donegal? I had been a child of the mist and the heather, never one to be kept indoors, not even when the fog floated in from the sea and the foghorn sounded mournfully across the cliffs.

Sounds from the street woke me when it was still pitch dark. I ran to the window, surprised to see that people were already hurrying along the street. Across the road a man was walking with a long pole and at each house he stopped and knocked with it on an upstairs window. As he walked away I could see gas jets being lit in the houses he had visited. There was a constant stream of people, men in flat caps and overalls, women in clogs and shawls, and I heard my aunt's voice calling to us to hurry.

The two girls turned over sleepily, and I dressed in a hurry without putting a match to the jet. My aunt was bustling round with an apron over her cream flannel nightgown and my uncle was already eating his breakfast of thick toast and marmalade, and there was a plentiful supply of hot strong tea in the pot.

'Where are all the people going so early?' I asked him.

'They works at some o' the mills a little way off. We're lucky. Foxland's is only five minutes' walk.'

'Shall I be working anywhere near you?'

'No, but don't worry about that, Katie, you'll find the women friendly enough. They'll play all sorts o' tricks on yer as it's yer first day, but yer must take it all i' good part. Don't get ruffled or they'll say it's yer Irish temper an' it'll make 'em worse.'

'What sort o' tricks?'

'Well, they'll be sending you on all sorts o' ridiculous errands, an' they'll be after tellin' yer stories that just aren't true. Take it all with a pinch o' salt, Katie, an' yer won't go far wrong.'

'There's no time for chatterin',' Aunt Martha said sharply. 'The first hooter's gone, they'll 'a' sounded the second 'afore yer out o' the 'ouse if yer don't 'urry.'

As we stepped into the street the biting wind almost took my breath away, and I heard hooters both near and far. We took to our heels and ran with the rest of them, and in a few minutes we were entering the factory gates. Already through the lighted windows came the sounds of clattering looms.

'There yer goes, Katie, that's your weavin' shed an' 'ere's somethin' for yer lunch.'

He handed me a small newspaper package and then he was gone, hurrying with the rest of them while I turned and entered the door facing me.

The noise was deafening – looms clattering and women

43

shouting across the noise. I wondered how on earth they could hear themselves speak but I soon learned that they were expert lip readers.

A girl about my own age showed me where to hang my coat and then she gave me a long-handled brush and instructed me how I should brush along the aisles of women working the looms. She was a tall lanky girl with lacklustre hair tied back with a piece of string, and she sniffed constantly as if she had a permanent cold.

Nobody paid any attention to me, I might have worked there for years for all the notice they took as I applied my brush around their feet. Promptly at ten o'clock the looms ceased their clatter and the women sat down on high stools and took out their lunches. I looked round for the other girl but she was nowhere in sight, and a plump apple-cheeked woman sitting at the end of her aisle said, 'Bring yer lunch an' 'ave it wi' us, luv. Yer new, aren't yer?'

'Yes, from this morning.'

'Yer not fro' Lancashire?'

'No, oi'me Irish.'

''Ave yer only just come ter live i' Lancashire then?'

'Yes, last Friday. I'm from Donegal.'

'Come ter relatives then?'

'Yes, my uncle and aunt. My uncle works here too, Turlough Cassidy his name is.'

'Oh ay, I knows 'im and Martha 'is wife. Got played off, 'asn't she?'

'Yes.'

'Oh well, that's 'ow it goes, some weeks there's plenty o' work, an' others we're on't dole. Are yer stayin' 'ere permanent like?'

'In England do you mean?'

'Ay, wi' yer aunt an uncle?'

'I don't know. Perhaps I shall go to America to live with mi mother when there's enough money.'

'I thowt yer said yer mother lived in Ireland?'

'No. I said I was Irish but mi mother'll be livin' in America soon, and I'm hopin' to join her there.'

She didn't understand, I could tell from the curiosity on

44

her face, but just then a man told the women to get back to their looms and the noise started all over again.

The whistle sounded promptly at twelve o'clock and the tall thin girl who had shown me my job said, 'Wc 'as an 'our fer dinner, so yer due back at one o'clock. If yer late they'll close the factory gates and dock it off yer wage at the end o' the week.'

'I shan't be late, my uncle will see to that.'

I had very little to report over the dinner table so I left all the conversation to my aunt and uncle, mostly about the factory, but on our way back my uncle said, 'Are you goin' to be 'appy at Foxland's, Katie?'

'It's too soon to tell, I spoke with a woman who was very friendly but she asked a lot o' questions.'

He laughed. 'Yer'll find most of 'em nosey, luv, but their hearts are in the right place. Played any tricks on yer yet?'

'No.'

'Well just watch out fer 'em, that's all.'

During the afternoon I was sent to the mechanics' shop for a glass hammer, which had the men hooting with laughter, and I was told the manager wanted to see me in his office so that he could deliver his welcoming speech. I was sent back from the office sharpish by a dignified man with a winged collar and a waxed moustache and told not to submit to any such foolishness in the future.

At five-thirty the last buzzer of the day sounded and en masse the women left their looms, grabbed their coats and shawls and made a beeline for the doors. I had seen two men working on the looms when the women were having problems. One of them was a plump elderly man with grey hair and a kindly manner but the other was small and wiry, with thin sandy hair and a pointed face that reminded me of a weasel. As I was putting on my coat he came up to me with a smile, saying, 'Enjoyed yer first day at Foxland's, lass?'

'Yes thank you.'

'What's yer name?'

'Kathleen O'Donovan.'

'Another Irish lass.'

'I'm afraid so.'

'Well if yer wants any 'elp, Kathleen O'Donovan, come ter me. My names Charlie Wheeldon, I'm what they call a tackler, that's somebody who looks after the looms when they're out o' flunter.'

'I see.'

'Livin' round 'ere then? If yer are I'll walk along wi' yer.'

'Thank you but I'm waitin' for mi uncle.'

'Suit yerself, but remember, if yer wants any 'elp see me. Yer a pretty lass, yer an' me should get along just fine.'

He put his arm around my shoulder and gave it a squeeze and I stepped back swiftly, a gesture that seemed to amuse him since he went off smiling broadly.

I didn't like Charlie Wheeldon and I decided there and then that if I wanted any help it would be the other man I would be asking. I said nothing of this conversation to my uncle however. I thought it was too early to start discussing the people I was working with and I didn't want Uncle Turlough to think the man had been familiar. I remembered his hot Irish temper and I wanted no part in that anger.

At the evening meal Frances said disdainfully, 'I shan't be workin' at Foxland's when I grow up, I'm not goin' into any factory.'

'You'll get what there is goin' and like it,' her mother snapped.

'Leave the lass alone, Martha,' my uncle said indulgently, 'there's plenty o' time 'afore she needs ter be thinkin' about work.'

'She's a young madam wi' 'er high-flung notions and she's got ter 'ave 'em knocked on the 'ead now.'

'She means no 'arm, yer wants 'er to 'ave some ambition, don't yer?'

'I don't want 'er to cry fer the moon like you 'ave many a time.'

'When 'ave I ever cried for the moon?'

'When yer first come over fro' Ireland. Oh, yer were goin' to be a fine gentleman with a big 'ouse and a stream of 'orses, surely you can't 'ave forgotten all that.'

'Oi 'aven't forgotten, besides I were only a young feller then, all young fellers dream a bit, ay and young lasses too. Oi'll bet Katie 'ere has more than one dream in 'er head.'

He was right, but I wasn't going to tell a single soul what they were. If they never came true I didn't want somebody like Aunt Martha reminding me of their futility.

Chapter 6

At long last, after I'd been a year at Marsdale, a letter came for me from my mother in America. She enthused about Uncle Shamus's fine house in Philadelphia, and the fine furniture he'd collected. Then she said the children had both settled down well, that Terrence was going to school and Eileen was a favourite with their neighbours and friends. She told me to be a good girl and heed my uncle and aunt, not to cause them any worry and to look after my job and save money. Of my going to join them in America she said not a word and, hurt and angry, I tore the letter into shreds and burned it.

How I hated the weaving shed with the clatter of the looms and the raucous voices, but most of all I hated and feared Charlie Wheeldon.

He followed me about and whenever I was sent on an errand into another room he came after me, losing no opportunity to put his arms round me, squeezing my small breasts and trying to kiss me. At first I struggled and tried to get away, but then he became more insistent, saying he loved red-headed girls, particularly Irish ones, and I was just the girl he had been looking for.

One of the weavers pulled me to one side one night when we were putting our outdoor things on ready to go home, saying, 'Watch out fer Charlie Wheeldon, Katie, I've seen 'im followin' yer around. E's wed, yer know.'

'I wouldn't fancy him if he wasn't wed and twenty years younger,' I snapped in reply.

'Sure yer wouldn't, but 'e's a good tackler an' the firm'll not dispense wi' im. It'll be yer that 'as to go if there's any funny business.'

'There's not likely to be any funny business, not between

48

me an' Charlie Wheeldon, I can tell you.'

'I'm only warnin' yer, luv, just watch 'im.'

It was several days after that when I had gone to get hot water in the huge urn from which the women brewed their tea. The urn was heavy and it took all my strength to lift it when it was full of water, so he came after me saying, 'I'll 'elp yer wi' that, Katie, it's too 'eavy fer yer to manage on yer own.'

I was already trying to lift the urn when I gave a gasp of astonishment. He had thrust his hand up my skirt and in a sudden fury I spun round, sending the urn crashing to the floor. There was water everywhere. With a muttered oath he stepped back, but by this time I had hit him over the head with a broom and he was shouting obscenities at me.

People were rushing in from the weaving shed by this time and Charlie Wheeldon was nursing a cut face.

'Serves yer reet,' a fat woman with a red face shouted at him. 'Yer've bin askin' fer this fer a long time, can't keep yer 'ands off the young lasses. It's about time yer got yer cumuppance.'

'I'll see yer pays fer this, Katie O'Donovan,' he shouted. 'Yer little hell cat.'

The sound of the women's laughter followed him out of the shed.

The woman who had given me the first warning shook her head. 'No good'll come 'o this, Katie. Yer'll be needin' to watch 'im fro' now on, 'e's a vindictive devil. I should tell yer uncle if I were yer.'

'I don't want to tell mi uncle, an' 'im thinkin I'm settled here.'

'Well, yer not settled now, luv. I'm just warnin' yer to keep yer eyes open.'

After that day my life at Foxland's was terrible. Time after time he accused me of being a slut, of not doing my job properly, and I swear that the aisles I had swept most carefully were later strewn with rubbish. I bit my lip in anger but started all over again while he watched with a sinister sneer on his thin face.

One thing more I learned in the weeks that followed. The

women who had been on my side on that fateful day now sat with closed lips and sullen faces. They feared for their own jobs, and work was scarce. They had no thought of jeopardizing what they had on my behalf.

One day I found a dead mouse in my pocket and another a cockroach, and I had come to the end of my tether. I decided I would tell my aunt and uncle what was happening. But during the afternoon break I heard two of the girls talking. They had only just begun to work in the weaving shed and they were a good deal younger than most of the other women. Mona was a tall thin girl with a pock-marked face and dark frizzy hair, but Mildred was pretty, with a short pert nose and flashing green eyes, so pretty that I had already seen Charlie Wheeldon lingering round her looms whether she required assistance or not.

'I 'ear yer sister Nellie's gettin' wed at Easter,' Mona said.

'That's right, to a chap fro' Settle way, but it's goin' ter be a quiet affair 'cause he's just lost 'is mother.'

''Ow did she meet 'im, then?'

''E worked at Carslake's as a groom but 'e's got a job nearer 'is 'ome so that 'e can care for 'is old father.'

'I take it Nellie'll be leaving Carslake's then.'

'That's right.'

'I wouldn't mind 'er job, I'm fed up wi' weavin' an' not knowin' whether there's work or not.'

''Er job's spoken for, the kitchenmaid's bein' promoted. But I reckon 'er job'll be goin'.'

'I wouldn't fancy that, workin' i' the kitchens all day, peelin' vegetables, an' I 'ear Mrs Tate's a right tartar wi' the young servants.'

'Oh I don't know, our Nellie's never said owt about 'er. Any road, what do yer know about bein' a parlourmaid?'

'I'm not too daft ter learn.'

'When they appoints a parlourmaid they expect 'er to know all about it.'

'Well, what will the scullerymaid know?'

'She's bin at Carslake's two years so she's 'ad the chance to keep her eyes open.'

'Well I'm better off 'ere on mi three looms than skivvyin' fer the Carslakes. Someat else'll turn up.'

For the rest of the day I couldn't get that conversation out of my mind, and the dead cockroach in my coat pocket was the last straw.

'Is somethin' wrong, Katie?' my uncle asked at our evening meal.

'Wrong, Uncle?'

'Ay, you've not said a word right through the meal. Yer not 'avin' trouble at the shed, I hope?'

'Why no, Uncle, no trouble.'

He was watching me closely so I bent over my plate, refusing to meet his eye. I knew how gossip ran rife around the weaving sheds and I wondered if he had heard something of my troubles at the hands of Charlie Wheeldon.

'Well, it's Friday,' he said, smiling. 'Yer can forget about the mill till Monday mornin'.'

Normally the mill was working Saturday morning, but through lack of orders it was now closed for the whole of Saturday and Sunday, and although the weavers missed the extra money, most of them looked forward to the long weekend.

Mechanically I went about my evening tasks, helping Aunt Martha clear away the dishes, washing my hair, helping Frances to clean our bedroom although she performed this duty with bad grace and I preferred to do it on my own. Frances was not my favourite person and we had come no nearer liking each other than on the day we met. Lucy was different, she was a happy uncomplicated child, but Frances entertained ideas of grandeur far above her station, largely emanating from the girls she mixed with at school, most of whom lived in better-class houses and whose fathers were better placed than her own.

She was clever at her lessons and she was studying hard for a scholarship to the local grammar school, but my aunt was constantly worried on this score.

'What shall wi do if she passes, Kathleen? We've no money to send her there, there'll be 'er school uniform an' 'er books, it's only the education we shan't 'ave to pay fer.'

I kept silent during these tirades, for I had no words to comfort her. I was confident that if ever Frances had the opportunity to leave her family she would take it, and I antagonized her further the following morning when I made an excuse not to go to the market with my aunt as usual so that Frances had to go in my place.

'You always go to the market with mi mother,' she stormed at me. 'Why can't you today?'

'Because I have something else to do, it won't kill you to go for once, surely.'

'I hate goin' to the market, I hate the vegetable stalls and the noise, nobody else in my class goes to the market.'

'And if they did you'd be ashamed to be seen there. Why are you such a little snob?'

'I'm not a little snob, I just don't see why we can't go to the shops instead of those cheap stalls on the market.'

'Perhaps it's because your parents haven't enough money to shop anywhere else but the market. If those girls were really your friends they wouldn't mind where you shopped.'

'Well you wouldn't know anythin' about girls like that, would you? You won't catch me sweepin' up in a rotten old weavin' shed when I leave school, I'll get miself a real job.'

'In the meantime why don't you just hush up and go off to the market with your mother?'

She flounced out, and several minutes later I saw her setting off down the street with her mother. I noticed Frances wasn't carrying the basket.

As soon as they had gone I set about making myself look as neat and presentable as possible. I shrugged my arms into my best tweed coat, whose lengthened sleeves were once more beginning to look too short. I had grown since I had arrived in England so that the length of the coat was shorter than was strictly fashionable. I pulled the woollen tammy over my red hair and checked in the mirror for a final reassurance that I was looking my best. Then I set off towards Tremayne Hill.

For the first time I sensed spring in the air. Although

there was a sharp nip in the wind, snowdrops were in bud in the gardens and there was a new cheerfulness in the people I met. It was only as I passed the wrought-iron gates leading to the Foxland house that I began to have qualms about inquiring if the Carslake family required a new kitchenmaid.

I felt intimidated by the fine houses and well-kept gardens but, squaring my shoulders, I pressed on. They could only say no, they couldn't eat me, I told myself doggedly.

I had almost reached the Carslake's house when a group of riders emerged from the drive. They were a party of men and women, some of the men wearing bright hunting pink, the women in severe black and riding side-saddle. I had to lean back against the wall to allow them to pass. They were laughing and chattering amongst themselves and none of them spared me a glance until the last rider to leave the gates was forced to control his frisky horse, otherwise they must surely have crashed into me.

He smiled down at me somewhat ruefully, then he said gently, 'I'm sorry to have frightened you, you may pass now, I have him under control.'

In spite of my fear, I returned his smile, then I stood quite still watching them canter down the road.

That was the moment it was born, that long enchantment that was to colour my young life with wonder and enslavement and despair. Was it his voice, so different from the English voices I had been hearing of late, or the graceful way he sat his horse? Was it the charm of his smile or his handsome air of good breeding? I didn't know then and I have never known since, and I could not turn away. I stayed rooted to the spot until they were out of sight and it was some moments later when I felt secure enough to make my way along the drive. I felt bemused. Something momentous had happened to me, destroying my common sense, making me feel totally insecure.

An elderly man was in the garden pruning rose bushes, and as I approached he raised his battered hat in greeting.

'Nice day we're 'avin', to be sure,' he greeted me affably.

'Yes indeed.'

He beamed at me. 'Yer not fro' round these parts then.'

'No. From Donegal in Ireland.'

'I knows where Donegal is, Oi'me fro' County Kerry miself.'

'Oh and isn't that the most lovely spot in all Ireland.'

'So they tell me, but County Donegal's mighty foine.'

'Oh yes, yes it is.'

'Are ye callin' on the family then?'

'No, I'm lookin' for work.'

'Work is it. An' what makes ye think there's work for you 'ere, mi dear?'

'I've heard that Nellie is leavin' to get married and there could be a job going.'

'Is that a fact? Well, I've heard nothin' but then I'm only one o' the gardeners. You'll be needin' to speak to Mrs Tate but don't be put off with 'er manner, 'er bark's worse than 'er bite.'

'Where shall I find Mrs Tate then?'

'Ye goes to the side door. Ring the bell there an' somebody'll be answerin'. I wishes ye luck, lassy.'

'Thank you, I'll be needin' it I'm sure.'

I hurried along to the side door. My heart was racing and I stood for a few moments to compose myself before I lifted the heavy brass knocker.

After several minutes I heard bolts being drawn back and then the door opened and a girl was eyeing me over suspiciously. She was older than myself and she was wearing a sacking apron stained, I suspected, from its contact with vegetables.

'Could I see Mrs Tate please?' I ventured.

'Who's callin' then?'

'My name is Kathleen O'Donovan.'

'Wait 'ere,' she said shortly and left me on the doorstep. I listened for voices but there was only silence and my heart sank, expecting I would be sent away.

At last she returned, and holding the door open a little wider she said, 'Yer'd best come in, Mrs Tate's in the kitchen.'

I followed her down a flagged corridor and into the largest kitchen I had ever seen. There was a huge whitewood table in the centre and a vast oven all along one wall, while along another was ranged a huge Welsh dresser furnished with blue and white crockery.

A woman was sitting in a rocking chair at the fire and at the table sat another woman decorating a cake with sugar icing. Both were middle aged, the woman in the rocking chair in a long black dress, with her dark hair caught in a bun. The woman at the table was stout and she wore a snowy white apron and had a white mob cap over her grey hair.

Both women eyed me over without speaking, then the woman in the rocking chair said sharply, 'I'm Mrs Tate. Get back to your work, Polly, there's plenty to do if we're ever to be ready for tonight.'

Polly scurried out and Mrs Tate continued to look me over until I began to feel nervous.

'Well, an' what might you be wantin' to speak to me about?' she said at last.

'I've heard there might be a job going here in the kitchen, I came to ask if I could have it.'

'Who told you there might be work here?'

'I work at Foxland's and I heard Nellie's sister talking to another girl.'

'What's wrong with Foxland's then that makes you want to go into service?'

'I'm not happy there, I hate the noise and I'm frightened of the shuttles.'

'You're lucky to be in work at all. There'd be many a lass glad o' the chance to work at Foxland's.'

'Then if I leave there'll be a chance, won't there?' I retorted. The woman at the table chuckled but Mrs Tate frowned ominously and I regretted my audacity.

'How old are you?'

'I'm fifteen next month.'

'Irish, aren't you?'

'Yes, I've been in England just over twelve months, I live with mi aunt an' uncle.'

'What do you know about working in a house this size?'

'I worked hard in mi grandmother's house and it was the biggest in Dunfanaghy.'

'Workin' for your own folk isn't like workin' for strangers.'

'I worked like a servant for mi grandmother, I scrubbed and cleaned and I did all the vegetables an' washed the dishes. Mi Grandmother Cassidy didn't believe in idle hands.'

'Your grandmother doesn't appear to 'ave been too fond of you.'

'No, she wasn't. She said I was an O'Donovan and she never liked mi father.'

'What sort of a job might you be expectin' to find here?'

'I don't care. Nellie's sister said a girl was to be promoted into her sister's job, so I was thinkin' I might have the job she was leavin'.'

Somewhat wearily she said, 'Polly's bein' promoted, but I've no great hopes that she'll be comfortable in a parlourmaid's job. Still, money's not what it used to be an' we all has to make sacrifices. What money are ye earnin' at Foxland's?'

'Two and sixpence a week.'

'Well, you'll not get that 'ere as a kitchenmaid. Two shillings is what you'd be getting', but yer'd get yer keep, three meals a day an' a little bedroom that's tucked up under the eaves.'

My eyes lit up with expectancy.

'Please, Mrs Tate, I promise ye won't regret it and I'd work real hard. Even mi grandmother never complained about mi work.'

She looked across at the other woman. 'Well, wi can't manage without a kitchenmaid, Cook, what do you think about this lass here, is she what we might be lookin' for?'

'Will you do as I tells yer an' no back answers?' Cook asked sternly.

'Oh yes, yes I will.'

'Yer'll get up punctual an' no philanderin' wi' the lads who work in the stables and gardens?'

'Of course not.'

'Well, they all sez that but it didn't stop Nellie fro' gettin' wed to one o' the grooms, an' yer wouldn't 'a thowt butter'd melt in 'er mouth when she first came 'ere. Do yer folks know yer've come 'ere lookin' fer work?'

'No. I'll tell them when I get home.'

''Ow are they goin' ter take it?'

'My cousins will be glad to have the bedroom to themselves and mi aunt won't lose by it, she'll not 'ave me to keep an' I can afford to give 'er somethin' out o' mi wages.'

She nodded, then turning to Mrs Tate she said, 'I reckon wi can take a chance on this one, the lass looks clean and tidy an' she's pretty. P'raps you'll need ter be warnin' 'er about a couple o' things.'

Mrs Tate nodded. 'Do you know anythin' about this family?'

'No, Mrs Tate.'

'Well there's Colonel Carslake an' his wife, an there's five children, Mr Humphrey, Mr Roger and Mr Jeffrey, then there's Miss Mary and Miss Nancy. There is another son, Mr Ambrose, but 'e's married and lives over at Coppelthorpe. You'll not 'ave anythin' to do with the family in your work but Mr Roger wants watchin', 'e's an eye for a pretty face an 'e's never bin against chattin' the servants up. You should know right from the outset that you 'ave your place and they has theirs and the gulf 'atween you and them is unbridgeable. Isn't that right, Cook?'

'Ay, if she remembers that she'll not go far wrong.'

''Ow much notice do you have to give at Foxland's?' Mrs Tate asked.

'A week.'

'Then you can come here a week on Monday, you can see your bedroom then. I 'aven't the time to take you up there now an' Polly's busy in the scullery, there's a big dinner party tonight an' I don't want to interfere with what she's doin'. It doesn't take much to put her off 'er work.'

I thanked her gratefully and was about to leave when she called after me.

'Did you say your name was Kathleen?'

'Yes, Mrs Tate.'

'Do they call you anythin' else?'

'Mi father always called me Katie and mi uncle does too.'

'Well, it's Katie you'll be gettin' here. A week on Monday then, at seven o'clock sharp.'

Outside in the early spring sunshine I danced along the drive in glee. Out on the road leading down the hill I took to my heels and ran, snatching off my tammy and swinging it gaily while my auburn hair escaped from its slide and blew wildly around my face.

Chapter 7

I had thought to break the news to my aunt and uncle that evening after the girls had gone to bed, but I was so elated my news wouldn't keep until then. It was received with mixed feelings.

Uncle Turlough shook his head. 'I doubt if yer mother'll take kindly to ye goin' into service, Katie. It's feudal, that's what it is. One day there'll be no masters and servants, the Good Lord never intended that one man should serve another.'

'But that day moight be a long time comin', Uncle Turlough, and in the meantime I have to have a job.'

'You 'ave a job, Katie, at Foxland's. I know it isn't much but there'll be looms waitin' for yer one day. A bit o' patience is all that's needed.'

'There'll be no promotion for me at Foxland's, Uncle Turlough.'

'Why are ye so sure?'

'Because two girls who started after me have got looms and I'm still waitin'. Besides I don't want to be a weaver, I'm frightened to death o' them looms.'

'Ye say yer've bin passed over in favour o' two others, Katie?'

'Yes, but I don't mind, it doesn't matter, Uncle.'

'It's Charlie Wheeldon isn't it? What's 'e bin sayin' to yer, Katie, 'as 'e laid a finger on ye?'

'Yes, and I hit him with a broom so hard that I cut his face. He'll never forgive me for that, Uncle, an' as long as I stay at Foxland's 'e'll be at the back o' mi.'

'How much are they payin' yer?' my aunt demanded.

'Two shillings.'

'That's less than yer gettin' now.'

'I know, but I get my keep, three meals a day and my own bedroom. I shall be able to give yer one and sixpence a week easy and 'ave some left out of that.'

'We'll not be taking one and sixpence a week off ye, Katie,' my uncle said firmly, 'not when we're not givin' ye owt for it.'

'I'll get a day a week off surely, and I'd like to think I can come 'ere. I don't want you an' mi aunt to be losers, if ye feeds me on that day. I'll be wantin' to give yer somethin' for it.'

'I'll take one and sixpence then, an' I'll do some o' your washin' an' sewin' too. You knows yer've got ter give a week's notice at Foxland's?'

'I know, Aunt Martha, I'm to start at the Carslake's house a week on Monday at seven o'clock sharp. I don't even know what it's called.'

'It's called Heatherlea,' my uncle informed me.

'That's a real pretty name,' I mused. 'Miss Kathleen O'Donovan of Heatherlea.'

'Scullerymaid,' Frances put in spitefully, and was admonished by a look from her mother while I only laughed. It was just as well that she then put me in my place.

The week that followed was quite the worst I had known so far. I gave my notice in first thing on Monday morning, and after that my duties were twice as heavy, until in the evening I could have cried from the pain of aching arms through too much shifting of baskets filled with spindles and lifting and moving the heavy tea urn.

Charlie Wheeldon was doubly spiteful, following my footsteps with snide remarks, and when I appeared to take no notice he became even more angry. The last straw came when I found a dead rat on top of a basket I was asked to move and to my utter shame I became hysterical while he laughed uproariously and swung the dead thing in my face.

Before I was completely aware of it my uncle was there, lifting Charlie Wheeldon up by the back of his collar, and threatening what he would do to him if he ever touched me or even spoke to me again. The outcome was that the three of us were hauled in front of the works manager where I was forced to tell him the entire story.

My uncle was cautioned to keep the peace and Wheeldon was threatened that if there were any more complaints about his conduct with the weavers he would be dismissed. Fortunately I was leaving the mill that evening, hopefully never to return.

Aunt Martha insisted on walking up to the Carslake's with me the following Monday even when I protested that I could manage my bag unaided.

'If they sees somebody's with yer they'll know yer a respectable lass and come fro' respectable folk,' she argued.

This time a boy answered the door. He looked about seventeen years of age and he was carrying a steaming cup of cocoa. He stared at us without speaking until my aunt said, 'This is Kathleen O'Donovan, mi niece. She's comin' to work 'ere.'

At that he opened the door wider and let us in.

About six people were sitting round the table, just finishing their breakfast: Cook and Polly, two older girls in white caps and aprons, and two men in working clothes – all staring at me without exception.

'O' course,' Cook said, 'I'd forgotten for a minute that yer were comin' this morning. Pull a chair up to the table, lass, and I'll pour yer a cup o' tea. Is this yer mother then?'

'No, this is my aunt, Mrs Cassidy.'

'Mornin', Mrs Cassidy, I take it yer'd like a cup o' tea?'

'Thanks, that'd be very nice.'

'This is Katie O'Donovan whose comin' 'ere to take Polly's place when Nellie leaves, an' this is Nellie who's leavin' to get wed, an Milly who's parlourmaid-cum-ladies' maid. This is Joe Grimley an' Ted Stringer, both of 'em grooms, and this is Ned, one o' the stable lads. After yer've drunk yer tea Polly can show Katie 'er room. Yer'll allus use the back stairs, Katie, the front stairs are only fer the family an' fer the cleaners.'

'I'll remember, Cook.'

61

'Oh, an' mi name's Mrs Jackson but I answers ter Cook.'

I knew that my aunt dearly wanted to look at my room but I kissed her cheek quickly and said, 'I'll come and see you on mi first day off, Aunt Martha. Thanks for walking up 'ere with mi on mi first mornin'.'

The room was only large enough for a single bed and a small washstand. A corner was curtained off and Polly said, pointing to it, 'Yer can 'ang yer clothes be'ind that, there's 'ooks on the walls.'

'But isn't this your room, Polly?'

'I'm movin' out today, into Nellie's room along the corridor there. It's bigger ner this so I'll 'ave more room fer mi things.'

'But Nellie is still here.'

'Fro' today she's livin' in the town wi' 'er folks, that's until she gets wed that is.'

'I see.'

The room was very untidy, with hairpins and a thin layer of dust covering the washstand. Several pairs of cheap shoes occupied the floor at the side of the bed and soap had congealed on a soap dish next to the wash bowl. A wet towel was screwed up and lying on the floor and I itched to set to work putting the room to rights.

'When will you be able to move?' I asked her.

'Well, yer 'eard what she said, I was to get straight back, so likely as not it'll be after dinner.'

'Then there's no use mi unpacking, I'll leave mi things at the side o' the bed until I can get them in the drawers.'

'Suit yerself. Are yer comin' back with mi then? Yer can start 'elpin' wi the vegetables.'

I smiled at her but couldn't help wondering what sort of parlourmaid she was going to make.

In the back kitchen she handed me a sackcloth apron. 'Yer'd best put this on, vegetables stains yer clothes someat shockin', an wi the family an' all the servants there's a lot of 'em ter see to.'

It didn't take me long to realize that Polly wasn't a very good scullerymaid. The eyes were left in the potatoes and the droopy leaves from the outsides of the cabbages were mixed in with the rest. The same sort of carelessness applied to swedes and carrots and all of them only received a perfunctory wash before they were placed in the heavy iron pans.

'Are you glad you're bein' promoted?' I asked her.

'I'm not sure. They're not givin' mi as much money as Nellie gets, cuttin' down Cook sez, but I'll give it a try. Cook sez I has to learn to speak better an' look after mi appearance. You're pretty, is that hair its real colour?'

'Yes of course it is.'

'I wish I 'ad 'air that colour, that or fair like Miss Mary's.'

'Have you seen the family then?'

'Well yer sees 'em about the gardens an' the stables yer know, I sees 'em on't road sometimes but they don't know me.'

'They don't know you an' yet you work here?'

'That's right. Mrs Tate's told me I 'as to keep mi place even though I'm gettin' Nellie's job. That Mr Roger's 'ad is arm round Nellie more ner once but I don't suppose 'e'll be fancyin' me.'

'Mrs Tate's the housekeeper isn't she?'

'Ay. She goes ter see Mrs Carslake every mornin' an' they talks about the meals fer the day, what sort o' food they want an' so on, then Mrs Tate tells Cook an' I 'ave ter get busy. When they give their big parties the work that's needed is someat awful. I've 'ad ter be down 'ere at six o'clock seein' to mi vegetables or they'd never 'a' bin ready, an' Cook's that cross wi' extra mouths ter feed an' all sorts o' fancy cookin' ter do.'

'Do they often have parties then?'

'Not as much as they did. Times is 'ard, Cook sez, an' cotton's not doin' as well as it did. My but I'd like to 'a' bin 'ere when they 'ad their big weekend 'ouse parties, but I bet the work were someat cruel.'

'When was the last big party then?'

'That must 'a' bin when Mr Jeffrey were twenty-one. We were allowed to watch the guests arrivin' because it were a buffet meal, not a dinner like. All them lovely frocks and furs, an' Sir Joshua an' Lady Dorothy come an' they browt some young folk wi' 'em, nieces and nephews 'cause they 'as no children o' their own, an' there was Miss Mary pretty as a picture dancin' with Mr Jeffrey an' Miss Nancy waltzin' round wi' a young chap i' uniform, an' the presents, there were so many of 'em they 'ad ter be displayed i' the library an' they took up all the table an' most o' the floor. Yer should just 'a' seen Mr Roger flirtin' wi' every pretty girl that was 'ere an Mr Ambrose came wi' 'is young wife an' Mr Humphrey announced 'is engagement to a girl fro' over Yorkshire way.'

'And Mr Jeffrey, does he 'ave a young lady too?'

'Sweet on Lois Foxland 'e is. Cook sez 'e can't see anybody else when she's around.'

'She's very pretty.'

'Oh ay, she's pretty enough, but Cook sez they're not real gentry, not like the Carslakes an' the Tremaynes, they're only second-class gentry.'

'Now then,' came Cook's voice from the doorway, 'less o' that chatterin' you two or them vegetables'll never be ready. Mrs Tate's in the kitchen, Katie, she wants a word with yer.'

I wiped my hands on my apron and followed Cook into the kitchen where Mrs Tate sat at the table with a cup of tea and a huge piece of fruit cake.

I bobbed her a little curtsey as I had seen one of the maids in my Aunt Moya's house do. Great-aunt Moya had kept two maids but she had left all her money to mother Church and my father always said he doubted if God would forgive her for her lack of feeling or generosity to her own kinfolk.

'There's no need to bow and scrape to me, Katie, just be respectful an' do as you're told. Are you settlin' in all right?'

'Yes, thank you, Mrs Tate.'

'You'll find there's plenty to do.'

'Yes Mrs Tate.'

'Well, get back to your work then, there'll be a meal on the table at twelve o'clock, the family dine at one.'

'Thank you Mrs Tate.'

The pattern of my life was set. Nellie left to get married at Easter and Polly donned her white cap and apron while I soldiered on peeling vegetables, blackleading the huge iron fireplace and washing the pots and pans.

On my day off I walked down the hill to visit my relatives. Aunt Martha seemed happy for us to look round the shops, and sometimes when I could take Sunday off we listened to the band in the park.

On one of my visits towards the end of the summer she seemed unduly preoccupied and I could tell that she had been crying. She shook her head when I asked if anything was wrong but she showed no interest in going out.

'I'm sorry, Kathleen,' she said, 'I'm not feelin' miself today, I shan't blame ye if yer decides to get off early.'

'Are you ill, Aunt Martha?'

She dabbed at her eyes, then reaching into her apron pocket she pulled out an envelope which she handed to me.

Curiously I took out a long official-looking sheet of paper and then my eyes lit up with delight. Frances had passed the scholarship for the local grammar school.

'But this is wonderful news, Aunt Martha, why is it making you so sad?'

'We 'aven't got the money to send 'er. I was dreadin' 'er passin' but somehow I knew she would. She's worked real 'ard, it'll break 'er 'eart when I tell 'er she can't go. It's 'er clothes I'm worryin' about, all that uniform an' them sports things.'

'What has Uncle Turlough had to say about it?'

"E sez we'll manage, that she's ter go. 'E's allus 'ad 'is 'ead in the clouds an' 'e' spoils our Fanny, far more than 'e's ever spoiled Lucy, an' she's the best o' the two of 'em.'

Silently I agreed with her, but keeping my thoughts to myself I said, 'Have you nothing put by, Aunt Martha for something like this?'

'Ay, I tries to put somethin' by every week, but it's fer our old age an' for when the mill's on short time, yer never knows when that's goin' to 'appen.'

'Perhaps I could give you a bit more.'

'Nay lass, yer gives me enough fer what I does fer yer. She'll 'ave to be told that it's impossible, there's nothin' else fer it.'

'I'm not going to be here when you tell her, I'll get back to Heatherlea.'

She looked at me piteously. 'Yer do see that I'm right don't yer, Kathleen?'

'I can see you have a problem Aunt Martha, it's hard for all of ye.'

I felt for Frances. I didn't like her very much but I recognized her ability to learn and she had tried so hard for this scholarship, to be denied it now would cause her the utmost anguish. Why oh why couldn't there have been some money to help with her clothes?

At Heatherlea that night I told Cook about the scholarship. She shook her head, saying, 'Yer aunt's wrong, Katie, that lass should be given 'er chance. If she isn't, where's she goin' to end up? In a weavin' shed most likely, or p'raps i' service like you.'

Like me! I didn't tell Cook that I had high-flung notions of being something other than a scullerymaid. I didn't know when or how I was going to accomplish my ambitions but I knew one day I would.

The family were away from home the following weekend and I had Sunday afternoon off, but I was reluctant to visit my aunt's house in case there were still tantrums from Frances and much weeping from Aunt Martha. Instead I walked in the park, and towards the dovecotes I saw Uncle Turlough, leaning on his stick and looking down at the rosebeds in wrapt contemplation.

His eyes lit up when he caught sight of me. 'Ave ye bin down to the house then?'

'No, I thought being Sunday you might all be out.'

'Ye didn't wait to see mi last Wednesday, Katie.'

'No, I thought you had things to discuss and you wouldn't want me there.'

'Yer kin, Katie.'

'I didn't think Frances would want mi there. Was she very unhappy?'

'She's goin', Katie. We've no right to deny the lass her education.'

'But will you be able to manage?'

'We'll manage. I'll cut out mi tobacco an' Martha'll take in a bit o' sewin'. It'll work out, Katie. I'll not 'ave mi daughter sayin' we stood in 'er way. She'll meet a better class o' girls there an' it could mean she'll meet a different type o' feller when the time comes for 'er to think o' gettin' married.'

'I hope she never forgets the sacrifices your're goin' to have to make for her, Uncle Turlough.'

'She'll not. Oh, I knows she sez things that make her mother angry but she's only a young lass. She'll mature an' she'll work 'ard, we knows that.'

'You're goin' to miss your pipe, Uncle.'

'That I am, but it's not as important as our Fanny's education.'

All thoughts of Fanny's education went abruptly from my mind the following week.

It was Tuesday morning and breakfast was on the table promptly at a quarter to seven, and still the men had not come up from the stables. Cook was irritable as she clattered the huge frying pan on the stove.

'Where are they?' she complained. 'The bacon'll be cooked to a frazzle at this rate an' then they'll do nowt but grumble. Yer'd best get down ter them stables, Katie, an' ask 'em when they're comin' up fer their breakfast.'

Near the stables I heard men's voices and as I entered the stableyard I saw six men surrounding a horsebox from which a young horse was being coaxed down the ramp. They took no immediate notice of me and because I loved horses I joined their circle, staring in admiration at the beautiful animal with his shining chestnut coat.

At last Ned the stable lad saw me, and shouted, 'Do ye like 'orses Katie? I'll bet Cook doesn't know yer 'ere.'

At that all the men looked at me, including a young man wearing faultless riding breeches and a tweed jacket. He was good-looking, with dark curly hair and bold brown eyes.

Forgetting the horse, he sauntered to my side saying, 'Hallo, I've not seen you before. Do you work at the house?'

'That I do.'

'I haven't seen you there.'

'No, I work in the kitchens.'

'And what do they call you?'

'Mi name's Kathleen O'Donovan, an' what do they call you, might I ask?'

There was a gasp of astonishment from the others, but with a merry smile the man said, 'They call me Roger Carslake, Mister Roger to you, Kathleen O'Donovan.'

'Oh Sir, I'm sorry, I didn't know you were one o' the young masters.'

'In that case I'll forgive you. What are they thinking about, hiding a girl as pretty as you in the kitchens? We've never had a kitchenmaid with glorious red hair before.'

'Cook says will ye be comin' for your breakfast or the bacon'll be spoilt,' I called to the men, and turning on my heel and with a little backward smile, I started back.

To my surprise he reached out and caught my arm. 'Before you go tell me where you're from, Kathleen O'Donovan. Not from around here, I'll be bound.'

'No. I'm from Dunfanaghy.'

'And where on earth is that?'

'In County Donegal.'

'Ah. So you're Irish.'

'I am.'

'Well, Kathleen O'Donovan, the sooner you are moved from the kitchens to the rest of the house the better I'll like it.'

Oh the impudence of him with his laughing eyes and his teasing voice. Shaking my arm free, I moved towards the stable gate and almost collided with another young man coming in. This time it was I who stared wide-eyed and tongue-tied and for the second time I was staring into his blue eyes, bewitched by the charm of his smile.

'This is Kathleen O'Donovan, our new kitchenmaid,' came Mr Roger's voice behind me.

The smile became wider and he said, 'You're the girl I

'almost knocked over on the road one day.'

'Yes Sir, I was comin' for a job.'

'And apparently you got it.'

'Yes, Sir.'

He smiled again and then they walked away from me towards the horse. I stood where I was, staring after them, listening to their conversation with the grooms and observing their pleasure in the horse, then one of the grooms spotted me.

'Tell Cook we're on our way,' he called, and I turned and fled.

'My what a time yer've bin,' Cook complained, 'are they comin' or aren't they?'

'Yes, they'll be here soon. Mr Roger and another man were in the stableyard with a young horse that'd just been brought in.'

'That'll be the 'orse Mr Jeffrey bought fro' the sales last week. Was Mr Jeffrey there?'

'I'm not sure. Mr Roger was there and then another young man came, a man with fair hair and blue eyes.'

'That'll be Mr Jeffrey. Not a bit alike those two brothers aren't. Mr Ambrose and Mr Jeffrey are alike, Mr Humphrey and Mr Roger are alike. Now finish yer breakfast, we're goin' ter be runnin' late this mornin'.'

The men came in a few minutes later and Cook told them 'I want no complaints about the breakfast, it's yer own fault if it's spoilt.'

'We couldn't come any sooner,' Ted Stringer said, 'Mr Roger an' Mr Jeffrey were down at the yard wi' the new colt.'

'And they'll be back upstairs now wantin' their breakfasts, and 'ere I am still feedin' you lot.'

'Mr Roger took a shine to Katie 'ere,' Ned said, and although I glared at him furiously he did nothing but laugh.

'Ye just watch yer step wi' Mr Roger, Katie, 'e's allus 'ad an eye fer a pretty face an' 'e's not much carin' where he finds one. Different as chalk an' cheese, 'im an' Mr Jeffrey.'

'I reckon 'e's more of a man though,' Ted Stringer replied.

'Not 'im. Mr Jeffrey's the sensitive one, far more a gentleman.'

''Is father doesn't think so, it's young Roger who's the favourite!'

'Then it's ashamed of 'isself he should be, makin' a favourite o' one of 'is sons. Katie, 'elp me to clear this table an' get back to the vegetables, or lunch'll never be ready.'

The rest of the day passed uneventfully until that night when there was a quiet tap on my bedroom door. On opening it I found Polly shivering in a thin nightdress, with a cardigan draped around her shoulders.

'Can I cum in fer a minute?' she asked plaintively.

I opened the door wider and she came in and sat on my bed while I pulled a blanket round both of us. The rooms on the top floor were draughty and mine was draughtier than most.

'Is something wrong, Polly?' I asked, and to my consternation she burst into tears.

'Oh Katie, I 'ates it upstairs, I were never cut out ter be a parlourmaid, I don't talk proper an' mi 'ands are rough fro' too much cleanin'. I breaks the china an' I'm that nervous 'elpin ter serve the meals I spills the soup and clatters the dishes. I can tell Mrs Carslake doesn't think I'm up to it an' the two girls giggle when I does owt wrong.'

'Has Mrs Tate said anything?'

'She doesn't 'ave to, 'er looks are enough. I wishes I could get back downstairs, but it's yer job now.'

'And I need a job, Polly. Why don't you speak to Mrs Tate?'

'I couldn't, not when this is supposed to be promotion fer mi. She'd send mi packin' an' that's fer sure.'

Polly wasn't aware of the fantastic idea being born in my mind at that moment. I wouldn't be afraid to be a parlourmaid, I could speak properly even if I did have an Irish accent – both my parents had been very careful about that. And if my hands were roughened by too much contact with carbolic and hot water I would get some hand cream and work on them until they were smooth again.

'Polly, are you quite sure you don't want to stay on as

parlourmaid?'

'I am sure Katie, but I got ter work.'

'Do you think *I* could be a parlourmaid? If you do perhaps we could ask Mrs Tate if we could change places.'

There was sudden hope in her eyes, then with her words tumbling over each other she said, 'Yer'd be a lot better ner me, Katie, but you'll 'ave ter ask if we can change, I'm that frightened o' Mrs Tate she might tell me ter go. What shall I do if she does?'

'She won't, Polly, leave Mrs Tate to me.'

'When? Tomorrer?'

'As soon as I get the chance.'

She smiled tremulously and her thin pinched face seemed suddenly happier.

'Get back to bed now Polly, it's so cold you'll catch your death.'

I watched her scurry down the corridor, then I sat on my bed and thought about what I would say to Mrs Tate.

My opportunity came after lunch, when she invariably came into the kitchen to drink tea and eat cake with Cook before they took their afternoon naps.

I smoothed my hair and took off my apron. I had put on a clean white blouse and my best navy-blue skirt under my apron, and I was looking my tidy best. They both raised their eyes when I entered the kitchen and Cook said, 'It's not yer half day today is it, Katie?'

'I wanted to speak to Mrs Tate.'

She eyed me stonily for several seconds then she said, 'Well, what is it?'

I had decided to take the bull by the horns right away so without further preamble I blurted out, 'Please, Mrs Tate, can Polly and I change places? She hates it upstairs and I'm ambitious, I want to do better for miself.'

'Have you bin talking about this between you then?' she demanded.

'I didn't know till last night that Polly was unhappy in her work, she came to my room and she was very upset.'

'Why didn't she come to me, then?'

'I think she was afraid.'

'But you're not afraid, it's plain to see.'

'No. I've nothin' to be afraid of. I does mi work an' Cook's had no complaints. I'm clean and tidy and I knows how to wait on table.'

'How? How do you know how to wait on table?'

'Well I waited on table for mi grandmother, and she entertainin' anybody in Dunfanaghy if she thought they were somebody. She'd have boxed mi ears if I'd done anythin' wrong.'

'There's seven in this family alone, an' more often than not there's more when they brings their friends home.'

'That's all right, there were four of us and mi grandmother, then there was Father McGinty an' the Widows Malone and Murphy and sometimes mi grandmother's friend from Ballymore.'

Cook threw back her head and laughed till the tears rolled down her cheeks, and even Mrs Tate's lips twitched as though she found my talk amusing.

'I'll give it some thought, Katie O'Donovan,' she said at length, 'but I'll have to ask the mistress, she has to know about these things. How much money are you thinkin' you'll be entitled to?'

'I'd be willin' to work for what Polly's gettin' until you think I'm suitable, then I think I should get a bit more.'

'Well, I'll say one thing for you, you've got a head on your shoulders, an' it's true that Polly's no good as a parlourmaid and never likely to be any good.'

'When shall I know, Mrs Tate?'

'Why are you in a hurry to know?'

'I'd like to be able to tell mi aunt and uncle when I visits them tomorrow.'

'Well I'm not sure about that, but we'll see.'

I thanked her, then I hurried back to the scullery and after putting on my apron started on the vegetables for that evening's meal. I would be so glad to see the end of peeling vegetables, and quite deliberately I kept my mind from straying on the true reason for wanting to get upstairs.

Chapter 8

I stood in front of the mirror in the corridor eyeing my reflection. I was wearing a long black dress that had belonged to Nellie and which fitted after taking in a bit here and there, with starched white cap and apron, and the whole picture was mighty pleasing to the eye.

At nearly seventeen I had grown tall and slender and my glossy red hair looked its best against the snowy white of the cap. My intense blue eyes complimented my fair pink and white skin and my mouth was warm and generous over small, even white teeth. I knew that I was beautiful. Men looked after me in the park and on the streets, the grooms flirted with me and Ned was hopelessly in love with me, but I kept to myself. If they teased me I answered back and if they reached out to touch me I danced quickly away. Once I heard Cook say to Mrs Tate, 'My but she's a beauty that Katie, rockin' all the men on their 'eels an' not carin' a toss of a button for a single one o' them.'

'It could be she's set 'er sights on somethin' a bit more prosperous than one o' the grooms,' Mrs Tate said darkly.

'Nay, she's too sensible fer that. Mr Roger'll get no change out a' Katie.'

'I wasn't thinking of Mr Roger, I was thinkin' of Mr Jeffrey.'

'Nay, I can't believe that, an 'im wi' not a thowt in 'is 'ead that doesn't concern Lois Foxland.'

'I hope she's more sense, there's only hurt in that direction. But I have seen her lookin' at him and Mr Jeffrey's always nice wi' the servants, she could get the wrong idea.'

I bit my lip in vexation, wishing I hadn't overheard. Were they so obvious then, my feelings for Jeffrey Carslake?

He was kind, he got up from the table and held the door open for me, and once he had even taken the heavy tray from my hands and laid it on the table. Not like Roger, who lost no opportunity of putting his arm round me or giving my bottom a little pinch if I had my hands full.

I didn't dislike Roger, he was the life and soul of any party and his father's obvious favourite.

Colonel Carslake himself was a rumbustical figure. He was tall like all his sons, with grey hair and a grey waxed moustache. He liked his whisky, which was evident by his red face, and sometimes he favoured wearing a monocle which gave him a debonair alien appearance. Mrs Carslake was pretty and gentle, as introverted as her husband was extroverted, and she presided over the dining table with a gentle grace that I admired.

Miss Nancy was gay and beautiful with black hair and green eyes and Miss Mary was her very opposite, with pretty fair hair and blue eyes, and she was very like her mother.

Mr Humphrey was an older version of Roger but since he had become engaged to a Miss Elsie Mountjoy from the South Riding his high spirits seemed singularly curtailed and he only ogled me from over his soup plate and kept his hands to himself.

Mr Ambrose and his wife lived a few miles away but sometimes on Sunday morning they would ride over, either on horseback or in their carriage with their two children, Master Robin and Miss Edith, and when they had gone Roger would be disparaging in his remarks about his oldest brother.

'He's living in the past over at Copplethorpe, why doesn't he get a motor car instead of riding about in that old carriage?'

'Lorna prefers the carriage, dear,' his mother would chide him, 'besides everybody doesn't want to go tearing over the country in a noisy two-seater like yours.'

'I'll take you to church on Sunday morning, Mother, you'll soon change your mind about motor cars.'

'No thank you, darling, I prefer to drive myself there in

the trap.'

'Why don't you get one, Jeffrey? You know Lois would love it,' he demanded.

'I might one of these days. I'd prefer to wait a while to see if business improves.'

'Better to get it now, old boy, if business doesn't improve you can always sell it.'

Jeffrey merely smiled and went on with his meal while Colonel Carslake said, scathingly, 'You'll not find Jeffrey doing anything as adventurous as buying a motor car. Give me a lad that likes his whisky and a romp in the hay rather than a lad who spends all his time walkin' on his own over the fells or with his head buried in a book.'

'That isn't fair, John,' his wife said gently. 'Jeffrey rides as well if not better than the rest of you and he's no less a man for being interested in books.'

I could not help but hear conversations of this kind because the servants were treated as if they were not there when they waited at table. Once after listening to such a tirade from Colonel Carslake, Mrs Tate said to me, 'Not one word of that conversation will you repeat out of this house, Katie. Good servants don't tittle-tattle.'

'Of course not, Mrs Tate.'

But we talked amongst ourselves and it soon became evident to me that while Cook adored mister Jeffrey, Mrs Tate preferred Roger, and long and many were their arguments on that score.

I was now earning four shillings a week and I was insisting that my aunt kept three of them in spite of her reluctance.

'Honestly, Aunt Martha,' I said firmly, 'I get all my food at Heatherlea and you do a lot for me.'

'What do I do then? A bit o' sewin' and a bit o' cookin'.'

'I don't care, I want you to have it and don't say it won't come in useful with Frances at the grammar school. I take it she's happy there?'

'She doesn't say much about it, but she's made friends and she visits their homes. I haven't asked her to bring 'em 'ere.'

'But they'd come, surely.'

'I mentioned it once and she didn't seem too keen. It'll change 'er, Katie, I just know it will. You mark my words, she'll not be our Fanny at all in a few years' time.'

'If she does change, Aunt Martha, it won't be the school that's changed her, it'll be Frances herself.'

She stared at me for a moment then, shaking her head, she said, 'Ay, yer right.'

One afternoon I saw Frances walking towards me with three or four other girls, but when she saw me she hurried across the road, making it quite plain that a cousin in service was not a desirable relative.

I said nothing of this to my aunt or uncle, but I had it in my mind to give young Fanny a severe shaking if ever I encountered her alone.

I seldom went to their house on Sundays now, keeping my visits to midweek when I knew Fanny would not be at home. On Sundays I preferred to walk in the park or over the fells, and it was on one of these walks I came across Mr Jeffrey sitting on a five-barred gate overlooking the town.

At first I thought I should turn back before he saw me, but then squaring my shoulders I walked on, hoping he would not turn round. As I drew nearer however he jumped down from the gate and turned as though he had decided he had sat there long enough. By this time I was level with him and there was no escape.

For a moment he stared at me without recognition, then he smiled. 'Hallo, it's Katie, isn't it?'

'Yes, Sir.'

'I haven't seen you walking on the fells before.'

'I do it often Sir on Sundays, if I'm not working.'

'Then that's why we haven't met. I don't often walk here on Sunday.'

He fell into step beside me and I was aware of a sudden and unfamiliar shyness.

'Do you find it very different living here after Ireland?' he asked.

'Not the countryside, Sir, but I'm missing the sea, there's always the sea at Donegal.'

'Yes. I've never been there.'

'Never been to Donegal! Oh but ye should, Sir, it's beautiful with the hills and the little islands and there's hundreds and thousands o' gulls on Horn Head.'

He smiled down at me, his slow gentle smile that charmed me utterly, and I blushed under his regard.

'If Donegal was so beautiful, Katie, how could you ever bear to leave it?'

'Well you see mi father died and mi Uncle Turlough offered me a home while mi mother and brother and sister went off to Uncle Shamus in America.'

'And you didn't mind your family being split like that?'

'Oh but I did mind, I minded a lot. I suppose if ever I have enough money I'll go out there to join them, but when mi mother writes she doesn't mention it any more.'

'Are you happy at Heatherlea?'

'Oh yes, Sir, particularly since I got promoted upstairs. I did so hate all them vegetables, I couldn't get the stains out of mi fingers.'

He laughed and it was nice to think I had the power to make him laugh.

It felt so natural and easy to be walking across the fell with him with the short tough grass under our feet and the soft wind in our hair. As we reached the ridge we turned and looked down into the valley where Marsdale nestled between its two hills. Because it was Sunday there was no smoke coming from its forest of mill chimneys and as if he knew my thoughts he said, 'That would be quite a pretty town if they took all the chimneys down.'

'It'd be a much poorer town, Sir.'

He smiled. 'Are you always so practical, Katie?'

'When you haven't much money and you're not so sure what the future holds you have to be practical, Mr Jeffrey. Mi Grandmother Cassidy said I was just like mi father, a dreamer with mi head in the clouds, but then she never really knew what I was like. She never took the trouble to find out.'

'Couldn't you have stayed on in Donegal with your grandmother?'

'Not likely. She would 'a' turned mi into a real skivvy, she did her best in the short time we were there. No, I'm better off here in England and I have mi aunt and uncle in the town.'

'And a boyfriend perhaps,' he added with twinkling eyes.

'Not me. I have more important things to do with mi life than waste it on a boyfriend.'

He threw back his head and laughed.

'On the day you leave Heatherlea to get married I'll remind you of that remark, Katie O'Donovan.'

'Then you'll be waitin a long time, Sir. I've no thoughts on leaving Heatherlea or getting married.'

He smiled, and how I despised the wild fluttering of my heart.

'I am walking on to the old pilgrims' cross, Katie, it's a fair distance.'

'Oh you carry on, Sir, I'm going to walk back now, there's afternoon tea to see to.'

'Of course, the function my mother looks forward to every day of the week.'

I flashed him a bright smile then I turned and walked briskly down the hill, nor did I turn my head to stare after him, a feat which required all my willpower.

Cook was terse with me as I set about preparing the afternoon tea tray, and I couldn't see why. After all I was allowed a few hours off on a Sunday afternoon as long as I got back for tea, and it was only when she slammed the tea pot down on the tray and I raised my eyebrows that she snapped, 'So yer've bin walkin' on the fell wi' Mr Jeffrey, then?'

I stared at her, startled. 'How did you know?'

'Ned told me. He started out after ye thinking he'd walk with yer, then 'e saw yer talkin' to Mr Jeffrey and yer walked on together.'

'I didn't know Mr Jeffrey was on the fell, I just happened to meet him and we got talkin'. It has nothin' to do with Ned, Cook, an' it was all very innocent.'

'It might start out that way but don't get any wild ideas about Mr Jeffrey. He's spoken for, an' even if 'e wasn't 'e's

78

not for the likes o' yer. Money marries money, Katie, and don't you ever forget it. No good'll come o' yer setting yer cap at Mr Jeffrey.'

'I'm not settin' mi cap at him. Oh, won't I just have somethin' to say to Ned when I see him.'

I picked up the tray and stalked out of the kitchen, hurt and angry that my innocent meeting with Jeffrey Carslake should have been reported to Cook. At the same time deep down in my heart was that haunting fascination that was colouring every hour of every day.

'You're late, Katie,' Mrs Tate remarked as we set out cups and saucers on a long low table in front of the mistress, and then as Mrs Tate started to pour the tea the doorbell rang and I hurried to answer it.

It was Lois Foxland standing on the front step, as pretty as a picture in a pale beige coat with mink ties at the neck and a stylish brown hat adorned with osprey feathers.

She favoured me with an absent-minded smile while she took off her coat to show a pretty beige dress decorated with brown velvet ribbon, and three strands of pearls. How I envied that fashionably clad figure as I held the door open for her to enter the drawing room.

Mrs Carslake greeted her warmly, saying, 'Why Lois, how lovely to see you, you're just in time for tea.'

I was sent to the kitchen for extra china, and Cook asked urgently, 'Who's arrived then?'

'Miss Foxland.'

She gave me a knowing look and said, 'She's come lookin' for Mr Jeffrey. Now just you be sensible, Katie, and see things as they are.'

I felt a vague elation at knowing Mr Jeffrey would not be back in time for tea but as Mrs Tate and I served the tea it became evident that Lois had not come to see him.

'Mother hasn't been at all well,' she was telling Mrs Carslake, 'so Daddy thought it would be a splendid idea if we took a cruise over Christmas, the Med probably.'

'That means you won't be at the Hunt Ball this Christmas, then. Jeffrey will be very disappointed.'

'I know, poor dear, but he'll have no difficulty in finding

79

somebody else to escort.'

'No, I'm sure he won't, but Jeffrey isn't Roger, he's very single-minded in his likes and dislikes and you are the only girl he gives a thought to.'

Lois laughed, obviously delighted. 'Perhaps he would like to come with us.'

'I'm afraid that will be out of the question. My husband wouldn't hear of him being away from the mills for several weeks and it really wouldn't be fair to the other boys. Jeffrey and his father don't exactly see eye to eye as it is.'

'No they don't, do they. I wonder why that is?'

'They're very different in temperament. Jeffrey is like me, Roger is like his father. My husband is a man of action and he considers Jeffrey something of a dreamer. Besides, we are having to lay people off at the mills through shortage of orders, it wouldn't be right for those poor people to see Jeffrey going off on a cruise at this particular time.'

'No, I suppose not. Trade is awful, we're having to cut down at Foxland's.'

'I believe it's pretty general, my dear, but we've seen bad times before. I'm sure we shall weather the storm once again.'

'Yes I suppose so, but Daddy is pinching and saving a bit. He's told me to go easy on the clothes I buy for this cruise.'

Mrs Carslake laughed. 'My dear, you always look quite enchanting. You don't need a lot of new clothes.'

Lois pouted prettily. 'Well, we get such wretched weather and it will be hot in the Med. I shall have to have things for the climate, and so will Mummy.'

Mrs Carslake smiled indulgently.

'I have no doubt, my dear, that you will both manage everything you need. You do remember that Sir Joshua and Lady Dorothy are holding a ball at the end of January to celebrate their silver wedding?'

'Yes of course, we shall be back long before then. I suppose there will be a lot of people congregating round the gates to see everybody arrive.'

'They come to admire you young ones in your pretty

clothes.'

'Sometimes I don't think they come to admire us at all, I think it makes them pea green with envy because we have so much and they have nothing at all.'

Mrs Carslake looked at me a trifle nervously and I was sent to the kitchen for more hot water. When I returned with it she said, 'I will ring for you to clear away, Katie,' but my dismissal didn't prevent me from hearing her say, 'I hope you are not in a hurry, Lois, Jeffrey shouldn't be long and I know he will want to see you.'

I was halfway across the hall when the front door was flung open suddenly and Miss Nancy ran in accompanied by two young men I recognized as the Halford twins who lived in a house a little lower down the hill. She was blushing and breathless as though they had been running and I knew from gossip that both young men were contestants for Miss Nancy's favours.

'Is my mother in?' she asked in a whisper.

'Yes, Miss Nancy, having tea in the drawing room.'

'Is she alone?'

'No, Miss Foxland is with her.'

She spun round to her companions, asking, 'Do either of you want to take tea with my mother and Lois or would you rather go into the library and practice the bunnyhug?'

'The bunnyhug every time, old thing,' Stuart Halford said, laughing.

They were not identical twins and Cook had told me that Stuart was the dark one whereas Mark had hair as red as my own.

'Will you ask Cook if we can have tea in there, Katie? I know Mrs Tate hates it but I expect Lois and my mother have almost finished theirs.'

'I'll ask her, Miss Nancy,' I said, and hurried to do her bidding.

I liked Nancy Carslake with her dark gay beauty. The men hung around her like flies round the honey pot and she flirted indiscriminately with most of them. When I told Cook who she was with, she sniffed, saying, 'Playin' one off against the other, that's what Miss Nancy does, and in the end no good'll come of it. It's my guess she'll marry neither of 'em.'

'They're both very good-lookin',' I said as though that exonerated her flirtatious behaviour.

'Looks 'as nothin' to do wi' it, Katie,' she snapped. 'They think they've all the world in a bant just 'cause they're all in cotton, but mark my words they'd do well to look outside cotton for their partners i' life.'

'Why is that?'

'Because if cotton goes down they all go down wi' it. If they 'as other fingers i' other pies at least they saves someat. It makes sense, Katie.'

'The Carslakes and the Foxlands are in cotton, so doesn't that apply to Mr Jeffrey and Miss Lois?'

'It's not a good match for either of 'em, Katie, but it wouldn't be a good match for Mr Jeffrey to go off wi' one of 'is mother's servants, neither. Use yer 'ead, girl.'

'I wasn't even thinkin' of that,' I stammered with a scarlet face, and snatching the tea tray out of her hands I made a sudden exit.

They had rolled back the carpet in the library and a gramophone with a huge horn occupied the top of the desk. Nancy was engrossed in teaching one of the boys how to do the bunnyhug. While I watched as I poured the tea, and under cover of the table my feet tapped out the rhythm.

'I've poured the tea, Miss Nancy,' I announced.

I was almost at the door when she pounced on me.

'Can you dance, Katie?' she demanded.

'I can do the Irish dances, Miss Nancy, but that's about all.'

'Then you should learn to do the bunnyhug, Katie. Come on you two, it's much better with the four of us. Stuart, you're better at it than Mark, so you teach Katie and I'll teach Mark.'

'Oh but I can't, Miss Nancy,' I protested. 'Cook'll be furious if I don't get right back.'

'Oh bother Cook, she's always furious about something. It's way off dinner time so you can't have much to do. Tell Cook I asked you to stay.'

'I don't think that's likely to satisfy her, Miss Nancy.'

'Well then, leave Cook to me. Now wind up the gramophone, Mark, and we'll begin.'

I was nervous, but soon the music cast its spell and we were leaping round the room without a thought for anything else. Stuart was an excellent teacher and he was easy to follow. I had forgotten how much I had loved dancing. Those country dances had served me in good stead and I was dancing the bunnyhug as well as Miss Nancy and far better than Mark, so that Nancy clapped her hands with glee, saying, 'You're good, Katie, really good. We must try the foxtrot.'

I had forgotten all about a quick return to the kitchen and it was only Mrs Tate frowning in the doorway that brought me to my senses.

'Get back to the kitchen, Katie,' she commanded, 'I'll have something to say to you later.'

'Oh Mrs Tate, don't be such a spoilsport,' Nancy cried, 'I asked Katie to stay so that one of the boys didn't need to sit out.'

I escaped quickly, leaving Miss Nancy to placate the housekeeper, but I waited in the kitchen with a fluttering heart until Mrs Tate came to eye me with a severity that brought the hot colour into my face.

'Fine exhibition that was, and no mistake,' she began. 'There she was in the library dancin' with Mr Halford and Miss Nancy dancing with the other one, an' the carpet rolled back and the gramophone on. You should have told Miss Nancy you had work to do.'

'I don't think I'm in a position to speak like that to Miss Nancy,' I objected.

'You're in no position to spend your afternoons dancin' in the library with yer betters,' she snapped angrily. 'Nellie knew how to keep her place an' I wouldn't have had such trouble with Polly.'

'I doubt if Polly'd 'a' bin asked,' Cook said drily, and I threw her a grateful glance which did not escape Mrs Tate's eagle eye.

'There's no call to stick up for the girl, Cook. Miss Nancy

should've had more sense than ask her to stay there but she'll know in future to decline anythin' of that nature. I shudder to think what the master or the mistress would 'a' said if they'd walked into the library instead of me.'

'I'm sorry, Mrs Tate, it won't happen again.'

'See that it doesn't, now ye can collect that tray from the drawing room and keep out o' that library.'

I hurried towards the drawing room, aware that my cheeks were burning, and I bit my lip nervously when I encountered Mr Jeffrey crossing the hall.

Nervously I filled the tray, upsetting some of the milk, but he was too busy greeting Lois to notice my failings. Later from the kitchen window I saw him escorting Miss Foxland along the drive, walking arm in arm and their laughter floating on the breeze. I had not noticed Cook standing at my side until she said, 'See what I mean, Katie, she's the girl Mr Jeffrey 'as is eye on, an' if it weren't Lois Foxland it'd be somebody like 'er.'

With a bitterness strange to me I murmured, 'What is there for us, Cook, what can there ever be for people like us?'

'There be plenty if yer learns to stick to yer own sort an' not go cryin' after the moon. Leave Mr Jeffrey for the likes o' Lois Foxland, and much good may she do 'im.'

'She's so pretty, like a piece of best china.'

'Ay, and about as useful, I shouldn't wonder. She's not as pretty as you, Katie O'Donovan, if yer 'ad 'er clothes an' 'er education yer'd knock spots off 'er.'

'Then why am I put down, why can't men see further than their noses?'

'Ye mean further than 'is nose. I'll tell yer why, Katie. They've bin brought up together, they runs wi' the same crowd, wantin' the same things, an' if luv didn't bring 'em together money would.'

'That's horrible.'

'It's practical, lass, an' instead o' moonin' round after Mr Jeffrey yer should be looking round for a young feller wi' a good trade in 'is fingers an' a bit of ambition. Mr Jeffrey's got no ambition, nice as 'e is. Aren't they all content to sit back waitin' for the old days to come back when cotton were King i' Lancashire. Them days'll never come back, Katie, they've gone fer good.'

'What about all those people in Marsdale and the other cotton towns then? Most of them work in the mills, what will they do if cotton's finished?'

'P'raps someat else'll take its place. If it doesn't there'll be a lot o' poverty in this area.'

I went into the scullery where Polly was busy scrubbing the potatoes for the evening meal. Cook's talk troubled me and I couldn't help thinking about my aunt and uncle, whose finances were already stretched to the limit so that their eldest daughter could take up her scholarship. Aunt Martha was working at her sewing machine from early morning until late at night, taking in sewing from people who didn't want to pay much, and all Uncle Turlough knew was farming and cotton. Most of the mills were on short time and even at the Carslakes' house the joints of meat were becoming smaller and rich cakes had almost entirely disappeared from the menu.

That night Mrs Tate went to bed with a sick headache and I was informed that Milly would help me to serve the evening meal.

I had seen very little of Milly since my first day at Heatherlea, as she spent most of her time attending to Miss Nancy and Miss May. Once I heard Mrs Tate scold her sharply for not pulling her weight in the household tasks, and Milly had tossed her pretty head, saying, 'I 'ave too much to do for my young ladies, Mrs Tate, I sees to their mending and looks after their clothes, then there's their hair to do an' now that Katie's 'ere I didn't think I would be needed as much.'

'You were needed when Nellie was 'ere, there's still only the same pair of hands.'

'I'll 'elp when I can, Mrs Tate,' Milly snapped.

She helped with poor grace and without addressing a word to me, and after we had taken the dishes down to the kitchen she made as if to retreat upstairs until Cook said, 'There's the dishes to see to, Milly, give Katie some 'elp.'

'I 'ave some sewin' to do upstairs, Cook.'

'Yer 'eard what Mrs Tate said, yer don't want 'er complainin' to the mistress, do yer?'

'She can complain all she likes, I knows what mi job is 'ere.'

'An I'll 'ave no back answers, Missy. 'Elp Katie wi' them dishes.'

I would rather have done them myself. Milly slammed the china about until I feared it would all be broken. Snatching the tea towel out of her hands, I said, 'Leave them, I'll finish them.'

She tossed her head and disappeared.

It was late when I went up to bed. Passing Milly's room, I heard laughter, and then a man's voice cautioning her to be quiet.

I wondered who she had spirited up to her room after she left the kitchen. Had there been some boy from the town waiting in the shrubbery for her to give him the word that all was clear?

The following morning Polly said, 'Did yer 'ear Milly laughin' 'er 'ead off in 'er bedroom last night? I couldn't sleep fer 'em.'

'Who was with her, do you think? She's takin' a risk invitin' one of her young men up to her room.'

She gave me a sly amused look. 'What makes yer think it were some lad fro' the town then?'

'I don't think, I haven't the faintest idea who it is.'

'Why not somebody fro' the 'ouse, then?'

'One of the men who work on the land or in the stables?'

'She wouldn't look at a one of 'em, not Milly.'

'Well it's none of our business who it is, but if Mrs Tate catches her there'll be trouble. Couldn't you warn her?'

'She'd take no notice 'o me, 'sides she's made 'er bed, let 'er lie on it.' Then she dissolved into loud laughter as if her little joke had undercurrents I knew nothing about.

Several days later I was returning to the house from the town and saw Milly tripping daintily down the road. Soon after, Mr Roger's car emerged from the drive and went racing after her. I watched her get into the car, then with a puff of exhaust smoke the car roared out of sight.

I wondered if it was Mr Roger she was entertaining in her room, and if she yearned for him as I yearned for his brother. She appeared to have made more headway than I ever would. Mr Roger seemed to have no other lady in mind, while Mr Jeffrey went about with a face increasingly sad in Lois Foxland's absence.

Several weeks after that I became aware of whispered conversations carried on between Cook and Mrs Tate, conversations that stopped abruptly whenever Polly or I entered the kitchen.

'What's goin' on, then?' Polly demanded of me.

'How should I know?'

'It's Milly, that's who it is. I've seen Mrs Tate goin' into 'er bedroom an' Milly's allus cryin' these days an' 'idin' in 'er bedroom. I reckon she's goin' to 'ave a baby.'

'Oh Polly, of course she isn't, she's probably not feeling well.'

'Well if that's all it is why are they whisperin'? I'm right, I know I am, Milly's goin' to 'ave a baby an' I know who's the father.'

'How could you know?'

'I knows all right.' Her face was sly again and she went on peeling and scrubbing, an amused smile on her lips.

That afternoon I saw Milly leaving the house, and I observed her dark-circled eyes and pallor. She saw me but she held her eyes averted, and I watched her hurrying along the path with her head bent against the wind.

When I returned to the kitchen Cook said, 'Who's that gone out the door then?'

'It was Milly, Cook. She doesn't look well.'

'No.'

I felt her eyes boring into my back as I put away some cooking pots, and when I turned round to face her she looked away quickly. Polly sat at the table polishing cutlery.

'What's up wi' Milly then, Cook?' she asked audaciously.

'None o' your business, mi girl, yer asks too many questions.'

87

'Well, what's goin' to 'appen when she leaves 'ere?'

'An' who sez she's leavin'?'

'Norah left when she 'ad a baby an' I reckon Milly's no different.'

'Yer knows too much fer yer own good, mi girl, now finish that polishin' an' get back to the scullery. I wants a word wi' Katie wi'out yer listenin' to every word I sez.'

'Why do I allus 'ave to go back to the scullery? I've bin 'ere longer ner Katie so why can't yer talk ter both of us?'

'Because if yer must know there'll be more temptations put i' Katie's way than there'll ever be in yours, now back to the scullery and shut the door after ye.'

She scurried away like a frightened rabbit. I said, 'That wasn't very kind, Cook. Polly's plain but I don't think she likes to be reminded of it.'

'Look, lass, I'm not agin' the girl, she's not a bad lass but I've no fears fer Polly. She's not likely to put temptation in the way of any man and like as not one day she'll marry some lad wi' about as much imagination an' know-'ow as 'erself. Yer different, both yer and Milly.'

'Is it true about Milly?'

She nodded her head sadly. 'Ay, it's true, an' she'll 'ave ter go. Oh, they'll no doubt give 'er some money an' she'll 'ave the baby taken care of. She'll 'ave 'er living' to earn but she'd do well to get well away fro' 'ere.'

'You mean she can't come back, not even after the baby's born?'

'There's no chance o' that.'

'And the baby's father?'

'He'll noan wed 'er, fer one thing 'is father wouldn't let 'im, and fer another 'e doesn't want to. She were nobbut an escape fro' boredom fer 'im, but I'd like ter think 'is father'll give 'im a talkin' to an', I wish, a jolly good 'idin.'

'Is it Mr Roger?'

She nodded. ''Ow did yer know?'

'I've seen them together along the road, I've seen his car waitin' for her. Doesn't he care?'

'Oh, 'e cares fer 'isself I've no doubt, but not fer Milly. Be warned, Katie, about what 'appens to young women in yer walk o' life if they tangles wi' their betters. A don't want what's 'appened ter Milly to 'appen ter you.'

Tears pricked my eyes as I jumped to my feet, and tossing my head proudly I stormed, 'They're not mi betters. They might have more money than I'll ever have but they're not mi betters.'

With deep anger in my heart I snatched my coat off a peg in the kitchen and ran out to the stable yard. Then I stood for a moment wiping the tears from my eyes and until I had calmed my pounding heart.

I was appalled by life and its unfairness but I made myself walk through the stableyard as if nothing was amiss. The new colt had his head over the stable door and I approached him to stroke his satiny neck. I often brought him titbits from the kitchens but today I had nothing, and he soon grew tired of my petting and retreated to the back of his stable.

Ned's voice hailed me from the back of the yard. 'Comin' to look at the others, then?'

I turned and walked towards the open doors leading into another yard.

He stared at me, his narrow, malicious eyes gleaming. 'Wat 'ave yer bin' cryin' fer?' he demanded.

'I haven't. The cold wind made my eyes water.'

'Why is it allus Mr Jeffrey's 'orse yer looks at afore the others?'

'I look at them all, I came to him first, that's all.'

'Still see 'im up on the fells, then?'

'No I don't and it's none of your business anyway.'

'One o' these days Mrs Tate'll know yer smitten' wi' 'im, I might tell 'er miself.'

'Don't talk to me if you can't talk anything but rubbish.'

'Yer'll end up like Milly if yer doesn't watch yerself, right mess she's got 'erself into an' 'e won't wed 'er, that's fer sure.'

He had his arms placed one on either side of me, his palms against the wall, and I could feel his hot breath on my face, see the perspiration shining on his brow. He smelled of horseflesh and manure and I was afraid of his

89

strong gnarled hands and short muscular body pressing against mine.

I struggled but he held me fast, then his wet mouth came down on mine and I felt I must suffocate while the pain of my arms pinioned against me hurt so much I felt sure I would faint. Suddenly I was released, and through a blur of pain I saw Ned struggling in the hands of Jeffrey Carslake. His face was purple with anger, then looking up into the white face of his attacker he seemed to visibly shrink.

Jeffrey said, 'You young savage, get back to your work or I'll have you thrown off the premises.'

Ned staggered after he was released, then he ran towards the back of the stableyard. Jeffrey turned to me, almost indifferently.

'Are you all right, Katie?'

'Yes, thank you, Mr Jeffrey.'

'No harm done then?'

'No, Sir. Thank you for helping me.'

'What are you doing here?'

'I came for a walk and I like the horses.'

'Well if you'll take my advice I should keep out of the stableyard for a while. That boy isn't to be trusted.'

With a cool nod he walked away from me, and I ran to the side door leading to the kitchen. I felt cheapened by Ned's embrace, soiled because we had been seen by Jeffrey Carslake, and degraded because he had nodded so coolly and walked away, as though he expected lesser beings to behave like animals.

I waited in the passage until I felt sufficiently composed to face Cook, smoothing my hair and my dress, laying my cold hands against my burning cheeks, but I need not have worried, she was too engrossed in upbraiding Polly for some misdeameanour. I escaped into the scullery and set about peeling vegetables until Polly returned, wiping her eyes with her apron.

Something else happened to disturb me profoundly before the day was over. As I passed Milly's room on my way to bed I heard her sobbing but I hesitated, reluctant to intrude on her grief. I couldn't sleep however, and lighting my candle and putting a coat over my nightgown I crept back along the corridor. She was still crying, and it was only when I heard her whisper 'Oh God, I wish I was dead,' that I knocked softly on her door.

The sobs ceased, and in a trembling voice she said, 'Who is it?'

'It's me, Katie, please let me in.'

There was silence for so long that I thought she would not open the door to me. After all we had never been close. Most of the time she treated me like a lesser servant, barely condescending to pass the time of day, so it was more than likely she would not want me to witness her distress. I was about to turn away when the door opened a few inches and Milly stood looking at me, her face pale and tear-stained, such a sad dejected figure that I pushed the door open wider and stepped into her room.

'I heard you crying,' I explained. 'Come and sit on the bed and put something warm round your shoulders, you'll catch your death.'

'They'd be pleased about that then,' she said tearfully. 'It'd solve a lot o' problems.'

'Cook told me, Milly. I'm sorry you're so unhappy, do you want to talk about it?'

'What's to talk about? I'm 'avin' a baby an' 'e won't wed me.'

'What will you do?'

'I don't know. I daren't go 'ome, that's fer sure, mi father'd kill me.'

'It's Mr Roger isn't it?'

She stared at me dully, suspiciously, then lifting her chin proudly she said, 'What do you know about it? I suppose they're all tittle-tattlin' in the kitchens.'

'I've seen you together a few times. I've seen him waitin' for you down the road and I heard his voice once when I passed your room.'

'I suppose you thinks I'm terrible, but I love 'im, I always 'ave, ever since I came 'ere, an' 'e said 'e loved me.'

'Well then, if he loves you why won't he marry you?'

With a wry smile that twisted my heart she said,

'Because I'm not good enough for 'im.'

'But you were good enough to sleep with, it's his baby, so why won't he marry you? What do the family have to say about it?'

'I'm to see Mrs Carslake in the mornin'. I told Miss Nancy, you see, an' she's told 'er mother. There'll be so much trouble, yer know what the master's like, an' they'll want nothin' to do wi' me or the baby.'

'That's monstrous. It's their grandchild whether they like it or not, and you're not dirt to be trampled under their feet. Mr Roger should be made to pay for what he's done, he should be made to marry you.'

'Oh Katie, what a lot yer 'ave to learn. Yer know what they'll do, they'll send mi away wi' some money an' that'll be the last 'e ever sees of me.'

'But if he loves you, Milly.'

'He doesn't love mi enough. 'E'll be relieved to see mi go.'

'But if you realize all this now, why didn't you think about it before?'

'Would you if yer loved somebody, would you ever think they could let yer down?'

I thought about Jeffrey Carslake and I knew I would be just like Milly. Shame filled my being as I sat with her, both of us shivering in the cold, and although I was filled with compassion for Milly I pitied myself just as fiercely. For the rest of the night we lay in each other's arms and it was only in the first light of day that I crept miserably back to my own room to lie awake, my mind tortured with Milly's problems and my own.

She didn't come down to the kitchen for breakfast, and Cook sniffed disdainfully, 'Off 'er food she is, the little madam, she'll be glad o' this food when she's sent packin'.'

I glared at her balefully. 'How *can* they send her packing? She needs care and attention.'

'You'll not be sayin' anything outside o' these four walls, I 'ope.'

'Well of course I shan't. I wouldn't want anybody to think the Carslakes were so unfeeling,' I snapped, and stalked out with my head in the air.

It was my half day and I longed to get away from the house but I had no real wish to visit my aunt and uncle. The last time I had seen them, there was an atmosphere in the house, a strange despondency, although neither of them had said anything of their problems. I decided, however, that I should go there.

There was a hint of rain in the air as I set off down the hill and before I had reached the bottom the heavens opened and the downpour became intense. I ran, my shoes squelching in the puddles and the rain trickling down my coat collar. By the time I reached their house my hair was saturated and my tweed coat hung heavy and damp.

Uncle Turlough came to the door, staring at me incredulously.

'Whatever brings you 'ere on a day like this, love?' he greeted me.

'It was fine when I started out, Uncle.'

'Well, yer'd best come in an' get out o' them wet clothes.' In no time I was sitting by the fire in a shapeless old dressing gown, drinking hot tea with a little whisky.

'Why aren't you at work, Uncle Turlough?' I asked curiously.

'I'm played off for a week, Katie, there's not much work in.'

'I see.'

The house was untidy. There was sewing on all the chairs and a pile of it on the table. The sewing machine was open under the window and seeing me looking at it, Aunt Martha said, 'I didn't intend taking so much of it in, but I'm glad of it now yer uncle's not workin'. They don't want ter pay much but every little 'elps.'

'Yes, I'm sure it does. How are the girls?'

I did not miss the look which passed between them, then busying herself at her sewing machine she replied tersely, 'They're well enough, Lucy'll be 'ome fro' school afore yer needs to get back.'

'Is Fanny doing well at her school?'

She nodded and my uncle buried his face in his newspaper. Something was quite evidently wrong but it

93

looked as though neither of them wanted to talk about it.

Lucy came home about four o'clock and immediately began to show me some of her drawings from her favourite lesson. I admired them before she turned to her mother, saying, 'I saw our Fanny on the way 'ome, Mother, she were gettin' into a trap wi' another girl.'

'Did she see you?' her mother asked.

'If she did she didn't let on. I don't want her to speak to me anyroad.'

'Now Lucy, you mustn't talk like that about yer sister,' her father reproached her. 'It's nobbut a phase she's goin' through, she'll come to 'er senses when she gets a bit older.'

'It's better anyway since she went away,' Lucy persisted.

I stared at my uncle curiously. 'She's gone away, Uncle, but where?'

My aunt jumped up sharply from her machine and ran into the kitchen with the tears streaming from her eyes, and Uncle Turlough shook his head sadly.

'Yer aunt's upset, Katie, it's all 'appened so suddenly an' she'll not be after wantin' yer to see her cry. She'll tell yer all about it in 'er own good time.'

Her own good time came after we had eaten and Lucy had gone up to her room complaining of a headache.

'I suppose yer might as well know, Katie, but our Fanny's bin stayin' wi' a friend over at Charnwood for the last few weeks. She made friends wi' this girl soon after she started at the school. Her folk are very well off, they live in a big old 'ouse on the outskirts o' Charnwood an' 'er father's a solicitor. They lost a girl wi' diphtheria three years ago, the twin to the one that's in our Fanny's form. They've taken such a likin' to Fanny, she's the same colourin' as the lass that died an' they takes 'er to concerts and the theatre, they've even asked if she can go away wi' 'em when they goes on 'oliday. I said at first that she couldn't go. She'll need clothes an' the like, but she threw such a tantrum yer uncle said we'd manage, an' Mrs Markham said she could wear Dorothy's clothes, Dorothy had been spoiled since 'er sister died an' she 'ad enough fer both of 'em.'

'She's not gone for good though, surely she'll come back?'

'I don't know. I made 'er a lovely dress for an end of term party at the school, it took most o' what yer uncle brought 'ome that week, but she said Mrs Markham 'ad bought 'er a dress an' it were prettier than the one I'd made 'er. She'll be spoilt, Katie, she'll never be our girl again. Why there's times when she meets Lucy in the street and she looks the other way. That's 'urtin, yer know. Lucy sez she doesn't care but underneath I knows she does.'

'I am sorry, Aunt Martha, I don't know what to say.'

'There's nowt to say, lass. If she comes 'ome we'll be glad to 'ave 'er back, if she doesn't we'll just 'ave to make the best o' things.'

I would dearly have liked to give Miss Fanny a piece of my mind but it was unlikely that she would listen to me, even if we ever met. I wasn't surprised. Right from the outset I had thought Fanny was going to be a handful, and she was proving me right.

'I thowt you looked a bit peaky when yer came in today, Katie. Is everythin' all right up at the Carslakes' house?'

'Yes, Aunt Martha, quite all right. I expect I was feeling cold and very damp. I should think of getting back, it's going to be a cold dark night.'

'Yes, I'll ask yer uncle to walk back with yer.'

'Really there's no need. There's no point in two of us getting wet.'

The rain was still coming down and I gritted my teeth and pressed on up the hill. My coat still felt damp from the earlier rain and I was glad of the scarf my aunt had lent me to cover my hair.

I was walking as briskly as I could in the wind, my head bent against the driving rain, when I heard a high screeching of brakes. I leapt to the side of the road, my heart pounding, as a low-slung car came to a shuddering halt beside me and a man's voice cried irritably, 'What the hell do you think you're doing walking in the middle of the road on such a night? I almost killed you.'

I was too frightened to speak, and shrank back against the wall, praying that he would drive on and leave me to continue behind him. He did no such thing however, but jumped out of the car and came to stand over me, staring down at me with hostile, angry eyes. I shrank back still further, trembling with cold and fright.

'What the devil are you doing out on such a night?' he demanded.

'I'm going home.'

'Home. Where is home? Don't you have any transport?'

'No,' I snapped back, recovering my lost spirit. 'It's no night for a horse and mi car's in the garage.'

He stared at me and I realized he was as frightened as I was, having come so close to killing me.

'What's an Irish girl doing halfway up Tremayne Hill in a downpour?' he asked.

Without thinking twice I snapped, 'How do you know Oi'm Irish?' at which he threw back his head and laughed.

'You should listen to yourself, my girl. It's not too evident but it's Irish all right, with all the charm and the lilt in it. Where do you live?'

'Further up the hill, I'll be home in no time.'

'Well you were nearly not going to be home at all. Now jump in the car and I'll see that you get home.'

'I'm not jumpin' in any car with a complete stranger.'

He took my arm in a firm grip and propelled me towards the car. 'Don't waste any more of my time, mi girl, get into the front seat there and hold your tongue. I've no sinister designs on you on such a night, it's doubtful if I'd have any such designs on you at any other time, with your lack of self-preservation.'

Seething with annoyance I watched him walk round the car and get into the seat beside me, then swiftly we climbed the hill and he asked, 'Which is your house?'

'We're coming to the gates now. You can drop mi here, I shan't come to any harm between here and the house.'

'I'd not like to bank on it. I'd prefer to deposit you at your front door.'

There was something about his voice, a strangeness, a drawl that bore no resemblance to the Lancashire dialect I had become familiar with, and yet it was not the clipped public-school speech of the Carslake family. This man's voice was low and undeniably charming, and I found myself wondering where he lived or where he might be visiting on the hill. As he brought the car to a standstill my curiosity got the better of me.

'Well you're not Irish to be sure, but you're not from these parts either.'

'No, but no doubt we'll be seeing each other again in more congenial circumstances. It's hardly a night for telling you the story of my life.'

He got out of the car and came to open the door for me. I thanked him for the lift, wishing that I could see him better. I only knew that he was tall and occasionally I could see the flash of his teeth when he smiled. To my utmost surprise he bent his head and lightly kissed the top of my head, then he walked quickly back to the car and drove off in a cloud of exhaust fumes.

I was at the front of the house and I sincerely hoped none of the family had witnessed my arrival. I ran along the path to the back door, feeling more than relieved to find it unlocked.

Cook and Mrs Tate sat in the kitchen in front of a bright fire. Mrs Tate was reading and Cook was knitting, and they both looked up at my arrival. Cook's eyes narrowed a little and she snapped, 'Didn't I hear a car just now, Katie?'

'Yes, I got a lift up the hill.'

I felt her eyes boring into my back as I went about making my usual cup of cocoa and I imagined them filled with suspicion.

'I 'ope yer didn't go acceptin' lifts fro' strangers, Katie, that's askin' fer trouble.'

'It's a terrible wet night, Cook, he was a very nice gentleman who offered me a lift and you must have heard the car arrive and drive off again very quickly.'

'Yer a very foolish girl, Katie O'Donovan. Gettin' wet's better ner gettin' strangled, and strangers is strangers.'

When I didn't speak Mrs Tate said, 'What was this man doing on the hill on such a night anyway?'

'Driving to one of the houses, and I was walking in the middle of the road. I didn't hear the car for the wind, he almost ran me down. He was angry with me but he insisted on driving me home.'

'There's not many with cars livin' on the hill, most of 'em are satisfied wi' their 'orses,' Cook snapped irritably.

'Well this man had a car, and he drove on up the hill,' I retorted.

'There's only three 'ouses further up Mrs Tate, p'raps 'e's a guest at one of 'em.'

'I'd like to get out of mi wet things now, goodnight,' I said quickly, glad to escape their inquisition.

My room felt cold and I wished I had had the foresight to put a stone hot-water bottle in the bed. My skin was clammy from the wet clothing and I was glad to rub myself dry and put on my flannel nightgown. I was brushing my hair when there was a faint tap on my door. Thinking it was Milly I rushed to open it, only to find Polly standing on the threshold, blinking owlishly in the candlelight.

'Can I come in, Katie? I don't want Cook or Mrs Tate ter find mi standin' 'ere.'

I pulled her into the room and closed the door behind her.

Her eyes were popping with excitement and no sooner had she made herself comfortable on my bed than the words came, tumbling over one another until I had to give her a little shake, saying, 'For goodness' sake slow down Polly, I can't make any sense out of what you're sayin'.'

'I 'eard Mrs Tate talkin' ter Cook 'afore they sent mi to bed out o' their way. There's bin such trouble, Katie. It were all goin' on when Mrs Tate took in the drinks tray after dinner. There was the mistress cryin' like a baby an' the master upbraidin' Mr Roger fer gettin' Milly inter trouble, an' then if 'e didn't start on Mr Jeffrey, callin' 'im a milksop, sayin' if 'e'd 'ad anything' about 'im 'e'd 'a' put a ring on Lois Foxland's finger 'afore she went off wi' 'er parents, cruisin'. 'E said 'e'd rather 'ave a man like Mister Roger who knew 'ow ter get 'is way wi' a lass than Mr Jeffrey who 'adn't the gumption ter know what a lass was there fer.'

'Oh, that's terrible. How can he be blamin' Jeffrey for

what Mr Roger's done? It isn't fair.'

'No, an' it made the mistress cry even more, an' 'e called Milly a trollop who set out ter trap Mr Roger, but she's ter be sent packin', 'e's not goin' ter wed 'er.'

'But what about the baby, surely they can't just send her away without making sure she's going to be cared for, Milly and the baby?'

'I don't know, Katie. Cook found mi listenin' at the scullery door so she boxed mi ears and told me ter get upstairs sharpish, an' Mrs Tate said if I said one word o' what I'd 'eard I'd be sent packin' along wi' Milly.'

'Then what are you doin' telling me, Polly?'

'I *ad* to tell somebody, Katie, an' you don't matter, yer nobbut a servant like mi.'

'Oh Polly, this is a terrible world to be born into if you haven't any money and nobody to look out for you.'

'Well I'll tell yer this, Katie, there's none o' them so-called gentry goin' ter get 'is 'ands on me, I'm lookin' fer a decent chap who'll marry mi, not think 'imself too good fer mi.'

I looked at her sitting huddled on my bed with her thin nondescript hair, protruding eyes and teeth, and slightly blotchy complexion. A plainer girl I could never have imagined and yet she had her ideals set firmly on a future in the home of a god-fearing upright man who would be proud to marry her. And there was Milly with her pert prettiness, and me who everybody said was a beauty, and both of us burdened with an impossible dream.

'Milly isn't a trollop, is she, Katie?'

'No, and I'm quite sure she didn't set out to trap Mr Roger. I hate him for what he's done to Milly, an' I hate his father for the things he's saying' about Mr Jeffrey.'

'Yer won't let on yer knows anythin' about it, will yer Katie? If yer do I'll lose mi job, an' work's 'ard ter get i' Marsdale.'

'You know I won't say a word, Polly, now get off back to bed.'

I lay for a long time shivering in my cold bed, but even in a warm bed I wouldn't have slept. I was troubled about

Milly, and I deplored the cruelty of the words Jeffrey's father had lashed him with.

A shadow seemed to hang over the house the following morning. Breakfast was a silent meal, with the men departing more quickly than usual, and Cook uncharacteristically taciturn. Milly did not come down to breakfast and when Mrs Tate knocked on her door she was answered by a tearful voice telling her to go away.

Lunch was eaten in silence. None of the male members of the family were present. The mistress sat with red-rimmed eyes and Miss Nancy and Miss Mary were unnaturally quiet.

'It's a shame to waste good food,' Mrs Tate complained. 'None of them 'ave eaten much. I reckon some of this food can be served up again for dinner, the way things are none of them will notice.'

I had never become accustomed to hearing the family chatter together as though the servants who waited upon them were pieces of wood without eyes to see and ears to hear. As soon as the master sat down to dinner he was in a mean mood. Mr Roger was unduly subdued and Mr Humphrey engaged his father in some complaint about the machinery in one of the weaving sheds, possibly because he could see the sort of mood the older man was in.

Mr Jeffrey seemed wrapped in thoughts of his own, and when Miss Nancy addressed him she had to repeat her remark three times before he roused himself.

I was nervous. Always sensitive to atmosphere, it seemed to me like one of those days in my grandmother's house when I could not do anything right for her, and when Mother had sat in tearful silence waiting for the anger to fall on one of us – usually me.

My hand shook as I served the soup and Colonel Carslake snapped, 'Do we have to have third-rate service after a hard day's work? Leave the soup alone, girl, and let Mrs Tate handle it.'

I stepped back, my face bright scarlet, looking quickly at Jeffrey, but he did not appear to have heard although I did receive a sympathetic glance from Miss Mary. The meal continued with the colonel complaining that the soup was cold, the vegetables burnt and the meat tough. Then turning to his wife, he snapped, 'I trust that girl's out of the house.'

'Do you mean Milly, dear?'

'I don't know her name, that trollop my son Roger's been foolish enough to tangle with.'

'She can't just go at a minute's notice, dear, it would be too cruel.'

'You mean she's still here, in spite of what I said yesterday!'

'The girl's a local girl, John, we have to be very careful, we can't send her away without making sure she has somebody to care for her and somewhere to go. The child is our grandchild whether you like it or not.'

He stared at her through narrow, red-rimmed eyes, his face black with rage. 'She'll be out of this house first thing in the morning, grandchild or not.'

'It's as much Roger's fault as Milly's,' Nancy snapped angrily at her father. 'He's never been able to keep his hands off her, and she's not a trollop, she's a very good lady's maid.'

'Lady's maid, lady's maid. There'll be no more lady's maids in this house, and don't raise your voice at me, young lady. I'll have some respect in my own house.'

'Why isn't Roger being blamed for anything then? It's as much his fault as Milly's,' Nancy persisted. 'Last night it was Jeffrey you picked on, tonight it's me. Why does Roger always get away with everything?'

'You can leave Roger to me, young woman, now leave the table immediately and go to your room. And take that girl with you, she's about as much use waiting at table as one of the gardeners would be.'

I glared at him angrily across my tray, and with as much force as I could muster I slammed it down hard on the side table, and with my head held high I stalked out of the room after Nancy.

I had red hair and an Irish temper to go with it, and no Colonel Carslake was going to talk of me like that. Outside

101

in the hall, Nancy suddenly burst into laughter.

'I'm glad you did that, Katie, Father's in a foul mood and we're all suffering, all except his precious Roger.'

'I'll probably be sent packing along with Milly.'

'Oh, he'll calm down, he's probably had a rotten day at the mills and then there's Roger and Milly on top of it. What a little ninny Milly's been. I really don't know what I shall do without her and father won't allow us to have another maid, particularly while trade is so bad.'

'I'm good with hair, Miss Nancy, and if there's time I might be able to do the things Milly did. That's if I'm kept on after mi show of temper.'

Her face brightened considerably. 'I'll speak up for you, Katie, and if you take over some of Milly's work I'll ask Mother if you can't have an increase in your wages. I don't suppose it will be much, they're forever cutting down these days. Will you ask Cook if she can let me have coffee in my room?'

'Yes Miss Nancy, I'll deliver it miself.'

But Cook delivered Miss Nancy's coffee while I was treated to a good scolding from Mrs Tate for showing that I was listening to the conversation over the dinner table.

'How can I help but listen?' I answered her sharply. 'They speak as though we weren't there, as though we were nothing.'

'Well you are nothing girl when it comes to mixing with your betters. Now let's have no more of it. Lucky for you the master is willing to overlook it on this occasion, but he won't a second time, you can be sure of that.'

Since Frances left home I had returned to visiting my aunt and uncle whenever it was convenient, but on this Sunday afternoon I decided I couldn't possibly listen to my aunt's tirade against her and see my uncle's sad, bewildered face. Instead I walked to the top of Evening Hill and then across the long reach of Grisebrook Fell. The sharp wind tossed the coarse grass until it resembled the sea, shimmering and dancing in the sunlight, and a strange stillness seemed to have descended over the length of the valley. For once the pall of smoke had lifted from the towns and villages, but I knew this wasn't a good sign. It was an indication that many of the mills would not be working the next day, or indeed perhaps for days and weeks to come.

I started to climb to where clumps of purple heather grew in profusion and dark moorland sheep calmly cropped the harsh grass. I picked my way gingerly across a shallow stream then, climbed a stile and scrambled between boulders towards the summit of Wisden Tor. On Good Friday walkers from every direction made their way towards it, just as they had done to that other green hill centuries before. Today, however, it was deserted and I was glad of the solitude and the silence.

It was said in Marsdale that on a clear day from the top of Wisden Tower it was possible to see the distant silver line of the sea, but today there were storm clouds in the west. Few people climbed the tower these days as the old stone steps were crumbling, and the safety rail had long since fallen into disrepair.

I intended to climb to the summit and sit for a while under the tower before making my descent. It was beautiful on the moor and, exhilarated by the climb, with the sharp wind ruffling my hair and my cheeks flaming with the cold, I found a dry grassy knoll and became totally absorbed in watching two curlews wheeling and diving over the fell, their long mournful cries filling the air.

I frowned a little at the sight of another climber ascending the hill, walking easily along the ridge and jumping the low stone walls as though he had done it many times before. He carried a walking stick and the bright sunlight gilded his hair. As he drew nearer however there was no mistaking his tall easy grace and my heart started to flutter as it always did whenever Jeffrey Carslake came near me. I wanted to take refuge in the tower or run round the side of it, but I knew that if I moved he would be sure to see me. I hoped that perhaps if I kept perfectly still he would walk on and I would be able to return to the house by another direction.

It was not to be, however. I soon realized that he too was making for the summit. I had ample time to watch him. He seemed preoccupied as he climbed, and for a little while he stood leaning against a gate, gazing towards the town. His face was pensive, sad almost, and I knew that his thoughts were turned inward and brought him little joy.

He turned away suddenly, tossing his folded raincoat over his shoulder as he continued his climb. When he reached the summit he strolled slowly towards me, seeing me so suddenly he seemed startled, and I did not miss the small frown of annoyance that told me he had wished to be alone on the hill.

The smile followed so quickly I could have imagined the frown, but I knew I had not. Neither of us had wished for company on the hill that afternoon.

'You must be feeling very energetic, Katie,' he said, smiling down at me, then to my utmost consternation he sat down beside me and commenced to point out various landmarks.

'I thought you visited your relatives in the town in your time off,' he said.

'Quite often I do, but I wanted to walk up here on the fell. Was your father very angry with mi display of temper last night?'

'My father is angry with everything and everybody at the moment, Katie. He is constantly out of countenance with me.'

'Then why do you stand for it, Mr Jeffrey? It's your brother he should be railin' against.'

'Ah, but then he'd be railing against himself. Roger and my father are very much alike, earthy and exuberant. Father doesn't understand me, he considers me a dreamer, lacking in both courage and resolve.'

'But you don't have to be like Mr Roger to have courage. Oh, I know what it's like to be looked down on, mi Grandmother Cassidy always looked down on me because she never liked mi father.'

He smiled, his eyes filled with amusement. 'Why was that?'

'Because she said he was a dreamer with his head filled with booklore. Mi father liked readin' when the other men

went fishin' ánd drinkin' in the taverns, but surely that was
better than spendin' all our money on such things. After all
the books didn't cost a lot, he bought them at Mrs
Cavanagh's on the second-hand stall.'

He laughed delightedly. 'You were very fond of your
father, Katie.'

'Oh yes, he was big and handsome and he could turn an
ordinary day into somethin' enchantin'.'

'I've never thought about my father in that way and yet
I've always wanted him to be proud of me. He doesn't know
how hurting he can be.'

'Sure he knows, my grandmother always knew, she
meant to be hurtin'.'

'I must say you're not very well prepared for a walk in the
hills. See those rain clouds coming in.'

I looked up and sure enough blue-black clouds were
rolling in, and mist lay over the valley. I hadn't thought to
bring a raincoat and I sprang to my feet. 'I'd best be gettin'
back, Mr Jeffrey, if I hurry I might just beat the rainstorm.'

'You'll never make it, Katie. We'd do better to shelter in
the tower till the rain passes. Look over there, there's the
sun, so the rain can't last very long.'

Taking my hand he pulled me towards the tower, and I
could see that the door was open and hanging awkwardly
on its hinges.

'It's not very prepossessing in there,' he said, 'but at
least we'll keep dry.'

It was dark in the tower and I could see the staircase
leading upwards and occasional gaping holes in the stone
walls. He spread out his raincoat on the lower steps,
inviting me to join him.

'Now tell me some more about your Grandmother
Cassidy and your life in Donegal.'

So I talked and he listened and the more I talked the
more the Irish came back into my voice, and outside the
thunder rolled around the hills and the dark room was
constantly illuminated with flashes of lightning. I had no
sense of time, I was happy sitting so close beside him that I
could smell the soap he used, feel the rough tweed of his

105

jacket against my arm and, when the lightning flashed, see his smile.

I wanted to feel his arms around me, I ached for him to kiss my mouth, but when the room became lighter and a shaft of sunlight fell across the floor he rose to his feet and pulled me up after him. For one brief heady moment I stood in the circle of his arms, then he let me go and I watched helplessly while he walked towards the door.

He turned with that smile which had the power to twist my heart, then holding out his hand he said, 'We can go out now, Katie, the storm is over.'

The sun shone brightly out of a pale watery sky, and as I looked out towards the town I was suddenly aware of a rainbow, perfect and beautiful, and like a child I clapped my hands with glee.

'Oh, will you just be lookin' at that, isn't it the most beautiful thing you ever saw?'

'Did you never see a rainbow before, Katie?'

'Oh yes, sure I did, over the sea from the cliffs, and I cried when it went away. Mi father said I shouldn't be cryin' over lost rainbows, there'd always be another one somewhere in the world.'

'Well, there you are then. Now hadn't you better be returning to the house before the storm clouds come back?'

At his words something seemed to go from the day. He was not walking back with me, the old barriers had returned, seeming so much stronger after that rare moment of intimacy with his arms around me.

I nodded, unable to trust my voice, then turned and scrambled down the hillside, seeing the wandering path through a blur of tears.

I did not see the man climbing upwards until I was upon him, then I heard an amused voice saying, 'Hold on there, not so fast.' Then with a little laugh he said, 'So it's you again, I might have known it.'

At first I couldn't see his face because of the treacherous tears, but I recognized his voice with its slow drawl, and indignantly I wiped the tears away with the back of my hand.

He was watching me with consternation, then he looked up to where Jeffrey stood watching my descent.

'What's this then, a lovers' quarrel?' he asked, smiling.

'No it isn't, it's the wind making mi eyes water.'

I made as if to pass him but he put out a restraining hand. 'All right then, so it's the wind making your eyes water, that's no reason to pass an old friend who almost ran you down on a dark night.'

'You're not an old friend, you're not even a friend at all.'

'Such gratitude,' he mocked. 'Well, I've had enough of the fells for one day, I'll walk back with you.'

'There's no need.'

'Oh but there is, if your friend isn't so inclined it's hardly chivalrous to allow you to walk home alone.'

'I don't need anybody to walk back with me.'

'It'll do him good to see he's not the only pebble on the beach, a pretty girl like you shouldn't be treated in such a cavalier fashion.'

As we descended the hill I stole a look at him. He was as tall as Jeffrey but he was dark and bronzed as though by suns stronger than ours, he walked with an easy grace and he was good-looking with dark sardonic eyes and a whimsical smile.

'Where've you been hiding yourself these last few days?' he asked. 'I've looked for you on the hill but there's been no sign of you.'

'Why should you be lookin' for me?'

'Oh, to pass the time of day, to see if you were no worse for being frightened nearly to death.'

'You were driving too fast.'

'And you were walking in the middle of the road.'

'I know, it was wrong of me.'

'And you won't do it again.'

'I might. Do you live on the hill, then?'

'Not permanently, I'm visiting relatives.'

'I see. There's only three houses further up than ours.'

'That's right.'

He was maddening. I knew he had no intention of telling me which house he was visiting and he knew I was dying

107

with curiosity.

'Did you see the rainbow?' he asked changing the subject.

'Yes, it was beautiful. It's years since I've seen one.'

'There's always one over the falls.'

'The falls!'

'Niagara.'

'They're in America aren't they?'

'America and Canada. So you've heard about Niagara?'

'Of course, but I've never been there. Have you really seen them?'

'Many times.'

'Then you're an American.'

'Canadian, there's a difference. You should go to Canada one day, it's a beautiful country.'

'I'd like to see the Rockies.'

'Yes indeed, they're very grand.'

He was looking down at me with that attractive whimsical smile, on his face and I knew he was curious about me. I held out my hand in a friendly gesture, saying. 'Thank you for walking home with me.'

'You haven't told me your name,' he said, keeping my hand in a firm grip.

'There's no call for you to be knowing it, we probably shan't be seeing each other again.'

'I guess it's Nancy, then,' he said, laughing down into my face.

I ran away from him towards the house and it was only then that I realized he believed I was the daughter of the house, and the people he was visiting had told him my name might be Nancy.

Miss Nancy was a tease, quite capable of misleading any young man by a bogus Irish accent. Oh well, he was a Canadian and it was highly unlikely we would meet again during his stay in England.

Chapter 9

I thought no more about the strange Canadian in the days that followed because so many more matters came to the fore.

Milly left, escorted down the back stairs and out of the door before any of us had a chance to say goodbye, but we watched her stepping into a cab, dabbing her eyes and looking up at the house in silent farewell, her face swollen from weeping. Polly was all for rushing out to speak to her but Cook restrained her sharply.

'She'll not thank yer for seein' 'er go off in disgrace, it's best yer stays 'ere in the kitchen.'

'Where's she goin', then?' Polly demanded.

'I can't rightly say. Mrs Tate'll know'.

When Polly asked Mrs Tate she was told, 'It's none of your business, Polly. Get back into the scullery and make a start on the vegetables.'

'That's unfair,' I cried, 'Polly's every right to know what is going to happen to Milly. I want to know too, and what is going to happen to the baby.'

She looked at Cook helplessly, and Cook said, 'It's only natural for 'em to be concerned, Mrs Tate. If they knows what'll 'appen to Milly it might stop 'em makin' a similar mistake.'

'Milly's going to work for Mrs Carslake's friend in Cumberland. She's a woman fond o' good works and she has some sort of interest in a home up there for fallen women. Milly'll be cared for when 'er time comes an' p'raps the baby'll get adopted. If not it'll grow up in a home. Milly'll have to work, her family won't help her and the money Mrs Carslake gave her won't last for ever.'

'Does that mean Milly'll never see the baby again?' Polly asked.

'Better she doesn't,' Cook answered her.

I said nothing but I was seething inside, wishing all sorts of dire things would happen to Roger Carslake to punish him, and later that afternoon I asked the Lord Almighty to forgive me for those wishes. Mr Roger had been set upon by a gang of men as he left the millyard.

He arrived home with two black eyes and a bloodied nose. His tweed jacket was covered with blood and one of the sleeves had been ripped out, but he adamantly refused to give any description of his assailants.

Colonel Carslake was all for calling out the police but Mr Roger said he hadn't recognized them in the dark, and it would only antagonize them further if the law was called in.

'I reckon it's Milly's kinfolk,' Polly stated. 'She 'as a brother an' two uncles livin' down in the town. Serves 'im right, it does.'

'Hold your tongue, Miss Polly!' Cook snapped. 'And don't you be talkin' about your betters like that. It was cowardly, six or seven of 'em to attack one man.'

I kept silent in the firm belief that it had been my prayers that had brought such swift retribution.

Dinner was a silent meal. Mrs Carslake toyed with her food in tearful silence while the master's face was brick-red with anger. Roger looked a sorry sight with his bruised and blackened eyes. The girls kept a discreet silence and only Jeffrey gave me a sad half smile.

Two days later Mr Roger informed his father that he had joined the army, which brought on a further flood of tears from Mrs Carslake and heavy disapproval from his father.

'Ye young fool,' he shouted, 'I suppose ye know there's trouble brewing in Europe and if it comes to a head we'll be in it like we always are.'

'I'd have joined the army anyway,' Roger retorted, 'this way I'll get a commission much quicker.'

'Why didn't you tell me you wanted to join the army? I could have pulled strings, and well you know it.'

'You've pulled enough strings, Father, this I'll do on my

own.'

He stalked out of the room, and at that moment, against all my better judgement, I admired him.

Meeting his youngest son's eyes, the colonel snapped, 'Well at least I've got a son who's a man, I doubt if I'll ever get the same proof from you.'

I saw the pain in Jeffrey's eyes – raw, blistering pain – then he quietly pushed his plate away, saying quietly to his mother, 'May I be excused, Mother? I find I am no longer hungry.'

'Do go and find Roger, dear, neither of you have eaten anything.'

The colonel was the next to leave, slamming the door behind him, and his wife said to her daughters, 'Oh dear, I wonder how long all this is going to go on?'

'Not long, I hope,' Miss Nancy snapped. 'It's the Hunt Ball on Friday and at this rate we'll all arrive with long faces and absolutely appalling hairdos now that Milly's gone.'

'There are more important matters than hairdos, Nancy, and it won't do you any harm to miss the ball for once.'

'Because of Roger and his carry-on! Oh Mother, you can't mean it. Besides, Mary and I have new dresses and I promised to go with Arthur Steadly. If I don't keep my promise he'll be off with Edith Atherton and I can't allow that.'

'You are fond of Arthur Steadly?'

'Fond enough. He's very rich and presentable, and Edith Atherton's father is terribly rich even if his daughter looks like a horse.'

'That isn't very kind, Nancy.'

'I know, but when Arthur's not with me she sits about waiting for him like a tarantula. Father's made it plain we shall just have to marry somebody with money because he will have very little for a marriage settlement.'

'You're only twenty, Nancy.'

'I know, but Mary's twenty-eight and we're getting older by the hour.'

'I don't like to hear you talking like this, Nancy, it is most unseemly.'

I saw her glance at me quickly but I kept a blank face as I went about clearing the table.

'Will you be taking coffee in the drawing room, Ma'am?' I asked.

I served their coffee and was about to leave when Miss Mary said, 'My sister tells me you are very good with hair, Katie. Perhaps you would be willing to assist us before the Hunt Ball.'

I glanced at the mistress, but she was reading a letter with a great deal of attention.

'I've had no experience as a lady's maid, Miss Mary, but I'll do what I can to help.'

'Thank you, Katie, I'm sure you'll do splendidly . . . Is something wrong, Mother? That letter seems to be causing you some concern.'

'It's from the Foxlands, dear. They appear to have left the ship at Nice and are staying for three weeks in a private villa there, friends of some man they have met on board.'

'That means they definitely won't be home for Christmas.'

'Apparently not.'

'What about this man, then?' Miss Nancy demanded. 'Is he young or old, has he got a wife or is he looking for one?'

'I don't know anything about him and the letter doesn't enlighten me. We shall no doubt be hearing all about it in due course. Jeffrey will be disappointed, he was hoping Lois would return home in time for the Tremaynes' ball.'

I returned to the kitchen rejoicing, and yet it was a very small crumb of comfort. Jeffrey would spend Christmas without Lois Foxland and yet I had no real thought that he would turn to me. I was a servant in his father's house, no better than Milly who had been sent away in disgrace.

I came in for delighted praise from both his sisters for my efforts with their hair, and in company with the rest of the servants I watched the family depart for the Hunt Ball in all their finery.

It was at the female members of the family that the others looked, but I had eyes only for Jeffrey Carslake in his faultless evening clothes.

His father and Mr Humphrey were Hunt officials, so they were wearing the mess jacket in bright hunting pink. Mr Roger had declined to attend, since he was still nursing a bruised face and, giggling, Cook said, 'There's allus a crowd round the town hall watchin' the gentry arrivin', I expect he thinks them as did it might be there.'

'Serves 'im right,' Polly said stoutly.

'Ay, well we didn't ask fer *your* opinion, Miss Polly.'

'Yer made Miss Nancy an' Miss Mary look loverly, Katie,' Polly went on. 'Are yer goin' ter be their maid fro' now on?'

'The master sez there's to be no more maids for the two girls i' this 'ouse, an' wi' 'alf 'is workforce out of a job 'e's quite right fer once,' Cook interrupted.

'Katie should get more money if she's two jobs ter do,' Polly insisted, 'and so should I 'cause she won't be able to 'elp me any.'

'Be lucky that yer in a job at all, both of yer,' Cook retorted. 'Now yer've seen all there is to be seen, yer can get back to yer work.'

Back in the scullery Polly carried on with her grumbling.

'It ain't right, Katie, they're savin' Milly's wage, Cook could speak out fer us if she would.'

'She's right about the people workin' at the mills, though. Mi uncle's bin on short time for weeks an' mi aunt lost her job just before I arrived and they've never taken her back. I don't know what sort of a Christmas they're going to have. I'd like to be able to give them something towards it.'

'Well, so you could if you got a bit more.'

'There's not much chance of that, so just drop it, Polly.'

Clattering her dishes she snapped, 'I 'spect they'll be cuttin' down on Christmas presents fer us too. Last year I got a box of 'andkies.'

'From the family?'

'Mrs Tate gets lots o' things, an' so does Cook. None of 'em really knows me but I 'spect you'll get someat fro' the two girls and mebbe fro' the master since yer waits on't table.'

113

'He doesn't think my waitin' on table is up to much.'

She giggled. 'Oh well, 'e's allus 'alf drunk over Christmas wi' 'is 'unt meetins an' such like. 'E even pinched mi bottom last year, an' 'e kissed Cook under the mistletoe.'

'The master!'

'Ay. 'E's not as quiet as 'e looks, Katie, I've heard stories about 'is carryings on over at Copplethorpe, an' I once heard Mrs Tate tellin' Cook 'e 'ad a woman wi' 'im at one o' the race meetings i' Kendal.'

'There was probably nothing in it, they have lots of friends they go racing with.'

'Ay, but the mistress never goes, does she? Cook sez she used ter go in the old days, now she's probably not welcome.'

'You shouldn't listen to gossip, Polly.'

She was watching me slyly. 'Yer never 'ear any scandal about Mr Jeffrey. I reckon 'e's savin' 'isself fer Miss Lois, allus supposin' 'e's savin' 'isself fer anybody.'

'You know nothing about it, Polly.'

'Yer don't like mi talkin' about Mr Jeffrey, do yer, Katie?'

'I don't mind, why should I?'

'Yer fancies 'im, though.'

'No I don't. I'd be a fool to fancy him.'

'I know, but it wouldn't stop yer. Are yer goin' ter yer uncle's fer Christmas then?'

'I expect so, some time over Christmas. What will you do?'

'Stop 'ere. I've no folks, I were brought up in an orphanage i' Manchester, I never 'ad no folks.'

'You never knew your mother or any of your folks?'

'A policeman found mi on a bench in the park.'

'And you stayed at the orphanage until you were old enough to find work?'

'That's right. The matron called mi Polly an' they kept mi till I were twelve, then I come 'ere. They must 'ave applied to the orphanage for a scullerymaid.'

I was looking at her in horror, but she went on washing her dishes, and at my silence she turned and a grin spread

114

over her face. 'It weren't really so bad, Katie, we 'ad outings in the summer the trustees paid fer, an' we 'ad a decent Christmas wi' a party an' such. I 'ad to work at the 'ome fer mi keep but I didn't mind that an' there were allus plenty o' company.'

'Did nobody try to find your parents?'

'I don't know, but yer know what I thinks? I'll bet mi mother were somebody like Milly an mi father some posh feller as wouldn't marry 'er. She probably couldn't do owt else but leave mi in that park fer somebody else to bring up.'

'And here's me feeling sorry for miself because mi mother hasn't sent for mi to join her in America.'

'An' so yer should be. I were nobbut a day old when mi mother parted wi' me. She's 'ad yer for thirteen years, yer were a part o' your mother.'

I felt the stupid tears pricking my eyes and I turned away quickly, hoping Polly wouldn't see them, but she was too sharp.

'I don't mind if yer cries about it, Katie, I used ter cry when I saw some o' the pretty ones bein' adopted. Nobody ever asked fer me. But yer the prettiest girl I ever saw, I can't understand yer mother ever lettin' yer go.'

'She was dominated by my grandmother.'

She shook her head sagely, and with the tears still bright on my cheeks I left her humming quietly to herself.

Chapter 10

On Christmas afternoon I stood with the other servants in the hall while the mistress presented us with brightly wrapped parcels and the family shook hands with us.

The master had a red face and as he took my hand I could smell whisky on his breath. Then came the rest of the family, and I tried to think that Jeffrey held my hand longer than was strictly necessary, but this was wishful thinking, I know.

My gift was a box of chocolates and Polly grumbled incessantly because for the fourth Christmas in succession she had been given a box of handkerchieves.

'Be thankful you've received anything at all,' Cook admonished her. 'It's more than you received in that orphanage.'

'What 'ave you got, then?' Polly demanded.

'A bottle o' port which I treats as medicine, an' well the mistress knows it,' Cook snapped.

'You can share my chocolates if you like,' I told Polly, and when her eyes grew round with pleasure I said, 'I'll swap you if you like.'

'Don't you like chocklits then?'

'I don't want to get fat, and you can stand a bit more flesh on your bones.'

She accepted the chocolates with delight and I was delighted to see the handkerchieves were made from fine Irish linen and bearing a small embroidered motif.

Family parties were the order of Christmas Day, which meant I was unable to visit my relatives until Boxing Day, but with all the comings and goings of family and friends I was kept busy. Mr Ambrose with his wife and two children arrived for luncheon, and in no time at all the children were

116

running all over the house and into the kitchen, so that Cook plied them with tartlets and Mrs Tate accused her of spoiling their lunch. Then guests were arriving, including a young lady escorted by Mr Roger and who until that morning none of us had seen.

It was three o'clock when the servants finally sat down to their Christmas lunch. I received the well-meant embraces of the grooms and gardener with fortitude; even Ned's too-ardent kiss under Mrs Tate's watchful eyes was easily turned aside.

The talk over the table was light-hearted enough until Ted Stringer said, 'And who's the young lady Mr Roger's fetched o'er fro' Merton, then?'

'She's Mr Roger's guest, that's all I know,' said Mrs Tate.

'It's noan taken 'im long ter forget Milly, 'as it?'

Mrs Tate sat tight-lipped and Cook silenced him with a stern look, but Polly, who never knew when to remain silent, said, 'It's a shame it is, an' 'er sent away i' disgrace an' 'im bringin' that girl 'ere as though he'd nothin' to be ashamed of.'

'Hold your tongue Polly,' Cook ordered, 'and make yerself useful clearin' these dishes.'

For the rest of the day I was kept busy in the dining room, which gave me a golden opportunity to observe the girl sitting next to Mr Roger. She was not pretty, but she had an air of well-bred refinement. She was plainly but expensively dressed and she wore her dark brown hair taken back from her face and caught by a watered silk ribbon the colour of her green gown. She had a long thin face and a prominent nose, and for the main part her expression was bored until Roger spoke to her, when it became more animated. He too appeared bored and I had the impression that his family had prevailed upon him to invite her.

Miss Nancy's guest was much older than herself and I wondered why she had not invited one of the twins until I remembered that their father was reputed to be going through a bad time financially, and of late neither of the boys had been visiting Heatherlea.

Miss Mary's guest looked decidedly ill at ease and he was hardly the type of young man I would have seen at the dinner table only months before. He had a loud laugh, and I could feel my face colouring at one of his risky stories which was received in silence by those sitting next to him.

Something was happening to this family, I could feel it and yet I could not put my finger on what it was.

As I stood with Mrs Tate at the side table, trying not to look at any of them and yet be ready to attend to their slightest whim, I could not but reflect on how the family had changed in the three years since I came to work for them. The mistress seemed more than usually preoccupied, sad almost, and the master was drinking more heavily. Neither of the girls seemed happy and only the two older sons, one with his wife and children, the other with his fiancé, seemed at ease. Roger was plainly making an effort to interest his companion and Jeffrey's thoughts were far away, possibly with Lois in distant France.

Mrs Tate's face was expressionless and I longed to know how she viewed the changes the last few years had wrought, but I knew I would not be able to ask her. In time Cook would talk about them because she couldn't resist dropping the odd remark.

On Boxing day I visited my aunt and uncle, taking the Christmas presents I had saved up for over many months – tobacco for Uncle Turlough, a warm woollen cardigan for Aunt Martha and chocolates for the girls. As I was leaving Heatherlea, Cook put a cardboard box into my hands, saying, 'Take these for yer folks, Katie, they're nobbut a few mince pies and cookies, but I know times is 'ard for them that works in't mills.'

My eyes lit up with appreciation and I thanked her warmly for her thoughtfulness.

My aunt and uncle received my gifts gratefully, although Aunt Martha admonished me for spending my hard-earned money on them. Lucy was attending a party at the church hall but Frances sat at the table, with her head as usual buried in a book, and she hardly raised it high enough to acknowledge my presence.

'''Ave the grace to thank yer cousin Kathleen for the chocolates she's brought yer, she could 'a' done wi' that money for 'erself,' my aunt told her.

She muttered something unintelligible, then snatching up her book she escaped to her room.

'She's sulkin',' my aunt said. 'She wanted to stay wi' her friends for Christmas but I insisted 'er place was at 'ome. I don't know what we're goin ter do about 'er, Kathleen. We 'ears nothin' except their posh 'ouse an' their way o' life which isn't ours. We've lost our girl, but yer uncle won't 'ave it. Come an' take off yer coat, Kathleen, and sit by the fire.'

'I can't stay long, Aunt Martha. I couldn't come yesterday, there were so many guests to see to.'

'Yer'll stay for someat ter eat though, won't yer, Kathleen?'

'No, I'd best get back. I'll come again when I have time off.'

'It's Fanny, isn't it? Yer not stayin' because she's 'ere.'

'No, of course not.'

But it *was* Fanny who sent me scurrying back to Heatherlea, to be received with raised eyebrows from Cook and curiosity from Polly.

Feeling they deserved some explanation I said my aunt had a bad cold and I hadn't wanted to put her to any inconvenience, and although my remarked satisfied Polly, Cook was not fooled for one moment.

Later she said slyly, 'How's that girl o' theirs goin' on, Katie, the one that passed the scholarship?'

'Very well, Cook. I haven't seen much of her.'

'Yer've seen 'er today though?'

'Yes, for a short time.'

'An' she's the reason yer came back so soon.'

'No, why should she be?'

'Because she's a right little madam an' yer've no great luv for 'er.'

'The feelin's mutual.'

'So I'm right, then?'

'Yes. I don't know what's goin' to happen there, she's

growin' away from them. Maybe they were wrong to let her go to that school.'

'Nay, it's not the school, Katie, it's the girl 'erself. They'll never do any good wi' 'er, best let 'er go 'er own way to make 'er own mistakes. Mebbe one day she'll come ter appreciate all she's thrown away.'

'What makes you so wise, I wonder?'

She chuckled, well pleased with herself. 'Nay, I'm not so wise, Katie, just old, an' yer can't put old 'eads on young shoulders.'

'Did you never make mistakes?'

She laughed. 'That I did, monny a time, an' lived ter regret it. There's somethin' very comfortable about bein' old enough to sit back an' watch others doin' all the daft things I did afore I learned some sense. I looks at yer sometimes and thinks yer the bonniest lass I've ever seen, yet 'ere yer are waitin' on folks as doesn't even know yer exists.'

'It's better than workin' in that weavin' shed an' bein' pestered with the likes of Charlie Wheeldon.'

'But yer wouldn't mind if Mr Jeffrey was to pester yer, isn't that right, Katie?'

I busied myself boiling milk for the cocoa so as to hide my blushing face, but undeterred she went on, 'Well, Miss Lois will be comin' back in the new year an' he'll need ter make 'is mind up; 'e's bin shilly-shallyin' long enough.'

'If he really wants her he wouldn't be shilly-shallyin', would he?'

'Don't be comfortin' yerself on that score, Katie. I'm fast changin' mi ideas about Mr Jeffrey.'

I put the mug of cocoa down sharply in front of her and she looked up with her narrow eyes filled with amusement.

'Yer don't like me sayin' a wrong word about 'im, I know, but 'im not being like Mr Roger doesn't make 'im perfect.'

'You're talkin' just like his father, Cook. Mr Jeffrey doesn't deserve that.'

'P'raps not, but time'll tell, Katie, we shan't 'ave long to wait.'

She was right. Halfway through January the Foxlands returned from their holiday, bringing with them a Mr Joseph Earnshaw, and Miss Lois was sporting a large diamond ring on her engagement finger.

The family seemed stunned by the news and although I scanned Jeffrey's face curiously whenever I got the chance it gave nothing away. The mistress was distressed, the girls were openly curious and the master scathing in his denunciations of his youngest son, who had allowed the girl to slip through his fingers.

Only Mr Roger's departure for service with the Yeomanry interrupted his spleen, and the following after- noon Mrs Foxland arrived to satisfy everybody's curiosity.

Mr Earnshaw, it appeared, was the owner of several mills on the outskirts of Manchester making clothing of the mass-produced variety, with contracts for the armed forces. He had a large house in the Ribble valley where he bred prize cattle and racehorses, as well as a house near the city where he was cared for by an admirable housekeeper.

His first wife had died over ten years before and there were no children, and he was fifty-two years old. When the mistress said this seemed rather old for Miss Lois, who was twenty-two, Mrs Foxland was quick to remark that Mr Earnshaw didn't look his age and was a well-set-up man who looked after his health and smoked and drank only in moderation.

Later in the day Mrs Tate informed us that the marriage was to take place in the spring, that neither the bride nor groom saw why they should wait.

'So she'll be leavin' these parts?' Cook asked.

'Naturally they'll live in his home, which I am told is quite beautiful. Mr Earnshaw is obviously a very wealthy man.'

'An' that o' course is why she's marryin' 'im. 'Aven't I allus said that young woman 'as 'er 'ead screwed on tight.'

'What do you mean by that, Cook?'

'Well, 'asn't she seen what can 'appen to cotton, she's only got ter look at 'er father's mills, and the Carslakes are no better placed. She's gettin' out o' cotton, an' Mr Jeffrey's wishy-washy courtship 'asn't bin strong enough to keep 'er.'

Mrs Tate made no comment. Inwardly I rejoiced. I had no thoughts that I could take her place in Jeffrey's affections, I knew my place, but all the same I had some vague hope that one day the world might change enough to wash away the barriers that so divided us.

A few days later, Mrs Tate informed me that the mistress wished to see me in the drawing room.

I thought of all my misdemeanours as I knocked timidly on the door. The smile with which she greeted me instantly dispelled my fears.

I stood dutifully in front of her and she said, 'I don't know if you are aware of it or not, Katie, but there is to be a big affair at Tremayne House at the end of January in honour of the silver wedding of Sir Joshua and Lady Dorothy, and all those people who live on the hill have offered the services of one or two of their servants should they be needed. I have spoken for you, Katie.'

'For me, Ma'am?'

'Well of course, Katie, you are a very presentable girl and I doubt if Polly would be suitable.'

'Oh Ma'am, what'll I have to do there?'

'One morning next week you will go up to Tremayne House to be interviewed by the butler, a Mr Johnson. You mustn't be afraid of him, even if he does appear to be very superior, he is only a servant like yourself. I am quite sure he will find you most presentable and efficient. He will want to know what you do here and what your past experience has been. He will not be interested in your work in the cotton mill but you could tell him about the work you performed for your grandmother in Ireland, that I think will be very important.'

My expression was doubtful and in a lighter voice she coaxed, 'Don't look so afraid, my dear, you will be splendid and when we know what your duties will be there will be a new pretty apron and cap for you to wear. Let everybody see what a pretty servant the Carslakes are blessed with.'

'I'll do mi best, Ma'am.'

'And that is all I expect from you, Katie. Now off you go and inform the others.'

Several days later I was instructed to make my way to Tremayne House, which I viewed with considerable uneasiness once I entered the huge gates. I had been told to go to the servants' entrance at the back, and I was glad to see several other people waiting there, both men and women.

We were ushered into a small room, which the man standing next to me said was the butler's parlour.

'Wait 'ere,' said the maidservant who had admitted us. 'The butler'll be 'ere directly.'

There was a square table in the centre of the room with a chenille tablecloth, and round it were several chairs. A bright fire burned in the gate and on a sideboard stood a bowl of fruit and a figure of a bronze horse. I was unable to look further because the butler came in – a tall thin man with black hair and a saturnine expression, clad in severe black and carrying a rolled up newspaper which he used to point to the chairs.

'I would like the girls to sit, the men can stand behind,' he said, eying us over with a decidedly jaundiced expression.

He consulted a list and proceeded to read out our names and duties, presumably supplied by our individual employers.

When he had satisfied himself that we were all present he said, 'I require two men to assist with conveyances in the courtyard and along the drive, and two more to take care of horse-drawn traffic. I need four women to help in the kitchens to prepare salads and vegetables, and two more to assist upstairs, serving food and drink. It is to be a buffet meal so the guests will help themselves, but there will be plates to replenish and glasses to refill.'

His eyes swept round the table and came to rest on a pretty dark girl sitting second from the end.

'Your name?' he demanded.

'Jennie Grady, Sir.'

'From the Foxland house?'

'Yes, Sir.'

'You will assist in the upstairs rooms. You will address me as Mr Johnson. There are two of you from the Foxland house?'

'Yes, me an' Mabel 'ere.'

His eyes slid over Mabel, sitting next to Jennie – a small thin girl with a freckled face and hair the colour of a freshly peeled carrot, then he turned away and his eyes swept along the girls until they found me.

'What is your name?' he asked abruptly.

'Kathleen O'Donovan, Mr Johnson, from Heatherlea.'

'The Carslake's house?'

'Yes.'

'You will assist me upstairs with Jennie here. I shall want you here at three o'clock in the afternoon. There will be a lot of preparation to be done. That will be all.'

We moved silently out of the house, but once we were on the drive one of the men said, 'Thinks a lot of 'isself, an' no mistake,' and another said, laughing, ''E knew who 'e wanted upstairs though, didn't 'e? The prettiest lasses i' the bunch.'

Jennie Grady turned to me. ''Ow long 'ave yer been in service then?' she demanded.

'Three years.'

'But yer not fro' round 'ere?'

'No.'

'Where are yer from, then?'

'Does it matter? But if you must know I'm from Donegal.'

'Well I've bin a parlourmaid fer nigh on five years, so I'll be able ter put yer right on what's what. I don't know why 'e couldn't 'ave picked Mabel 'ere, we're used to workin' together.'

'Well, the choice was his. It had nothing to do with me.'

With a bright smile I left them to hurry on ahead, and later when I told Cook and Polly, Cook snorted with satisfaction.

'Don't yer be 'avin 'er telling' yer 'ow ter do things, Katie, yer've as much idea as she 'as an' it's about time she were taken down a peg or two.'

124

'Ought I to inform the mistress, do you think?'

'Mrs Tate'll tell 'er later. The mistress and the two girls 'ave gone to tea over at Mr Steadly's 'ouse. I reckon someat might come o' that 'atween Miss Nancy an' Mr Steadly.'

'There won't be need to serve afternoon tea, then.'

'No. Yer can go out if yer wants to, but get back i' time to 'elp wi' the evening meal.'

I set off towards the fells, climbing steadily, surprised to find my uncle standing moodily staring down at the town over one of the low stone walls. He failed to see me until I gently touched his arm, then his pensive face lit up with a smile.

'Why aren't yer visiting us on yer half day, Katie?'

'It's not mi half day, Uncle Turlough, I just have a couple of hours off before I need to get back.'

'Oh well, we might as well walk on together then, I'll be glad o' your company.'

'How's Aunt Martha?'

'Not well, Katie, she's that worried about our Fanny, but I tell her it's no use worryin', the girl'll come to 'er senses soon enough.'

'And if she doesn't?'

'Then we've lost 'er, Katie.'

'Why don't you have a word with the family she's been living with, tell them about your fears, how unhappy her being away is making her mother?'

'We've thought o' that, Katie, but if we did they'd probably stop invitin' 'er and she'd blame us for it. She'd be that resentful there'd be no living with 'er.'

'Then there's nothin' you can do except sit back and wait.'

'I reckon so.'

For a long time we walked in silence until I became aware of a flurry of snow in the wind and a mist creeping down across the fell shutting out the town.

'We should be gettin' back, Katie. Snow's comin'.'

Dutifully I turned, quickening my steps to match his.

'Have you no good news about the mill, Uncle?' I asked anxiously.

His face brightened considerably. 'Well, I moight 'ave, Katie, I saw one o' the works managers this mornin' an' he said they were 'opin' any day to 'ave a government contract for the armed forces. It were all hush-hush at the moment. I've bin thinkin' for some time now that there's trouble brewin' in Europe.'

'How could that affect us, Uncle Turlough?'

'Haven't the English always pushed their noses into trouble, Katie wherever it was?'

'But not Europe, Uncle. Europe isn't part of the Empire.'

'Nor does it 'ave to be. If there's trouble the British'll be there. They 'ave their fingers in so many pies, Katie. Yer've only to look at Ireland.'

'Oh Uncle, I don't want to look at Ireland, I've been listening to tales about the British as long as I can remember. If they're as bad as all that why do the Irish come over here to make a living?'

'That's treason yer talkin', Katie O'Donovan.'

'So what if it is? It's common-sense treason.'

'I'll not 'ave yer runnin' the Irish down to put the British in a good light.'

'Then why didn't ye stay in Donegal with Grandmother Cassidy an marry a good Irish Catholic girl then? It'll be the same with Uncle Shamus, and him not bein' able to get to America fast enough.'

'Work was 'ard to come by in Donegal, Katie, that's why we got out.'

'Sure an' ye couldn't get on wi' mi grandmother. All I ever heard was the Irish talkin' about the old country an' how much they loved her an' how beautiful she was, yet when they left they never went back, leastways not to stay back.'

'If Michael O'Donovan could be listenin' to his daughter right now, he'd be spinnin' in his grave he would.'

'And wasn't mi father always talkin' about when he had enough money to leave Donegal he would? I reckon he meant it too.'

'I don't know what to think about ye, Katie O'Donovan, indeed I don't. Yer every bit as bad as our Fanny.'

126

'Oh no, Uncle, I'm not at all like your Fanny. I'm loyal to mi own and I'll stand up for what's right and proper and for folk I love, even though they be as poor as church mice, but you'll never get mi to say black is white against all mi better judgement.'

He was looking at me so sternly I began to fear that he was really angry, then I saw the twinkle in his eyes, and throwing my arms round his neck I cried, 'There now, you've bin baitin' mi all this time. It's ashamed of yourself you should be, Turlough Cassidy.'

'I'm not surprised ye got on the wrong side o' your grandmother, Katie.'

Chapter 11

I had never been in a place like Tremayne House before.
Twice Mr Johnson had to ask me to attend to my duties, I
was so busy staring at the sweeping shallow staircase and
the great bowls filled with exquisite blooms. The huge
dining table groaned under masses of platters piled high
with food, whole salmon and turkeys, suckling pigs and
hams, and there were side tables bearing trifles and sweets
of all descriptions and others covered with drinking glasses
for champagne, wines and brandies.

'You will circulate among the guests, Kathleen, to make
sure that their glasses are filled,' Mr Johnson instructed.
'And you, Jennie, will see that they are helped to sweets
from this table. When one dish is empty you will bring up
another from the kitchens.'

For the rest of the afternoon I was instructed into the way
of wines and spirits and the various glasses I would need to
supply by a supercilious young wine waiter.

He looked down on women servants as lesser beings, but
I was quick to learn, and when I had grown tired of his
condescension I gave him as good as I got. After that we got
along reasonably well.

Promptly at six o'clock we were told to discard our
working overalls and prepare ourselves for the evening's
work.

As Mrs Carslake had promised I had been given a new
cap and apron, pretty, snow-white frilly things. The cap sat
on my red hair at a most becoming angle and the dainty
apron over my long black skirt reminded me of the picture
of a French maid I had seen in one of Miss Nancy's
magazines.

'Are those new?' Jennie Grady asked with raised eyebrows.

'The mistress likes her servants to look the part,' I answered, hoping she would think I was similarly attired every day.

Later I stood behind the drinks counter with shining eyes, watching the guests entering the ballroom, and listening to the small orchestra with my feet tapping.

Many of the gentlemen and the older guests drifted into the supper room and away from the music and the more energetic pursuits of the younger element. Back in Donegal, this was how I had believed all English people lived in their great houses, the women in exquisite gowns wearing priceless jewels and fabulous furs, the men in dazzling uniforms or formal dress.

My companion handed me a huge silver tray filled with glasses of sherry.

'Take this among the guests and try not to drop it,' he said shortly.

The tray was heavy and would have been better carried by himself, but I gripped the handles firmly, and soon it became much lighter as the glasses were taken one by one. I was well aware of the admiring glances from the men, some of them old enough to be my grandfather, and the women too were not averse to watching me move from group to group. I was glad of my slender figure in its long graceful skirt.

I could see the master standing near the fireplace surrounded by a group of his hunting friends, all of them wearing their mess jackets in hunting pink. He had a glass of whisky in his hand, his face was already red and glistening, and he seemed in high good humour. I looked round anxiously, but could not see any of the Carslake sons.

It was ten o'clock when the younger guests entered the supper room and then I saw him, looking so incredibly handsome in his evening clothes, escorting a dark pretty girl in the company of her mother.

Mr Humphrey was there with his fiancée, then I saw the mistress with Mr and Mrs Foxland, and then there was Miss Lois with her fiancée, and I stared in amazement.

How could she possibly prefer this short plump man to Jeffrey? He was no taller than Lois. He looked affluent, judging from the diamond pin in his lapel and the huge diamond ring on his right hand.

I had the opportunity to observe Miss Lois's ring also as she took a glass of wine from my tray. It was an enormous solitaire diamond, almost too large for her dainty hand.

I was aware of many things as I went about the guests, of the mistress's approving glances and the master's conspiratorial leer as he informed his friends that the pretty Irish lass was a member of his household. Jeffrey smiled at me across the room and I felt the warm rich colour flood my cheeks, then a voice at my side was saying, 'So here you are, not Miss Nancy at all but still the prettiest girl in the room.'

I looked up into the laughing dark eyes of the man who had almost knocked me over in the lane. He too was wearing faultless evening dress, his tanned face was filled with devilment and his eyes were tantalizingly warm.

'I wonder why I got the impression that you were the daughter of the house?' he insisted provocatively.

'I never set out to give you that impression.'

'No, but you have a distinctive air. What *is* your name, by the way?'

'I can't be talkin' to you, people are watching us.'

'Let them watch, can't a fella talk to the prettiest girl in the room without causing a disturbance?'

'I knows mi place, Sir, an' I'll not have you upsettin' things.'

'Kathleen,' came the wine waiter's voice at my elbow, 'there are glasses to be filled. Hurry girl.'

'You can start by filling mine, Kathleen,' said the most maddening man I had ever met. 'I'll know what to call you the next time we meet on the fell.' Then with another gay smile he was moving away to join his host and hostess.

I felt bemused as I watched him in laughing conversation with them, then Lady Dorothy was walking towards the tables to assure herself that all was well. I bobbed a small curtsey and to my utmost consternation she paused to speak with me.

'You are Mrs Carslake's housemaid, I believe.'

'Yes, Milady.'

'Charming, quite charming.'

With a brief smile she moved on, leaving me pink cheeked but unreasonably happy, and catching Mrs Carslake's smile I knew that she was equally gratified.

The dancing had started again and I was instructed to go with my tray into the ballroom, where I was surprised to see Jeffrey dancing with Lois Foxland while her fiancé looked on indulgently. Looking away, I became aware of two dark sardonic eyes watching me, eyes that were filled with dark malicious amusement.

It was almost three o'clock when the last vehicle trundled down the drive, yet the servants were still at work, clearing the ballroom of glasses and putting the supper room to rights. I began to realize how tired I felt, and six-thirty, my normal time for rising, didn't seem very far away.

Eventually Mr Johnson called out, 'There is nothing more to be done now, you are all free to go.'

As we struggled into our outdoor clothing Jennie Grady said, 'The kitchen staff went off duty hours before. I'm that weary don't know where ter put miself.'

'I hope somebody's going to walk down the road with us, it's very late.'

'Early, yer means. Some o' the men are still 'ere, they've bin seein' ter the traffic.'

'It was a splendid occasion wasn't it?'

'Ay. A saw yer Mr Jeffrey were dancin' wi' our Miss Lois.'

'Well, why shouldn't he?'

'Well, she's passed 'im over, 'asn't she? He fancied 'er, yer know, we all thought 'e'd 'a' wed 'er.'

I decided not to speak as I walked quickly towards the door where Mr Johnson was evidently anxious to see the back of us. He handed each of us a small parcel.

'Her ladyship has asked me to thank you for your services, and to present you with this small gift in appreciation,' he said pompously, and we were out in the frosty air, walking quickly to catch up with the little band of men ahead of us.

''Urry up, girls,' one of them called, 'it's long past yer bedtime.'

'Did you know most of the people present?' I asked Jennie hopefully.

'I've seen a lot of 'em afore, but a lot o' them folks came a fair distance.'

She began to air her knowledge, and I listened with a desire to know more of English society. Against all my better judgement I asked, 'Who was the man who spent some time with Sir Joshua and Lady Dorothy in the supper room?'

'Yer mean the young man, tall, wi' dark hair an' that smile that turns mi legs to water?'

I stared at her in surprise. 'You mean you think he's attractive?'

'Do I not. He's a stranger i' these parts but 'e's stayin' wi' the Tremaynes.'

'I didn't know.'

'Well, this is your gate, I'll probably be seein' yer about. Hey, wait for me,' she called, and ran down the hill in pursuit of the men.

I had been given a key to let myself into the house. The kitchen fire had gone out and the room felt cold and forbidding. My bedroom too would be unwelcoming.

In my room I unwrapped the parcel, then I gave a little cry of pleasure. I had expected an unimaginative gift of chocolates, sweets or the inevitable handkerchieves, but it was a pure silk scarf in green and primrose, the colours that suited my red hair more than any others, and it pleased me to think that perhaps Lady Dorothy had decided on my gift after she had seen me.

What had she given to Jenny, I wondered? And who was the Tremaynes' Canadian guest? I fell asleep thinking of his impudent dark eyes and flashing smile, but it was Jeffrey Carslake's face that haunted my dreams: he was dancing with Lois Foxland in any empty ballroom, his eyes gazing sadly down at her pale head, while I stood in the doorway holding my tray of empty glasses, ineffectual and unseen.

Chapter 12

They were all anxious to hear how I had fared at the Tremayne ball, the following day, but I had only just launched into my story when there was a loud knock on the side door. It was my uncle, asking for me.

I looked at Cook in some dismay, but she said quickly, 'Bring 'im in 'ere Polly, don't keep the man waitin' on the doorstep.'

He came clutching his cap, apologizing for interrupting.

'Is something wrong, Uncle, is it Aunt Martha?'

'No Katie, it's yer grandmother.'

'She's ill?'

'She's dead, she had a stroke, and 'er never having a day's illness that I can remember.'

'When did you hear, Uncle?'

'Father McGinty sent a message through the police last night.'

'I see. Will you have to go over there, then?'

'We've talked about it, Katie. Shamus and yer mother won't be able to get over from America for the funeral, but one of her children ought to be there as a sign of respect. Would you be able to come with mi, Katie?'

There was no grief in my heart for Grandmother Cassidy, only a wild desire to see the sun setting over the wild cliffs and listen to the haunting cries of the seabirds circling low over the sea. In that moment only the dear loves of my childhood filled my heart, the sea and the wind and the clumps of pink thrift on the limestone cliffs, the winding lanes that led to the headland and the lilt of Irish voices round the stalls on market days.

He was staring at me intently, waiting for my answer, and I said hesitantly, 'It'll cost a lot, Uncle Turlough, I don't rightly know if I've got that much.'

'Yer aunt says we'll pay, Katie, it hasn't got to cost you a penny.'

'But you can't afford it. I'll pay you back, every penny.'

'We'll talk about that later, Katie. Does that mean you'll come?'

'I'll have to ask the mistress, Uncle . . .'

Cook interrupted: 'When's the funeral to be, Mr Cassidy?'

'The day after tomorrow, we'd have to be goin' in the mornin'.

'She'll be there, the mistress 'as never said no yet when it's bin sickness or a death.'

He nodded, satisfied. 'There'll be a taxi sent up at seven o'clock, Katie, to take us to the station. Can ye be ready?'

'I'll be ready,' I said, walking with him to the door.

Promptly the following morning we were bound for Liverpool and home.

How strange it seemed to be walking again along the narrow country road edged by whitewashed cottages, most of them with their curtains drawn as a mark of respect for the woman few had liked but all had respected.

Men we met on the road raised their caps and many greeted us by name. Shawl-clad country women curtsied in the old way, and Uncle Turlough said, 'Nothin's changed, has it, Katie?'

'Not on the surface, perhaps.'

I was glad that my grandmother's coffin lay in the church. All the same the house felt cold, and there was a sweet sickly scent which spoke to me of death. While Uncle Turlough talked to Father McGinty I escaped out of the back door and ran as fast as my legs could carry me towards the cliffs. A young crescent moon hung low in the sky and the sound of the birds was stilled. I could hear the sea crashing on the rocks, and a vague desperate sadness brought the stinging tears into my eyes and they rolled down my face unchecked.

The church was crowded by the townsfolk in their best Sunday black, silently listening to Father McGinty's eulogy on my grandmother's blameless life. My mind wandered, to my father's neglected grave with not even a posy laid on it, next to that marble edifice they would place over my grandmother.

Back at the house there were great tables waiting piled with all manner of fare. Since the funeral was taking place at noon, Uncle Turlough was hoping they would all be gone by three o'clock, when he was due to meet her solicitor. We had talked about it earlier:

'I don't suppose I shall need to be there will I? There'll be nothin' in mi grandmother's will to concern me.'

'Ye don't know that for sure, Katie.'

'Perhaps not, but I've a good idea.'

'All the same, Katie, I'd like you to be there. Father McGinty'll be there as well.'

'He's not family.'

'That is so, but knowin' your grandmother she'll 'ave left somethin' to the church.'

'Buyin' her way into heaven, do you mean?'

He hadn't answered me, and now looking round the congregation I knew that more than one person present would be wondering just how Janie Cassidy had left her money, and how much she had had.

It was over at last, the praying and the singing, the feasting and the drinking, and the last one was trundling down the path, trying without much success to maintain a steady gait.

The lawyer was shuffling his papers and Father McGinty sat with lowered head, over which my eyes met my uncles' with their faintly mocking gleam.

Janie Cassidy had scrimped and saved all her life, mostly at the expense of poor old Alice, and now to my utmost astonishment I learned that she had left the princely sum of just over ten thousand pounds. The lawyer's voice droned on: 'To my three children, Shamus Cassidy, Turlough Cassidy and Mary O'Donovan, I leave the sum of two thousand pounds, and to my dear friend Father Patrick

McGinty I leave two thousand pounds with the proviso that he installs in his church, close to the altar, a suitable memorial to myself and my dear husband James Terrence Cassidy.

'To my grandson Terrence O'Donovan I leave the sum of five hundred pounds and to my two granddaughters, Frances Cassidy and Lucy Cassidy, two hundred and fifty pounds to be spent on their education, and the same sum to my granddaughter Kathleen O'Donovan, to be kept in trust until she reaches the age of twenty-one when she may, God willing, have learned enough sense to handle it wisely.

'To my daughter Mary O'Donovan I leave my gold watch and chain and to Martha Cassidy my daughter-in-law I leave my jet beads and pearl brooch. To my granddaughter Kathleen O'Donovan I leave my gold locket which I promised her mother should be hers before I became aware of her many failings.'

I took little account of the rest of her will, which consisted of bequests of furniture, clothes and such to her cronies, then the lawyer was shuffling his papers and the whisky was being passed around.

That night my uncle said, 'You see Katie, yer grandmother didn't forget ye.'

An idea had been forming in my mind ever since I had heard the will and now I asked, 'When can I have the gold locket, uncle?'

'Now, Katie if ye wants it. It's upstairs in yer grandmother's strong box.'

'It's mine, to do what I like with, isn't it?'

'Well o' course, but you'll be wearin' it, Katie, it's a pretty thing.'

'No, Uncle, I'll be pawnin' it. I'd be a hypocrite to wear it, and the money I'll be gettin' for it'll do more good than havin' it hangin' round mi neck.'

He was staring at me aghast. 'Katie, ye *can't* pawn it, what will folks think?'

'I don't care what they think, like as not I'll never set eyes on any of 'em again. I don't want the money for miself Uncle, please let me have the locket and I'll tell you what

I've done with the money when I know how much I'm goin' to get for it.'

Early next morning I faced old Paddy Fitz across the counter in his dingy little shop while he handled my grandmother's locket appreciatively.

'So you're pawnin' it already, Kathleen O'Donovan, and your grandmother hardly cold in her grave,' he said sternly.

'The money's not for me, Mr Fitzpatrick. How much can you give me for it?'

'Well there's not much money about, and like as not it'll be on mi hands a long time. How much were you thinkin' on?'

'Well, it's solid gold and mi grandmother laid much store on it. If you don't want to buy it I could always sell it to one of the jewellers in Manchester and get well paid for it.'

We were disturbed by his wife, who shuffled into the shop and came to stand beside him, looking curiously at the locket.

'It's a wicked girl you are Kathleen O'Donovan, to be pawnin' that,' she scolded. 'How much is she askin', Paddy?'

She took the locket in her hands, allowing the chain to fall through her fingers while Paddy looked on, frowning.

'We've come to no arrangement yet, Bridget,' he said warily.

'Offer her twenty-five pounds then, it'll not be far off.'

'Are ye mad, woman? I'll never have it off mi hands at that price.'

'Ye don't need to have it on your hands, I'll wear it miself. I've had mi eye on this every time I saw it on Janie Cassidy. Will you take twenty-five pounds, Kathleen?'

I hesitated, but faced with her gratification and his indignation, I accepted it.

'And what's a girl like you goin' to do with twenty-five pounds?' she asked. 'Spend it on fripperies, most likely.'

'I'm puttin' a stone on mi father's grave, a nice grey granite stone with bright gold letterin' with his name and with love from his wife and children.'

She stared at me dumbfounded for several minutes, then

pressing the money into my hands she said, 'Bless ye, Kathleen O'Donovan, wi all 'er money your grandmother never put a flower on his grave, an' 'im lying next to yer grandfather. I 'opes somewhere she'll know it's 'er locket that's payin' for that stone to be put up.'

Chapter 13

It was a grey dawn when I stood for the last time on the windswept cliffs watching the grey waves come tumbling in, with the seabirds crying all around me as they swept on snowy majestic wings on the bitter wind. The time when I had stood with my father on these same cliffs was now remote in my memory, and I have tried to remember that child with her red curls, holding on to the big man's hand, her blues eyes filled with joy at the sight of the gulls she loved.

Well, I would stand no more on Horn Head with my heart searching for memories and my eyes for shimmering rainbows. My feet were planted firmly on the ground, except for that ridiculous infatuation for Jeffrey Carslake with which Fate had been unkind enough to afflict me.

A slight sound made me turn round quickly. My uncle was clambering over the boulders to reach me.

'I thought I'd find you here, Katie, when you weren't at the house. Sayin' yer last farewell to the sea are ye?'

'I don't think I'll ever come back to Donegal, Uncle Turlough.'

'Nor me, Katie, this is the last I'll ever see of Ireland.'

'I can tell you now what I've done with the money I got for mi grandmother's locket.'

'The money must have been more important to ye, Katie.'

'Twenty-five pounds Paddy Fitz gave me for it, and every penny's gone on a stone for mi father's grave. I couldn't bear to see that black monstrosity over mi grandparents and nothin' above mi father. Now it won't matter so much that there's nobody to put flowers on his grave.'

He smiled gently. 'That was a rare thing ye did, Katie, a

139

rare nice thing ye did.'

'And what are you going to do with that fortune she's left you? You're a rich man now, Uncle.'

'I've bin thinkin' all night about it, couldn't sleep for thinkin' about it. I'll suggest to Martha that we move and find ourselves a nice little house out o' town, with a big garden for the girls. Frances's always wanted that, she'll be glad to stay with us and not bother so much about her friends.'

When I didn't immediately answer him he looked at me doubtfully. 'Ye don't think much of that idea, Katie?'

'I should let Aunt Martha have a say in what's done with your money, it's only fair.'

He chuckled. 'I knows what Martha's going to say. Save it for our old age. She's a practical soul.'

'Oh well, spend a bit and save a bit, perhaps that'll please you both. Had we better be getting back now?'

'Ay. I'll not be likin' the look o' them rain clouds. We'll be 'avin' a rough crossin'.'

I followed his gaze where the grey sky had taken on all the tints of red and crimson and where the rays of the hidden sun slanted over the raging sea. I shuddered a little, thinking of that other crossing I had taken in the company of Liam Clancy, and as if my uncle read my thoughts he said, 'One of these days, Katie, we must look up Liam Clancy and his relatives. We did promise, ye know.'

I said nothing. Liam Clancy and Ireland had little to do with the girl I had become.

My uncle had been so sure that his wife would view his changed fortunes with complete delight, and was totally unprepared for her tight-lipped silence.

He stared at me doubtfully across the table where we had just partaken of a large breakfast which she insisted I should eat before returning to Heatherlea.

'What are yer aimin' ter do wi' all that money? For no doubt you've bin makin' plans, high-falutin plans if I'm not mistaken,' she asked her husband.

'I thought we could move, luv, p'raps look for a nice little house on the other side o' Marsdale, with a nice garden.'

'And 'ow about your work? Yer'd 'ave further to travel.'

'There *is* no work, Martha. I'll 'ave to look around for somethin' else.'

'There's work. The works manager called to see yer when yer were away. That government contract's arrived, yer to report at the mill next Monday.'

'There, didn't I always say we'd turn the corner sooner or later? Now there's work and we 'ave money. I don't mind travellin' a bit further and it would be nice to 'ave a garden for the girls and a nice little house with a bathroom and a sittin' room.'

'For the girls, did yer say?'

'Well, ye know how Fanny's allus hankered after a garden.'

'Fanny's not 'ere.'

'Well, she's at school but they'll both be at home tonight.'

'Lucy will be 'ere, but not our Fanny.'

We stared at her pale face and angry eyes, and before my uncle could ask further questions she said bitterly, 'I left 'er upstairs in 'er bedroom the first night you were away. I 'ad a dress to deliver but I were only away half an hour. When I got back she'd gone, taken all 'er clothes and 'er books.'

'Did they come for 'er then, 'er friend's folks?'

'No, she walked it, all that way wi' a full suitcase. They came to see me the next day, 'im and 'is wife, they said she'd cried and pleaded with 'em to let 'er stay. She said she could never come back 'ere even if they didn't want 'er there.'

'What did ye say, Martha?'

'What could I say? They both stood there just inside the door and I saw 'er looking round the room at the chairs littered wi' mi sewin' and the fire burnin' low in the grate. I told 'em if she felt like that about 'er parents and 'er 'ome then she's best stay away from us.'

'She's coming back 'ere, Martha, if I've got to bring 'er back miself tonight.'

'I'm not 'avin 'er back, Turlough, to sulk and cry in 'er

141

room. I'll not 'ave yer temptin' 'er back wi' talk o' the money yer mother's left us. If we weren't good enough 'afore we're not good enough now, and yer 'ave another daughter. Lucy'll make twenty o' Fanny.'

'What good is the money goin' to do us, Martha, if it can't unite us as a family?'

She started to gather up the breakfast things and I sprang up to help her. He stared at us bleakly, then in a firm reasonable voice she said, 'Don't think I'm not grateful for the money, it's just that I don't want it used in silly ways just to tempt Fanny back. I want her to come back of 'er own free will, because she loves us and misses us, not because we've moved into a house wi' a garden. There's a lot we can do wi' this 'ouse, we needs a new carpet and some new curtains, p'raps even a new tiled fireplace and a new bed, we've 'ad that since we were married and the springs aren't so good. We could educate Lucy when she's a bit older and save for the next time cotton's in the doldrums, we could . . .'

Tears rolled down her cheeks, and my uncle reached out to comfort her, while I hurried into the kitchen with the tray. By the time I returned to the living room they were seated once more at the table.

'Mi mother left two hundred and fifty pounds to each o' the girls, Martha, the will said for their education, but Katie has to wait until she's twenty-one for 'ers.'

'Yer can send our Fanny's to the folks she's decided ter live with. It'll 'elp pay for 'er keep, but if they don't want it they can save it until she's wed, then she can 'ave it.'

'Wed, Martha?'

'Ay, ter some chap i' their walk o' life. She'll not go to 'im wi' nowt.'

'Eh luv, she'll be back wi' us long before 'er weddin' day.'

She sniffed. 'You'll be walkin' up the 'ill wi' Katie to 'elp 'er wi' 'er bag, Turlough?'

'That I will. Are ye wantin' to be off, Katie?'

'I think I should.'

We walked up the hill in silence. At last he squared his shoulders and gave me a self-conscious smile. 'I'm sorry, lass,' he said gently, 'I am poor company but I can't 'elp thinkin' about Fanny, she were such a pretty little thing, and such a lovable lass when she were little. I can't believe how she's changed. Do ye think it'll all come right in the end?'

'I wish I could read the future, Uncle, but sometimes it's better we don't know.' The widow Murphy used to read the tealeaves and grandmother Cassidy used to say, 'I only want to know the good things, none of the bad.'

At the house I took my valise from him and thanked him for carrying it.

'You'll be comin' to see us on yer next day off, Katie?' he said urgently.

'You know I will.'

I watched him walk away, and it seemed to me that in these last few hours he had aged fifty years.

Polly sat at the kitchen table with her head buried in a magazine, and one look at Cook's face told me that she was not in the most amiable of tempers.

'So yer back at last,' she said crossly. 'I expected yer back yesterday.'

'It took us a full day to get there, Cook, and we had to stay on after the funeral. There were things to see to.'

'Oh well, yer 'ere now, I suppose it couldn't be 'elped. What sort o' things did yer need to see to?'

'Mi grandmother's furniture and the rest of her things, then the lawyer came to read her will and mi uncle had to make arrangements about selling the house.'

Polly's eyes became round and curious at the mention of a will, and Cook's narrowed with speculation.

'There was a will was there, did she leave much?'

'She left me two hundred and fifty pounds.'

Polly gasped and even Cook's eyes flew open in amazement.

'I thowt yer said yer grandmother didn't like yer.'

'She didn't, but she couldn't very well leave the others somethin' and leave me out. It'd cause too many tongues to

143

wag. I can't have the money till I'm twenty-one.'

'All the same it's rich yer are, Katie O'Donovan. I'd 'ave ter work a year or two to earn that sort o' money. 'Ow much did she leave yer uncle then?'

'Two thousand to each of her children and two thousand to the church. She left mi brother Terrence five hundred and when the house is sold the money they get for it will have to be divided.'

'Yer'll not need to stay on 'ere wi' that sort o' money,' Polly said shrewdly.

'Well of course I shall, I told you I shan't get it until I'm twenty-one. I'm no better off than I was before mi grandmother died.'

'And what about yer uncle?' Cook said. 'I suppose that flighty lass o' theirs'll come ter 'er senses now that there's money in't family. She'll know which side 'er bread's buttered all right. Do yer suppose yer mother'll be sendin' fer yer now she's come inter brass?'

I had no such illusions. My mother's letters came regularly and were warm and tender, but I felt pretty sure that Uncle Shamus wouldn't want to be burdened with yet another member of the O'Donovan family.

I said nothing to Cook about Fanny. I had had enough of Cook's pontificating for one day.

No doubt there was much to be done, so I hurried to put on my apron. 'What do you want me to do, Cook?' I asked.

'There's ter be a dinner party for twelve tonight, Katie, so yer'd best look sharp about it an' join Mrs Tate in the dining room.'

'They don't usually have dinner parties on Friday.'

'P'raps not, but Miss Nancy's got 'erself engaged to Mr Steadly an' 'is uncle's comin' for dinner as well as Mr Ambrose and 'is wife. I've a big joint ter cook and the trifle ter decorate, right welcome the family's givin' 'im, and no mistake.'

Mrs Tate asked no questions about my visit to Ireland, and after only a few minutes it seemed as though I had never been away, she kept me so busy. It was only when the table met with her satisfaction that she said, 'You can go upstairs now and see if Miss Nancy needs you for anything, then there's Miss Mary. Hurry along, then.'

Miss Nancy was impatiently brushing her hair, which was at the best of times fine and always unruly. She greeted me with delight. 'Thank goodness you're back, Katie, Mrs Tate didn't know how long you were to be away. I'm hopeless with my hair, just look at it, and tonight I'm supposed to be the centre of attention.'

'Cook tells me you are engaged, Miss Nancy.'

'Yes, to Arthur Steadly.'

'I wish you every happiness, Miss.'

'Thanks, Katie. Arthur's quite a pet really, so I expect we'll get along together. I couldn't possibly allow Lois Foxland to beat me to the altar.'

'You're getting married before Miss Lois, then?'

'At the end of May, Katie, I believe she gets married in June.'

'You'll be moving away from Marsdale then, Miss Nancy?'

'Only to the next town, where Arthur's family have cotton mills. Thank goodness Arthur has other irons in the fire though, I couldn't have borne hearing him going on about short time and laying people off like I've heard from my father and brothers for as long as I can remember.'

'My Uncle works for Foxland's. He's going back on Monday because they've got a government contract in.'

She stared at me through the mirror. 'Father won't like that, and I don't intend to tell him. He'll be in a foul mood if I do and I don't want my engagement dinner spoilt.'

'Perhaps Carslake's will get a government contract too. Mi uncle says there's trouble in Europe and it's not a good sign when the forces start placing work in the mills.'

She laughed. 'Not you too, Katie, we've already had Mother in tears because Father's convinced there's going to be a war and she's thinking about her four precious sons. I think war could be terribly exciting with all those men in lovely uniforms, and nothing diabolical is going to happen in England. It would all be so far away.'

I didn't speak as I went about curling and teasing her

hair into the shape she preferred. I felt impatient with her shallowness, her total assumption that come what may her life would remain the same, without any thought for her brothers and her future husband, and no interest in me and my reasons for being absent in Ireland.

So impatient was I that I tugged sharply at a strand of hair and she gave a little cry. 'Ouch, that hurt, Katie, you're not usually so rough.'

I murmured an apology and went on with my work in a more restrained manner. After a while she said, 'I think my sister might want you to help her, Katie, she's invited Albert Rice although heaven knows he's not our sort. I hope he doesn't tell any of his risky stories this evening, it was quite dreadful the last time he was here. I hope Mary's told him how to behave.'

When I didn't speak she said, 'You must have heard him when we had that dinner party a few weeks ago, Katie, didn't Mrs Tate say anything?'

'Not to me, Miss Nancy.'

'Oh well, Mary *is* twenty-eight, she can't afford to be too choosy and all the boys she was friendly with are married. I can't think why she didn't snaffle one of them when the going was good.'

I stepped back and invited her to look at her hair.

'It's lovely, Katie. We *are* lucky to have found such a treasure, and you've never been trained as a lady's maid. I declare you're even better than Milly, so perhaps it's as well she's gone off into the blue, never to return.'

'Where has Milly gone, Miss Nancy?'

She met my steady gaze and for a moment had the grace to look disconcerted, then airily she said, 'She's really been most awfully fortunate Katie, she's gone to work in a home for old people run by a friend of Mother's in Westmorland. This lady is full of good works for the old and for so-called fallen women. When the baby's born I'm sure it will be well taken care of, either in an orphanage or given to some childless couple Mrs Fairbrother knows.'

'And what about Milly, suppose she wants to keep the baby?'

'My dear girl, she can't. Milly will have to work for her living and what good will an unmarried mother be for the child?'

I said nothing and after a while she said, 'I know this must all seem quite terrible to you, Katie, but my brother couldn't possibly have married Milly. They would have had absolutely no friends and she would have been as miserable as he. It's such a pity that Roger didn't have enough sense to leave her alone and she hadn't the courage to send him about his business.'

'Perhaps she loved him, Miss Nancy,'

'Well I've no doubt she thought she did. I hope you're not going to be foolish about anything so impossible, Katie. It's far better to have both feet firmly on the ground instead of putting all your faith in love. Love is such a silly emotion really, it can lead a girl into all sorts of mischief.'

'But you're in love, Miss Nancy, or you wouldn't have got engaged,' I couldn't resist saying.

For a fleeting moment a shadow crossed her face, then with a gay trill of laughter she said, 'My dear Katie, how frightfully old fashioned. I love Arthur for all the material things he can drop into my lap. I'll be a perfect wife, a good hostess and a delightful companion and he will cosset me in considerable comfort in return. Don't look so disapproving, Katie, I'm only doing what Lois Foxland is doing, but she's marrying a man old enough to be her father, even when she's in love with my brother.'

'If I was in love with one man I couldn't marry another.'

'Well of course not, and you will never have to, my dear. All our servants have left us to marry good solid citizens who either work in the mills or on the land, men without too much imagination but of strong upright moral fibre. Every year you will go to the seaside in August for the local Wakes Week and you'll end up being the pillar of your church with your children holding the banner strings during the processions at Whitsuntide. You don't know how lucky you are to face such an uncomplicated future.'

When I didn't speak she said, 'Now what are you thinking, I wonder. I can tell you're not agreeing with me.'

147

I turned to her, only too aware of the bright spots of colour burning in my cheeks, and eyes that might be too stormy.

'I think my life's going to be very different from what you say, Miss Nancy. The sort of life you think might be mine wouldn't suit me at all. Mi father said I'd spend most o' mi life chasin' rainbows, and I'd rather do that than settle for mediocrity.'

She laughed somewhat self-consciously. 'Well, all I can say is that you're wrong, Katie. Rainbows have a nasty habit of disappearing into thin air, and I know to my cost that the right sort of man isn't waiting round every corner.'

'Is it all right if I go to Miss Mary now, Miss Nancy?'

'Oh, very well then, if I need you again I'll send for you.'

I found Miss Mary sitting in her robe, busy stitching tiny pearl buttons on her white petticoat, and she smiled with relief at my appearance.

'I'm so glad you've come, Katie. I suppose my sister found endless things for you to do.'

Miss Mary was less demanding. After I had adjusted the shoulder straps on her pale pink gown and attended to her fine fair hair, she nodded with complete satisfaction.

'You might pop in to Mother, Katie. She always declares she has no use for a maid but that is only because she thinks Nancy and I are more in need of one. She always had a maid of her own when she was my age.'

I had seen Mrs Carslake's gown twice before, a soft lavender silk with which she wore a three-strand pearl necklace, and I began to appreciate Cook's remarks that she denied herself so that her daughters might have more.

She allowed me to dress her silver hair and when I had finished she said, 'I was sorry to hear about your grandmother, Katie. I trust her funeral passed off satisfactorily.'

'Yes, thank you, Ma'am.'

'Have you no other relatives in Ireland?'

'No, Mrs Carslake, mi mother's in America.'

'Perhaps one day you will be able to join her.'

'I have no mind to go there, Ma'am.'

'Or back to Ireland, Katie?'

'No.'

'Is there much poverty there, Katie?'

'Yes, Ma'am, there's poverty in plenty, indeed when I was a little girl I thought all Englishmen rode fine horses and lived in mansions and their ladies were that beautiful in their silks and satins. I couldn't believe mi eyes when I first saw English folk on the streets o' Liverpool.'

She laughed. 'And now, Katie, you have no illusions about the English and their way of life.'

'No, Ma'am.'

I didn't tell her that I had illusions, illusions to be equal to the best of them, and that one of them concerned her youngest son.

That night as I waited on table I missed nothing. Miss Mary's friend was suitably subdued, so perhaps she'd had a quiet word with him about his previous behaviour. The master was red-faced and jovial, sitting next to pretty Mrs Ambrose, and now and again I saw the mistress glance in his direction with a worried frown as though she expected him to be indiscreet.

Miss Nancy was all pretty smiles, basking in the attentions of her fiancé. Jeffrey toyed with the stem of his wine glass and seemed strangely uninterested in their celebrations. Once he caught my eye and smiled, that sweet impersonal smile that had the power to twist my heart so that I set down a serving dish with unnecessary force, earning a severe glance from Mrs Tate and another from Colonel Carslake.

Toasts were drunk to the health of the happy couple, and Nancy trilled, 'Well, there's only Mary and Jeffrey left. I wonder who will be the next one to flee the nest?'

'There's Roger,' her mother murmured unhappily.

'Oh, we don't count Roger, Mother, he's likely to have dozens of girls before he settles down.'

'And Jeffrey here lets 'em slip through his fingers,' her father said sourly. 'He seems to think if he pets 'em and flatters 'em it's enough, he doesn't realize a woman needs to have her mind made up for her and she wants more than pretty speeches. She needs to know if she's marryin' a real man she can rely on, not a pretty boy with his head in the clouds.'

Jeffrey sat white-faced and silent while the rest looked uncomfortable, then Mrs Carslake said, 'I think the ladies should retire to the drawing room to drink their coffee and leave the men to enjoy their port.'

Mrs Tate and I followed, to serve the coffee. How I hated the master for belittling Jeffrey, and even Mrs Tate said, 'Never misses an opportunity to let the lad down. Family feuds should be kept discreetly within the family.'

Much later, when I went in to clear the dining table, I stopped dead at seeing Jeffrey still sitting staring morosely in front of him.

He looked at me in a bemused fashion, then visibly pulled himself together. 'Are you wanting to clear away, Katie? You can do so, I'm just leaving.'

'Do you never answer him back, Mr Jeffrey, at what he says?'

He stared at me, then smiled. 'I was brought up not to answer my elders. Perhaps you'd have got along better with your grandmother if you'd afforded her more respect.'

'I did respect her, Mr Jeffrey, I just didn't love her.'

'And you answered her back?'

'Yes, when I thought what she said was wrong.'

'My dear, it isn't worth it. My father and I have never seen eye to eye and if I answer him back it only prolongs the antagonism. Surely you must know something about that.'

I did, but I didn't care, I only knew that he had called me my dear, and even those two words unthinkingly spoken and carrying no importance to him had the power to send my naive immature heart racing with joy.

Chapter 14

During the following weeks it seemed Nancy's wedding took pride of place over everything except the government contract that Carslake's secured – in line with most other cotton manufacturers in the district. The mills were at full strength, smoke poured from their chimneys and their resonant hooters called out the work people at seven o'clock both morning and evening.

There was a new affluence in the bearing of the people in the streets. There were more goods in the shops and the children were better dressed and bonnier, and in the spring of 1914 young ladies in floral voile hung on the arms of young men in white flannels and straw boaters, and few thoughts were on Europe where old empires were tottering and men were on the march at the command of a despot whom England complacently called the old girl's grandson.

Mr Roger arrived home for his sister's wedding in early May wearing the uniform of a subaltern, smart as paint and already a hero in the eyes of his father. In no time at all the house was filled with the laughter of young people while the master restocked his wine cellar and Cook and Mrs Tate had their heads together discussing the master's latest indiscretions with a certain Miss Annabel Hanson during various racing weekends.

All this I learned from Polly, who was never averse to listening at doors. Through it all Mrs Carslake remained dignified and aloof, even though there was a sad expression on her hitherto serene face. More and more time was spent in the company of her youngest son, earning him the scathing remark from his father that he was a mother's boy.

The day of Miss Nancy's wedding dawned bright and sunny but there was so much to do we only just had time to

151

scamper to the front of the house to see her leave for the church on the arm of her father, a lovely vision in clouds of white lace and a frothy veil. Later we saw her with her bridesmaids on the lawn, all of them attired in sweet-pea shades of pink, blue and lavender.

Lois Foxland simpered on the arm of her fiancé and Jeffrey stood at the edge of the group, looking lonely and not a little lost. Mr Roger flirted with all the bridesmaids, and once across the room I looked into the eyes of the young Canadian, who favoured me with a flashing smile and wink which I haughtily ignored, much to his obvious amusement.

There was a great deal of chatter and laughter as they stood around the bridal car, particularly when Miss Mary caught her sister's bouquet, and then the guests began to drift away and we were clearing the mess they had left behind.

Cook sank into her rocking chair, fanning her face with a newspaper and proclaiming that she was exhausted, so Polly and I put the kitchen to rights and made a strong cup of tea for Cook and Mrs Tate.

'Oh, but it was gorgeous,' Polly enthused. 'Them dresses must 'a' cost the master a pretty penny. I reckon 'e'll be cuttin' down on someat else to pay for 'em.'

When I didn't answer she went on wistfully, 'I wonder what sort o' weddin's we'll 'ave? Not like this one, fer sure.'

'Don't you want a white wedding with loads of bridesmaids, then?'

'Wantin' an gettin' is two different things. It'll be someat serviceable an' sensible fer me, like as not a costume an' a new white blouse. I reckon I could allus put a few flowers in mi hat, though.'

I laughed. 'Oh Polly, on your wedding day you're going to have a silk dress and a pretty hat if I have to pay for it miself. Mi aunt could make the dress for you, she charges next to nothing.'

'Is that what you want then, a silk dress and a pretty hat?'

'I don't know what I want, Polly, but I don't want to go

152

to mi weddin' in any old thing.'

'You're pretty, Katie, any old thing could look real lovely on you, I needs fol-di-rols ter make me look anythin' like.'

'One of these days I'm going to do something with your hair and your face, just as if you were Miss Nancy,' I promised her.

Cook appeared to have revived and was busy filling a cardboard box with fancy cakes and patties, and seeing my inquiring glance she said, 'I'm puttin' these up fer yer ter take down ter yer aunt's. I reckon that young lass o' theirs'll appreciate 'em.'

'Oh Cook, that *is* kind of you.'

'Well, they'll be wasted 'ere. I reckon we've 'ad enough fancy fare ter last fer a while, an' the family won't want 'em.'

'Are you sure?'

'Well, the mistress never keeps tabs on the food and if *she* doesn't nobody else does. Now get off into the town straight away and don't be late back.'

The box was heavy, and I was only halfway down the hill when to my utmost consternation a car stopped alongside me and an amused voice said, 'How far are you going, Katie O'Donovan?'

I looked into the smiling dark eyes of Sir Joshua's Canadian guest, who leaned over and opened the passenger door. 'Hop in, I'm going into the town. Tell me where I can take you.'

Still I hesitated, and in some exasperation he said, 'Come on, Katie, I have no ulterior designs on you and that box looks a bit cumbersome.'

Hurriedly looking back over my shoulder, I took my seat beside him, holding the box on my knees. I didn't look at him, but I was very aware of his amusement. Anybody seeing me would have been convinced I was like Milly, who had often met Mr Roger on the hill. They would assume there was something going on, and that I was no better than Milly.

'Why are you so afraid of somebody seeing you? You're a respectable girl, aren't you?'

'That I am, but if anybody saw me gettin' into this car they'd think I was just like Milly.'

'And who was Milly then?'

'She worked at the Carslakes' house and left in disgrace.'

'Thrown out in the snow was she, on Christmas Day?'

'There's nothin' to laugh about. She was thrown out but it wasn't Christmas Day and it wasn't snowin'.'

'And what had she done to merit such dastardly treatment?'

'She'd only had an affair with Mr Roger and was going to have a baby.'

'And Mr Roger didn't feel like honouring his obligations?'

'Well he wouldn't, would he? Not with Milly.'

'Oh, Katie, Katie, didn't all that teach you a lesson, not to go setting your cap at one of the Carslake heirs?'

'I don't know what you mean.'

'I think you do. I've watched your eyes following Jeffrey Carslake, and it's my guess he doesn't know yet what he's looking for.'

'What rubbish you talk. Jeffrey Carslake was in love with Lois Foxland and now she's got herself engaged elsewhere he's unhappy about it. I've no doubt he'll get over it, she's gettin' married in a week or two.'

'But will he turn to you, Katie? That's the question.'

I could feel my scarlet cheeks in tune with my racing heart, and with a toss of my head I said, 'You can drop me here, my aunt lives along the next street.'

'I'll drop you at the front door, my girl. Let us by all means give all those nosey parkers behind their lace curtains something to talk about. They'll be quite sure you've taken your first step towards perdition.'

'Mi aunt won't like it, it's her they'll be getting at.'

'Perhaps if you introduced me to your aunt I could assure her of my respectability.'

I thought about Aunt Martha's forbidding expression and the house untidy with her sewing, and snapped, 'I can do all the reassuring that's necessary. Thanks for the lift, it was kind of you.'

This time he walked round the car to open the door and take the box from my hands, while from across the way lace curtains moved and eyes peered.

'There, what did I tell you?' he said, smiling. 'It seems to me your reputation is for ever damned.'

To my utmost consternation he planted a light kiss on my mouth. With a chuckle of amusement he leapt into the car and roared away down the street, while I rubbed my mouth with the back of my hand as if to erase every vestige of his kiss.

There wasn't a chair to sit on, every one in the room being covered with sewing of one sort or another. Half-completed dresses were piled one on top of the other, and from the picture rail were hung cotton voile and rayon dresses in all the colours of the rainbow. Aunt Martha sat at her sewing machine, peddling as though her life depended on it, but my uncle was not in the house and there was no sign of Lucy.

She took the cardboard box out of my hands with a swift smile.

'It's kind of Cook, Kathleen, but we're not short of money. There might be folk more in need of it.'

She saw my glance at the untidy house cluttered by her sewing.

'I know what yer thinkin', but it gives me somethin' ter do and stops mi thinkin' too much. Move some o' the things off that chair while I makes yer a cup o' tea.'

'Please don't bother, Aunt Martha. I can't stay long and I'd rather we sat and chatted. Where's mi uncle, then?'

'He's on shift work and Lucy's at a meetin' for the procession.'

'The procession?' I echoed in surprise.

'Ay. It's Whitsun. All the churches i' Marsdale'll be walkin' next Sunday. Brass bands and banners, wi' all the children carryin' flowers and holdin' ribbons on the banner strings.'

Suddenly her eyes filled with tears and she looked away quickly.

'Are all these dresses for the procession, then?' I asked

curiously.

'Ay, and there's not much time. I haven't started on the ones fer St Luke's, and they're gettin' anxious.'

'That's a pretty one,' I said pointing to a peach voile sprigged with tiny white flowers. 'Is that Lucy's?'

'No, she's not tall enough yet fer a banner string. I made it for our Fanny. She were picked 'afore she left 'ome, but she won't be wantin' it now.'

'Whyever not, if she was chosen? It's a beautiful dress, she'll love it.'

'She'll not be takin' part. She's gone wi' 'em to the coast fer a week's 'oliday. Methodist they are, and wi' our Fanny being Catholic they thought it were for the best to get right away.'

'I'm sorry, Aunt Martha. Did Fanny come to tell you she was going away?'

'No. They told me. She'll be Methodist 'afore she's much older, that's the way it's goin', I can tell.'

She fixed me with a stern eye. 'You've not bin attendin' yerself, 'ave yer, Kathleen?'

'No.'

'Why's that?'

'I'm busy on Sundays and the Catholic church is at the other side of the town.'

'That wouldn't 'a' stopped yer if yer'd bin a good Catholic.'

'I know.'

In the face of her stern frown I felt obliged to defend myself. 'I've nothin' against God, Aunt Martha, but I grew to hate Father McGinty an' his cowtowin' to mi grandmother.'

'Father O'Reilly's a different sort o' man. He'd be glad to welcome ye to the church. There's an envelope on the mantelpiece for ye. It's fro' yer uncle.'

Mystified, I reached down the envelope and took out six crisp five-pound notes.

'But there's thirty pounds here, Aunt! What is it for?'

'Yer grandmother's 'ouse has bin sold. Four hundred pounds they got fer it from a businessman fro' Cork who

156

was lookin' for a house near the sea. Yer uncle's seen to it that Shamus and yer mother got their share and the rest was divided between the grandchildren.'

'I see. What has he done about Fanny?'

'I don't know an' I've asked no questions. I reckon if she'd walked in the procession 'e'd 'ave given it to 'er then. I know 'e looks for 'er if 'is shift's finishin' at the same time as the school's loosin', but 'e never tells mi if they've spoken. Ye know, Kathleen, there's times I 'ates that girl fer makin' 'im suffer like this. 'Ow could she do this to us? She could never 'ave luved us, Kathleen, none of us.'

'Perhaps one day when she's older and wiser she'll come back, Aunt. But will you be able to forgive her?'

She sat staring at the wallpaper, then with a fatalistic shrug she said, 'She'll not come back, Kathleen, an' even if she did things'd never be the same. Now don't you go spendin' all that money on fripperies. Put it in the bank fer when it's needed.'

'Like when, Aunt?'

'When yer gets wed, yer'll be needin' ter furnish, an' things is that expensive I don't know 'ow young folk are managing.'

I put the money back in the envelope and pushed it into my purse. My aunt's advice was sound, but I was making no promises. Fripperies I had never had, but if fripperies could attract Jeffrey Carslake the money would be well spent.

Chapter 15

The house settled down to normality after Miss Nancy's departure and Mr Roger's return to his regiment two days later. He seemed to think we had no recollections of his affair with Milly and was not averse to smiling at me when I served the meal, or giving my waist a squeeze when we met in the hall. When I mentioned this to Cook she snapped, 'If yer tangles wi' Mr Roger ye deserves all that yer gets.'

'I'll not be tanglin' with him, Roger Carslake's not what I want.'

'Or any other son o' the family,' she went on darkly.

The master was away most weekends but often in the evening we could hear his voice raised in the drawing room and I believed Jeffrey was the recipient of his ill humour.

On the Saturday before Whit Sunday the mistress departed with Miss Mary and a great deal of luggage to spend a week with her sister who lived in Cumberland. No sooner had they gone than the master too left the house, wearing country tweeds and carrying binoculars, followed by a groom carrying his suitcases, which were placed in the back of the large tourer he had just acquired.

'We all knows where 'e's goin', don't we?' Cook said from her vantage point at the side window. 'Off ter pick up that Annabel, I'll be bound, an' then off ter the races. The poor mistress can 'ardly 'a' reached the station an there 'e goes off wi' that little baggage who's like as not done up to the nines an' actin' as if she was Mrs Carslake. An' not one of 'is sons wi' the guts ter tell 'im what they think about 'im.'

With the family away there was little to do, and early afternoon found me climbing swiftly up the hillside where I had seen Jeffrey riding only a little while earlier.

A warm wind stirred the grass, bringing an overpowering scent of hawthorn blossom and clover, and as I sat on the stile looking down upon the town I snatched off my ribbon to let the wind blow through my hair. It was so quiet here, the only sounds the droning of bees and birdsong, yet below me the market place would be thronged with people intent on their Saturday shopping and oblivious to the beauty of the wild sweeping fells.

As I climbed onwards an overpowering shyness filled my entire being. I wanted to meet Jeffrey, but another part of me, a more sensible part, acknowledged the futility of such a meeting. Yet when I saw him riding towards me with the sun gilding his fair hair I went on bravely, foolishly even, when that other part of me wanted to run away.

Why could I never be sure if his eyes lit up at the sight of me, why did I always believe his smile was welcoming, his eyes warm and encouraging?

I stroked his horse's velvety nose, and when it reached out its long neck and nuzzled my ear Jeffrey laughed, saying, 'It's evident you have a way with horses, Katie. Is that the Irish in you?'

'Mi father used to bring some of the horses home so that we could see them and make friends with them. I used to ride 'em too, across the shore bareback, like one o' the tinkers, with the gulls screaming all around us.'

'Then you must ride very well Katie,' he said soberly.

'Nay, I wasn't all togged out in ridin' clothes, I rode wi' mi skirts above mi knees and mi hair flyin' in the wind. Not your sort o' ridin' at all, Mr Jeffrey.'

'I doubt if many people would have the courage to ride your way.'

'Oh well, I was only a young girl then.'

He laughed. 'And are you so very much more than a young girl now, Katie?'

'Well, I'm not a schoolgirl now, am I?'

'No, that's true. Would you like to ride him now, Katie?'

'Oh no, Mr Jeffrey, I couldn't, it wouldn't be right, would it?'

He jumped down from the horse's back and I stared at him in dismay. Then he lifted me up on to the saddle and I

159

was sitting high above him with my hands on the reins. The fearlessness of childhood abruptly changed to an agony of apprehension.

He smiled his encouragement as he adjusted the stirrups to my feet. 'There's nothing to be afraid of, Katie. Nothing has changed except that now you are better equipped and Drummond is very predictable.

I didn't feel better equipped. All these trappings seemed unnecessary to me, and I was aware of my long skirts stretched uncomfortably across the horse's back, restricting and unbecomingly taut. Girls didn't ride astride, they sat elegantly on side saddles, much as they sat on chairs, and I could feel my cheeks colouring at the spectacle I was making.

'Please, Mr Jeffrey, I should get down,' I cried dismally. 'It doesn't feel right, it's nothin' at all like it was then.'

'See, Katie, I'll lead him a little way until you get the feel of him, then you must try. Just think you are a little girl again back there in Donegal.'

He led the horse, with me sitting trembling and afraid, until we came to the wall above the road, then he placed the reins firmly in my hands and said, 'Now Katie, just like you did as a child, urge him on gently, nothing is going to happen to you.'

The horse walked on, leaving Jeffrey behind. I would have died rather than give him the satisfaction of thinking I was afraid. After a while, and with my courage restored, I urged the horse faster, and then we were cantering gently along the line of the wall, and unbidden the years fled away and I was a child again, riding Tara along the sands with the keen salt wind in my hair, the taste of it in my mouth, Tara's hooves sending the salt spray flying around us as we raced through the rippling surf.

Everything my father had ever told me about horses and riding came back to me and soon we were galloping, and the exhilaration of that ride was in the horse's flying mane, his pounding hooves and my red hair streaming in the wind. I knew well the picture we made as we crested the hill, and I knew that never in his life would Jeffrey Carslake

160

have seen a girl ride with such complete and easy abandon, while praying at the same time that I would have the strength to pull up the horse at the crest.

Drummond was predictable, as Jeffrey had said. We came trotting back to where he waited near the wall and I could see that he was smiling, well pleased with my exhibition.

'Well done, Katie,' he said, his words bringing a happy glow into my heart. 'That was splendid.'

He reached up and I slid into his waiting arms. I was in no hurry to leave them, for I had dreamed of this moment, standing in the sunshine with my arms around his neck, his arms holding me against him, our eyes locked in shocked amazement. Before my feet touched the ground our lips were pressed together, and all I was aware of was the depth of the passion that consumed me so that afterwards I could not remember whether the kiss had been mine or his, whether they were my arms that desperately held us close, or his. When he released me I reeled and would have fallen if he hadn't held out a hand to steady me.

I don't know what I expected, but certainly not his calm voice saying, 'It's a pity you don't get many opportunities to ride, Katie. Have you never thought you might like to work with horses?'

I stared at him, bemused and uncertain. Shouldn't we be talking of love, or when we would meet on the fells again? Instead he had fallen into step beside me, leading his horse by the reins.

I didn't answer, but walked in silence until we reached the path that led down from the fells. Then he turned and, taking my hands in his, he said, 'You are a dear sweet girl, Katie, and a very brave one. Now hadn't you be getting back before Cook gets an opportunity to scold you?'

Hurt and bewildered I nodded and turned away, then as if he understood my hurt he took my hand and turned me to face him.

'How old are you, Katie?' he asked gently.

Miserably close to tears I murmured, 'Eighteen.'

'Eighteen, and beautiful, very beautiful.'

His hand lay along my cheek and my tears rolled slowly on to it. He bent his head and lightly kissed my forehead. 'Run along my dear, we'll meet up here again one day and you shall ride him again.'

'When, when shall we meet?' I persisted.

'Well, not tomorrow because you will be watching the processions like everybody else in Marsdale.'

'I don't have to watch the processions.'

'Oh but you do, everybody does.'

'Do you?'

'Well no, but Mrs Tate and Cook will be there. It will be expected of you, Katie.'

'I see.'

I lifted my head proudly and set off down the hill. When I reached the bend in the lane I turned back to find he was still standing where I had left him. He raised his hand in farewell then he called, 'Next week Katie, I'm often up here on the fells.'

I was uncertain as to whether it was a plea for me to be there or a gesture of remorse, possibly even the sort of promise one might give a child. But I would look for him on the fell, every day if needs be. Beyond that my heart had derived no real pleasure or satisfaction from the afternoon's events.

From the direction of the town from early morning had come the strains of martial brass bands as they marched to the various churches from which the processions would start.

Breakfast was a rushed meal. I helped Polly to wash the dishes and set the kitchen to rights, then Mrs Tate appeared, smartly dressed in a pale grey costume and wearing a pink crêpe-de-chine blouse and a small pull-on hat. She looked years younger without her drab black housekeeper's gown, and she had left in the gig, driven by one of the grooms.

Cook's voice came from the direction of the house-keeper's parlour. 'Get a move on you two, if we're to get a

162

good place to watch the walks.'

'Is she coming with us?' I asked Polly.

'Oh ay, she likes ter get i' the town hall square where all the churches stand together ter sing hymns.'

I decided the day merited a summer dress and chose one my aunt had run up for me in pale green with a floral pattern in primrose and white. It had a pretty demure bodice and a very full skirt, and I wore my one straw hat, which was cream, with a wide cream petersham ribbon.

Cook was ready before me, and I stared at her in some surprise for I had never seen her without her large all-enveloping white apron.

She wore a tight navy-blue costume and white blouse, but her hat was disconcerting. It sat upon her head as conspicuously as Britannia's helmet, a tall navy-blue straw confection decorated with bunches of cherries and as many feathers and flowers as there was room for.

She looked at me proudly, inviting my admiration, which I was quick to give, much against my better judgement. I had decided early in our acquaintance that if I wished to get along amicably with Cook, I would have to think the way she thought and like the things she liked.

I was to be shocked for the second time that morning by the appearance of Polly wearing a cotton dress which reached her ankles in three frills, a mustard-yellow dress on which red flowers bloomed profusely, topped by a white straw hat with a floppy bunch of daisies and scarlet poppies.

Cook eyed her dispassionately, saying, 'That 'at were a lot better wi'out them flowers,' a remark which seemed singularly unjust in view of her own attire.

Polly hung back uncertainly until Cook said, 'We'd best get off, there's no time ter do anythin' about yer 'at now.'

'Yer looks lovely,' Polly confided to me in a whisper, 'I likes yer dress.'

'Thanks, Polly, it's one mi aunt ran up fer me.'

'Will she make one fer me one day do you think? I could get some material off the market.'

'Yes, I'm sure she will.'

163

'Then will ye 'elp me to pick somethin out?'

'Of course.'

We were hurrying down the hill, Cook puffing and panting from the tightness of her corsets, and of her new shoes which she complained were pinching something shocking.

I had never seen so many people in Marsdale. The streets were crowded and wooden seats had been placed along the side of the thoroughfares through which the processions would walk. When I suggested that we sit there Cook said, 'We'll only see one or two of 'em 'ere, we wants to be near the town hall. That way we sees 'em all and 'ears 'em sing.'

The town hall square was already crowded but we followed Cook as she elbowed and pushed towards the front. Those about us complained that they wouldn't be able to see anything above her hat, and she gratefully accepted a seat when those already seated moved closer together to make room for her.

We stood behind and I looked around with great interest. It seemed that all Marsdale had turned out, and the sun shone on people in holiday mood, all wearing their Sunday best: flower-bedecked hats and summer dresses, straw boaters and starched white collars, the men with flowers in their buttonholes. When I remarked on the absence of children Polly said, 'Oh the little 'uns'll be walkin wi' their flowers. Don't they do anythin' like this in Ireland, then?'

'Not in Dunfanaghy they didn't, although mi father used to tell me they were always marchin' in the North. But their marches had nothin' to do with God, only their memories of old wars.'

The memory of that morning in the warm sunshine has stayed with me as fresh and joyful even when other memories deserted me. The music from more than a dozen brass bands was all around me, the ribbons and the massive banners carried by stalwart men, pretty girls wearing identical dresses holding on to banner strings, and the children carrying baskets of flowers walking with their teachers, each church led by its priest or vicar and the church officials, and following the children the older

164

parishioners, some of them so old they were pushed in wheelchairs.

Their singing of the hymns brought tears to my eyes, and all around me the people joined in. Cook's rich contralto could plainly be heard above all those around her.

They sang for half an hour, then once again the bands struck up and one by one led their various processions out of the square.

'What do we do now?' I asked Polly.

'We'll 'ave to ask Cook an' 'ope she gives us the day off.'

People were drifting away from the square, following the processions. Others stood chatting in small groups before they went away to their homes. Cook was in conversation with the woman sitting next to her and when we went to her she said, 'This lady's bin kind enough ter invite me back to 'er 'ouse fer a cup o' tea. What are yer two intendin' ter do wi' yerselves?'

'Can we go ter the field day?' Polly asked hopefully.

'Ay, but don't go gettin' into any mischief, and I wants yer both 'ome fer six o'clock sharp. 'Ere yer are, there's threepence a piece fer yer, an' 'ere's a packet o' sandwiches. Six o'clock, mind yer.'

'Where are we going?' I asked Polly curiously.

'The churches 'ave their field days now, all over the place. We'll go ter St Anne's. Last year A went ter St Luke's but it weren't as good as St Anne's, and it's nearer 'ome. We'll only 'ave ter walk up the 'ill when we gets fed up.'

'What's a field day then?'

'Well, they 'ave sports, races like egg and spoon and sack races, an' there's ice-cream stalls an' side shows. It's a lot o' fun. I'm glad Cook's not comin', she's 'a' bin wantin' ter go back 'alf-way through the afternoon.'

'Are the processions going there now?'

'Bless yer, no. They're goin' back to the churches ter get rid o' their banners. There's pies an' buns laid on fer 'em, an' all the children get an apple an' an orange.'

'So what time does it start, this field day then?'

'Oh, about two o'clock.'

'It's only just twelve. Perhaps we should sit here and eat

our sandwiches, then.'

'Ay, it's a pity we can't get a cup o' tea, though.'

'We could call at my aunt's house if you like, we can eat our sandwiches there.'

'Won't yer aunt mind yer takin' a stranger round?'

'Of course not, besides she knows about you, Polly. I've told her about all the people at Heatherlea.'

'I'm shy wi' strangers.'

'You don't need to be shy with mi aunt and uncle, they'll make you very welcome.'

The house was tidy, with all the sewing put away. The table was spread with its best chenille cloth and there was a vase of roses in the centre. My aunt was still wearing her hat, although my uncle was taking off his shoes and getting into his slippers. Of Lucy there was no sign and when I asked if she was still with the procession my aunt said, 'The Catholic church doesn't walk today, Kathleen, they walks tomorrer, but she's goin' wi' 'er friend to their field day.'

For the first time that morning something seemed less than perfect.

'Why can't all the churches walk on the same morning?' I asked curiously.

'Well it wouldn't be fittin' would it, an' ours bein' the only true church an' the others comin' later an' sproutin' up like mushrooms.'

She bustled into the kitchen after telling us to make ourselves at home. Aunt Martha wanted no argument with me, but she must have known that my thoughts were back with Grandmother Cassidy and Father McGinty and the rigidity of their beliefs.

We were treated to strong cups of tea while we ate our sandwiches, then she brought out home-made fruit cake and my favourite macaroons.

Polly soon forgot her shyness and began to talk to Uncle Turlough.

'If Polly buys some cotton will you run her a dress up, Aunt Martha?' I asked as we washed up.

'Ay, I don't think much o' the one she's wearin' this mornin'.'

166

'That's her Sunday-best dress. Heaven knows where she got it from.'

'A jumble sale more than likely,' my aunt retorted.

Then she said, 'Your uncle sent Fanny the money, yer know. 'E said she'd 'ave someat ter spend on her 'oliday wiout takin' it fro' them. I were dead agin it but 'e took no notice. We never talk about 'er, Kathleen, it's as if she never lived i' this 'ouse.'

'I'm sorry, Aunt. The hurt's still there, isn't it?'

'It is. I 'opes yer never 'as the same sort o' trouble wi' a lass o' yers.'

I said nothing. I had no thoughts on marriage and children. I had no dreams in my heart that did not include Jeffrey Carslake, and without him the idea of husband and children was as remote as the memories of the sun glinting on the waves beyond Horn Head in distant Donegal.

The field day was in full swing when we eventually arrived at the large field which a local farmer had loaned to St Anne's for the afternoon. Races were in progress and the brass band that had played for the procession now played popular airs.

Ice cream and pop were being sold at an alarming rate, and Polly was in her element cheering the children in the egg and spoon races and the morris dancers in their colourful costumes.

It was during one of their dances that two young men approached us. I was surprised at Polly's blushing face and coy manner. The taller one had a round boyish face made owlish by the round steel spectacles he was wearing. The shorter man was plump and had a pale spotted face and buck teeth. I found neither of them very prepossessing although they were neatly dressed in blazers and pale grey flannels.

'Do you know them?' I hissed to Polly at the first opportunity.

'This is George Plummer. 'E works as a gardner fer Major Fearnley,' she explained hurriedly. The other young man was introduced as Ronald Dexter who worked for Major Fearnley as a groom.

167

From the general conversation I soon gathered that both young men had walked in the St Anne's procession, and I also gathered that Polly had been well aware of the fact.

'George told me 'e were walkin' this mornin',' she confided in me. 'I met 'im on the road last Thursday.'

'Is that why you wanted to come to St Anne's field day?'

She blushed bright scarlet. 'George is all right, A went ter the pictures wi' 'im once.'

'So you like him?'

'A suppose so. 'Is pal likes yer, A can tell.'

I said nothing. For Polly's sake I watched the races, ate ice cream, listened to the band and danced round the bandstand, and I listened to Ronald Dexter's boasting that Major Fearnley would not be able to exist without his expert advice on the breeding and handling of the horses which were the pride of the local hunt.

By three o'clock I longed to escape, particularly when Polly intimated that she and George were going into the tea tent, and Ronald, who was more reluctant to spend his money, suggested we walk into the woods behind the field.

Catching hold of Polly's arm, I whispered, 'If we get separated, remember you have to be back at the house by six.'

She nodded and went with George into the tent, then turning to his friend I lied: 'I have to get back to Heatherlea.'

'Polly didn't say owt about it,' he murmured sulkily.

'Why should she? You'll meet somebody else, but I must go now. Nice to have met you,' I ended, holding out my hand, which he took with barely disguised annoyance.

I escaped, running until I was half-way up the hill.

I couldn't go back to the house. If Cook had returned I would only have to explain Polly's absence. My eyes scanned the fells above the town. Somewhere up there Jeffrey Carslake would be exercising his horse, and I started to climb. The memory of that lovesick naive girl troubled my thoughts long afterwards, but on that warm sunlit afternoon I climbed towards the fell with my eyes shining with expectancy, swinging my straw hat and my red hair tumbling around my shoulders. Birds sang and bees hummed in the waving moorland grass, in my nostrils was the scent of honeysuckle and clover, and in my heart was all the deep consuming passion of young love.

He waved to me from the summit where he sat with his back against a crag while his horse champed the moorland grass, and laughing happily I threw myself down beside him.

'So you grew tired of the merriment down there,' he said, 'what happened to the others?'

'Oh, Cook found somebody who invited her round for a cup of tea, and Polly found a friend.'

'And didn't you find a friend?'

'I found a man who would have liked to be one.'

He laughed. 'Did you enjoy the processions?'

'Oh yes, they were beautiful, the children and the flowers, and I loved the brass bands, then mi aunt spoiled it by tellin' mi the Catholics walk all on their own tomorrow.'

'I suppose you are a Catholic, Katie? I'm sure my mother will allow you to walk with your church.'

'I never go to the church so I couldn't very well turn up on their walk.'

'And that doesn't bother you?'

'Why can't they all walk on the same day, they all believe in the same God, don't they?'

'Perhaps tradition has something to do with it.'

'Bigotry more like.'

'You'll feel different when you marry a good Catholic boy and have children of your own. I'm quite sure you'll want them to be brought up good Catholics and walk with the processions on Whit Monday.'

I turned my head away angrily. He had no right to talk to me about marrying good Catholic boys and bringing up children. Twice that day I had had to listen to such talk. Springing to my feet I walked away from him and stood looking towards the town.

He rose to his feet and came to stand beside me. 'Would you like to ride the horse?'

'Not in mi Sunday-best dress I wouldn't.'

169

'And very charming you look. I'm not surprised that young man wanted to be more than a friend.'

'And I'd rather not talk about him.'

'Very well then, you shall tell me all about the place in Donegal with the quite unpronounceable name, and young Katie O'Donovan sitting out on the cliffs looking for rainbows.'

I laughed. 'And never finding them. Better than that, why don't you tell me about you and what you want out o' life?'

'But that would make very boring telling, Katie.'

'Not to me it wouldn't. You must have some thoughts about the future, time isn't goin' to stand still for any of us.'

He was staring out across the fell and his expression was suddenly bleak and remote. Then gathering his thoughts, he turned and smiled.

'I don't know what I can talk about that might interest you, Katie. My life at the mills, you know all about my life at home with my family, and what I like to do when I'm not at the mills.'

'But you must think about things, you must dream a little, I do.'

'Then you would be far more interesting than I Katie.'

'What do I do? Only work for your mother. You don't want to hear about waitin' on table an' cleanin' the house. I've never been anywhere outside Ireland and Marsdale, I've never even been to Manchester except passin' through.'

'Well, there's nothing very exciting about Manchester, my dear.'

'P'raps not, but it's different, isn't it? What do you do when you goes into Manchester?'

'I go there every Tuesday to the cotton exchange.'

'So that's why you're always late for dinner on Tuesday.'

'Yes. Occasionally I go to the theatre when it's something I particularly want to see. Do you like the theatre?'

'How do I know? I've never been there.'

He stared at me, then in a lighter voice he said, 'Well then, Katie, if ever we meet in Manchester I will personally see that you visit the theatre.'

'I'm never likely to be in Manchester.'

'Whyever not? You could go there on your day off and look at the shops. I must warn you they are very expensive.'

'That doesn't worry me. I have some money mi uncle gave me to spend, all of thirty pounds, and mi grandmother left mi a fortune.'

'Did she, indeed? I hope you are not aiming to spend all that in the Manchester shops.'

'No I'm not, but it's not only the folk in their big houses down there that have money. Mi grandmother lived in a fair-sized house and she left her children and grandchildren well provided for.'

In my naivety I believed that talk of my money might place me on the same level as Lois Foxland, but he seemed completely unconcerned about the size of my fortune, and on that golden afternoon I did not put it down to indifference.

Chapter 16

I told myself that for the first time in my life I was completely happy. I went about my duties with a song in my heart, and when the day's work was done I escaped to the moors where I walked with Jeffrey Carslake, believing that we were drawing closer as I listened to his talk about his childhood, his schooldays and even his thoughts on the gathering clouds over Europe.

Sometimes he would take my hand and hold it as he talked to me, and at those times I longed to put my arms around him and hold him close, but some invisible veil kept him distant.

At night in my lonely bed I tossed and turned, knowing that on the floor below he slept, unconcerned that I could not sleep because of my need for him.

'Yer lookin' pale,' Cook said to me, 'I 'opes yer not sickenin' fer somethin'.'

'I don't sleep very well these warm nights.'

'Well, make the most of 'em, you know them attic bedrooms are cold in the winter.'

Polly sang over her work, and Cook said slyly, 'Got someat to sing about, 'as she? A never thowt a feller'd look at Polly.'

She had bought two lengths of cotton and my aunt had made dresses for her. I had helped her to choose them – one a pretty blue, the other a flowered material in shades of pink and mauve, and as promised I brushed and teased her hair into some semblance of normality. It was dry, wiry hair with a tendency to frizziness, but gradually it was taking shape, and an inner happiness made her seem suddenly comely.

She talked to me about Major Fearnley's gardener, and

when I asked her if he was serious she blushed, saying, 'Well, 'e's talkin' about one o' the cottages the major owns in the town. They're all taken now, but he did say as 'ow we might get the next one that comes empty.'

'That's a proposal surely, Polly.'

She giggled. 'I never thowt I'd get wed. When you came 'ere I thowt yer'd not stay long, some feller'd snap yer up i' no time.'

'Well you were wrong, you're the one that'll be gettin' wed.'

'It's Mr Jeffrey, isn't it, Katie?'

I stared at her dully for several seconds and then the tears rose to my eyes and rolled down my cheeks.

'Gracious, Katie, yer 'aven't done anythin' daft like Milly, 'ave yer?'

'No, of course not. But I love him, Polly, and I don't know if he cares the toss of a button about me.'

'But yer meets 'im up there on the fell, I've seen yer together. Doesn't 'e 'old yer and kiss yer like my George kisses me?'

'No we just talk, but he likes me. It's always him that asks to meet again.'

She was watching me sorrowfully, and somewhat sharply I snapped, 'Well we always knew he wasn't like his brother Roger, he's far more sensitive.'

'Does 'e talk ter yer about Miss Foxland? She'll soon be wed, so it's no use 'im 'ankerin' after 'er.'

'He's never talked to me about her.'

It was true he hadn't, and only a week later the entire family attended her wedding at the parish church in Marsdale, and we were all in time to see the bride and groom leaving the church.

Lois Foxland was a beautiful bride in masses of white lace. The bridegroom seemed old enough to be her father, but he looked at her with pride as she hung on his arm.

My eyes sought for Jeffrey among the guests gathered round the church porch. He looked so elegant in his formal morning clothes as he stood chatting easily to the people around him. Once I saw Lois Foxland look at him and could not miss the colour that suddenly suffused her cheeks.

Several days later when I referred to the wedding Jeffrey admitted that it had been a splendid affair, and when I remarked on the bride's beauty he merely smiled, saying, 'Lois is a very beautiful girl, naturally she made an exquisite bride.'

'Everybody thought you would have married her yourself,' I couldn't resist saying, and I watched his face carefully, but he merely smiled.

In the middle of July the mills closed down for the annual wakes week and Marsdale became a dead town as those who could afford it left en masse for the coastal towns. War clouds might be gathering in Europe and the mills might have urgent government contracts to fulfil, yet on that first Saturday morning there were few people round the market stalls. Families could be seen hurrying to the railway station, the children carrying buckets and spades, the men toting large suitcases.

Lawson's, the large drapers in the square, started their summer sale, and for the first time I entered their imposing doors. I loved the thick carpets and the smell of perfume that lingered over the counters. I had thirty pounds burning a hole in my pocket.

A thought that had occurred to me several weeks before and had gathered momentum with every passing day.

Every Tuesday Jeffrey Carslake went into Manchester to the cotton exhcange, and the next time I had my day off on a Tuesday I too would go into Manchester.

Surely everybody in Manchester must know the cotton exchange, so I would find it all right. Jeffrey always lunched at a small restaurant in the square, and I would surprise him. Nor would I disgrace him. I would buy something entirely suitable at Lawson's, something that Lois Foxland would not be ashamed to wear.

The assistants seemed supercilious, and I felt they were putting a price tag on my home-made cotton dress and lisle stockings. When I paused to look at scarves I was shown the sale items, which creased when they were handled. I asked for pure silk, much to the assistant's surprise. I purchased two pairs of delicate pure silk stockings, and her manner became decidedly more affable. She escorted me to the lift that would take me to the first floor where the garments were to be found.

I tried on beautifully tailored skirts and costumes, silk and shantung dresses and delicate lace blouses, and at last I decided upon a pale green skirt and jacket and with it a crêpe-de-chine blouse in pale lemon.

In the millinery department I sat entranced as confection after confection was placed upon my head. Finally I selected a pale green straw tricorn trimmed with pale primroses, well pleased that those gathered round seemed enchanted by the picture I made.

I gazed ruefully at the remains of my thirty pounds, but in my heart was a glow when I remembered my picture in the long mirror in the store. A picture of elegant beauty. I would show Jeffrey Carslake that in the right clothes I was every bit as beautiful as Lois Foxland. Besides, what was thirty pounds? In two years I could get my hands on the money my grandmother had left me.

I had to be careful about smuggling my purchases into the house, and I made sure that Cook was in the midst of her afternoon doze before I tiptoed into the kitchen. She was snoring gently in her chair and there was no sign of Polly. I still had to creep up the stairs, hoping I would not meet anyone, and for once luck was with me.

It seemed a sacrilege to hang that beautiful outfit in my curtained alcove, but there was no other place for it. Many times in the days that followed I took it out to look at it, and handling the delicate blouse afforded me the most perfect aesthetic pleasure.

On my next afternoon off I visited Lawson's again and I bought a pair of soft leather shoes, with three-inch heels which my aunt would have declared extravagant and unsuitable.

I didn't see Jeffrey all that week. He was in Oxfordshire visiting friends, and I missed him sorely. The rest of the family, including the master, went off to Bournemouth – a signal for Mrs Tate to clean the house from top to bottom.

Carpets were taken up and beaten, walls were brushed and curtains washed, and not until she was satisfied that the entire house shone with cleanliness were we allowed to relax.

Polly grumbled because she was not seeing as much of George, although he could be seen hovering about the shrubbery in the early evenings, and once Cook snapped, 'Yer'd best invite the lad in fer a cup o' tea, he gets on mi nerves, 'e does, peerin' through the winders.'

So George was invited in, clutching his cap nervously while Cook pushed a pint pot of tea in front of him and cut him a huge chunk of fruit cake. She took her place across the table, watching him nervously eating the cake, and I knew an inquisition was on its way.

'So yer courtin' our Polly, are yer?'

He gulped over his cake and his face became brick red, and Polly, clattering her dishes, muttered, 'She's got a nerve, what's it got ter do wi' Cook?'

'She's looking after your interests, Polly,' I replied calmly.

'She's not mi mother, she's got no right.'

'It's because you haven't got a mother that she thinks she has a right.'

'She'll frighten 'im off, she will.'

'Not if he's genuine she won't.'

'Does the major pay yer a decent wage?' Cook was asking.

'I gets twelve shillins a week, that's not bad fer gardening.'

'No, but yer've only yerself ter keep. Do yer live wi' your parents?'

'No, I lives wi' mi brother an' 'is wife, but a don't smoke an' I only 'as a glass o' beer now an' agin.'

'Reckon yer could keep a wife on that then, pay the rent on a cottage an' bring up a child or two?'

He didn't answer, and beside me Polly gulped angrily.

'Well,' Cook prompted.

'A could if mi wife worked fer a while. T'rent wouldn't be much on one o't Major's cottages, an I 'as a bit o' furniture mi mother left mi.'

Cook's voice warmed to him. 'Yer know Polly 'as nowt. She were an orphan wi' no folks to leave 'er owt.'

'A know, she's told mi.'

'Well, yer seems like a decent lad, an' Polly'd like as not get a decent present fro' the mistress. Would yer like another piece o' cake?'

There was silence while Cook cut the cake, and in the scullery Polly looked at me with a question in her eyes.

'He is genuine, Polly,' I reassured her. 'He does want to marry you.'

Her face lit up until it became almost pretty.

'Oh Katie, I'm goin' to save up like mad, I've got ter 'ave someat decent to get married in, an' I want to furnish that little cottage lovely.'

At that moment I felt ashamed of my extravagance. I had wantonly spent thirty pounds on clothes I would find little chance to wear, and here was Polly unsure where her wedding dress was coming from. I determined then that I would save as much as I could out of my wages to give her a good wedding present, and perhaps even buy her a pair of silk stockings for the big day.

Chapter 17

The family were back in residence and the townspeople returned from the coast. Once more smoke billowed from the mill chimneys and the sound of looms could be heard all around the factories.

The talk over the dining table was of war, and Mrs Carslake was often in tears. She had received a letter from Roger saying that all leave had been cancelled and his regiment had moved suddenly to the south coast.

Jeffrey and his father were not on speaking terms. Jeffrey had spoken out on the futility of war, and his father had called him a coward. They no longer set out together to the mills every morning. Jeffrey strode down half an hour early, and came home later in the evening.

On the last Sunday in July I met him on the moor for the first time in weeks. I came upon him lost in thought, looking dismally down on the town.

He stared at me with a frown, until my tentative smile chased it away, then holding out his hand, he said, 'Why Katie, you've come at the right time to cheer me up.'

'It's your father, isn't it?'

'No, Katie, he ceased to affect me a long time ago. No, it's the war, because be very sure, there is going to be one.'

'But it won't be here, will it? It's all going to be miles away and it has nothing to do with us.'

His smile widened. 'Oh Katie, so young and so sure. It *is* going to affect us. Why do you think all the mills are working to capacity, why are we all so affluent these days?'

'Well, mi uncle says they're all making cloth for the soldiers and sailors, but that doesn't mean they'll be in any war.'

'But they will, Katie, and not just the present soldiers

178

and sailors. All the young men are going to be called to the colours.'

For the first time the enormity of war became significant, and a wild fear filled my heart.

'But you won't have to go, you'll be needed here – the mills, your mother. Oh, it just isn't possible that you'll have to go to war.'

He was looking down at me, smiling gently, then surprisingly he changed the subject.

'What did you do with yourself while all Marsdale was on holiday?'

I laughed. 'I've bin spendin' mi fortune at Lawson's in the town. I bought some pretty clothes and I'm goin to go into Manchester to see some folks I knew in Ireland.'

Until that moment Liam Clancy hadn't entered my thoughts. Now he quite suddenly became the excuse I had been looking for.

'So you are going to set Manchester alight and turn the heads of all the men you meet.'

'It's mi day off next Tuesday, so I'll probably go then.'

'Tuesday. That's the day I go on the cotton exchange, so if you're in the vicinity of St Anne's Square we could meet.'

'Oh yes, that would be lovely, and you could tell me what you think of mi finery.'

He laughed. 'You cheer me up, Katie, you have no idea how much.'

He made no definite arrangement to meet me, much to my chagrin, but in my stupid romantic young heart I believed he would be glad to see me in the city and I made my plans accordingly.

I told Cook the same story I had told Jeffrey, that I was visiting the city to see friends I had known in Ireland, and she merely murmured darkly, 'Just you be careful in them city streets, they're no place fer a girl to be wanderin' unescorted. Are yer friends meetin' the train, then?'

'I expect so, but I've got a tongue in mi head.'

'That yer 'ave, but just yer watch out fer yerself, that's all I'm sayin'.'

My next problem was how to get out of the house without

179

being seen in my finery, so I decided it had to be extremely early.

The first train to the city was six-thirty and I was so determined to be on it that I hardly slept. Next morning I crept down the side stairs, carrying my high-heeled shoes. As soon as the kitchen door had closed behind me I stepped into them and tottered through the garden to the side gate. By the time I reached the station they were pinching my toes something dreadful, and I had to take them off in the waiting room until the train arrived.

Few people boarded the train, mostly workmen, with a sprinkling of smartly dressed men carrying small valises and wearing an air of importance.

I was stared at, even leered at, but I adopted an air of indifference, and sat staring out of the window while the train ate up the miles to the city. It was my first adventure on my own, and I hoped that before the day was out Jeffrey Carslake would view me as a desirable companion, not just his mother's servant. After all, it wasn't every girl in service who had a fortune of her own.

The city with its big shops was an enchantment, even Lawson's paled in comparison. All morning I wandered through the scented halls of large department stores, oblivious of my pinching shoes.

I had coffee in one of the restaurants, sitting at the same table as a fashionably dressed lady laden with parcels. She chatted amiably and was very precise in her directions so that I knew exactly where to find the cotton exchange. It was a large imposing stone building on one of the main shopping streets, and I had no trouble finding the entrance on to the square where Jeffrey said he often ate lunch.

There was a café on the square and I was lucky enough to find a window seat where I could keep an eye on the exchange doors, so I dawdled over another cup of coffee, determined to stay there until Jeffrey left the exchange and I could accidentally meet him crossing the square.

My heart raced, my shoes pinched and the fingers on the clock opposite moved so slowly I began to wonder if my nerve would fail me. But then I only had to remember how desperately I loved him to renew my flagging courage.

The café was becoming crowded, and I knew I could not linger much longer. Then I saw him on the steps outside the exchange building, in conversation with two other men.

I paid my bill hurriedly and left the café, waiting in the entrance until he was alone. The two men left him and still he stood, staring across the square as if he waited for someone, and my foolish heart lifted. By some happy chance was he hoping that I would find my way into the square? I saw him raise his hand in greeting, then he smiled, but it was not in my direction.

He moved forward and then I saw her, hurrying across the square, dainty, elegant in pale peach and wearing a small hat trimmed with osprey feathers. He took her hand in his and she smiled up into his face, then taking her arm he walked across the square with her, and I hung back, turning my face to the wall.

Lois Foxland was a newly married woman but here she was lunching with Jeffrey Carslake, who had met her eagerly. And she had smiled up into his face with a warmth she had not tried to disguise.

I felt sick and my eyes were streaming with tears as I ran across the square, oblivious to staring eyes. I didn't know where I was going, I just had to put distance between me and them. My feet slithered on cobbles, and suddenly I pitched forward on to the road when one of my high heels broke on the crumbling footpath.

A man came to help me up and a crowd gathered round. A woman wearing a shawl over her head held out my broken shoe, and the man said, 'Yer not goin' ter be walkin' far on that, luv.'

I looked at it in dismay, wiping my cheeks with the back of my hand, and another woman said, 'My, but yer've got dust all down that loverly costume. Were yer goin' somewhere special, luv?'

I thanked them tremulously and shaking my head I walked away, limping because I had hurt my ankle and I was wearing only one shoe.

I had to get back to Marsdale as quickly as possible, but

now I was walking down narrow streets where water ran in the gutters and poorly dressed men loitered on the pavements. A woman giggled at my plight, laughter that was taken up by others standing near her, and taking off the other shoe I took to my heels again and ran, panting for breath, until my headlong flight was pulled up short by contact with a stout man carrying a large pot of paint, some of which splashed on to my jacket. I stared at him through a blur of tears.

'Sorry, luv,' he said, 'but it were yer own fault, yer weren't lookin' where yer were goin', an A couldn't see yer fro' round the corner.'

I was sobbing incoherently now and he put a clumsy arm round my shoulder, saying, 'There now, it's nobbut a dress, like as not it'll wash.'

It wasn't the dress or the broken shoe, it wasn't my aching ankle or the fact that I had lost my hat, it was the ending of a dream, the feeling of betrayal, unfair and illogical as it might seem.

I hated Jeffrey Carslake and Lois Foxland, at that moment I hated everything and everybody. Reason had deserted me and I was alone and terrified, in a strange city with a big man staring down at me nonplussed and helpless.

'What's goin' on 'ere, Sam?' said another voice, and then with blessed relief I heard yet another: 'Will ya be after carryin' that paint where it's wanted, Sam, and not be dawdlin'. There's men idle up there.'

I opened my eyes wide and found myself staring into Liam Clancy's, pale blue under a shock of straw-coloured hair.

'Why if it isn't Katie O'Donovan. And what moight you be doin' in the city?'

I replied by bursting into tears again, and Liam drew me into the side of the road after handing me a large red handkerchief.

He didn't speak again until I had more or less composed myself, then he said, 'Sure an' oi thought ye were livin in Marsdale. What are ye doin' 'ere?'

'I came for the day to look at the shops,' I answered him tremulously.

'Well, there's no shops round 'ere, this is a buildin' site. And what are ye doin' without shoes an' lookin' as if yer've bin dragged through a hedge? Has somebody bin chasin' ye?'

'No. I was frightened in those narrow streets an' mi heel broke so that I couldn't walk properly, then Sam came an' I bumped into him. Look what he's done to mi dress.'

'Well, it wasn't his fault, ye shouldn't be runnin' wild down the middle o' the street. Oi moight 'a' known if some girl'd act that crazy it 'ad to be you.'

A retort was quick on my lips but I repressed it. I needed Liam, I desperately needed a friendly face and somebody who would tell me how to get back to Marsdale quickly.

'It's nigh on two o'clock,' he said, 'and we don't lay off for a brew till four. Oi don't know what Oi'm to do with ye till then. Stay 'ere, Oi'll foind mi uncle an' see what he suggests.'

I waited trembling on the pavement, while passers-by looked at me curiously, making me very aware of my dishevelled state. At last Liam returned with his Uncle Joel, who eyed me with some disfavour.

'What's yer Uncle Turlough thinkin' about, allowin' yer to come into Manchester on yer own?' he snapped.

'He doesn't know, I didn't tell him.'

'Ay well, that's like young folk these days, don't care 'ow they mess folk about. Liam'd best take yer 'ome. Mary'll be in, she'll give yer someat to eat, and then 'e'll put yer on the train fer 'ome.'

'But isn't Liam working?' I faltered.

'Ay 'e's workin'. I'm givin' 'im time off, aren't I? It's plain yer can't get 'ome on yer own i' that state.'

'How far do we have to go?' I asked.

'Yer'll 'ave to go on the cart. We lives out o' the city, but not as far as Marsdale.'

'I am sorry to be puttin' you to all this trouble.'

'Ay. Well, get off with ye. An see to the 'orse when ye gets 'im stabled, Liam.'

We climbed up behind the big cart-horse and Liam took the reins, urging him on along the narrow street with his shoes clip-clopping on the cobbles.

We did not pass along any of the main thoroughfares and in a short while we were driving along wider and quieter roads with a distant view of the Pennine hills.

To say that Liam's Aunt Mary greeted us with amazement is an understatement. She fussed about my ruined attire, and for the first time I found myself thinking miserably about the thirty pounds I had so recklessly spent and of how I could have put it to better use.

She made sandwiches for us, followed by home-made cake and scones washed down with several cups of very strong tea.

'I'd like to take a sponge to that dress, Katie, but I thinks I might make it worse than it is at present,' she said ruefully.

'It doesn't matter. I'll take it into Lawson's where I bought it, they might have some suggestions.'

'Lawson's, is it? That's a mighty expensive shop.'

'I know. I got some money from mi grandmother.'

'Ay, we heard she'd died. Did ye not think o' savin' that money, Katie?'

'It was thirty pounds from the sale of her house. I get the rest when I'm twenty-one.'

'Why are ye 'avin' to wait fer it, then?'

'She said I'd be able to handle it better then.'

'Ay, I reckon she were right. An' are ye workin' i' one o' the cotton mills, then?'

'No, I'm in service.'

Her eyes opened wider. 'Didn't yer aunt an' uncle mind yer goin' into service? What sort o' family are ye with? I'd 'a' thowt the mill'd 'a' suited ye better.'

'I'm in one of the big houses on Tremayne Hill, they're cotton manufacturers. I hated the mill, the noise and some of the men who worked there.'

'Give ye a bad time, did they? Well that's as may be, but just watch out fer some o' them rich young men who thinks a servant girl's fair game. I've heard some shockin' stories

184

o' the carryins on i' some o' them big 'ouses.'

'I have no complaints about the family I'm with.'

'That's good then. And 'ave yer got yerself a young man?'

'No. I've not been lookin' for one.'

'But yer've bin attendin' church an' visitin' yer folks?'

'I visit my aunt and uncle when I can, but the church is too far away.'

She pursed her lips with a little frown, while I wished Liam would come back from attending to the horse.

'I remember yer Grandmother Cassidy, right upright God-fearin' woman she was, she wouldn't like to think yer weren't goin' to church, Katie.'

'No, I suppose not.'

'Ah well, it'll be different when yer gets wed, yer'll marry a nice Catholic boy who'll see that yer gets ter church. I wish Liam'd find himself a decent girl. 'E did bring one 'ome, but is uncle an' me didn't take to 'er, Methodist she were an' cocky with it.'

'Are they still friendly?'

'No they're not. Mi 'usband and me made it plain we didn't like 'er. We've no children of our own and Liam'll come in fer the business one day, so we're particular who 'e weds.'

Liam came in from the stables and Aunt Mary said, 'Yer'd better get spruced up now, Liam, so yer can take Katie to the station for 'er train.'

'Won't I do as I am?' he objected. 'It isn't far.'

'No yer won't. Yer'll put a collar an' tie on an' show Katie yer a presentable lad when yer all dressed up.'

Liam looked eminently presentable in collar and tie, while I wore one of Aunt Mary's coats over my pale green ensemble and a pair of her shoes on my feet.

I was glad of the coat, not wishing to encounter Cook's scathing remarks and Polly's stares.

We walked mainly in silence. Liam had always been a laconic boy, not given to idle chatter. At the station he looked at me somewhat shyly and said, 'My aunt says I should be askin' you to come for tea next Sunday, Katie. She'll be wantin' her coat and shoes back.'

I couldn't resist the amusement which trembled on my lips. 'Be sure I'll return your aunt's things, Liam. But couldn't you just say you'd like me to come for tea?'

'I do of course,' he said, blushing furiously. 'But it was mi aunt who mentioned it.'

I laughed. 'I'm trouble to you, Liam Clancy. You'll not have forgotten that wretched boat trip when I lost mi luggage, and today mi dress smothered with paint. You've bin very kind to me, Liam, and I'm grateful. You don't have to put yourself out further.'

'I'd like ye to come, Katie, really I would. Mi aunt likes you and you sure are the prettiest thing, or you would be if ye were dressed proper.'

We were still laughing when the train pulled into the station and my last words to him were that I would try to go for tea the following Sunday, but would be sure to let them know if it wasn't possible.

I sat back in the corner of the compartment and thought about the day's events. I would go no more to meet Jeffrey Carslake on the fell. From now on I would go about my duties without an eye on the clock and an ear attuned to his footsteps leaving the house. I would obey the housekeeper and cook and I would stop all those silly ridiculous dreams that I had been a slave to for far too long.

Neither Cook nor Mrs Tate commented on my borrowed attire, not even when my slack shoes clip-clopped across the kitchen. They had their heads together across the table and the only words that I heard were war and more war.

All night long I tossed and turned in my narrow bed, the tears rolling unchecked down my cheeks. I was crying for something irretrievably lost, for a dream that had died, and for my new acceptance that in this class-conscious world I was of little account.

I was crying too for the squandered thirty pounds, and for a future in service in the same house as a man I had adored and who had disappointed me sorely.

For hours it seemed I lay staring into the darkness, listening to the sounds of the night.

I thought at last about Liam Clancy, and with the

memory of his face came hope. Wasn't the familiar a thousand times better than the unknown? And Liam had prospects, good prospects. I would show the Carslakes that I didn't intend to spend my life waiting on them hand and foot, I would survive and prosper and I would be somebody one day.

That thought sustained me throughout the week, even when Cook commented on my eyes swollen by weeping and the fact that I went about my work as if my life depended upon it. I went no more on to the moor in search of Jeffrey Carslake, and when he saw me alone in the dining room before the others had come down to dinner and inquired if I had deserted him, I smiled politely and said I had other things to do.

I went to tea with Liam's aunt and uncle and by the end of July Liam and I were walking out.

Chapter 18

By the end of the summer we had all been carried along by a tide so strong it left us gasping and helpless. War against Germany was declared at the beginning of August and Polly married George, who was called to the colours to serve in an infantry regiment.

She was married quietly, in a pale grey dress made by my aunt and a flowered hat loaned by Mrs Tate. I was her only bridesmaid and the wedding breakfast, provided by the mistress, was eaten in the kitchen. Polly received house linen from the Carslakes, and the rest of us clubbed together to buy china.

She was staying on as scullery maid and all talk of their removing into their own cottage was deferred until after the war. I stood with the others in the kitchen while we admired George in his new ill-fitting uniform, then after Polly had gone off with him to the station I sat with Cook and Mrs Tate, listening to their doubts about his survival.

The following Tuesday Jeffrey was late for dinner, and somewhat savagely I thought that he was probably with Lois Foxland, and I took a grim satisfaction in having his father declare angrily that they would wait no longer. Indeed the meal was almost over when Jeffrey arrived.

'Dinner is at seven,' snapped the master. 'What time do you call this?'

'I'm sorry, Father, I was delayed.'

'Not at the exchange, I'll be bound.'

'No.'

There was a long silence before the master, now red in the face, growled, 'Well, I'm waiting for your explanation.'

'Explanation?'

'Yes, do I have to spell it out for you? Why were you so

late?'

'I joined the army, Father, I preferred to join up rather than be called up.'

I saw the mistress's face visibly pale while his father sat back stunned. Then he said angrily, 'You young fool, the mills'll be working to capacity. You would have been protected in your occupation.'

'I thought you would have been pleased, Father. You've always regarded me as something less than a man, and I joined up to prove you were wrong.'

His father sat back shaken, and across the room my eyes met Jeffrey's and the old enchantment was back – and oh, so much stronger than before.

The meal progressed in silence, each of us busy with our own thoughts until the master snapped, 'Stop whimpering, woman, he's done the right thing for once.' Then looking across the table at his son, he said earnestly, 'I *am* proud of you son, I never thought you had it in you.'

He got heavily to his feet and I saw him wipe away a tear with the back of his hand.

'I don't want coffee, I'll have a glass of port in the study. Perhaps you'll join me there when you've finished your meal, Jeffrey.'

'Yes, Father.'

As soon as his father had left the room he smiled across the table, saying gently, 'Don't mind so much, Mother, I'll get a commission almost immediately and I don't think for a moment my job at the mills would have protected me. It's far better to do what I have done.'

She nodded, then asked tremulously, 'When will you have to go?'

'Within days. Things are livening up out there.'

'Oh, how I hate this wretched war. Why are we involved? We didn't need to be.'

'It won't last long, Mother, then we'll all be back and things will go on as usual.'

Nobody in that room believed him, and later when I met him on the stairs I hissed savagely, 'You didn't have to go. Why are you throwing your life away?'

189

He smiled down at me gently. 'Why Katie, I believe you're as concerned as the rest, in spite of your having other things to do.'

His smile was tantalizing and I steeled myself against its charm. I was remembering his eyes scanning the crowded square for a sight of Lois Foxland, and my degradation. Besides, I had troubles of my own.

Aunt Mary was organizing my life. She now made sure that whenever I visited them on Sundays, Liam and I went with her to church, and the parish priest greeted me with every courtesy as a newfound member of his flock. I was introduced as our Liam's young lady, and one evening she began to plan our wedding.

'It'll not 'ave ter be a white wedding, Katie, as much as yer've probably set yer heart on it. Not wi' a war on, but yer aunt'll run up somethin' pretty, I'm sure.'

'But we hadn't thought of getting married so soon,' I cried.

'There's no call ter wait as I can see,' she said, frowning. 'Yer don't know 'ow long yer job's goin' to last, wi' all the sons gone ter the war. They'll noan be needin' as monny servants, yer could be called up fer munitions. And Liam might be called up for the war. Yer'd want to be married before then, surely.'

Before I could respond, her husband added, 'There'll be little doin' in the buildin' trade. The men'll be called up an' materials'll be 'ard to come by. We'll be shuttin' up shop i' no time.'

'But yer've got plenty o' work in,' his wife protested. 'Yer told me yer'd work for at least four years.'

'Things is different now, luv. Like A said, we're goin' ter lose the men an' we'll be lucky if we keep goin' on a bit o' joinery.'

She pursed her lips unbelievingly, then turning to Liam she said, 'Yer'd best get goin' if Katie's ter catch 'er train.' And with a meaning look: 'Yer should 'ave a quiet talk about yer future an' make sure o' some permanence in yer lives.'

We walked in silence to the station, each of us with our

own thoughts. I felt trapped. One half of me wanted marriage and security. The other, the flighty half, hungered for the unknown, the impossible dream.

When I could bear the silence no longer I asked anxiously, 'Is Aunt Mary pushing you into something too soon, Liam? Don't be afraid to tell me if you're not ready for marriage.'

'How about you, Katie, are you ready for it?'

'I'm not sure, marriage is for such a long time and we're both so young. I'm not even sure if we love each other enough.'

'P'raps you love somebody else better Katie, sure an' Oi never seem to be able to get near to you somehow, and you with your head in the clouds.'

'It isn't in the clouds, I just don't want us to make a mistake we'll be sorry for. You never liked me much in Donegal.'

'Well, you were such a funny scrawny little thing then, now you're the prettiest girl I've ever seen. There's nobody as pretty as you, Katie O'Donovan.'

I was touched, for compliments did not come easily to Liam's lips, and he was looking down at me with eyes that reminded me of my father's old sheep dog, anxious and pleading, and I was so desperately needing somebody to love me.

I smiled up at him shyly. 'All right Liam, we'll get married. But I'll have to ask mi aunt and uncle if they approve, and we'll have to talk about where we're going to live.'

He nodded eagerly. 'I reckon Aunt Mary'll have some suggestions to make, Katie. She's right set on this weddin'.'

'And you, Liam, are you set on it?'

'Oi am.'

His goodnight kiss was unusually passionate, so passionate that I felt startled. I wanted to love Liam Clancy as I believed I loved Jeffrey Carslake, but God help me, I couldn't, and I was being swept along upon a tide I was afraid of. Oh, why wasn't my mother near me so that I could pour out my problems to her? Instead there were

191

Aunt Mary and Aunt Martha, both believing they knew what was best for me, and there was Cook, saying, 'I'm glad ter see yer've come to yer senses at last. 'Ere's a lad fro' your own walk o' life wi' a good trade in 'is fingers, not Mister Jeffrey who's goin' to the war and might not 'ave so much ter come back to.'

'He'll have the mills, Cook. He'll have plenty to come back to.'

She shook her head sagely. 'I'm not so sure about that, it's the war that's put cotton back on its feet, things'll be different when the war's over.'

Two evenings later I went into the study to light the fire. The evening had grown chilly, and the mistress was spending more time in the study, which didn't need as much heating as the large drawing room. I was surprised to find Jeffrey alone, and he came immediately to take the heavy hod.

He watched as I knelt and applied matches to the fire, then when I was satisfied that the wooden sticks had caught, he held out a hand and pulled me to my feet.

'I got my papers this morning, Katie. I leave the day after next.'

I stared at him miserably. 'Oh Mr Jeffrey, why didn't you wait till they sent for you?'

'It's better this way, Katie. It's made things easier between me and my father and I would have had to go sooner or later.'

'But what about your mother? It's not made it easier for her.'

'There are a great many mothers losing their sons, Katie. My mother will accept it, she has no alternative.'

'They've not given you much notice, two days'll soon pass.'

'I know, and there are so many people to see before I go.'

'Like Miss Foxland,' I couldn't resist snapping, and then wished I had bitten off my tongue.

'Miss Foxland is a married woman now, with other matters on her mind. I'm not even certain that we shall meet before I have to go.'

'Oh, I rather think you'll manage that, Mr Jeffrey,' I retorted, and picking up my matches from the hearth I left him.

My behaviour had been childish and immature, but the hurt had been too intense. Only time would take it from me. I was to speak to him only once more, and that was the night before he left to join his regiment.

The master was in the habit of leaving lamps burning in the study when he went out, and Miss Mary too was careless.

'I'd better go and see to the lamps,' I said when it came near bedtime. Cook was reading and Polly was knitting socks in thick khaki wool, occasionally muttering over dropped stitches.

'The master's gone to his club,' Cook said, 'and the mistress and Miss Mary'll 'ave gone to their rooms. I daresay Mr Jeffrey and Mr Humphrey are out.'

The rooms were in darkness and I was crossing the hall when the front door opened and Mr Jeffrey came in. 'Is my mother up, Katie?'

'No, Mr Jeffrey, she's gone up to bed.'

He stood looking at me with a strange awareness in his eyes. 'Will you drink a glass of sherry with me on my last night, Katie?'

'Oh, Mr Jeffrey, I shouldn't. Suppose somebody sees us?'

'On my last night in this house I should be able to do what I like. One glass of sherry and we'll say goodbye.'

Willingly then I went with him into the study where the firelight lingered on polished mahogany and silver, on a large bowl of late summer roses and the tray of glasses sparkling on a side table. He flicked on a lamp, leaving much of the room in darkness.

'Not too much sherry, Mr Jeffrey, I'm not used to it.'

'We should drink a toast, Katie.'

'Oh yes, we must, that you will soon be home and the war will be over. That you will be safe.'

'Thank you, Katie, and we will drink to you, that one day quite soon you will find the rainbow you've been looking for.'

I could feel my eyes filling with tears as I set my glass back on the tray. We stood so close together and I wanted him as I had never wanted anything in my life. I wanted to take him in my arms and hold him close, I wanted him to make love to me, to hold me and kiss me. I wanted to sleep in his bed and have his warm naked body next to mine, and in my torturing desire I swayed close to him, so that his arms were around me and his mouth on mine.

The passion was mine. I would have given myself to him there in the flickering firelight, oblivious to anything except the passion that consumed me, but he was pushing me away from him saying, 'No, Katie, no.' Then after kissing me briefly on the lips he left me, striding out of the room and leaving me to sink to the floor, shivering with frustration and despair.

After that night events crowded upon me so fast I was like a leaf blown in the wind with no thoughts of my own and no direction that wasn't planned by others.

Aunt Martha agreed with Liam's Aunt Mary that there was no need for us to wait, and when I started to talk about looking for a home of our own Aunt Mary was quick to say there was plenty of room with them. When I complained bitterly about this to Cook she merely said, 'It's not a bad idea, Katie, it'll give yer a chance ter save up for somethin' of yer own when the war's over.'

'But it might be years,' I wailed.

'Not it, we'll soon 'ave 'em routed.'

When I complained to Aunt Martha that things were moving at too great a pace she said, 'I suppose yer does want to marry 'im, Kathleen? Sometimes I get the impression yer none too sure.'

'Perhaps I'm not.'

In some exasperation she said, 'Yer don't know when yer well off, Kathleen, 'e's a decent God-fearin' young man wi' good prospects, an' 'is folks like yer. If yer asks me yer don't know which side yer bread's buttered.'

So at the end of October I married Liam Clancy at a quiet ceremony attended by my aunt and uncle and his. Lucy was my bridesmaid. I received house linen from the

Carslakes and a china tea service from the servants. I wore a serviceable saxe-blue costume, my only concession to frivolity being a small felt hat of the same shade trimmed with one pale pink rose and a good deal of veiling. After the wedding repast we caught the evening train for Southport where we spent three days.

I remember standing in our bedroom at Aunt Mary's, staring into the mirror with a feeling of utter disbelief. I was nineteen years old and a married woman, but I didn't feel married. I had dreamed as all girls must dream of a marriage compounded of joy and tenderness, love and mutual delight, but it had been nothing like that. I had been an object on whom Liam had vented his lust and passion, after which he had quietly turned over and gone to sleep, while I had lain awake for the rest of the night listening to him snoring beside me.

I could not believe that all marriages were like this, and in my misery I thought about Jeffrey Carslake, who was sensitive and gentle but who had not wanted to make love to me.

I lived in limbo. There was little to do in the house, for Aunt Mary liked to do things her way. I soon grew tired of accompanying her round the local shops. I read books, indeed I was the public library's best customer, and I spent hours in the museum and art gallery because money was scarce and in these places I didn't have to pay.

Business was bad. The young men had been called up and only old Simeon was left besides Liam and his Uncle Joel. All those order books that had been filled meant nothing. There were not enough men left to do the work, and people grew tired of waiting. It seemed that all I ever heard was that the war would soon be over and customers would come flocking back.

By the end of November I knew that I was pregnant, and in December Liam decided he had had enough at the builder's yard and arrived home one evening with the news that he had enlisted in the Manchester Regiment.

After that he suffered a tirade from his aunt and uncle, who called him a young fool for doing something he hadn't needed to do.

'I'm fed up o' folk lookin' at mi an' thinkin' I'm a conchie,' Liam snapped.

'And what about Kathleen 'ere?' Aunt Mary said sternly.

'She'll be all right, she's got you an' 'er aunt an' uncle, and she were always independent, even as a little 'un.'

'It's no time ter be leavin' a girl who's expectin' a baby.'

'Oh, don't fuss,' I retorted, 'there's hundreds of girls expecting babies with their men away.'

So just before Christmas I stood on the platform of Piccadilly Station watching the men march off to war. They went so gaily, with a song on their lips and laughter in their eyes, but the eyes of the women were filled with pain and helplessness.

'Don't wait, Katie,' Liam said. 'Get off home with you, it's too cold to be hanging about the station platform.'

I nodded. 'Write to me when you can, Liam. I'll send you whatever I can.'

'Nay Katie, ye mustn't do that, keep it for the baby.'

Suddenly I felt a warm rush of affection for him, and throwing my arms round his neck I cried, 'Oh Liam, take care, may God keep you safe.'

I ran along the platform and out into the station yard, and then I saw Jeffrey, embracing his mother and shaking his father's hand. He looked so tall and handsome in his officer's uniform and I hung back with my eyes devouring every gesture, every line of him until he turned and walked in my direction.

I stood riveted to the spot, and then Jeffrey was there, smiling down into my eyes, saying, 'Why Katie, what are you doing here?'

'I came to see mi husband off to the war.'

'But of course, my mother said you had left us to get married. Am I too late to wish you every happiness?'

I shook my head, and next moment he bent his head and gently brushed my cheek with his lips.

He was gone, and I spun round to watch him shouldering his way through the crowd. Through a blur of tears I set off across the station yard and found myself pulled back roughly by strong hands. There were shouts of alarm and the high whinnying of a horse, and I felt the brush of cartwheels against my skirt.

'You young fool,' said a man's angry voice. Then it changed to one of amusement: 'Oh no, not *you* again. Katie O'Donovan, you are going to be the death of me.'

In some anger I looked up at the man who was still holding my arms tightly, and a dark laughing face came into focus.

'Please let me go, you're hurting me!' I cried.

'You were in danger of being hurt a great deal more,' he retorted. 'Didn't you even see that horse and cart bearing down on you?'

'No I did not.'

'I believe you. You were too intent on seeing our friend Jeffrey off to the war with stars in your eyes and all those tears.'

'I was not. I've been seeing mi husband off, I didn't even know Jeffrey Carslake was goin' at the same time.'

His smile was mocking, disbelieving. 'So you're a married woman, are you? I wouldn't have thought it.'

I glared at him. 'What are you doing here anyway? You're a Canadian.' He was wearing an officer's peaked cap and white trench coat.

'We Canadians *are* still part of the Empire. I'm off to war, Katie, so shouldn't you be sending me off with a smile on your lips and a kind word or two? At least with as much affection as you afforded Jeffrey Carslake.'

He gathered me into his arms and his lips pressed against mine, and if at first I struggled furiously, in the end I relaxed against him, enjoying the first really passionate kiss I had ever received.

He let me go at last, then with a gay wave of his stick he was gone, striding rapidly across the square while I stared after him, confused, and with my heart beating painfully against my ribs.

The idea came to me one morning after breakfast. We no longer sat down to bacon and egg and thick buttered toast, now we were lucky if there was jam or marmalade on the table, and it was not entirely due to rationing. Money was scarce.

'I'll walk down to the yard with you,' I said to Uncle Joel, and if he was surprised he agreed that he would be glad of the company.

There was a keen wind blowing right off the moors, and those we met on the streets looked chilled to the marrow. The yard had an air of dejection. Old Simeon was working on window frames, constantly sniffling and with watery eyes, and he eyed me in some surprise until Uncle said, 'She felt like a walk this mornin', Simeon. I'll just let 'er in the office, p'raps she'll make us a cup o' tea now she's 'ere.'

I spent the entire morning in that office, brewing cups of tea, making it tidy and looking through the files and order books. By lunch time an idea was forming, and preposterous as others might find it, I believed it had possibilities.

'Hadn't you better bi gettin' 'ome, luv?' Uncle Joel said. 'Mary'll 'ave a meal ready fer yer.'

'I need to talk to you, Uncle. I think you're not doing anything to keep this business runnin'. You've got orders you could fulfil if you had the men to do it, and that woodyard's full of seasoned timber.'

As though lecturing a child, he said, 'That's just it, Katie, we need the men and they're all gone to the war.'

'But there must be men like Simeon, retired joiners and brickies who could well do with jobs in these hard times.'

'You can't put old men on scaffoldin', lass.'

'I'm not talkin about men in their eighties, Uncle, I'm talkin' about men who are qualified builders in their late sixties or perhaps a bit younger. Why don't we advertise for them? If we have to go under we shouldn't go without a fight.'

'We can't put men in their *late sixties* on scaffolding,

Katie.'

'But they can make doors and windows, they can build cupboards and restore furniture. Those books are filled with orders wantin' small things. You can't be expected to put up houses or warehouses with a war on, but there's no call to stop doing lesser work.'

I knew my words had sunk in when I saw the first faint stirrings of hope in his eyes.

'Do yer really think there's a chance, Katie?'

'Yes I do, and I'll run the office. Aunt Mary doesn't need me at home.'

'We'll 'ave ter talk it over with 'er, Katie.'

'Of course. But it'll work, I just know it will.'

We talked it over with Aunt Mary that same night.

'I doubt folk who've bin retired'd want ter come back ter work,' she said. 'Besides, the lads'll want their jobs back when they comes back fro' the war.'

'Well of course they will,' I urged, 'and by that time these men'll be glad to step down.'

'We're not guaranteed to get anybody.'

'Well we won't if we don't try.'

'I don't know, Katie,' she said doubtfully, 'I don't know 'ow Liam would think.'

'Well of course we don't, but there'll be no business left for him to come back to if we don't try to keep it goin'. Please, Aunt Mary, let us at least try.'

'I don't like to think of you goin' down to the yard in the winter, there's the baby ter think about and it'll do no good if yer gets yer death o' cold.'

'I must do something, or I'll go mad. You don't need me to help you here, and I'm not sitting back to watch that business die on its feet.'

After days of wrangling with Aunt Mary, while her husband merely sat there shaking his head doubtfully, I got my way. An advertisement was put in the local paper for men who had been joiners, workers in the building trade and furniture restorers.

When Uncle Joel read the last bit he said, 'We've never bin interested in restorin' furniture, Katie, that's nothing' ter do wi' building.'

'I know, but we're looking at something that can be done by men who are no longer young, perhaps even semi-invalids.'

'Invalids!' Aunt Mary snapped. 'We want no invalids, we'll be payin' good money to men who are off as offen as they're workin'.'

I wished she didn't interfere so much. She meant well but there was no adventure in her, she was cautious and frightened when I felt she should be daring and brave.

Several days later Simeon appeared at the office door accompanied by an older man and a man who looked to be in his early twenties.

'This is mi wife's brother Harold, Mrs Clancy,' he introduced the older man. 'He's bin retired three year now but 'e were a joiner, and a good 'un. Money's scarce an' 'e's willin' ter come back if yer can find work fer 'im.'

I shook Harold's hand and looked inquiringly at the other man.

'This is 'is lad,' Simeon explained. 'E's bin trained ter restore furniture, ye know, French polishin' and the like. Yer did mention it in yer advert.'

'Yes, that's right, but isn't he very young? Aren't you likely to be called up?' I asked him.

'They won't take mi,' he said softly, then his eyes slid away unhappily.'

Meeting my inquiring gaze, Simeon said, 'The lad's epileptic, Mrs Clancy, but 'e's not a bad case, 'e's a lot better now than 'e were when 'e were a lad. The forces won't 'ave 'im and 'e can't work on munitions. 'E's good at 'is job, I've seen some o' the work 'e's done.'

'What happened to him in his last job?'

'The firm went bankrupt, couldn't get their money in, an' when the war come the owner joined up and Joe 'ere were thrown out o' work.'

'When you say he's much better now, does that mean that he no longer has epileptic fits?'

Joe answered for himself. 'It's three year since I 'ad one, Ma'am, but I 'aven't ter work wi' machinery in case A does.

There's no machinery called for i' polishin' furniture.'

I nodded. 'Well, Simeon, I'm goin' to employ yer brother-in-law and I'm goin' to advertise for work in the restoration line. As soon as we receive an order I'll send for Joe here.'

They were both loud in their thanks, and in the afternoon Isaac arrived. He spoke very little English but was able to explain that he was a Jewish immigrant from the Balkans. He ushered me out to a handcart in the road where he produced whitewood furniture he had made for himself and his neighbours since they had arrived in this country with nothing except the clothes they were wearing.

Simeon and Harold examined the furniture and proclaimed that it was expertly made, and then I saw Joe running his hands along the wood, his eyes gleaming, and there was a tenderness in his hands as if he loved it and needed to beautify it.

That night I faced Aunt Mary with the news that we had two more employees. After she had heard me out, tight-lipped and unimpressed, she snorted, 'That's all wi need, a foreigner, an old man, an' then p'raps a lad who's likely ter start 'aving fits all o'er the place.'

'We can at least give it a try.'

'It'll not work, Katie, an' what does a lass who's bin in service know about runnin' an office an' takin' on work folk?'

'Bein' in service doesn't mean that I haven't a head on mi shoulders. I intend to make somethin' of mi life, an' I won't sit back an' go under without a struggle.'

'Ay well, time'll tell. In the meantime mi 'usband's payin' good money to four men we 'aven't got work for. None of 'em can go up on a scaffoldin', an' it's that sort o' work that's fillin' the order books.'

'Nay, lass,' Uncle Joel put in staunchly, 'all that sort o' work's gone by the board fer the duration, we 'as to turn our 'ands ter someat else. Maybe Katie's got the right idea.'

The second advertisement went in the paper the following Saturday, advertising joinery of all descriptions, making of furniture and restoration work. Before Wednesday we had orders for five kitchen cupboards, two back-yard gates, and one garden fence to keep out a next-door neighbour's dogs.

To be sure such work bore no comparison to the erection of a house or factory, but it was a start and it kept the men busy. Joe appeared daily to inquire if there was anything for him and when I shook my head dismally he went away saddened.

I was beginning to understand Isaac's guttural English, and one day he brought in an oak bookcase he had made. It was a lovely thing even to my inexperienced eyes. When I praised his workmanship he smiled happily, and extending his hands and shrugging his shoulders he said, 'I make for you, you like books no?'

'Oh yes, Isaac, I love books but I don't have very many of them.'

'You vill 'ave. I cannot polish.'

'You think it should be painted?'

'Ach no, sacrilege to paint. Stain and then polish. Leave to Joe, 'e vell make it beautiful, vu see.'

My eyes lit up and when he saw that I had guessed what he was about he chuckled. 'That's right, now you see.'

So Joe came into the workshop and every day I saw my bookcase take shape as he lovingly stained and polished until it stood in the cluttered room resplendent and beautiful. We all admired it while Joe beamed with delight. When Uncle saw it he gasped with amazement.

'It's beautiful, Katie, an' it's worth a bob or two. Are yer sure 'e's given it ter ye?'

'I'm sure, and it's staying here so that I can show our customers. Oh, surely one of them must have something special put away in an attic that would be worth a lot more if Joe worked on it.'

'It's a shame ter keep it 'ere.'

'I know. I'll take it home when people know about us.'

A month later I took it home and installed it in my bedroom. Aunt Mary knew little about fine furniture but she did admit that it was pretty enough, particularly since it now had a glass front to it.

'If 'e'd made yer a cradle fer the baby it'd 'a' done yer more good than a bookcase. 'Ave yer any books ter put in it?'

'A few I brought from Ireland. They belonged to mi father.'

'Ay, I remember yer father, allus 'ad 'is 'ead in the clouds 'e 'ad. It'd be like 'im to 'ave books.'

'He didn't have his head in the clouds the day he saved Maureen Wilcox, did he?'

'No 'e didn't. I'm sorry, Katie, A shouldn't 'a' said that.'

I heard no more about wasting money in employing Joe. He was busily working on an old corner cupboard one of our customers had dismissed as of little account until she saw my bookcase and had invited Joe into her parlour to view the cupboard. We had watched as he ran his hands lovingly along its sides and the intricately carved front-piece.

'Well,' Mrs Sommers snapped, 'is it worth owt?'

'It's beautiful,' Joe said, 'it could be more beautiful.'

'Ay, but is it worth owt?' she persisted.

'It's Georgian. It's not worth anythin' like it is now, but it could be worth a lot o' money when it's done up.'

''Ow much would it cost?'

Joe looked at me anxiously, and gathering my wits I said, 'I can't tell you exactly now, Mrs Sommers, it will depend on how much time he has to spend on it.'

'Oh well, I'm not sure,' she faltered.

'I'll give you an estimate when we've worked out his time and the materials he'll need to use.'

'Ay well, I suppose that's fair enough. It belonged ter mi 'usband's uncle. It were the only thing 'e left 'im, the old skinflint.'

The following morning I closed the office and set off into the city and the most expensive furniture shop in the most elegant shopping arcade.

I knew of this shop because Miss Nancy had told me her dining-room furniture had been purchased there, and I well remembered her saying, 'I'm having the best, Katie, my husband can afford it.'

How I loved the elegant chairs and tables surrounding me, the deep-cushioned velvet chairs and settees, the polished walnut and mahogany and the richness of English oak. A tall supercilious young man approached, and I was glad that I had put on my wedding costume and hat – minus its veiling.

'Can I help you, Madam?'

'I hope so. I am looking for a corner cupboard in walnut. It must be Georgian and I would like some carving on it.'

'I'll show you what we have, Madam.'

So I followed him into another room where there were three or four corner cupboards, not one of them like Mrs Sommers'.

'Are these all you have?' I ventured.

'At the moment. Georgian furniture is very hard to come by and you would need to go to an antique dealer for the genuine thing.'

'Of course. Have you any idea how much I would have to pay for one?'

'In the region of a hundred pounds, Madam. I can only offer you a good copy.'

'How much would I be paying for the copy?'

'Twenty to thirty pounds, Madam.'

'Is that all?'

'Well, Madam, it would only be a copy. Real Georgian furniture is something that has been handed down in families and perhaps only parted with as a means to obtain money.'

'Thank you for your help. Is there a good antique dealer near here?'

'I will write his address down for you, it isn't far.'

I thanked him again and after bestowing a warm smile on him I left the shop in search of the antique dealer.

I could tell the difference as soon as I looked in the window. Here period furniture was arranged tastefully and I recognized it as such from my memory of the Tremayne house. Large silver trays and tea services were arranged on delicate walnut side tables and there was a profusion of bronze horses and marble busts.

The antique dealer did not have a Georgian corner cupboard to show me but he knew exactly what I had in mind.

'I may be able to obtain one for you but it may take some time,' he said. 'Is it urgent?'

'I would need to buy one quickly, but I have another alternative.'

'Oh, what is that?'

'A friend of mine has one stowed away in an unused room of her house, but I'm afraid she has let it deteriorate. It would need restoring before I could even contemplate purchasing it.'

'Is it very decrepit?'

'Oh no. It needs stripping and repolishing, the handles on the drawers need some attention and the glass will need replacing. The cupboard is sound.'

He appeared to be thinking hard. Joe had told me what needed to be done to the cabinet and now I waited anxiously for a price.

'How much would you expect to pay your friend for this cupboard?' he asked thoughtfully.

'I would have to ask her, the cost of its restoration is more important.'

'Perhaps if I were to see the cabinet.'

He was staring at me through narrowed eyes and there was a faint inflection in his voice that seemed familiar. I did not think he was English but neither was I, and by this time I was wondering what he made of my accent when most of the Irish in England were as poor as church mice.

'I cannot take you to see the cabinet until mi friend has said she's willin' to part with it. Can't you give mi some idea?'

He pulled a gold watch out of his pocket and consulted it with a slight frown.

'It is almost lunch time, Madam. Perhaps you would call another day after you have talked with your friend. I will give you my card.'

I took it and was ushered politely from his shop. I felt quite sure that he had seen through my ploy and he was determined not to assist me in whatever scheme I was about. Looking at his card I read that his name was Maurice Abrahams, dealer in antiques and fine furniture. I returned to the yard feeling inadequate and for the first time for weeks, less than sure of myself.

When I showed his card to Isaac he chuckled. 'Ach, but you should get a Jew to catch a Jew. I vil talk to Maurice Abrahams.'

'You know him, Isaac?'

He spread his hands and gave his expressive shrug. 'Sure, ve all know one another, but he in England many years. I see 'eem tonight.'

'Does that mean you will tell him you know me?'

'I tell 'eem, and he vil laugh. Tomorrow I 'ave news for you.'

I had been in the office only a few minutes the following morning when Isaac came in, smiling broadly.

'Maurice see through you. He asks to come 'ere.'

'To see me. Oh, Isaac, I hope he's not going to make an issue out of this.'

'An issue?'

'Why yes, Isaac. He must know I didn't really want to buy a cupboard at all, I was picking his brains.'

'Ach yes, Maurice is good at that. He veel come and you laugh together.'

I wished I had the same optimism but I was remembering Mr Abrahams' speculative narrowed eyes as he showed me from his shop.

Isaac brought him in that afternoon, his dark eyes gleaming with amusement, and to my utmost relief I saw that Mr Abrahams too was smiling.

As he took my hand he said, 'We will start again, eh, Mrs Clancy? Now you shall tell me what it is you want to know, and I will listen very carefully before I give you my answer.'

I nodded, then invited him to sit down in the one visitor's chair, and Isaac bustled about with the kettle and our assortment of cups and saucers.

'This time I will be honest with you, Mr Abrahams,' I began.

'Yes, that will be best.'

'I'm sorry to have wasted your time yesterday. I expect Isaac explained to you.'

'Not entirely, it is for you to explain and Isaac's English is still very limited.'

'But you are both Jewish.'

'That is so, but he is from the Balkans while I came here from Germany where I was taught to speak English as a child.'

'I see.'

He smiled. 'In Germany we were considered wealthy. My father was a banker, indeed most of my family are still there. Isaac is one of our people who is constantly on the move from country to country. Perhaps he will find sanctuary in England.'

'I hope so. He is a good workman.'

'No, Madam, he is a good cabinet maker, a craftsman. There is a difference.'

'Yes, I know, or at least I am beginning to know. I take it you have seen samples of his work, then.'

'I have seen some of the things he has made, but I have seen nothing completed. It is the staining and the polishing that beautify and enhance.'

'I have a bookcase that Isaac has made for me. And Joe, a boy who wants to work for me, has made it so very beautiful. I would like you to see it.'

'Of course, where can I see it?'

'It is in my bedroom, just a few minutes' walk from here. If you have the time, of course.'

'I have made the time, Mrs Clancy. Shall we go?'

I let myself in the house and, ignoring Aunt Mary who was pottering about in the parlour, we went immediately to the bedroom.

I watched anxiously as he ran his hands over the smooth polished wood. A few minutes later Aunt Mary came and stood watching with a frown of caution on her homely face.

At last he turned and I did not miss the gleam of excitement in his eyes.

'It is good, Mrs Clancy. You say this boy wants to work

207

for you?'

'Yes. Up to now he has found it difficult to find work because he is epileptic. I want to employ him and I have a customer with a corner cupboard that needs restoring. I have no idea what to charge her and that's why I visited your shop.'

'She will probably not be inclined to pay for this work to be done. So many of these people have priceless treasures put away in their attics, they neither know nor care anything about their value and are unwilling to spend money on their restoration. Tell her the work will cost sixty pounds.'

Both Aunt Mary and I gasped, and he smiled. 'You do not think she will be interested when she knows the price?'

'No, I'm sure she won't, and I can't think it will fit in with the rest of her furniture anyway.'

'Then we will go and see the cupboard and I will make her an offer for it.'

'I doubt if she will sell it, it was left to her husband in somebody's will.'

'It is plain this good woman is not aware of its value. Come, Mrs Clancy, we will find out if she will take money for it.'

He passed Aunt Mary with a nod and murmured good morning, and my eyes cautioned her to silence.

During the next half hour I stood on one side marvelling at Mr Abrahams' business acumen, which made mine look infantile indeed. He ran an experienced eye over Mrs Sommers' corner cupboard, pursed his lips and shook his head until the poor woman burst out, 'It's noan worth spendin' money on, that's what yer tryin' ter tell me.'

He shrugged his shoulders more eloquently than words, and she said sharply, 'I towd Fred it were o' no value,' is uncle'd 'a' done better ter 'ave left 'im a bit o' brass.'

'Well, to make it anything like we are speaking of, a figure in the region of fifty or sixty pounds, isn't that right, Mrs Clancy?'

Mrs Clancy remained silent, but Mrs Sommers threw up her hands in shocked amazement before saying, 'I'm spendin' no fifty pounds on that.'

'Then why not sell it, Mrs Sommers? I could part with it to a friend of mine who is on the lookout for second-hand furniture, poor immigrants, you know, who came into the country with very little. I could give you fifteen pounds for it.'

Her eyes narrowed and for a moment became crafty. 'Well, I don't know, Fred'll noan be so pleased if A sell it, an' fifteen pounds is soon spent.'

He pretended to examine it again. 'Well, how about twenty then? I can't pay more, Mrs Sommers, indeed I am losing money by offering twenty.'

We waited in silence while she thought about it, then making up her mind quickly she said, 'All right, yer con 'ave it. To tell the truth I'll be glad ter see the back on it, an' we'll 'ave a bit more room when that's gone.'

Mr Abrahams took out his wallet and handed her twenty pounds, which she shoved into the large apron pocket.

'It's a pleasure to do business with you, Mrs Sommers,' he said, smiling. 'If there is anything else you wish to part with, tell Mrs Clancy and she will contact me.'

She nodded. 'Well, there's that bowl in the middle o' the sideboard, that came fro' 'is aunt's too, and I've 'allus 'ated it.'

'Come then, we will look at it.'

I watched as another crisp note changed hands, then we were walking down the street with the bowl clutched firmly in Maurice Abrahams' hands.

'Is it valuable?' I whispered to him anxiously.

'It is Spode and old. I gave her five pounds for it and she will think she has done a good morning's work. The bowl is worth well over thirty pounds and prices will rise after the war.'

'It seems awfully like sharp practice to me, Mr Abrahams.'

'Mrs Clancy, this morning we have purchased two articles of great beauty from a woman who hated them. Bah, it was sacrilege that she should have possessed them at all.'

'But she wasn't educated into assessing their worth.'

'No matter. Things of great beauty should be where they are loved and appreciated. Mrs Sommers will look at her twenty-five pounds and think she has been very clever, then she will go out and spend it on something quite inferior, like a hideous ornament or a ridiculous hat.' He shivered delicately. 'You are unconvinced, Mrs Clancy,' he observed with a sly smile.

'Yes, I am.'

'Do you want to survive in this harsh world in which you find yourself, my dear? Because if you do a degree of ruthlessness is necessary. Do you want to give young Joe a job in your establishment and do you want to make your business fit for a hero to return to?'

I stared at him wordlessly.

'Go ahead, employ your Joe, and I myself will put work in his way. Isaac shall renovate broken furniture and Joe will beautify it, and I will pay them, nor will I use sharp practice on you, Mrs Clancy, for Isaac will be watching me with those sharp eyes of his. Believe me, my dear, it takes a Jew to know a Jew.'

I laughed, suddenly light-hearted. There was something about this man I liked, and my spirits soared.

'Are you really going to sell Mrs Sommers' old cabinet in your shop?'

'But of course, when Joe has done everything that is necessary. I will pay you the same money I would have had to pay any craftsman and when I sell the cabinet I will reward you for leading me to it. I think you and I are going to have a very rewarding partnership, Mrs Clancy.'

Chapter 19

After that morning I was amazed at how well the business prospered, although I got little thanks from Liam's aunt and uncle, who objected to me having dealings with Jews. I didn't care. Uncle Joel paid me only a bare pittance for looking after the office, attending to the order books and paying the men's wages, but I was making a nice little bit on the side, thanks to Joe and Isaac and Mr Abrahams, although by this time I was calling him Maurice and we were good friends.

I banked my money religiously every Friday morning and was gratified how steadily it grew. My entire life centred round that poky office and the builders' yard, but the workforce grew and now we had six men working for us and I decided it was time to ask Uncle Joel for a rise in pay.

'Well, A don't know, lass,' he replied, scratching his head thoughtfully. 'Yer nobbut the office girl an' it's more important fer the men ter be paid decent wages. Yer 'as a good 'ome with us, an' Liam'll be sure o' work when the war's over.'

'And who is that thanks to?' I retorted angrily. 'Who had the idea that put this business on its feet and who placates the customers when delivery's late and who sees that the men are on time and attend to their work? I might have a good home with you and Aunt Mary, but I wants mi own home after the war, that's what I'm savin' up for.'

He stared at me, nonplussed. 'Nay lass, Mary'll noan be takin' ter that. Yer 'ome's with us.'

I decided it was no moment to be arguing about where we made our future home, and in the hope that I would shelve that idea he upgraded my wages by three shillings a week.

'Does that satisfy yer?' he asked grimly.

'I'd be getting four times as much on munitions,' I retorted.

'Ay, well there's a baby on the way, so munitions is out fer you, Katie. Suppose A makes it five.'

'Thank you, Uncle, five will do very nicely for now.'

At the beginning of January I heard from Liam, from a field hospital behind the lines. He had only been slightly wounded, and was soon expecting his release and a return to the front. In a rush of compassion and as a penance because I did not think about him as often as I should, I began to knit feverishly, socks and scarves, gloves and sweaters, and I baked endless batches of biscuits until even Aunt Mary remarked that I was overdoing it.

There was snow on the ground now as I trudged to the yard and I was always cold, for the coal was poor quality and we burned anything we could get our hands on in the tiny grate. I hated the loss of my trim waistline, and the thickening of my body vied with the problems in my heart. I was a married woman who didn't feel married, I was soon to be a mother and I didn't want a baby.

In France the war raged in undiminishing ferocity, and we were suffering appalling losses. There were times when I wondered what all this had to do with Kathleen O'Donovan, whose heart was still rooted in distant Donegal. But there was no going back, today was the only thing that mattered.

Every day I scanned the paper for the names of those who had been injured or killed in Europe, and every day I heaved a sigh of relief that Jeffrey's name was not amongst them. At the beginning of February I bought my usual paper at the end of the street and stood leaning against the wall, reading the names under the light from the gas lamp before making my way home, as I always did. My heart gave a sudden leap as it reached the letter C, for there were two of them, then I collapsed, weeping, against the wall. Major Humphrey and Major Roger Carslake had both been killed in action, but there was no mention of Jeffrey, and I breathed again. Then I looked down further for the name of Clancy of which there were several, but no Liam.

That night I retired early, complaining that I was weary, and felt duly ashamed when Aunt Mary fussed over me, bringing hot milk to my bedroom where I lay unsleeping. I was thinking of Colonel and Mrs Carslake, with two sons dead and two others in France. I was remembering Roger's laughing impudent eyes and Mr Humphrey smart as paint as he basked in the adoring eyes of his fiancée. Most of all I was thinking about Jeffrey, particularly when I remembered that Grandmother Cassidy had always maintained that bad luck came in threes.

I shall remember the first winter of my married life always for the snow that lingered on the pavement for weeks and the biting winds that swept down from the moors as I battled to the yard every morning. I shall remember the cheerless little office and the smoking fire and I shall remember Aunt Mary's scolding that my baby was not being given a chance, that it would probably be born a poor pathetic creature that would develop rickets and God knows what other disastrous ailments through my neglect and the evils of the world it would be born into.

Only one thing sustained me in those winter months – we had plenty of work. True to his word Maurice Abrahams kept both Isaac and Joe busy and he paid good money for their services. The other men were kept busy on minor building and joinery work so that in March I was able to give them a bonus, much against Aunt Mary's better judgement.

'They deserve it,' I retorted. 'It's not the money, Aunt Mary, I'm paying for their loyalty, and we need them. Without those men the yard would have been finished months ago.'

She pursed her lips and said nothing more, but while she was busy in the kitchen her husband said, 'She can't help interferin' Katie, but she means well.'

Spring came slowly as though reluctant to face a world torn by war, and the papers were filled with woeful tales of wholesale slaughter, and of how the men were dying in their thousands in rat-infested trenches. It was months since we had heard from Liam, and Aunt Mary was pessimistic about his survival.

On the Saturday after Easter we received a visit from Aunt Martha and Lucy, who immediately joined forces in an endeavour to persuade me to stay away from the yard now that the birth of my baby was coming closer, until I began to feel trapped by their insistence.

'You owe it to Liam as well as to the baby,' they said.

'I also owe it to Liam to keep the business on its feet,' I retorted.

'Well, yer'll 'ave to stay at 'ome after the baby's born,' Aunt Mary warned me.

'Do you hear anything of Fanny?' I asked Aunt Martha in an attempt to change the subject.

Her face set angrily. 'No, it's as if she never existed and we never sees 'er.'

'She's still living with her friend's parents, then?'

'They've moved out ter Cheshire. It's more residential, so I heard they'd said, an' better fer Frances as they calls 'er.'

'We don't care, do we, Mother?' Lucy piped up. 'I 'ates her, I do, I never wants to see her again.'

I changed the conversation again, this time by asking if they ever saw anybody from Heatherlea.

'I saw Cook in the town and asked 'er back fer a cup o' tea,' Aunt Martha said. 'Did yer know that Polly's 'usband 'ad been posted as missin'?'

'Oh, I am so sorry. Poor Polly, she'll be so unhappy.'

'Ay, she will. She were lucky ter get a man ter marry 'er, fer she weren't much ter look at. It's not likely she'll find another.'

'She'll be missing George too much to be even thinking about another,' I retorted, thinking how terribly unkind people could be. 'I'll write to her, perhaps one of these days I'll get up to see them.'

''Ave yer got a name for the baby, then?' Aunt Martha asked.

'I thought if it was a boy I'd call him Michael, and if it's a girl I'll call her Marisa.'

'Marisa!' they all echoed.

'Well, yes, I've always thought it was a pretty name. Mi father had an aunt called Marisa and he always said she was the luckiest woman he knew, she never wanted for a thing and died in her sleep at a hundred and one. I used to wish they'd called me Marisa.'

None of them approved. They would both have preferred a girl child to be named after them, but there was no way my daughter was being christened Mary Martha or vice versa. Sure as anything they would have quarrelled as to which name came first.

'Well, I don't think much of Marisa,' Aunt Martha said on leaving the house, 'so let's 'ope the baby's a boy. I've nothin' against Michael.'

I was touched when Isaac appeared in the office carrying a wooden cradle he had made. It was beautifully carved and set on gentle rockers, and immediately Joe set to during his dinner hour to stain and polish it. When Maurice Abrahams saw it he walked round it with obvious delight, then with twinkling eyes he made me an offer of sixty pounds for it. When I hesitated he threw back his head and laughed uproariously.

'Why Kathleen Clancy, I do believe you'd trade your baby's cradle to the highest bidder.'

'I would not,' I retorted. 'You took me by surprise, that's all.'

'Well, it's a handsome piece of furniture, it deserves to become a family heirloom.'

With my eyes filled with laughter I said, 'When the baby's old enough to do without its cradle I might think of selling it to you.'

'Oh no you won't, it'll surely be wanted for all the other little Clancys that'll come after.'

I stared at him in some amazement. I had certainly had no thoughts beyond the one baby who was soon to arrive in the world.

Indeed Marisa Clancy made her appearance four nights

later and I saw her for the first time through a blur of pain as she was held up in the midwife's arms – a tiny, red, wrinkled creature – before I closed my eyes and drifted off into a sleep of utter exhaustion.

In the morning I saw her again, pink and white and beautiful, sleeping peacefully in the cradle beside my bed, and I lay back marvelling in contentment at the miracle I had wrought.

I was young and strong and I soon recovered from the birth of the baby, but still Aunt Mary insisted that I rest, plying me with endless milky drinks which I found nauseating. She was rapidly warming to Maurice, who appeared with fruit and poultry as well as a huge teddy bear for the baby.

'I don't know where 'e gets all the things 'e brings,' she said. ''Ow is it a Jew can get things when we can't?'

'He knows a lot of people in business, he's been very kind.'

'Oh, ay, I've no intention o' lookin' a gift 'orse in the mouth, but it makes yer think.'

The men called with their offerings, a money box from Joe and posies of garden flowers from the others. On one of these visits Joe said, 'What's goin' to 'appen in the office now you're not there, Mrs Clancy? The master doesn't seem to know what we're about.'

'As soon as Aunt Mary lets me out of the house, Joe, I'm coming down. I knew this would happen.'

'But will ye be coming back, Mrs Clancy?'

'Why yes, of course I will.'

Aunt Mary had other ideas. 'Yer can't go back, not wi' a new baby. Who's to care for it?'

'I'll look round for a reliable woman, there must be dozens of them simply crying out for work of this sort.'

'There'll be no woman lookin' after Liam's daughter, not while I'm 'ere.'

'Does that mean that you'll care for her, Aunt Martha?'

'Ye shouldn't be wantin' to leave 'er, ye should be content to be a good mother an' not concern yerself wi' the yard.'

216

I had an unexpected ally in Uncle Joel, who said, 'I could do wi' Katie some part o' the day, Mary. Ye knows I'm no good wi' paper work an' she's better wi' the customers.'

'I'll pay ye for looking after Marisa,' I told her eagerly. 'You know how much we need to keep the business going.'

Once we had won her over I suspected she looked forward to having the baby to herself, and I began to look forward to taking up my life as it had been before it was interrupted by the birth.

I was putting Marisa back in her cradle early one afternoon when Aunt Mary announced that I had a visitor, and the next moment there was Cook, armed with a large parcel which she pushed into my hands.

'Yer can open it when A've gone,' she said. 'I 'ad 'alf a day off so I thowt it were time I made the effort ter see yer. Is that the bairn then?'

I stepped back so that she could see into the cradle and, her face wreathed in smiles, she peered and crooned into the depths of the canopy. Straightening up, she said, 'She's beautiful, Katie, but she's not got yer red 'air.'

'No, she's more like Liam, at least she has his colouring.'

'Ay well, they often changes as they gets older.'

I pulled a chair forward for her to sit on in front of the fire, and Aunt Mary made a cup of tea.

'How are things at Heatherlea, Cook? I read about Mr Roger and Mr Humphrey.'

'Ay, terrible it were, and the mistress 'as taken it that badly, eats no more than a sparrer she doesn't, an' the master too. It's brought 'im ter 'is cake an' milk.'

'How do you mean?'

'Well, 'e stays 'ome now, 'e doesn't even go off at the weekend, just lives fer the mills an' the letters they get fro' the other two.'

'I hope they're all right.'

'So far they are. Mr Ambrose an' Mr Jeffrey are both i' France, nobody knows from one day ter the next. I 'opes yer 'usband's all right. I expect yer 'eard about Polly's George?'

'Yes, has she had no more word?'

'None. She spends every minute o' the day cryin', an we just can't be sharp wi' 'er. I don't suppose yer knows that Milly's wed.'

'Milly?' I echoed stupidly.

'Ay, Milly that left ter 'ave Mr Roger's baby. I saw 'er in the town last week an she'd 'a' passed mi by without speakin' a word if I 'adn't called 'er back. All dressed up she were, wi' paint on 'er face, an that hoity-toity yer'd 'a' thowt she couldn't say boo to a goose.'

'Who did she marry, then?'

'Some farmer fro' one o' the villages. She looks nowt short, an like A said she wouldn't 'a' spoken if I 'adn't made 'er.'

'Did she mention the people at Heatherlea?'

'No. When I told 'er about Mr Roger, 'er face grew that 'ard, as if she were glad, as if she 'ated 'im.'

'Perhaps she does, Cook. Perhaps I would if that had happened to me.'

'Ay well, she should 'ave 'ad more sense ner tangle wi' 'er betters.'

I was saved from answering by a knock on the front door. Maurice stood on the doorstep, carrying several paper bags and a bunch of white daisies and pink carnations.

Cook eyed him curiously after he had been introduced, missing nothing of his smart polished shoes and well-cut dark grey suit. The paper bags contained vegetables and fruit, chicken and several pieces of steak. After he had gone Cook pursed her lips, saying, 'It seems some folk can get 'old o' good food.'

'He's a business associate, Cook, he knows a great many shopkeepers.'

' 'E's Jewish isn't 'e?'

'Yes, I believe so. He's lived in England a long time.'

'Why isn't 'e at the war then?' E's not too old.'

'I don't ask him any questions, Cook. Perhaps he hasn't been called up yet.'

'Or perhaps 'e'll wriggle out of it,' she ended darkly.

Aunt Mary exclaimed delightedly over Maurice's gifts, while Cook watched with a sour expression.

To ease the tension I said, 'May I open your parcel, Cook? You really shouldn't have brought anything.'

'They're only odds an' ends, there's no steak or chicken in that parcel.'

'I'm grateful for everything and to everybody who is kind,' I said gently, and proceeded to open it.

There were boxes of little cakes, and home-made knitted garments for the baby – little gloves and bootees, matinee jackets and warm woollen vests – and I raptured over them, they looked so sweet, little bigger than dolls' clothes.

'We did 'em all in white,' Cook said, 'not knowin' whether yer'd 'ave a boy or a girl, but the pink one's fro' Polly. She would insist on knittin' in pink wool, said it were 'er favourite colour, an' look out fer the dropped stitches.'

It was a little jacket and indeed the dropped stitches were very evident, but that was the one that brought tears into my eyes because I could picture Polly working on it laboriously in the dim light of the scullery, in between constant demands on her to do other things.

There was another parcel wrapped in coloured paper, and I unwrapped it curiously, watched by two pairs of inquisitive eyes. It contained a delicately chased silver christening mug, and turning to Cook incredulously I said, 'But this is beautiful! Surely you didn't buy anything so expensive.'

'No, it's fro' the mistress. Mrs Tate told 'er about the baby an' next day she gave 'er this to bring yer. She said it 'ad belonged to one of 'er own children.'

I wondered helplessly if it had belonged to Jeffrey.

'I'll write to her tomorrow, Cook, to thank her, and as soon as I can I'll call in to see Polly and Mrs Tate. Tell them how much I loved their gifts and how much I shall treasure them.'

'Ay well, yer were allus a nice sort o' girl, flighty an' a bit independent, but yer were a pretty little thing an' there's noan so much beauty i' this world that we can't appreciate it when we sees it. I'd best be gettin' back now, it's a fair walk to the station.'

'I'll walk along with you,' I said. 'The walk will do me

good, I've hardly been out of the house since Marisa was born.'

'You stays where yer are,' Aunt Mary said sharply. *'I'll walk wi' Cook, an' if Joel comes in tell 'im 'is dinner's cookin' in the oven.'*

After they had gone I put the garments away carefully in tissue paper, reflecting all the time on their kindness and the increasing kindness of Maurice Abrahams. I knew that Maurice admired me. He was a bachelor, and had told me he had never wanted to marry, believing that he travelled fastest who travelled alone. But there were times when I found him looking at me so closely he brought the blushes to my face, and then he would smile and turn airily away.

Once after such an encounter Isaac had chuckled maddeningly, saying, 'Ach, but he likes you, that Maurice, vat a pity zat you are married.'

'What nonsense, Isaac, I'm a respectable married woman, and even if I wasn't Maurice is Jewish. Can there be anything more odd than a Jew and a good Catholic Irish girl?'

'Not so good the Catholic, Mees Clancy, when vu last go to church.'

'That's only because I'm as big as a house and I can't get up and down in the pew.'

'Vel vait and see then,' he had muttered darkly, and went off chuckling to himself.

After that I tried to avoid being on my own with Maurice, but his behaviour was always circumspect if his gifts were more than generous.

Chapter 20

Autumn and winter came again and by this time Marisa was my joy. She had Liam's fair hair but her eyes were like mine, dark blue, not pale like Liam's. She was a happy baby full of laughter and with a placid disposition, and the aunt and uncle adored her and spent all their spare money on her, so that I was forced to remonstrate with them.

It did no good, and I soon found Aunt Mary encouraging me to leave Marisa with her at the weekends when I had more time to spend with her myself.

'Make the most of yer spare time now while she's too young ter mis yer,' she admonished. 'An' isn't it about time yer went up to Marsdale ter see yer friends as well as yer aunt an' uncle?'

I went to see my folks just before Christmas, taking their present with me. Aunt Martha showed me over the house proudly, the new bathroom and the new fireplace, new carpets and a new kitchen, which was an extension beyond their old kitchen, now a dining room.

'So you've been spending Grandmother Cassidy's legacy,' I teased her.

'No we haven't, that's still in the bank, all this 'as bin done on what yer uncle brings in.'

'I'm glad the mills are doing so well, but I wonder what will happen after the war is over.'

'What do yer mean, Kathleen?'

'I wonder if cotton will slip back into the doldrums. The government contracts will surely come to an end.'

'Oh, cotton's allus 'ad its ups and downs, but it'll allus be wanted.'

'I hope so, Aunt Martha.'

There was no time to visit Heatherlea that day, and by

221

this time the fells were covered with snow and I made this my excuse to stay away. How could I ever go back to Heatherlea? It would remind me too much of an emotion I wished to forget.

At the beginning of January Maurice came into the little office where I was making up the men's wages. Perching on the edge of the table he laid an envelope in front of me, and when I stared at him curiously he said, 'Why not open it Katie, and tell me if you would like to take advantage of it?'

It was a ticket for a concert in the Manchester Free Trade Hall in which a famous orchestra and many famous singers and choirs would take part. I had heard their names, read about their accomplishments, but I had never been in a concert hall in my life.

'Oh Maurice, I'd love to go, but it's impossible.'

'Why is it impossible?'

'Well, it's very expensive, and I've nothing to wear for such an occasion. I couldn't go on my own.'

'Of course not, I would like you to come with me.'

'But Maurice, Aunt Mary would be horrified! She'd say I'd no right to be goin' to concerts while mi husband was away at the war.'

'But the concert is in aid of the war effort, Katie. All these famous people are giving their services on the night quite free, to provide funds for the Red Cross and the Salvation Army. The work they do is invaluable.'

'But what would I wear?'

'Isn't it time you spent some of your earnings on yourself? Surely a new dress wouldn't be a cardinal sin.'

'I don't know,' I said dubiously.

But he knew I was wavering, and he said, 'Think about it, Katie, see how the land lies this evening when you've talked to them about it.'

'I'd love to go, Maurice. I love music but I know nothin' about it. Grandmother Cassidy said there were other things in life, more important things than books and music.'

'Grandmother Cassidy's been dead these many years and she was wrong, Katie. Books can bring the world to your doorstep without your ever needing to step outside of it, and music was surely created in heaven.'

'When will you need to know, Maurice?'

'Very soon, Katie. If you are not able to accompany me I must see that some other person takes advantage of the ticket.'

'I will tell you tomorrow, Maurice, I won't keep you waiting any longer.'

I told them about the ticket that night after our evening meal, and immediately Aunt Mary found a dozen reasons why I should not go. It would be over too late for me to get home, it was unfitting that I went with a man who was not my husband, and a Jewish man at that. And why did they have to have a concert, why couldn't the money simply have been given for the war effort? The concert was an indulgence for rich people who had too much money for their own good.

Uncle Joel sat in silence, quietly puffing his pipe, and I realized I was going to get little help from that quarter.

'I'm twenty years old, Aunt Mary, and I've never set foot in a concert hall or a theatre. I don't know anything about anything except the work I do at the yard and cleanin' and polishin'. I don't want to be ignorant, I want to learn about beautiful things and listen to beautiful music before I begin to accept that I'm not fit for anything else.'

'Can't yer learn all this fro' Liam after the war's over? 'E'll not want to come back ter a wife who thinks she's better than 'e is.'

'Oh Aunt Mary, what will Liam be able to teach me except war and people dying and being killed? When Liam comes home we'll do things together, but he isn't home, is he?

'Yer 'ardly knows that Maurice, 'sides 'e's foreign.'

'He's not foreign, he's a naturalized Englishman.'

' 'E's Jewish.'

'Oh, for heaven's sake, what does that mean? I thought I'd left all the bigotry behind me in Ireland.'

'Well, yer'll please yerself, I've no doubt, but we don't approve neither of us.'

I told Maurice the following day that I would go with

him to the concert, and I was aware that he understood my defiance in the face of much opposition when he asked gently, 'You told them last night, Katie?'

'Yes. Aunt Mary made her disapproval very obvious but Uncle never said a word.'

'No, I rather gather that she is the deciding force in that household. Are you quite sure you can live with that disapproval?'

'Oh yes, Maurice, I want to go so much, and this afternoon I'm going into the city to buy a new dress. I never buy anything for miself, would you believe I still have an old tweed coat I bought out of mi wages from a second-hand stall on Marsdale market?'

He laughed. 'Buy the prettiest dress you can find, Katie, and you shall wear my mother's wrap that hasn't been out of mothballs since she died.'

'My, but they'll smell me coming a mile off.'

'Oh no, I'll take it out of the tissue paper and let it hang in the bedroom. Katie, you'll look like a queen.'

It was a night of enchantment such as I had never known. I wore a jade-green silk dress I had purchased in Manchester and which, after the pale green costume I had bought to captivate Jeffrey Carslake, was the most expensive garment I had ever owned.

Maurice arrived in a taxi, carrying his mother's wrap. He was careful to show it to Aunt Mary and ask her permission for me to wear it. It was made of heavy black velvet, with a huge white ermine collar which fell back from my neck to show the low-cut neckline of my gown. The neckline was not to Aunt Mary's liking, but I knew I was beautiful by the admiration in Maurice's eyes, and the reluctant and grudging praise from the aunt and uncle.

For two and a half magical hours I let the music pour over me, at the same time confidently aware that I was dressed as correctly as all the other women. Maurice looked distinguished in his evening dress. I stole a quick look at him as he chatted to an acquaintance. He was not handsome, but he had an air of elegance and his clever aquiline face made me feel that if I had not known him, I would have wished to.

I sat with stars in my eyes, stirred by the sheer patriotism of the music, the songs from Merry England, the *Pomp and Circumstance* of Elgar, and when the war songs were performed I was not ashamed of the tears in my eyes.

We were invited to eat supper with a group of Maurice's friends but he could see that I was anxious to get home.

'You go,' I urged him, 'I can quite easily go home on my own if I can find a taxi.'

But he refused to allow it, and when we stood at last on the doorstep I thanked him tremulously for the most perfect evening I had ever spent.

'Your enjoyment is thanks enough, Katie. When you are next in the city we will go into the art gallery and look at the paintings.'

'Oh Maurice, I don't want to be a nuisance but you can teach me so much.'

'Indeed, I shall be the proudest tutor in the whole of Manchester, or England too for that matter,' he said gallantly.

Once or twice a week now I made excursions into the city, ostensibly to pay accounts and order materials. Sometimes I would lunch with Maurice, and we spent time in the city art galleries and museums. I learned to recognize a Constable and a Rembrandt, a Leonardo and a Rowney. I learned about priceless porcelain and about Chippendale and Hepplewhite, the sheen of walnut and the glow of mahogany, the stoutness of English oak and the dark brooding beauty of ebony. He taught me to judge the quality of jade and marble, alabaster and onyx, and the exquisite carving of ancient yellowing ivory brought gasps of delight from my lips.

It was spring again and I shall always remember one warm afternoon when we walked through a city park after leaving the museum. Cherry blossom bloomed along the paths and ducks splashed merrily in the lake. Men in uniform and girls walked arm in arm across the grass, and

Maurice suggested that we sit for a while by the water.

He was very thoughtful as he sat with his stick tracing patterns in the dust, so quiet that I faltered in my chattering and stared at him doubtfully. 'Why are you so quiet, Maurice?'

'Have I been wise, I wonder, in leading your mind and senses into things that will have little bearing on your life, Katie?'

'I'm not sure what you mean.'

'Are you going to be discontented when Liam returns home, Katie? A young man coming home from the war will want a loving wife waiting for him, not a girl who has outgrown him. I have changed you, Katie, and I had no right to do so. I have not been fair to Liam.'

'You mean you would rather have left me as you found me, ignorant and uninformed. Oh, the audacity I had in thinkin' that to be young and pretty was enough. I know now that it was nothin', Maurice. I have to grow, I have to be somebody and make Marisa somebody. She's not going to grow up like I grew up in Donegal, she's going to be a match for all those people I was told were mi betters. And I'm not going to let anybody talk mi out of it, not mi folks, nor Liam nor his folks, and not you, Maurice Abrahams. You can't just leave me as you found me, I won't let you.'

He looked at me soberly. 'Not even if it does something to your marriage, Katie?'

'Oh Maurice, Liam's just got to climb up there with me. If he doesn't he'll lose me.'

'Has he got it in him to climb?'

'I've scrimped and saved everything I could lay mi hands on for a year and a half, I've had a baby. I've kept the yard together – not Uncle Joel or Aunt Mary, but me, so that he'd have something worth while to come back to. He owes me a lot. Surely it isn't too much to expect him to try to be the man I want him to be?'

He smiled slowly. 'I wonder if he deserves you, Katie. I'd change for you, I'd climb every mountain you'd set your sights on, I'd find the crock of gold for you. But I'm not your husband. I'll be just an onlooker in your life, and only time will tell if I was right to have opened your eyes to the beauties that life has to offer.'

'You were right, Maurice, I know you were.'

Rising to his feet he pulled me after him, and for a moment he held me in the circle of his arms, then with a smile he let me go and we were once more walking side by side.

Chapter 21

The war that everybody had thought could not possibly last beyond that first Christmas was now almost three years old. Letters from the front were few, and Liam's stilted and wandering epistles were pitifully inadequate.

Letters from America were arriving spasmodically, sometimes even three or four arriving together, and in them my mother showed her concern for me living in a country at war and praised God that Terrence was too young to be called. She made polite inquiries about Liam but I felt he was not the man she would have chosen for me to marry, though she never actually said so. She always referred to him as Liam Clancy, which somehow made him seem like a stranger, and after a brief mention her letters were filled with Eileen's prowess at school and Terrence's high hopes that one day he would come in for Uncle Shamus's business.

All mention that one day we could ever meet had long passed into limbo.

When Whitsuntide came round, I decided to return to Marsdale, but Aunt Mary said, 'I doubt if the churches'll be walkin', if that's what yer thinkin' on seein'.

'I'd like to visit Cook and Polly. I did promise.'

'Well, I wouldn't take the child, yer'll get about much better on yer own.'

Aunt Mary didn't like me to take Marisa far out of her sight. I was also discovering that Marisa was content to stay with her and showed little interest in where I was going.

On Whit Sunday I went to Marsdale, arriving well before ten o'clock. In the old days the streets would have been thronged, but today it was evident there would be no procession, and no brass bands. I headed towards the hill, and when I reached St Anne's field I found it was crowded with children, and a boys' pipe band was there in place of the brass band. I was about to turn away when I saw a woman standing dejectedly watching the activities. With a little cry I ran towards her, calling, 'Polly, Polly it's me.'

A bright smile illuminated her face and she threw her arms around me, exclaiming happily, 'Katie, yer 'ere at last. I thowt yer'd never come.'

As we walked up the hill arm in arm, I said, 'I see they're going on with their field day even though the processions have stopped.'

'It's fer the children, they're missin' so much. The processions were so lovely wi' all the ribbons an' the flowers. These little 'uns'll grow up not knowing what it were like.'

'It'll come back after the war's over.'

'I don't think it'll ever be over. It's just goin' on an' on. Does yer 'ear from Liam, then?'

'Not often, Polly, and his letters say so little.'

'But at least 'e's alive.'

'He was three weeks ago. Have you no news of George?'

'No, but the Germans are all over the part where 'e was. I keeps 'opin' 'e's a prisoner somewhere. They've not said 'e's dead fer sure. I prays every night that one day I'll see 'im walkin' up the path clutchin' 'is cap just like 'e used ter. I used ter tell 'im 'e didn't need ter take it off till 'e come into the 'ouse, but 'e were that nervous o' Mrs Tate.'

'Weren't we all.'

'Cook'll be that glad ter see yer, Katie. She's right morbid these days, allus sayin' the old life's gone, an' things'll never be the same again.'

'Well, they can't be any worse for you and me, Polly. Remember those cold attics and those mornings when we shivered in the kitchen because we were cuttin' down on coal?'

'I don't know what's goin' ter happen, Katie. Heatherlea'll be too big fer the family now wi' only Mr Jeffrey left, an' 'e's at the war. One day 'e'll be getting wed an leaving the 'ouse supposin' 'e comes back safe.'

'What about Miss Mary, then?'

'Eh, Katie, Miss Mary's married an' livin' near Lancaster. There's only the master an' mistress left. Most o' the time we 'as nowt ter do.'

I was thoughtful as we walked through the gardens towards the house. The gardens were well kept as always, so I assumed one of the gardeners at least was still about. The house looked in need of a coat of paint, but apart from that nothing was changed that I could see.

When Polly entered the kitchen Cook said, 'I didn't expect yer. I thowt yer wanted to go down ter the field.'

'We've a visitor, Cook. Katie's 'ere.'

Cook spun round, a broad smile on her homely face, and next moment her arms were round me and I was crushed against her not inconsiderable bosom.

''Ave yer browt the little 'un with yer?' she asked at last, peering behind me.

'No, Aunt Mary thought the journey would be too tiring for her.'

'It seems ter me yer Aunt Mary's takin' the child over. Just mind the lass knows it's you whose 'er mother, that's all.'

'She's very good to us, Cook, and I do have to work. Without Aunt Mary I don't know what we'd have done.'

'No, just as long as she knows it's not going ter be like this for ever. One day yer goin' ter take over, an' I reckon yer'll 'ave a job makin' Aunt Mary see it.'

'Polly's been telling me about the changes here. It's a sad house these days, Cook.'

'Ay it is, more so now that Miss Mary's gone. The chap she's married's not 'alf good enough fer 'er.'

'Why is that?'

'Brash 'e is, an' too sure of 'imself by 'alf. Miss Nancy 'ardly ever comes 'ere, an' Mister Jeffrey out there in France – 'ardly a letter from 'im. No wonder the mistress looks miserable and 'ardly a word fro' the colonel. Food's 'ard enough ter come by wiout it bein' sent back fro' upstairs untasted. This war's goin' on too long, it's time it were over an' the lads comin' back.'

'Will things change here after the war, Cook? Polly seems to think so.'

'I don't know what's goin' ter 'appen. It'll depend on whether Mr Jeffrey comes back in one piece, and 'ow cotton fares. 'Eaven knows it's bin in the doldrums time an' time again. I've allus said it did no good showin' them 'eathens round the mills, showin' 'em 'ow clever we were an' them listenin' and standin' back marvellin'. Like as not they'll beat us at our own game one o' these fine days.'

I'd heard it all before, Cook's pontificating about what was right and wrong with the family, with cotton and with the world. I accepted Polly's cup of tea gratefully, watching Cook cut a slice from a large fruit cake.

'This tastes as good as ever,' I said gratefully.

'There's not much fruit in it but we gets what we can. Yer'd be surprised if I told yer what went into that cake. I'll be glad when we can get proper food again wiout 'avin' to make do wi' makeshift stuff. Now tell us about yer little 'un.'

So for the next half hour I talked about Marisa, her charm and her prettiness, until Cook said, 'Yer've not told us owt about yerself, Katie. I suppose yer still workin' at the yard?'

So I told them as much as I thought would interest them about the yard. I didn't tell them about my excursions with Maurice.

I was encouraged to eat tea with them and it was after seven when I walked down the hill. Smoke was still billowing from the mill chimneys and in the air was the clatter of looms and the heavy clip-clopping of dray-horses pulling heavy carts over the cobblestones.

Marsdale was prosperous, but on the faces of the townsfolk there was anxiety, and often the pinched look of despair. A great many families had suffered the slaughter of a brother, a husband or a son, and flags flew at half mast in the square and on public buildings. Manchester was impersonal, a big city where few people were known to me, but here in Marsdale families were so close that when your neighbour was hurt you limped in sympathy.

I was just locking up the office at lunchtime several days
later when I turned to see a man standing in the middle of
the yard and gazing round curiously. There was something
vaguely familiar about him.

He was well dressed in a dark grey lounge suit and trilby.
He was of middle age, portly and clean shaven, and carried
a silver nobbed stick. Catching sight of me he raised his hat
politely.

'Do you work here, Miss?'

'Yes, I am Mrs Liam Clancy, my husband's uncle owns
the yard.'

'You are builders?'

'Yes, but there is little going on in the building trade just
now so we are concentrating on joinery work and lesser
things.'

He nodded. 'I've seen your advertisement in the newspaper. I'm requiring some work done on my home but I'm
not sure if you will have the scope for it.'

'I'll open up the office. Perhaps you would explain what
you are requiring.'

He followed me into the small room, remarking, 'This is
a strange occupation for a girl to be engaged on.'

'I don't think so, Sir. Mi husband's away at the war and
his uncle was runnin' it on a shoe string with all the young
men away. It was my idea to advertise and we've got some
good workers, even though most of 'em are old and Joe
doesn't enjoy good health.'

'And has the venture been successful?'

'Indeed it has. We have work a-plenty and the men are
all craftsmen and good at their jobs.'

'I don't live round here, indeed my house is some
distance away. Would the men be willing to travel?'

'Where is your house, Sir?'

'In the country over at Repperton. I would see that they
were met at the station and taken back there in the late
afternoon. All the work is inside the house, there is no

232

structural work.'

'What sort of work, Sir?'

'I should explain that my wife is an invalid, and unfortunately her illness is progressive. She will not recover, she will only deteriorate.'

'I'm sorry, Sir.'

'Yes, it is very sad. At the moment she can get around the house with the aid of a stick but eventually she will need a wheelchair, and I sense her frustration which, alas, will only increase. I want ramps made and railings along passages so that she will have some sort of independence. At the moment she can get by, but eventually if something is not done to help her she will become bitter in her helplessess.'

'Yes, I can understand that.'

'Would you or your husband's uncle be prepared to visit us so that you could decide if you could do the work?'

'I'll talk to him tonight. I'd like to help you, and if he's willin' perhaps we could call to see you this coming weekend.'

'That would be very satisfactory. Here is my card, and if you will let me know I will see that you are met at the station. Good day, Mrs Clancy.'

After he had gone the thought nagged at me. I should know this man, and yet his card conveyed nothing to me: Mr Joseph Earnshaw living at Merton Hall, Repperton. I had no idea where Repperton was.

When I gave the card to Uncle that evening he nodded, saying, 'It's in the Ribble Valley, a bit of a beauty spot. But I reckon it's too far for the men ter go. They'd 'ave ter leave 'ome very early, an' they'd get back too late.'

'Couldn't we ask them?'

'We could. We'll go up on Saturday an' 'ave a look at what's wanted. P'raps we could take Simeon with us.'

'Oh yes. I feel so sorry for Mrs Earnshaw. It's awful to think that she's only going to get a lot worse.'

'What sort of age were 'e?'

'In his fifties I should say.'

'Ay well, she'll not be a young woman, so that's a

blessin'.'

There was really no need for me to accompany Simeon and Uncle Joel to Repperton, but I was curious about the Earnshaws. After we had left behind the industrial part of Lancashire, the views became enchanting: low purple moors and lofty Pennine hills, stone villages and ancient churches, bubbling streams and forests of evergreens. We might have been a thousand miles from Manchester and yet we had hardly travelled any distance at all.

Mr Earnshaw was waiting for us outside the pretty station, driving a smart trap pulled by two handsome ponies, and soon we were heading towards an imposing mansion set on the hillside. Long lawns swept down to the river and the drive wound between avenues of azaleas. Low stone steps led up to a wide terrace along which bright red geraniums bloomed in white urns, and long windows lay on either side of the entrance door.

A manservant opened the door for us and took our coats. I stared round the entrance hall, agog with admiration. The walls were panelled in dark oak and the staircase swept up from the centre, its shallow steps carpeted in bright turkey red. My eyes were drawn to a portrait of a middle-aged woman which was hung where the staircase divided.

My eyes met his and he smiled, shaking his head. 'No, that is not my wife, it is the portrait of Lady Castlemere, whose husband owned this house before me. They were a childless couple, and indeed I have been unable to find any member of the family who would care to have that portrait.'

'It's a very beautiful house.'

'Yes, we think so, and now we are having to deface it by ramps and railings, but my wife is more important than bricks and mortar.'

I felt the tears pricking my eyes as I turned away. To be loved like that was surely every woman's dream, but here was Mrs Earnshaw with this beautiful house and a husband who cared so desperately, and it was almost as though she had been given too much, so that now Fate was conspiring to punish them both.

'Perhaps you would like to meet my wife, Mrs Clancy.

She doesn't have too much company because we are rather isolated here and I have my business to attend to. She is probably in the morning room. I'll take you in there and have some coffee sent in to you.'

As he entered the room he said, 'Here is Mrs Clancy to see you, my dear. I have asked them to serve you with coffee.'

I could not have said what was in that room. I saw nothing of the colours, the furnishings or the flowers, for my eyes were drawn to a woman sitting in a deep armchair drawn close to the window so that she could see out. A walking stick rested against her chair and there was a footstool for her feet. A tiny Yorkshire terrier bounded forward, barking, and Mr Earnshaw picked him up, admonishing, 'Quiet boy, this is no way to behave.'

The woman turned her head and I stood in shocked dismay, for the eyes I looked into were those of Lois Foxland.

Now I knew why he had looked familiar, for I had seen Joseph Earnshaw twice before, at Tremayne House and at Heatherlea. By this time he was beckoning me forward with the words, 'Sit here, Mrs Clancy. Lois likes to look out on the rose garden and the flowers.'

Lois held out a languid hand and smiled. There was no recognition in her gaze, no hint that she might have observed me moving around the rooms of Heatherlea. But then how could I have expected if from this beautiful pampered girl who had drifted through life surrounded by admirers and in a haze of perpetual bliss?

A maidservant came in and busied herself prettily with the task of pouring coffee. I racked my brains on what we should talk about. We could have nothing in common, unless it was our love for Jeffrey Carslake, and my life would be of little interest to her. I bent down to pet the little dog, who had come to nose around my feet, and Lois smiled.

'Benjie is very belligerent but he soon makes friends. Poor little dog, he misses his walks but I am not too well at the moment and not very steady on my feet.'

The maid lingered by her side to hand round the tray of tiny cakes. I wondered what we would say to each other now as Lois sat back in her chair and regarded me with a set smile on her lovely face. I need not have worried, Mrs Earnshaw was well versed in the niceties of polite conversation.

'My husband tells me you actually work in the building trade, Mrs Clancy.'

'Yes, but we have had to adapt to smaller things.'

'I see. Do you think your workmen will be able to do the work?'

'I believe so, but the men will soon know if it is possible.'

'At the moment I can manage perfectly well with the aid of my walking stick, but Joe is anxious I should not be too dependent on others.'

'How long have you been ill, Mrs Earnshaw?'

A shadow crossed her face and I regretted my question, then with a bright smile she said, 'It came on very suddenly. One day I was running across the lawns and the next I was feeling unsteady without being able to account for it. I have seen the best doctors in the North of England and last week I was taken to see a man in Harley Street. None of them hold out any hope that I shall get better, indeed I shall become much worse.'

A wave of pity swept over me when I remembered Lois waltzing round the ballroom in Tremayne House and hurrying on her incredibly high heels across the square to meet Jeffrey Carslake. Sitting in her pretty dress, with her fair hair fashionably coiffeured, she looked no different from the old Lois, except for the thin blue-veined hands resting on the arms of her chair and the haunting sadness behind that too-bright smile.

'I'm sorry, Mrs Earnshaw,' I replied with words that were too inadequate, too banal.

'Oh I am really very fortunate, Mrs Clancy. I have this beautiful house with this lovely garden to look out on and I have Benjie here to keep me company most of the time.'

'You also have a very caring husband, Mrs Earnshaw. He does not seem to mind how much it costs or what work is entailed to make sure you are made as independent as possible.'

She nodded. 'Yes, it is dear of him, but Joe is a very special man, a very kind man. When we married some of our friends were quick to point out the difference in our ages, they even accused me of wanting a father figure instead of a husband. I knew what I wanted. We met on a cruise, you know, and we came back engaged to be married. The age difference hardly mattered, I had found what I was looking for.'

Against all my better judgement I couldn't let that pass, not when I remembered that morning outside the cotton exchange in Manchester, or the opinions of people in Marsdale who had expected her to marry Jeffrey.

'I lived in Marsdale before I was married, Mrs Earnshaw. You didn't know me but I often saw you around the town, sometimes with your mother, sometimes with Mr Carslake.'

Her eyes never wavered nor did the colour suffuse her cheeks as it would have mine when faced with such a hidden accusation.

'How strange that you should have lived in Marsdale, Mrs Clancy. Did you live in the town?'

'I lived for a time with my aunt and uncle. My uncle is employed in one of the Foxland mills.'

'What a small world it is, and I am so bad with faces. Jeffrey and I were brought up together, it was natural that we went to the same dances and parties. I believe quite a lot of people thought we would marry one day.'

'Yes, I'm sure they did.'

There was uncertainty now in her face as her eyes met mine, and perhaps there was something in mine that brought the sharp retort to her lips.

'It is because of Jeffrey Carslake that I looked for something very different in the man I married.'

I waited for her to explain her words but she was biting her lip nervously, afraid that she had said too much to me, a stranger. I couldn't let the words stop there, I had to know why she had looked for something different in her husband,

and I prompted her by saying, 'Mr Carslake was very handsome, you looked so well together.'

She smiled then, the saddest most disillusioned smile I had ever thought to see on that exquisite porcelain face.

'Oh yes, Jeffrey was handsome, everybody said we were perfect together, and Jeffrey liked to be seen with me. He liked the way I looked, the way I dressed. He liked it that we had been brought up in the same way, knew the same people, it was all so effortless. But he did not love me, Mrs Clancy. Jeffrey has never loved any woman, nor will he.'

'I don't understand.'

'I'm not saying that he prefers men, merely that he is completely sexless where women are concerned. He likes to kiss them and fondle them but he would never commit himself to loving one body and soul, or caring for a woman who is less than perfect. I am less than perfect now, Mrs Clancy, and had I married Jeffrey Carslake he would not now be contemplating how he can make his home a suitable residence for an invalid wife.'

I felt shaken by her frankness, shaken and incensed by it. I wanted to say that it wasn't true, that she had been the one to put him aside in favour of another. But even as the words were forming in my mind I was remembering Jeffrey's constraint, the holding back.

Her expression was bitter. 'I loved Jeffrey Carslake, he was my universe when I was eighteen years old, my joy and my hope for the future, but he was incapable of the sort of love I wanted, incapable of giving himself, and still I loved him. Both his family and mine conspired to push us together and at first it delighted me until I realized it would be an alliance that had no substance. Then I went away on that cruise and met Joe. He was almost as old as my father but he was all kindness, all tenderness, and I began to realize what I had been missing.

'It would have suited Colonel Carslake to have me marry Jeffrey, to have the Foxland mills and his own become one massive combine. And though Jeffrey does not give the impression of being over-proud and snobbish, he enjoys having the men doff their caps to him and the weavers bob their curtsies in the aisles.'

I stared at her, nonplussed. This was a Jeffrey I had not known, and I found myself disbelieving her, resenting the picture painted of him.

Unaware of my resentment, she went, 'I hadn't realized it was so easy to fall out of love.'

Trying hard to keep the resentment out of my voice, I couldn't resist asking, 'But when you saw Jeffrey again didn't you think that perhaps you had made a mistake?'

She nodded. 'Yes, I thought so. Jeffrey was young and handsome, all the shared years of our childhood and our growing up drew me to him, but I found myself remembering his selfishness, his inadequacies.'

I was bemused to be here, with Lois Foxland talking about Jeffrey Carslake in a way I had never thought possible, and almost as if she knew my thoughts she said, 'I have never told any of this to another person, Mrs Clancy. It seems strange that I should tell it to you, a comparative stranger.'

'Do you feel better for having told me?'

'Strangely enough I do, and I feel you will respect my confidence.'

'Have you not seen Mr Carslake since you married?'

'Yes of course. We met at parties and such like. It was inevitable, and he asked me to have lunch with him in Manchester, once. I told Joe where I was going and he didn't object. Men know men, Mrs Clancy, he didn't feel he had anything to fear from my meeting with Jeffrey.'

'And you haven't seen him since?'

'No, and now Jeffrey is away at the war and we are very isolated here.'

'In spite of his inadequacies he was brave enough to volunteer for the army.'

I could have bitten off my tongue, but she seemed not to attach any importance to my knowing so much about him, and she was quick to retaliate.

'I have not thought that Jeffrey would be a coward, Mrs Clancy, he has all the attributes of his class and upbringing. I would have expected him to be a fine officer and

239

gentleman. But where any woman is concerned he would not have the ability to make her happy. He is selfish.'

At that moment Mr Earnshaw came into the room. He was smiling and, taking his wife's hand in his, he said, 'Well, my dear, something is going to be done for you. The workmen are moving in next Monday to start work on ramps and railings.' Turning to me, he said, 'I am very well satisfied with the estimate. Your uncle has been telling me how hard you have worked to keep the business together. Mr Clancy is a very lucky young man.'

'Men are not always too happy to find their wives interfering in their business.'

'Then he would be supremely ungrateful. Have you two ladies enjoyed your chat?'

Lois's eyes met mine, composed and unruffled. 'Mrs Clancy lived in Marsdale for a time, Joe, we discovered we had mutual acquaintances.'

'I think Lois misses some of her friends,' he told me.

'I don't really miss them, Joe. Many of my friends have scattered since we married and I wouldn't be able to keep pace with them as I am now.'

I saw his hand grip hers tightly, and then he was saying to me, 'We had better get you back to the station, Mrs Clancy, I wouldn't want you to miss your train.'

I had a great deal to think about on the way back. Looking into Lois's eyes on parting, I had wondered if I would ever see her again. She had told me far more than she intended, but she had relieved herself of a burden which I now carried. I too had loved Jeffrey Carslake, but had been too naive and foolish to recognize his inadequacies.

I slept badly that night. One half of me refused to believe the things Lois had told me, but the other half was remembering the quarrels at the dining table and the harsh words his father had showered on him. I remembered Cook's sly insinuations, but most vividly of all I remembered his withdrawal, the singular remoteness that had left me trembling with mortification. I had believed his remoteness was due to our different stations in life, now I saw it as somethings else, a deficiency in him, an inability to relate closely to a woman.

Lois had found consolation in Joseph Earnshaw. I had married Liam Clancy. But I could not easily forget that I had loved Jeffrey. That enchantment, I knew, would die slowly and painfully over the coming years.

Chapter 22

At last the war was over and victory was ours, but it was a sad and hollow victory when the cost was counted.

I stood in the rain with my daughter in her push chair, trying to shelter under Aunt Mary's large umbrella while we waited for the returning regiments to march past. The air was full of sound, church bells and mill hooters, the clip-clopping of horse's feet and the martial music from a dozen brass bands, and then they came, weary but unbowed, in ill-fitting battle-stained uniforms, but with brasses and shoes polished to incredible brightness, swinging along with military precision under the commands of the men they had obeyed with unquestioning courage through four long years of war, and all around we women wept with pride and the children watched with wide-eyed wonder.

They looked neither to right nor left, not even when many of the women cried out to them, or had to restrain the older children from running towards the fathers they recognized.

I was so busy watching Jeffrey Carslake riding his black horse at the head of one of the groups that I completely failed to see Liam until Aunt Mary gasped, 'Did yer see 'im, Katie? Two stripes 'e's got an' 'e said nowt about 'em in his letters.'

She pointed ahead to where the column of men were swinging right. It was easy to see Liam's tall gangling figure, and Aunt Mary said, 'Didn't yer see 'im' Katie, 'ow could yer 'a' missed 'im?'

I nodded, avoiding her eyes, but inwardly I trembled with shame.

''E'll be 'ome tomorrer. We'd best get back, there's a lot

ter do.'

'Don't you want to watch the rest?'

'Nay, we don't know anybody, an' there's bakin' ter be done an' the 'ouse ter be got ready.'

I would have like to have stayed. I loved the sound of the brass bands. But she was pushing her way through the crowd and I had to follow, asking folk to make way for the push chair, listening to their grumbles. Heaven knows the house was as spick and span as the two of us had been able to make it, and as for baking, the larder was filled with pies and puddings, for she had been saving from our meagre rations for weeks in anticipation of Liam's homecoming.

Aunt Mary walked stoutly ahead so that I was almost obliged to run to keep up with her, and many were the disgruntled glances I encountered as people fell foul of the chair wheels. In the side streets she was prattling happily. 'Not a bit different 'e isn't, Katie, except that 'e's filled out a bit. I recognized 'im 'alf a mile off, I'm surprised yer didn't. Oh well, now Liam's 'ome 'e'll soon take over at yard an' yer'll not need ter see as much o' that Mr Abrahams, 'e can deal wi' Liam an' 'is uncle.'

'Liam doesn't know anything about that side of the business,' I retorted.

'Well we shan't be *needin'* that side o' the business now the war's over, the men'll get back ter buildin'. It were only a makeshift.'

I didn't argue, but I was determined that Joe would stay. There would be room for that side of the business, I had worked too hard for it to be shelved now.

For the rest of the day we dusted and polished where it was quite unnecessary and she fussed so much even Uncle Joel said, 'Stop worryin', woman, yer polishin' the varnish off the furniture an' Liam'll noan see all yer doin', 'e never did afore.'

'Two stripes 'e's got, Joel, a corporal. I'm that proud of 'im. Yer'll stop at 'ome now, Katie, an' make 'im a good wife. P'raps next year there'll be a new baby on't way.'

Like a wild thing I felt trapped. And yet wasn't this what was expected from a young wife and mother? What was so different about me that I wished I could take to my heels and never stop running until I had found somewhere to hide, somewhere where I could be myself again, Kathleen O'Donovan, free and unfettered?

But surely I loved Marisa. I adored her. But it was Aunt Mary she went to to dry her tears, Aunt Mary who took her to the shops and knitted endless garments for her. I was just somebody who came home in the evenings, often tired and disinclined for conversation. Yet it was my work that kept me alive, that filled my mental needs. Was I some sort of freak, as inadequate as Jeffrey Carslake?

I had no idea when Liam was coming home, so the following morning I opened up the office as usual. Shortly after ten Maurice entered, looking particularly prosperous and wearing a white carnation, which he took from his buttonhole and laid on the table.

I picked it up absently and held it to my nose.

'Well, Katie,' he began, 'did you see the arrival of the men yesterday?'

'Yes, did you?'

'I watched for a while. Pomp and pageantry will not replace the men who have died.'

'Maurice, what shall I do? Will Liam want me to stay at home, do you think? He has no idea about this side of the business.'

'I don't know, Katie.'

'But who's to see the customers and pay the men's wages, who's to write the letters and order supplies?'

'Who saw to all that before you came on the scene?'

'I suppose Uncle Joel did it, but he's older now and he's never had much interest. All Liam knows is building.'

'They may be disinclined to continue with the furniture side.'

'We can't get rid of Joe, it'd kill him. Besides, it would be ungrateful after all he's done these last years. If they want to finish off all this I'll fight them every inch of the way.'

'Then your married life is going to be one long battle, Katie. Take it gently, don't fight them, convince them.'

'That's the Irish in me, Maurice, I haven't got your

244

temperament, I don't know how to coax and flatter.'

He spread out his hands in the familiar gesture. 'The Jewish temperament comes from a history of coaxing and flattering in order to survive. The Irish have enjoyed beating their heads against a stone wall.'

I laughed into his narrow twinkling eyes.

'I'm going to miss the museums and the art galleries. I don't suppose there'll be many opportunities to visit them when Liam gets home.'

'Whyever not? Take him there, make him see what beautiful things there are in the world. He might even surprise you.'

I did not argue, but I was remembering the Liam Clancy who was never one for the beauty of Horn Head and the wheeling gulls, who had never run across the shining sands looking for seashells or searched for a rainbow beyond the storm clouds.

It was early evening when Liam came home, and I knew his long stride and firm tread before he even opened the door. Aunt Mary was the first to greet him, throwing her arms around his neck while Uncle Joel stood behind her with his outstretched hand. Then Liam was looking into my eyes across the room before I went forward uncertainly into his embrace. Almost immediately Aunt Mary was beside us, holding Marisa by the hand, and he was bending down awkwardly to greet his daughter.

We ate supper and talked, about the war and the yard, about the neighbours and the activities of the church, but of the future nothing was decided, and soon after supper Liam stated his intention of going to bed to catch up on lost sleep. Aunt Mary looked at me meaningly but I busied myself at the table and the kitchen sink. Then I sat with my accounts until, completely exasperated, she snapped, 'Shouldn't yer be wi' Liam after all these long years? Surely them accounts can keep till tomorrer.'

I shook my head. 'Liam's weary, Aunt Mary, and these can't wait.'

It was late when I finally entered the bedroom but I need not have worried. Liam lay sprawled on his back in the middle of the double bed, snoring noisily. I pulled the bedclothes gently round him and crept quietly downstairs, and curled up in the depths of the armchair where I intended to spend the rest of the night.

Chapter 23

Liam was not convinced that I had done my best for the business, indeed he regarded the workmen with a very jaundiced eye and was not forthcoming with any praise for my efforts. The older men were not averse to seeking retirement for the second time in their lives, but I needed Isaac and I needed Joe. Liam looked at their efforts with ill-disguised impatience, which made me angry, and I told him that he should learn to appreciate first-class workmanship that did not involve scaffolding and the erection of large premises.

I showed him the bookcase Isaac had made and which Joe had embellished, but he merely shrugged his shoulders. 'I suppose books 'ave their place, but I'm after buildin' houses an' factories, not playin' bonny wi' bits o' furniture.'

'I don't want you to get rid of Joe. Where else would he find work?'

'He'll be a passenger, Katie, we've no room for passengers.'

'I haven't worked mi fingers to the bone to have it all thrown away now you're back. Joe and Isaac have made money for us and they'll continue to do so. I'll keep them on as *my* part of the business. You owe me that much, Liam Clancy.'

So they stayed and from their efforts I paid their wages and saved every penny I could. Maurice helped me, although he seldom came to the yard now. If I needed him I had to visit his shop or meet him at the restaurant where he took lunch.

On one visit to the city I found myself in St Anne's Square just before lunch time, and I yearned to stay there in the hope of seeing Jeffrey, but common sense got the better

247

of me and I hurried away. I had been a fool long enough.

One day in the summer I took Marisa with me to Marsdale and while I chatted to Uncle Turlough and Aunt Martha, Lucy took her to the swings in the park.

'We're thinkin' o' buyin' a little business over at Copplethorpe,' Uncle Turlough said. 'Newsagents and tobacconist it is, with a nice living room behind the shop and wi' a nice turnover.'

I stared at them in surprise. 'But I thought you were happy here now that you've modernized the house and Uncle Turlough's in full employment.'

'Things are slowin' down,' my uncle replied doefully. 'The government contracts 'ave finished and orders are slow comin' in. Lucy leaves school at the end of August an' I don't want 'er workin' in the mill when work's hard ter get.'

'It'll be a nice little job fer Lucy,' Aunt Martha went on. 'There'll be the mornin' papers ter see to an' we're not doin' any o' this wiout thinking carefully about it.'

'Is Lucy pleased with the idea?'

'Ay, she is.'

They seemed ill at ease and I guessed there was some other reason why they wanted to leave Marsdale. The opportunity came to ask Aunt Martha later in the kitchen.

'There is another reason, Kathleen. The Markhams that Frances went ter live with 'ave come back to the town and our Frances 'as just got 'erself engaged.'

'To somebody in Marsdale?' I said. I hadn't thought of Frances the schoolgirl as now a young woman.

' 'Is father's a solicitor in the town an' they live at the bottom o' the 'ill there. I've never seen the lad but they do say 'is father's in a big way an' 'is mother's one of these women full o' good works in the town. I don't want to see 'er an' I don't want our Lucy to see 'er. When she gets wed we shan't be asked an' I shan't be able to stand the neighbours tellin' me about 'er weddin'.'

'No. That I can understand.'

'She's gettin' wed mid September, I 'ear, an' by that time we'll be in our business over at Copplethorpe. I'll be that busy settlin' and learnin' about the business I'll not 'ave much time for thinkin'.'

'No. I don't believe I have ever disliked anybody quite as much as I dislike Fanny, Aunt Martha. What sort of woman is she, what sort of a wife is she going to make for any man? Doesn't this man see her for the superficial woman she is, or is he too besotted to care?'

'Nobody could be nicer than our Fanny when she had a mind ter be. She was so pretty an' she could make yer feel that proud when she were sweet and nice ter people.'

'Well, I saw very little of that side of her, what I did see was her petulance and her unattractive snobbery. I thought she was a little monster, and I still do.'

'It'll 'urt Turlough, yer know, not ter be givin' 'er away.'

'Oh, wouldn't I just like to give that little monkey a piece of my mind.'

'Ay. Well, save that fer yer own daughter, Kathleen. When our Fanny were the same age as Marisa we didn't know what we were in fer.'

I reflected on this during the journey home as I sat watching my little girl leafing through a picture book Lucy had given her. She was so pretty with her dresden-china daintiness and her cornsilk hair. She looked up and smiled, the smile that captivated Liam and endeared her to everybody she met, but instinctively I found myself distrusting it. Then with an impatient frown I told myself not to be foolish. Marisa was nothing like Frances Cassidy. Marisa was a normal sunny child who would grow up loving us and needing us.

As we entered the house Aunt Mary greeted me with the news that I had a visitor, and picking up Marisa took her into the kitchen for hot milk and biscuits.

It was Polly who waited for me in the living room, sitting at the table where Aunt Mary had evidently given her tea. Her eyes lit up and I went forward to embrace her.

'Why, Polly,' I exclaimed, 'you should have let me know you were coming.'

249

'I made up mi mind sudden like. It's not easy ter talk ter Cook, an' I'd rather talk ter you anyway.'

'Let me get out of mi hat, then, and I'll bring in some hot tea. I shan't keep you a minute.'

Aunt Mary looked at me meaningly while I brewed another pot of tea. 'It's 'er 'usband,' she whispered. 'She wants ter talk to yer about 'im.'

'Is he alive, then?'

'Ay, but yer'd best get back, I don't want 'er ter think I'm discussin' 'im.'

I hurried back and helped us both to tea. She sipped it nervously, while I looked for some sign of joy that George was alive.

She blurted her news out to me in short jerky sentences.

'He's alive, Katie. Taken prisoner 'e was, sufferin' fro' shell shock. I heard fro' the War Office. I've bin ter see 'im in 'ospital, 'e'll be comin' 'ome soon.'

'How is he, Polly?'

' 'E didn't know me at first. 'E does now, but 'e's not the George 'e used ter be.'

'How do you mean?'

'Well, 'e doesn't remember much an 'e forgets things that 'appened only yesterday. The only thing 'e remembers is gardenin'. 'E loves flowers an' plants, they 'ave 'im gardenin' up at the 'ospital.'

'Then he's going to be able to do his old job, Polly. Is he being taken back?'

'Oh ay, the major says 'e can 'ave 'is job back 'an we can 'ave that little cottage nearby, but it's not goin' ter be the same, Katie. George doesn't really want a wife, 'e doesn't allus want ter talk ter me, not even when I've travelled all that way ter see 'im.'

'It'll be different when you have your own home, Polly, an' your own furniture about you. You're goin' to have to be very patient, you do see that, don't you?'

'I suppose so. I've been offered a bit o' part-time work at Heatherlea, but I don't rightly know 'ow long they're goin' ter go on living there. The colonel's a sick man an' the mistress seems ter 'ave aged a 'undred years.'

'But Mister Jeffrey's home now?'

'Ay, but there's not the money about. The mill's on short time again an' there's talk o' big combines takin' over most o' the factories.'

'But surely the Carslakes won't lose by it, there'll be good jobs for the Carslake boys.'

'Oh ay, Mr Ambrose an' Mr Jeffrey'll be made managers, but Cook sez the old days've gone. She were right, weren't she, Katie?'

'Right about what, Polly?'

'Why about all them 'eathens comin' over fro' the Far East an' us showin' 'em 'ow to weave cotton and run the mills. Now they're takin' our orders an' doin' 'em for 'alf the price.'

'How can they do that?'

'Slave labour, that's what it is, that's what Cook sez anyway.'

'What about the Foxland mills, are they going into a combine too?'

'Old Mr Foxland's retired an' they've gone ter live somewhere in the Ribble valley ter be near Miss Lois. Yer won't know about 'er, will yer, Katie. In a wheelchair she is, an' they do say 'er 'usband's 'ad 'is 'ouse made so that she can get about wiout 'avin ter be pushed all the time.'

'I knew about Miss Lois, Polly. It's terrible sad for all of them.'

'It is, an' 'er allus so dainty an' pretty. A wonder what Mister Jeffrey thinks about 'er, an' 'im allus so much i' love wi' 'er.'

'Does he visit them, Polly?'

'That I don't know, Katie. 'E seems ter spend all 'is time walkin' on the moors an' ridin' that 'orse of 'is. They've only one groom workin' at the stables now, an' only one gardener. Cuttin' down right left an' centre, they are. Cook sez our jobs aren't worth a fig an' they could finish tomorrer.'

'Did all the men come back safely from the war, Polly?'

'All except Ned. 'E were killed on the Somme. My, but 'e used ter fancy yer, Katie, but yer never even looked in 'is

251

direction.'

I was sorry about Ned. I hadn't liked him spying on me, particularly when he related my comings and goings to Cook, but I was sad to hear that he had been killed.

As I walked with Polly to the station, listening to her talk about the changes that were happening in what seemed like every household on Tremayne Hill, I felt inordinately sad. It seemed that a whole way of life was ending and the future was shrouded with uncertainty.

What sort of England would my daughter grow up in, I wondered, and if the old gentry left their big houses on Tremayne Hill what sort of people would take their place? Money would take the place of breeding, and I thought about my cousin Fanny and the boy she was expecting to marry. Would they be the newly rich who might aspire to the properties vacated by the old order?

One thing was sure. I was going to work hard and save every penny. Marisa was going to be somebody in the new way of life that seemed inevitable, if I had to scheme and shape her future every step of the way.

Chapter 24

Only months after Liam's return from the war I realized I could not continue to live with his aunt and uncle. It was not my home and I had no say in the running of it. Aunt Mary was the organizer, and insisted on shopping for our food as well as theirs. When I remonstrated with her over this she merely said, 'Well, you're all tied up wi' that business o' yours, and it's easier shoppin' for us all.'

She doted on Marisa and Liam and they bothed seemed quite content to bask in her adoration while I grew more frustrated with every day. The crunch came one evening. Liam and I had been invited to a builders' dinner in the city and I dressed happily in the gown I had worn for the concert I had attended with Maurice, then I hunted in the wardrobe and the drawers in our bedrooms for the wrap he had given me. When I could not find it I went downstairs to ask Aunt Mary if she had seen it.

Her face flushed bright crimson and I had never thought to see her look so uncomfortable.

'I didn't think yer'd want ter wear it again, Katie. Liam's not one fer concerts and the like.'

'What have you done with it, Aunt Mary?'

'Well it were allus wrapped up at the top o' yer wardrobe, probably collectin' moths. I shook it out every week but I didn't like it up there.'

'Where is it, Aunt Mary?'

'I never thowt yer'd want it, besides Liam wouldn't 'a' liked yer to wear somethin' that Maurice gave yer. I asked Father O'Reilly's 'ousekeeper if she'd like it. She's a great one fer 'er concerts, they're allus off into the city fer some concert or another.'

Rage filled me and it took all the power I could muster to

253

control it.

'You had no right to give anything that belonged to me away, and she had absolutely no right to take it. Surely she knew it belonged to me.'

'Ay, and when I told 'er who'd given it ter yer she agreed yer shouldn't be wearin' it now yer 'usband's 'ome.'

'I'll bet she did. Well when I see her I'll tell her a thing or two about wearin' other people's property. The wrap belonged to Mrs Abrahams and it was kind of Maurice to give it to me. Why couldn't you have asked me if I intended to wear it again?'

'I shouldn't 'ave to ask about anythin' in mi own 'ouse.'

'It's a cruel and wicked thing you've done, Aunt Mary, you should be ashamed of yourself and so should Mrs Minty for takin' it. I shall tell her so miself.'

'Yer'll be needin' ter go to the church ter tell 'er anythin', an' yer've bin conspicuous by yer absence these last few months.'

'And tricks like this don't exactly encourage me to attend. It wasn't a Christian thing to do, Aunt Mary.'

Liam came in. 'What's goin' on now, then? The neighbours'll 'ear you the length of the street.'

Quickly I explained about the wrap, but Aunt Mary interrupted me to tell him how I had come by it, and, most galling of all, she ended with, 'I thowt it'd save trouble between you and 'er. I knew yer wouldn't want 'er ter wear that wrap 'e'd given 'er.'

'That I don't,' Liam said. 'Hurry up and get ready, the taxi'll be 'ere directly, an' yer not got yer coat on yet.'

It was no use. No argument of mine could combat the stand they made together, but I was determined that after this night I would find somewhere else for us to live. I would take Marisa and Liam away from Aunt Mary. She'd got her own way with me for the very last time.

Every day for the new few weeks I walked about the area looking at houses with For Sale signs in their windows or front gardens but it was a woman who came into the yard seeking some joinery work on her back windows who made up my mind for me.

'We're movin' away ter live with our son an' 'is wife,' she informed me, 'but I'm right sorry ter be leaving mi nice little 'ouse.'

'Is it very near here?' I asked her.

'It's three streets away, opposite the little park in Edgley Road. It's a terraced 'ouse but we 'ave a little bathroom an' a nice little garden front and back.'

'Do you think I could come round and look at it?'

'Certainly yer can. Are you wantin' somethin' for yerself, then?'

'Yes, and pretty quickly.'

'Yer'll be wantin' ter bring yer 'usband with yer, then?'

'No, he'll leave it to me, I'm sure, but I might bring my little girl.'

I made arrangements to go in the early evening and, although they were all present in the living room when I left with Marisa, the two men seemed uninterested in where I was going and Aunt Mary had begun to learn that our relationship had changed. I no longer confided in her or felt inclined to answer her questions.

I knew immediately I entered the house that this was what I wanted. It had a neat little parlour and a comfortable living room overlooking a long back garden. There was a good-sized kitchen and two good-sized bedrooms, but it was the bathroom I cared about most. The house shone with cleanliness and as we went from room to room, in my mind I was already arranging furniture and ornaments.

We had very little of anything. The bookcase Isaac had made me and a coffee table Maurice had given me. It was doubtful if Aunt Mary would allow us to take our bedroom furniture, but I had every faith that Maurice would help me. I placed no faith in Liam, indeed I was not even sure that he would leave his aunt's house to live with me, but I was determined to fight for what I wanted for my daughter.

'I'll tell you in the morning,' I told the owner. 'I'll speak to mi husband tonight but this house is just what I want.'

When Marisa was tucked up in her bed I faced the three

255

of them across the table, telling them exactly where I had been and that I wanted this house, and quickly.

The dismay was on their faces was evident and at another time I might have been amused by it, but not now.

Aunt Mary wept and accused me of ingratitude. Uncle Joel said nothing but sat there sucking on his empty pipe. Only Liam concerned me, however, and he sat there indecisive, looking from his aunt to me with increasing frustration, not quite knowing which way to jump.

Then Aunt Mary started to cry, great choking sobs accompanied by tears which rolled down her round face in ever-increasing volume, and consternation took the place of doubt on Liam's face.

'You've no right to upset mi aunt like this, Katie. Hasn't she given you and our daughter a home while I've bin away, an' hasn't mi uncle said the business'll be mine one day?'

'Yes I'm grateful for all that, Liam, but there wouldn't have been any business or much money if it had been left to your uncle. We should have our own home and we should bring up our daughter ourselves. Please, Liam, it's a lovely little house and it's only a little way from here. At least you should take a look at it.'

'We're comfortable enough here, I don't see why you're wantin' to move.'

'I want what every married woman wants, a home of my own. I'm a lodger here and well you know it.'

'I've allus tried ter do mi best fer you all,' Aunt Mary wailed, 'now yer wants ter leave an' take the child with yer. Well, she'll not want ter leave her Aunt Mary, I'll tell yer that. She thinks more o' me than she thinks of 'er mother, that I can tell yer.'

She was not intelligent enough to realize that by those words she had signed her own death warrant. Triumphantly my eyes met Liam's and he looked away quickly, but I knew I had won. I stood up and said calmly, 'We'll go round in the morning, Liam. Marisa loved the garden and the park is right opposite.'

'Yer've no furniture,' Aunt Mary said vindicatively. 'It's

goin' ter cost yer a fortune.'

'We'll get furniture.'

'I suppose that Maurice'll be 'elpin yer.'

'If I asked for help he would give it willingly, but we're going to have to get furniture like every other young couple. We'll manage, Aunt Mary.'

'And who's ter look after the child while yer at the yard?'

'She's old enough to start school. I shall take her there in the morning before I go to the yard, and I shall meet her at twelve and when school has finished in the afternoon.'

'It won't take yer long to realize 'ow much I've done fer yer. Yer'll soon get fed up o' what yer lettin' yerself in for.'

'Oh, Aunt Mary, we're not going to live on the other side of the world, we're just moving round the corner. And Marisa loves you, she'll be in to see you every day, I feel sure. Now I'm going to make a cup of tea. Does anybody else want one?'

In spite of all his reluctance Liam liked the house across from the park, but when the owner had gone into the kitchen to make coffee he whispered, 'Can we afford to be buyin' it?'

'Yes we can. All through the war I saved money. I paid Aunt Mary for our livin' there and lookin' after Marisa out of your allowance, and I saved mi wages. Uncle Joel gave me an increase an' I saved that, so we can afford this house.'

I decided to say nothing about the money my grandmother had left me. There would be many times in my married life when Liam would question my spending, and I had an eye on Marisa's education, which I was determined she would get.

'But what about the furniture?' he asked.

'We'll get by. I'll go to salerooms and buy what we need.'

'I don't want that Maurice helpin' yer.'

'You shouldn't listen to Aunt Mary, Liam. Maurice has been a good friend to me and nothing more. If you don't want his help I'll not ask him for any, but you'll be cuttin' off your nose to spite your face, that's what you'll be doin'.'

257

His face was sulky, unsure, but just then Mrs Haslam came in from the kitchen carrying a loaded tray.

'I couldn't 'elp over'earing yer talkin' about furniture, luv. We 'ave a bit fer sale, an' we shan't be wantin' much for it, we've 'ad it since we were wed.'

My eyes brightened visibly, and even Liam looked up with interest.

'What have you for sale?' I asked eagerly.

'Well, most of it. Yer see, mi son's 'ouse is fully furnished an' they were 'opin' we wouldn't be taking much with us.'

I couldn't believe our good fortune or that we had enough money for everything. By the time we had finished my bank balance was sadly diminished but, as I was leaving the yard on Friday evening, Uncle Joel called me over to his little office at the top of some crumbling stone steps near the entrance to the yard.

' 'Ere's a hundred pounds for yer, Katie. I don't 'old wi' everythin' Mary's done, but she's mi wife and I 'ave to live with 'er.'

I threw my arms round his neck and kissed his cheek warmly.

'Put it in the bank, luv, and don't say owt ter Liam. Most o' yer own money's gone on that 'ouse. Does that include the money yer grandmother left yer?'

'No, I still have that. But even if I'd spent it mi grandmother'd think I'd spent wisely for once.'

'Yer intends keepin' on at the yard, Katie?'

'Yes. I want the best for Marisa, I want her to have a good education and a good job when the time comes.'

'Eh lass, there's not many good jobs for women, 'cept i' shops an' the factories.'

'There will be, Uncle Joel. Times are changing and my daughter isn't going into any factory or into service either.'

He shook his head ruefully. 'Yer've got some high an' mighty ideas, Katie, I just 'opes they don't let yer down.'

'They won't,' I assured him. I now had a hundred and thirty-five pounds in the bank, and I was going to add to it.

Chapter 25

As I decorated the cake for Marisa's fifteenth birthday I found myself reflecting on the many changes the years had wrought. We stayed in that small terraced house for three years and then I found I was pregnant again and even Liam decided the house would be on the small side for four of us, particularly if the new baby was a boy.

My son Arthur was born four weeks prematurely and lived for only three days. At first they thought I too might die but with the resilience peculiar to my character I survived, although the doctors warned me I should not think of having another child for some considerable time. Aunt Martha came to look after me until I was stronger, and Liam sulked, so that I felt I had failed him lamentably in not producing the perfect son he had longed for.

Marisa was doing very well at a girls' private school I had moved heaven and earth to get her into, and we were now installed in a larger house on the outskirts of Marsdale. Liam had acquired a motor car. It was not new but it had been well looked after by its previous owner and it was a reasonably ostentatious model. He had also acquired a mistress by the name of Geraldine McClusky, about whom I was not supposed to know anything, although I had been aware of her existence for several years.

We no longer shared the same bed, since Liam had little patience in making love to his wife unless it was for the procreation of children. A mistress was something different, a mistress was for loving, a wife was for increasing the population. I was not averse to this arrangement. I did not love Liam but I was a good wife to him. I kept the house nice and I kept a good table. I loved and cared for Marisa, her well-being and her wants, and she was mighty good at wanting. When I accompanied Liam to functions in the city I sat besides him wearing elegant clothes and jewellery, admired by the men and frequently envied by the women, and I was glad that I had kept my slender figure and graceful carriage.

My auburn hair had lost none of its lustre and I knew I had good taste in both clothes and jewellery, most of which I bought for myself out of the money I was making in the fine furniture and antique business I had embarked upon in partnership with Maurice Abrahams.

Uncle Joel had been retired two years and the business now belonged to Liam. He managed to squeeze me out gradually over the years and was not pleased that I knew how to recognize a good piece of furniture or a fine picture, nor was he pleased when I was offered a partnership with Maurice. He frequently accused me of having got above myself and forgotten what life had been like in Donegal. I hadn't forgotten, I just didn't see why I constantly had to remember it.

He accused me of trying to lose the Irish accent I should have been proud of, and asked me why I thought it necessary to acquire an upper-crust English accent which I had no right to.

'You should be remembering that the English are our old enemy,' he argued. 'Didn't they invade Ireland and fill it with Scots they'd been glad to get rid of? This should never be forgotten or forgiven, Katie O'Donovan.'

'Then what are we doing here?' I asked. 'Why aren't we back in Donegal scratchin' a livin' from the soil?'

'I'm sayin' we should remember, that's all. The English owe us somethin', we've every right to be livin' 'ere.'

'Well, the English were invaded by the Normans in 1066, I haven't noticed them nursing their bitterness to posterity.'

'You think you know everything, don't you? Well just you be rememberin' that you're Irish, not English. You should be proud to be Irish.'

'Oh I am, in spite of the fact that Ireland's done nothin' for me and when everythin' I have and am is because we're over here.'

It was an argument he constantly lost and he hated losing it. I believe there were times when he actively disliked me. Liam had never been good with words even as a schoolboy, and I had always had a sharp tongue in my head.

There were days when I smiled to myself to see him riding off in his motor car, dressed in his best weekend tweeds and with a flower in his buttonhole, oblivious to the fact that I knew perfectly well that he was calling for Miss Geraldine McClusky before setting off for the races.

Geraldine was a big, raw-boned girl with a wealth of blue-black hair and a pair of bright blue eyes, and she was good-looking. Whenever we met on the street she greeted me respectfully, and more so when I visited the yard, where she acted as Liam's secretary.

Uncle Joel and Aunt Mary came for lunch every other Sunday, and Aunt Mary made no bones of informing me that Geraldine was worth her weight in gold to the business. She was a good girl at home and looked after her widowed father and four younger brothers and sisters devotedly. She was a good Catholic girl and wasn't ashamed to be seen with her sleeves rolled up working around the church.

Privately I believed her work around the church was a penance, after confessing her sins, but I said nothing to Aunt Mary. Self-opinionated as always, and perhaps even more so with her increasing years, she was ill-disposed to hearing anything detrimental about Geraldine McClusky, and it suited me to appear oblivious to Liam's wanderings. There seemed no point in making an issue out of something that was relatively unimportant to me.

My thoughts were dragged back into the present by the sound of girls' voices, and then Marisa was in the kitchen with six of her friends, all enthusing over my efforts with her cake.

'Everything's laid out in the dining room. Put your things in the cloakroom on your way in there,' I advised.

The party was a success. I was pleased with the way I

261

had laid out the buffet meal and there was plenty to eat, then we stood round watching her open her presents. She was a popular girl and she was pretty. She was tall for her age and slender, with Liam's pale blond hair, although in Marisa's case it was fine and shining.

I had given her an evening bag covered with pearl and silver beads, a pretty extravagant thing, but she was attending parties all over the place and I thought it was something she should have. She got a great many gifts from her friends, and from her father a single row of cultured pearls with a heavy gold clasp. She had chosen it herself and he had merely paid for it. As I fastened it round her slender neck I debated on whether Liam had even seen it.

Marisa played the piano and the girls gathered round and sang in clear young voices while I cleared away the remains of the feast with the help of Mrs Laurie, our daily.

'She's a lucky young woman wi' all them presents an' all that food,' Mrs Laurie said somewhat sourly. 'I 'ope she appreciates it.'

'I'm sure she does, Mrs Laurie, but she's all we have, we have to do all we can for her.'

'Yer can spoil a child wi' too much,' she muttered. 'My three children'll 'ave ter do wi' less.'

I found a large box in the pantry and began to fill it with a selection of food, finally cutting a huge chunk of cake which I wrapped up in a serviette. She watched curiously and I said, 'If this is too heavy for you to carry, perhaps Mr Laurie would come for it this evening. I've made a little parcel of clothes up for you, mostly things Marisa has outgrown.'

'Yer very good to us, Mrs Clancy, I expects yer thinks I'm allus grumbling.'

'It's hard trying to manage when there's not much money coming in, Mrs Laurie. I understand about things like that, we haven't always been so well placed.'

'I likes polishin' yer furniture, Mrs Clancy. I tells mi 'usband 'ow beautiful it is but I'm that frightened o' breaking yer china. Valuable, isn't it?'

'Some of it is valuable. I've enjoyed collecting it.'

'Does Mr Clancy like pictures an' the like?'

'He doesn't like anything that isn't functional, he's more interested in building houses than in what goes in them.'

'My, but that Geraldine McClusky doesn't 'alf give 'erself airs since she got that job at yer 'usband's firm. It might be 'er firm for all the airs an' graces she puts on.'

I didn't answer, and slyly she went on, 'She's smartened 'erself up these days, allus somethin' new she 'as in church on Sundays. I reckon yer 'usband must pay 'er a tidy wage for 'er to afford all them falderals.'

'I have no idea how much he pays her, Mrs Laurie.'

'Yer'd see 'ow she dresses if yer went ter church more, Mrs Clancy.'

It was an accusation I chose to ignore. 'You'll soon be finished, Mrs Laurie. Put the catch on the door when you leave, I shall be in the sitting room.'

I wondered how many people knew about Geraldine, and inwardly I became angry that Liam had chosen to play around with an employee. It wasn't fair to Marisa and it wasn't fair to me. Perhaps I didn't deserve fairness from him but I had been a faithful wife, though I didn't love him. I wondered somewhat savagely if any of the girls laughing with Marisa around the piano knew that her father was playing around.

The girls left just before seven o'clock. Liam had not returned, and somewhat sulkily Marisa said, 'Doesn't my father know it's my birthday?'

'Of course he does, darling, didn't he buy you the pearls? Something must have detained him.'

Although she had a book in her hands I knew she was not reading it. There was a frown on her pretty face, and I could tell that something was worrying her.

Eventually she said, 'Mother, do we have to go to Grange for our holidays this year? We never seem to go anywhere else.'

'You've never said anything about it before, dear.'

'I know, but I'm so fed up with it, aren't you?'

'Well, it's a very good centre for the Lake District and the hotel is nice.'

'Can't you persuade Father to take us somewhere else instead?'

We had gone to Grange-over-Sands for our annual holidays since the first year after the war. Liam was a creature of habit and I knew his mind did not extend beyond the regulated sameness of our lives. The aunt and uncle every other Sunday, Grange in the summer, Aunt Mary's Christmas Day, Aunt Martha's New Year and the same functions in the same hotels throughout the winter. I had grave doubts that he would take kindly to altering the summer vacation.

'If you don't want to go to Grange, where do you want to go?' I asked.

'All the other girls go abroad with their parents, they go to Italy and France and Switzerland. Why can't we?'

'Gracious me, your father'd never go abroad. He doesn't even want to cross the water to Ireland.'

'Well, he's always going on about Ireland. My friends will all come back talking about Europe while all I can talk about is silly old Grange and those dark lakes and mountains. Will you ask him when he comes in, Mother?'

She had come to sit on the rug near my chair, looking up at me with those big dark blue eyes of hers, and I could only feel that I was going to disappoint her. I knew that Liam would not take us abroad. He didn't like foreigners and he didn't like travel. He would want to go where he could drive us in the car, and Grange was just about far enough. Liam was not a long-distance driver, he preferred short trips and a degree of comfort at the other end of his journey.

'I'll talk to him when he comes in, Marisa. Now how about getting on with your homework?'

I could tell immediately Liam came through the door that he had had a frustrating day. Tonight instead of burying his face in the newspaper as usual, he snapped, 'I've had a hell of a day. The timber didn't arrive and Boswell came down to the yard an' started throwin' his weight about. You'd have thought I'd done it deliberately. Threatened to cancel unless the premises were complete by the end of July. What can I do when the orders don't arrive?'

'You have a secretary,' I said sweetly. 'Couldn't she have hurried the timber through for you, or at least make inquiries as to why it was late?'

He scowled. 'What are all those parcels lyin' about there?'

'Had you forgotten it was Marisa's birthday? They are her presents.'

His face coloured. 'I had forgotten. I've had too much to remember today. Is she in the house?'

'She is. Upstairs doing her homework, so I'd rather you didn't disturb her just now. I'll see to your meal.'

'It's mi daughter's birthday, Katie, you've surely no objections to mi wishin' her many happy returns. I'll eat in the kitchen, you needn't take the food into the dining room.'

I bit my lip in exasperation. Liam always had the unhappy knack of putting me in the wrong. He had blithely forgotten her birthday until I had reminded him. Now he would fuss over her as though she had been in his thoughts all day.

I grilled steak and cooked vegetables and, because he didn't care for sweet things, I laid out cheese and biscuits for afterwards. He sat down with a satisfied nod to eat the meal I set in front of him.

When he returned to the sitting room he immediately hid his head behind the newspaper, and in some annoyance I snapped, 'Have you thought about the summer holiday at Grange?'

He lowered his paper and looked over it in some surprise. 'The hotel's booked. What's there to think about?'

'Marisa doesn't want to go.'

'Well she's too young to go off with her friends, or her friends' folks, so she comes with us as usual.'

'She is quite happy to come with us, but not to Grange. She thinks it's time we had a change.'

'What's wrong with Grange?'

'Nothing at all except that she's never been anywhere else. It is limiting her, particularly when her friends talk about where they've been.'

'Oh, and where's that then?'

'Italy, Switzerland and France perhaps.'

'I had all the abroad I wanted during the war, I'm certainly not spending my holiday there.'

'It was different then, Liam, the war's been over a long time. Marisa is growing up and should see more of the world, and if not abroad, then more of England or even Ireland.'

'Why should we alter all our arrangements just because those silly people go abroad every summer? A lot of snobs that's what they are, as though this country wasn't good enough. We're not letting her have her own way about this, Katie. You'll tell Marisa we want to go to Grange and she's not spoiling it for us.'

'I too want a change from Grange. You booked and didn't even ask us. Why shouldn't we go somewhere else?'

He stared at me in amazement. 'Where do you want to go, then? You've never said anything about wantin' a change before.'

'I'm not sure. What's so wrong about wanting to go to Europe?'

'Well, if you goes you goes on your own. I shan't be comin' with you.'

'You'd let us go on our own, Liam?'

'If you're so set on it, I would. I wouldn't be happy in Grange with both of you sulkin' at me.'

'What would you do then?'

'I wouldn't be wantin' to stay at Grange on mi own, would I, settin' all their tongues a-waggin'? Don't we meet the same people there year after year?'

'What will you do, then?' I didn't really need to ask, I knew exactly what Liam would be doing, and he confirmed it.

'Oh, I'll get out to the race tracks and play a bit more golf.'

I felt pretty sure Geraldine McClusky would not accompany him to the golf club, but I had no doubt she would be with him at the race meetings.

I was soon overwhelmed with Marisa's talk of the South of France and Italy and I picked up brochures in the shops

266

and wrote off for others. I did not want to go to the South of France without a man, it seemed too busy and sophisticated, and I did not want Marisa's friends to think they should look after us.

It was Maurice who said, 'Why not go to Italy? The cities are beautiful and full of history, and the coast is fabulous, but you would like the Italian lakes. They are surely the most beautiful scenery on God's earth.'

When he saw that I was still unsure, he prompted, 'Dotted around Lake Como are the most beautiful villages in the world. Try Bellagio or Tremezzo. From either of them you could visit Venice and Milan, you could see Lake Garda and Lake Maggiore, and Switzerland is on the doorstep.'

'I'm not sure about Marisa.'

'She wants to go abroad, doesn't she? Why follow the fleshpots, Katie? Let Marisa see real beauty and absorb a little culture at the same time.'

'She's a little young to think about culture. She's more inclined to prefer lazing all day on a beach and splashing about in the sea.'

'All of which she could have done at Grange.'

'The sun is often reluctant to shine at Grange, Maurice.'

He laughed at that. 'Never mind Marisa for a moment, Katie . Where do *you* want to go?'

'Somewhere beautiful and peaceful, Maurice. I want to linger in old towns and cities where old times have not been forgotten. I want to listen to good music and see nature at its most spectacular. I want to recapture the sort of values I grew up with and seem to have lost with the years. Oh Maurice, how do I know what I want? Life's been nothing like I wanted it to be.'

'Life seldom is, Katie, but you've come a long way from that girl who first came into my shop seeking the price of a corner cupboard.'

'How? How have I come a long way?'

'You're a beautiful woman, Katie, with soaring ideals, ideals that are hardly likely to be filled if you stay with Liam.'

267

'He's my husband, Maurice.'

'I know, but you don't love him, Katie, you never have. Why did you marry him?'

'It seemed so easy to marry Liam. We'd always known one another and there were pressures from our families at the beginning of the war. He's not a bad man, Maurice. He's unimaginative and none too generous, but I've failed him in so many ways. I have to make up for that by making a good home for him. Besides, he adores Marisa.'

'In a little while, Katie, you'll hear the whisperings; the talk and scandal about that girl in his office. Liam isn't subtle enough to keep his mistress in the background and that young woman will not be satisfied to stay in it. She loves him more than you do, Katie.'

'Nothing permanent will come of it, Maurice. Liam won't ask me for a divorce so that he can marry her.'

'Does that mean that you are going to sit back and condone it? Why should you, Katie? In time it could hurt you both, you and Marisa.'

'Why should I do anything? Liam is happy enough with his comfortable home and his mistress. I'm happy with my work and I save every penny Liam gives me for Marisa. I'm his housekeeper, not his wife, and he's never quite forgiven me for the death of his son. I hate myself for the times I despise him. If Liam was a faithful husband I wouldn't deserve him, as we are we deserve each other.'

He shook his head sadly, then with a wry smile he said, 'But you did love somebody once, didn't you?'

'Yes, and quite ridiculously as it turned out. I was so young, just out of the egg; I still had feathers sticking all over me. I thought I knew everything there was to know about love but I knew nothing at all. The man I thought I loved didn't love me, I doubt if he had the capacity to love any woman. I never think about him now.'

'You are quite sure about that?'

'Only to think what a fool I was, how naive and abysmally stupid.'

'You know I care for you, don't you Katie?'

'Yes, Maurice, I do, and you are very important to me. I

shall never fall in love again.'

'You will, Katie. How old are you, thirty-four? A very beautiful woman with so much spirit stagnating in this backwater you call life. There'll be somebody else some day, Katie, and he could change your whole life.'

'Then I don't want to meet him. I have a daughter and a husband. I'm set in my ways and I can't afford for anything to change. I was only a little girl when I learned not to search for rainbows, they're too quickly gone. That was the first truth I ever learned; there's been a good deal more since, but love, Maurice Abrahams, is something I can do without.'

Chapter 26

Marisa was so pleased to be going abroad, she showed little desire to dictate the destination, and allowed me to make the booking. I took Maurice's advice and made all arrangements to visit Tremezzo on Lake Como at the end of July. I would have preferred to go earlier but we had to wait for the end of term at her school.

We crossed the Channel in a fine drizzle of rain, but nothing could have dampened our spirits, not even the sight of Liam's tall figure receding into the distance as the train pulled out of the station in Manchester.

A gentleman assisted us with our luggage and saw us settled into our first-class compartment in France. It was night, but I was still wide awake when the train started its journey across France and into Switzerland.

As long as I live I will remember the sight of those majestic peaks covered with snow as the train snaked its way through the emerald-green fields of Switzerland. This was the view that met my eyes when I raised the blind the next morning.

They filled the horizon like a frieze from some musical-comedy setting, exquisite peaks coated with sugar icing. The train thundered past villages where delightful wooden chalets edged quaint village streets, their walls decorated with colourful murals, their window boxes filled with geraniums and begonias. There were lakes too, blue enchanting stretches of water, and the sun shone warm and golden so that the people lunching in the dining car appeared smiling and carefree.

We left the train at Lugano, where a car waited to take us the remaining miles. It was an enchanting ride along the banks of Lake Lugano, through groves of orange and lemon trees. Then from the top of a mountain pass we saw Lake Como, dreaming deep blue and silver, far below. It lay like a huge letter Y, overpowered by the mountains, and along its rim were strung tiny fishing villages, their red roofs gleaming in the sunlight. I was enchanted, with the shimmering lake and the dramatic backdrop of mountains, with tall stately dark cypresses reaching heavenwards in the gardens of sugar icing villas, and with the aura of peace that lay over the most beautiful scenery I had ever seen. The peasants we met on the way bobbed quaint country curtsies, and now and again an old man ambled past with his donkey, or dark-eyed children ran to the windows of the car, holding out posies of wild flowers.

At Tremezzo, gardens edged the lake, and across the narrow promenade stretched an avenue of shops, with others meandering up shallow steps above the town. Ferry boats plied across the lakes but, before we could absorb more, the car was pulling up before the doors of a palatial hotel and the doorman, a striking figure in his green and gold livery, was holding the car door open for us.

The foyer was majestic with its marble floor and shallow marble stairs, crystal chandeliers and velvet chairs. There were flowers and plants everywhere, and behind the desk stood smiling dark-eyed men and woman anxious to be of service.

I was glad that my travelling attire was fashionable and in good taste, and that Marisa's pretty navy and white dress with its snowy collar and cuffs looked fresh and charming.

We followed the boy with our luggage into the lift, and soon he was unlocking our bedroom doors and flinging open the windows so that we could walk out on to our balcony. It was too perfect, like every picture postcard I had ever seen. Then for the first time I looked into Marisa's face and saw doubt and disappointment there.

'Why, what is it, darling? Don't you think it's absolutely beautiful?'

'But the hotel's so stuffy, Mother, and they all look so old.'

'Who does, dear? I haven't seen any old people.'

'Of course not, you were talking to the people at the desk. All those people sitting in the foyer were old, with walking sticks and grey hair.'

'I'm sure they're not *all* old; it's very hot outside, I expect the older ones rest in the afternoon. The young people will be out enjoying themselves. Look over there, the ferry seems to be filled with people, and those people sailing will be young.'

'Oh Mother, why couldn't we go to the coast? There's no beach here and no sea. What shall we do all day?'

'We shall go sailing, look at all those lovely little villages, and we'll go to Milan to see La Scala, and surely you want to see Venice. I thought all the people in the world wanted to see Venice.'

'I don't want to spend all the holiday travelling about in a bus or a train, I want to lie in the sun and get brown. We never get the chance at home.'

I stared at her in dismay.

They were Liam's eyes that stared at me accusingly and I began to have doubts about this holiday I had arranged with such joy. Perhaps for the first time I was seeing that Marisa was not like me. She was more like Liam, with all Liam's indolence, for she had contributed nothing to the preparation for our holiday but was now busy finding fault with it.

Liam had no interest in history unless it was the bigotry of Ireland. He was happy in the present and if the present didn't suit him then he looked to the future. He said the past was gone for ever, so why take the trouble to worry about it? Whereas I believed the past had shaped the present and the present would shape the future.

I knew now that if I took Marisa to some of Italy's oldest cities, she would merely wander round their streets in sulky silence, bored and resentful, and she would spoil it for me. The resentment in her heart would ignore the beauty of sunlit squares and ancient art. By this time I was heartily wishing we had gone to Grange.

'Why not go across to the lake while I unpack?' I

encouraged her. 'We can meet in the foyer for tea in about an hour's time.'

'I don't want to go on my own.'

'The cases won't unpack themselves, so you can help me unpack and we will go down together.'

Going out was preferable to helping with the luggage, however, and, watching from the balcony, I saw her sauntering across the road looking neither to right nor left, kicking the dust with her sandals and then idly picking up pebbles and tossing them into the lake. There was boredom in every line of her dainty figure, boredom and resentment, and I turned away with a feeling of acute disappointment.

She was in no happier frame of mind when she returned an hour later, and she was quick to inform me that the shops were tiny and they all sold the same things – musical boxes, peasant dolls and silk scarves – that the cakes were stodgy and the fruit covered in flies. The people sailing were quite as old as me, and I was to look at the old people sitting in the foyer, two of them actually in wheelchairs.

Finally I was stung to retort, 'Marisa, you haven't given yourself time to like the place, you are determined you won't like it. In fact you are behaving like a silly spoilt child.'

'No I'm not; it's just nothing like I thought it would be.'

'Well, why not be glad that it's different? When your friends are talking about their beach holidays you can talk about the lake and the mountains and all the lovely places you have visited.'

'I wanted the sea and the beach, you never asked me.'

'No and you never said what you wanted, only that you wanted to go abroad. You haven't got the sea and the beach, have you, so you'll just have to make the best of it. This holiday has cost a great deal of money, so you could at least try to look as though you're enjoying it.'

'Why, when I'm not? Who wants to look at a lot of silly old buildings and smelly canals?'

'A great many intelligent, educated and cultured people who can see nothing very glamorous in lying on a beach to get cooked and then spending the rest of the day in some

273

second-rate bar. If you want to do that sort of thing when you are are older then you'll do it with your father; it's not my idea of a holiday.'

'I suppose it was Mr Abrahams who told you to come here. You take more notice of him than you take of Daddy.'

I was shaken by the vindictiveness in her pretty face, but I was determined not to lose my temper. 'Your father has never been abroad except during the war, how could he tell me anything about Europe? Wasn't it perfectly natural to ask advice from a man who enjoys travelling on the Continent?'

'It would be like him to recommend a place like this. All that antique furniture and those stuffy pictures.'

'Well for your information those pictures and that antique furniture are worth a great deal of money.'

'Oh, money . . .'

'Yes, money. It's money that sends you to that expensive school and pays for your clothes and the concerts you go to with your friends. It's money that has brought us here, so please don't be so disparaging about it.'

Tears filled her eyes and, instantly contrite, I leaned across and put my hand on hers. 'Don't let's quarrel, darling, you've only been here just over an hour. Why not wait a little while before deciding you're not going to be happy here?'

I watched helplessly as she flung herself down with a magazine.

'Don't you want tea, then?'

'No, I don't want to sit with all those old people. And I'm not thirsty. You go down if you want to.'

I decided that was the best thing. She would be poor company and I needed to see for myself how much truth there was in her grumbles.

People had returned to the hotel for afternoon tea, and my heart sank a little when I looked round the beautifully appointed tea lounge. Many of them were old, and the younger ones were about my own age. There were a few young married couples with small children, but girls of Marisa's age were conspicuously absent.

I was served with tea and exquisite small cakes, then because I didn't want to return to our rooms I went out into the sunshine and strolled by the lake. All joy in the scenery seemed to have left me and I looked across the lake through a blur of tears. Three weeks stretched before me and I wasn't sure how I was going to bear it.

When I returned to the hotel I was surprised to see Marisa waiting for me on the front steps, and relieved to see that she appeared to have recovered a little from her ill humour.

'Did you go to the shops?' she asked in a far more friendly tone than she had used upstairs.

'No, I just walked through the gardens and looked across the lake.'

'There's an island in the middle of the lake, the doorman says there's a little monastery on it.'

'If we take one of the ferries we shall be able to see it, perhaps.'

'He says we can sail from here to Como, and Como is famous for its silk. I suppose that's why all the shops sell silk scarves.'

'Of course, and talking about silk, what are you going to wear this evening?'

'I haven't thought. The doorman says everybody dresses for dinner, isn't that terribly Victorian?'

'Not really, darling. Dressing for dinner is something the best hotels insist on.'

'Jenny Palmerston says they don't bother what the younger people wear in Cannes.'

I had met the Palmerstons. He was making a lot of money in the retail clothing business and Mrs Palmerston was blonde and fluffy, with ideas of grandeur since they moved into their new property in Copplethorpe. I doubted if either of them would be happy in this hotel. They led a chromium-plated existence, indeed when I informed Mrs Palmerstone that I was in the antique and fine furniture business she merely raised her plucked eyebrows as much as to say, 'How quaint.'

'I think I'll wear the pale blue dress, my party dresses are not going to be much use here, are they?'

Ignoring that remark I said, 'Did the doorman tell you anything else? You appear to have struck up quite a friendship with him.'

'He says the gardens of the Villa Carlotta are world famous and that little village we can see across the lake is called Bellagio. We can go there by ferry.'

'My, but you have been busy. What would I do without you?'

I was grateful to the doorman for having momentarily removed that sulky expression from her face, and I favoured him with a particularly gracious smile as we entered the hotel.

The foyer was deserted now and I guessed that people were in their rooms changing for dinner. The sun was setting in a blaze of glory across the lake and almost immediately the dark descended and a pale new moon was shining above the mountains. How strange it was and how I missed the dusk of an English evening.

Chapter 27

I dressed for dinner with great care but I was not looking
forward to the evening. Entering the restaurant without a
male escort would tax all my newly acquired sophistication. It wasn't enough to look soigné and beautiful. The
pale beige heavy georgette gown had cost a great deal of
money, my money. It was deceptively simple as it fell in
heavy folds to the floor, its only claim to adornment being
the silver and gold beading round the neckline and edging
the graceful sleeves.

My shoes were an exact match to the dress, and my only
jewellery was the pair of gold earrings Maurice had given
me at Christmas after what he described as the best year's
business he could remember – largely thanks to our
partnership. By the same token he had bought Marisa a
gold locket and presented Liam with a large bottle of
expensive brandy.

The pale neutral colour of my gown complemented
perfectly my gleaming red hair and, when Marisa came
into my room wearing her pretty pale blue dress, she
gasped in admiration. 'Oh Mother, you look so beautiful.
Shall I ever be as tall and slender as you are?'

'Well of course you will, you've plenty of time to grow.'

'But I'll never have that lovely red hair.'

'No, but you'll be a cool blonde; a perfect English rose.'

She laughed, showing small, pretty teeth. 'What, with
Irish parents?'

'That won't matter. You are English, you were born in
England.'

She spun round for me to appraise her, and hugging her I
said, 'You look lovely, darling.'

'Mother, aren't you nervous having to do downstairs

without Daddy?'

'Yes, I am a bit, but I think I would have been equally nervous with your father. He would have hated this hotel.'

'I'm like him, aren't I, more like him than you?'

'Only in some things, Marisa, in others you must surely be like me.'

She shook her head stubbornly. 'No, I'm like him most of the time, I look like him and I like a lot of the things he likes. I want to be like you, Mother. You could be anybody, a princess even, but Daddy'll always be Daddy. Look how he clings to his Irish accent and the way he goes on about things at home like the furniture and the silver. You love it so and he never really sees it.'

'But you see it, darling, *you* appreciate it.'

'Yes, but only when you point it out to me. I never feel I would want to buy it.'

'You will when you're older, dear. When I was your age I didn't even know what good furniture looked like, not even the decent stuff in my grandmother's house. I shudder to think of all those nice ornaments we let go with the house. There must have been something worth while. If only I'd known the things I know now.'

'Daddy says they're dust collectors.'

'Of course, and he leaves tobacco dust on polished surfaces and his golf clubs cluttering up the hall. I shall never change him, Marisa, but I shall change you just as Maurice Abrahams changed me.'

'You like him, don't you, Mother? Aunt Mary doesn't.'

'Aunt Mary is bigoted and set in her ways. Maurice has been a good friend to all of us and I don't forget such things. Now are you ready to go down to dinner?'

It took all my courage to walk down the long curved staircase and cross the hall, but I managed, and the admiration in the eyes of the men and women at the desk bolstered up my flagging spirits.

The dining room was vast. I followed the head waiter with my head held high, looking neither to right nor left but smiling at him graciously as he indicated we should occupy a table for two near the far wall, then I looked around

278

casually as though I dined in such exalted atmospheres every night of my life.

The room had marble pillars and enormous chandeliers, and the windows were open on to a terrace so that we could see the pale moon shining on the surface of the lake. Rose-coloured lamps were lit on every table, sparkling on cut glass and silver. Marisa looked around with awe before she leaned across the table and hissed, 'They *are* old mother, all of them.'

'Hush, dear, they'll hear you.'

'Well, just take a look for yourself.'

'I will in a minute.'

A lady at the next table bowed graciously when I plucked up enough courage to look up, and the man across the table from her lifted a monocle to his eye and followed her example. It was true that many of them were old, beautifully gowned and coiffured women, men who might have been retired naval or army officers. I felt sure that in such an exalted gathering there were titles galore, but there were some men and women of my own age, and even younger, the parents of the children I had seen earlier.

My dress compared with the best of those present, but I was aware of Marisa's accusing eyes across the table as she waited for me to agree with her. I was saved from doing this because at that moment the head waiter marched across the room escorting a woman and three men, and immediately I became aware of the stillness, the absence of voices as all eyes followed the procession.

The men were impeccably dressed in white tie and tails, but it was the woman upon whom all eyes were turned. She was tall and slender, and her blue-black hair shone against her pale face under a sparkling tiara. She was beautiful, wearing a dark-blue velvet gown and diamonds at her throat and wrists. As she chatted to her companions, her dark eyes flashed with amusement and there was a great deal of laughter at their table.

I was so intoxicated by the woman, I had not looked at her companions, but now my eyes were drawn to the man sitting directly opposite her and I gasped with something akin to shock. Surely I knew that handsome dark head and those laughing dark eyes? He was leaning towards her in conversation, and just at that moment our eyes met and I turned away quickly in some confusion.

'Isn't she beautiful?' my daughter was saying. 'Who do you suppose she is?'

'I have no idea, darling.'

'But she must be somebody very important, she's wearing a crown.'

'No, Marisa, she is wearing a tiara. I expect she is a member of the Italian nobility.'

'Mother, will you look at those diamonds! Are they real?'

'Yes, I'm sure they are. Darling, don't stare.'

I could not say what we ate that first night. I felt bemused by the man and enchanted by the woman. I hoped he would not recognize me and I was determined that as soon as we had eaten, we should leave the restaurant in the most inconspicuous way.

The last time I had looked into those dark amused eyes was at the railway station during the war, and the memory of that farewell embrace brought the rich colour into my face. He might think he knew me, but he would not expect to find Katie O'Donovan dining in this sumptuous hotel. I stole another surreptitious look in his direction but they were all in earnest conversation. There was silver now at his temples. As our eyes met again and clung, I finally looked away filled with the utmost apprehension and glad of the waiter's attention.

Marisa said, 'Mother, who is that man who keeps staring at you?'

'There is no man staring at me, Marisa; we don't know anybody here.'

'One of the men who came in with that lady with the diamonds keeps looking over here and he's not looking at me.'

'He probably is, after all you are the prettiest girl in the restaurant.'

'You see, you've actually admitted that they're all old, every one of them.'

'If you've finished your meal we might as well go into the lounge for coffee,' I said tersely, and having made her point she sat back smiling, and I could cheerfully have slapped her.

Without looking again at the table near the window, we left the room, seeking a table placed unobtrusively in the furthest corner of the coffee lounge.

Marisa soon grew bored watching a steady procession of elderly residents coming and going. Music floated in through the open windows and I suggested we went in search of it. A small orchestra played in the lounge, and on the terrace couples were dancing while old people tapped their feet and others went to the bridge tables.

Marisa merely shrugged, saying, 'There's nobody of my age to dance with and nobody's going to ask you to dance, they all have their wives with them.'

'I'm quite happy to sit and listen to the music. We'll get to know people as the holiday progresses.'

'I don't want to get to know any of these people, besides most of them are foreign and we wouldn't understand them anyway. Can't we go out and look at the shops?'

'I thought you didn't like the shops.'

'Well, anything is better than sitting here. The doorman said they stayed open quite late, and we can look for presents. Do you think Aunt Mary would like a musical box?'

My dinner gown wasn't suitable for walking along the promenade and when I said as much Marisa pouted disdainfully. 'Couldn't you wear a wrap or something?'

Since the loss of the wrap Maurice had given me, I didn't possess one but I did have a soft cashmere stole that would have to serve as one, so to placate Marisa, I sent her up to my room to fetch it. The night was warm and fragrant with blossoms but I was glad of its soft warmth around my shoulders. All the same I felt conspicuous in my graceful skirts as we walked along the promenade, and that the shopkeepers were enhancing their prices accordingly.

We bought several silk scarves and a beautifully inlaid musical box that played 'Come Back to Sorrento', and

281

which Marisa said was for Aunt Mary.

I didn't sleep well and at first light I was on the terrace looking out to where the mist lay low across the lake and at the mountains towering over it, ethereal and awe-inspiring. I went into Marisa's room but she was sleeping soundly, one rounded arm lying outside the coverlet, her pale hair spread across the pillow.

She looked so beautiful and innocent lying there that I was filled with such a surge of love I could have gathered her close into my embrace, but I crept out of the room, closing the communicating door quietly behind me. I dressed in a plain grey skirt and twin set, thinking that the early morning air might be chilly, then I went downstairs and out at the front door.

I went to stand by the lake where I could watch the fishing vessels returning after their night's work. Lights still burned on most of them, and the men were singing, melodiously and gloriously, some song of Italy.

I don't know how long I stood there absorbing the peace and the feel of the early sun becoming warm against my face. I heard light footsteps behind me and then the beautiful woman I had seen the previous evening was standing beside me, listening to the music and looking out across the lake.

'How beautiful it is,' she said, smiling. 'I never tire of listening to the fishermen; they sing all the time, when they sail and when they work at their nets.'

She spoke English with only a hint of an accent and her voice was musically low, and shorn of her diamonds and wearing only a loose wrap over her night attire she was still beautiful. Her face was creamy peach and tinted by the sun, and her eyes were large, with long dark curling lashes, and I was surprised to see that they were blue. She wore her hair loose around her shoulders. It was thick and shining. As I contemplated what I should reply, she went on, 'I love this place. Europe is changing everywhere one goes but nothing ever seems to alter here. I want it to go on like this for ever.'

'Do you come here every summer?'

'We come several times in the year. We live in Rome but

we have friends and relatives in the area. My daughter will be joining us today, she is at school in Switzerland.'

'She doesn't mind it that most of the people seem old?'

She smiled. 'I can see that you have been having trouble with your daughter, and it is true that many of the guests are old. They come here year after year to absorb the peace and meet old friends. They know the hotel is comfortable and the food is always very good. In a changing world it is good to find certainty. Do you not think so?'

'Yes, oh yes I do, but the young are not looking for permanence, they thrive on change.'

A shadow seemed to cross her face for a moment but then she smiled brightly. 'You are English, Signora?' she said.

'I *live* in England, actually I was born in Ireland.'

'Your husband is not with you?'

'No. He doesn't care for foreign travel and Marisa desperately wanted to come abroad; all her schoolfriends spend their holidays on the Continent.'

'They have their wants, these young people. Do you have only this one daughter?'

'Yes.'

'I too. Catrina will find plenty to do here. Our friends have children of her own age; they live in villas dotted around the shore between here and Como, so they will take her sailing and there will be garden parties and soirées for her to attend. I see very little of her when we come here but I know she is quite safe.'

I smiled politely, and she went on. 'My name is Valeria Lestriani, the Contessa Lestriani. What is your name?'

'Kathleen, Kathleen Clancy.'

'We must talk again, Mrs Clancy and perhaps I will find something nice for your daughter to do with Catrina; they are about the same age. It would be a pity if she went away disliking Tremezzo simply because most of the hotel guests are old.'

'You are very kind, Contessa.'

Together we strolled back to the hotel and she kept up a constant chatter on things we should see and the gardens and art galleries we should visit. On leaving, she said, 'I have enjoyed our chat, Mrs Clancy, we must meet again. It is lonely for you, I think.'

'Yes. I have been wondering if I have made a mistake in coming here.'

'No, no of course you have not. You will love Lake Como but how can you judge after such a short time?' She smiled at my raised eyebrows. 'I can tell you are newly here from England, the sun has not had time to colour that lovely complexion.'

'Do your friends also live in Rome?' I asked her.

I had to know, there was every possibility I could be wrong about one of them.

'No. Stephano lives in Genoa and will be returning there, Nicholas is a business friend of my husband's whom we have known for many years. He is Canadian and travels extensively. I believe he has relatives in the North of England; indeed it is possible you might know them.'

I smiled politely. So I had not been wrong after all. I had never known his name, but I had the strangest feeling that I would soon learn more about him than I had known in the past, and a note of anxious warning crept into the peace of the morning.

I had not come to Tremezzo looking for complications in my life; life was complicated enough.

I did not tell Marisa about the contessa's daughter. We took the ferry across the lake to Bellagio and fell in love with the entrancing little town with its steep cobbled streets and avenue of pretty shops. We sat in its hotel gardens drinking iced lemonade which the waiter made for us at the table from fresh lemons and sugar, finally adding ice and mint stems.

The sun was warm on our bare arms and already it was gilding our skins although with my fair skin I had to be careful.

It was pleasant in the gardens, watching the pageantry of bold-eyed Italian boys ogling the pretty foreign girls in their light summery dresses, and the older visitors bargaining in the shopping arcades for wood carvings and musical boxes. After the siesta time when all Bellagio seemed to sleep we caught the ferry back to our hotel. Marisa's eyes brightened at the sight of a group of younger people splashing in the pool and I said, 'There, you see, younger people *are* coming to the hotel.'

'I don't suppose they'll want to bother with me.'

'Whyever not? They look a friendly crowd to me.'

'Well, they'll all know one another, won't they? I shall be a stranger.'

'Let us not be too pessimistic, Marisa,' I was saying, just as one of the boys waved and Marisa waved back, favouring him with a bright smile.

'Do you want to sit round the pool and watch them?' I asked.

'Oh no, if they want me to join in, they'll have to ask me.'

'And you will have to meet them half-way, dear.'

'I'll watch them tomorrow, Mother. Today I'm all sticky and I haven't combed my hair.'

'You look very nice to me.'

'No, Mother, no, I don't want to sit around the pool now, I want to get out of this dressed-up dress and into something more like the thing that girl over there is wearing.'

The girl she referred to was wearing a full colourful skirt and a low-necked sleeveless blouse. She was pretty, with a wealth of dark cloudy hair and a small piquant face alive with laughter. There were other girls standing around the pool and splashing in the water and I wondered which one of them was the contessa's daughter.

'You go and change, Marisa, I think I'll go into the lounge for tea. You can join me there.'

'You only have to look in the tea lounge to know which are the English,' she grumbled, 'nobody else cares so much about tea.'

'Oh I don't know, it seems to me entirely civilized to drink tea on a hot afternoon.'

'Oh Mother, you are getting to be so stuffy.'

With a gay smile she left me and I watched her run lightly up the steps with her blonde curls tossing around her shoulders.

As usual the tea lounge was full of elderly people. The waiters performed their duties as if this was a ceremony to be savoured. As I took my place at an empty table, the contessa entered the room, and seeing me walked across.

'Do you mind if I join you, Mrs Clancy? Most of the tables appear to be occupied and some of these older people will not like a stranger at their table. How the British enjoy their afternoon tea.'

I smiled. 'Yes, that is what my daughter said.'

'She is not joining you then?'

'No. She's gone up to her room to change. She saw some young people round the pool and didn't seem to think she was suitably dressed.'

Her eyes filled with amusement. 'How alike they are, these young people, how they run to meet life in case it escapes them. They want everything and they want it now; they do not understand that the things we most value in life are those we have had to wait for.'

I didn't comment but how I agreed with her. The waiter served us with tea but she asked for lemon with hers and disdained the cakes and sandwiches. When I hesitated to help myself from the plate he proferred she said, 'Please, Mrs Clancy, you will offend me if you do not eat. I had a late luncheon and I watch my figure.'

'Then perhaps I should watch mine. Surely you do not need to watch yours?'

'Oh yes, I am Italian and as we grow older we get fatter. My mother was quite fat and my grandmother tremendous. I can't possibly end up like them.'

'I'm sure you won't. The entire restaurant was open-mouthed in admiration last night when you entered it.'

'That is very sweet of you, Mrs Clancy, but then you can afford to be generous, you too are a very beautiful woman.'

'Thank you,' I murmured, and quickly, to save my embarrassment, she said, 'My daughter has arrived, she is with her friends at the pool, it was they you saw as you came in. Tonight after dinner I will introduce your daughter to Catrina. No doubt they will make plans and your daughter can meet Catrina's friends and relatives. There will be

286

much for them to do, and you will not have to feel unhappy about bringing her here.'

'You are very kind, Contessa.'

'My kindness serves a dual purpose. Catrina will have a friend in the hotel and you and I will not be burdened by sulky little girls who ask too much too soon.'

Just then one of her companions came to our table. He was handsome in spite of his silver hair,' and was considerably older than the contessa. There was a fond smile on his thin aristocratic face. He raised her hand to his lips and lightly kissed it, then taking his place at the table he said, 'I thought I might find you here, my dear.'

'May I introduce my husband Carlo, Mrs Clancy? Mrs Clancy is from the North of England and is staying here with her daughter. I have promised to introduce her to Catrina this evening. Have you seen them? They are round the pool.'

He had risen and, after bowing correctly, raised my hand and lightly kissed it.

'I have been watching them from the gardens. I told Catrina it was time for her to come in; Nicholas is driving the rest of them home.'

'They will come again in the morning.'

'It is doubtful if we could keep them away. You are enjoying your stay in Tremezzo, Mrs Clancy?'

'Very much, it is beautiful here.'

'Yes indeed. I lived in Como as a boy. My parents had a villa there, so I know the area well. We come back year after year and never seem to tire of it.'

'I don't believe I would ever tire of it. The combination of scenery and sun is unforgettable.'

We chatted for a few more minutes then I made the excuse of wanting to bathe before dressing for dinner.

The conte stood up as I left the table and the contessa said, 'We will meet this evening, Mrs Clancy, indeed you and Marisa must join us in the restaurant.'

I merely smiled. I would make quite certain that we would go down to the restaurant early so that we would almost have finished our meal before they arrived. I wanted

Marisa and Catrina to meet, I wanted her to meet other young people and have the time of her life, but I was afraid of those amused dark eyes and that slightly puzzled air which told me he was trying to remember where we had met.

How could he expect a woman who had once been a servant in the home of his friends to be accepted in the eyes of these wealthy and noble Italians? They were charming because they knew nothing about me, but that could change once they knew my history, and I had to think of Marisa.

Marisa was thrilled with the idea of meeting Catrina and the conte and his wife.

'Are they very important, Mother?' she enthused. 'Are they related to royalty? Oh, won't there be something to tell the girls at St Clare's. You will let me go to their parties and anywhere they want to take me? I'll just *die* if you won't.'

'Don't get too carried away, darling, you might not even like them and we don't know how well they speak English.'

'But the contessa speaks it, doesn't she? Mamselle Decoret says all Continentals speak English, it is us who are too lazy and won't take the trouble. But there are so many languages in Europe, how can she expect us to learn every one of them?'

All the time she was speaking she was hunting through her wardrobe and I watched doubtfully. She was so excited, so sure she wanted to meet Catrina and her friends. It was I who was afraid of facing a past I believed I had lived down.

'I shall wear the blue dress I wore last night,' she announced.

'Oh, but darling, you have so many dresses, why not the pink one?'

'I hate it. It makes me look ten years old.' Then catching my hurt expression, 'Oh all right, but not with my hair hanging down like this. Can you do something with it? Anything to make me look a bit more foreign and at least three years older.'

I laughed at the anxiety in her face. 'When you get to my age, Marisa, you'll be wanting to look younger. I agree with the contessa.'

'Why? What did she say?'

'She said the young were too impatient with their lives, that they rushed to meet it in case it ran away from them.'

'Well, what is so wrong about that? The contessa's made the most of her life with all those lovely diamonds and three handsome men dancing attention on her. One day I want to sweep into a crowded room just like she did, wearing diamonds and a heavenly gown, and I want to have handsome men with me and others staring at me. I don't care if the women are pea green with envy as long as the men think I'm beautiful.'

'And I think you are in for a period of adjustment, Marisa Clancy. Walk before you run and don't be in such a hurry to grow up. Now let me see what I can do with your hair.'

I combed and teased its shining strands into a long gentle curl that fell over one shoulder and, as fast as she pulled the neckline of her gown off her rounded shoulders, I pulled it up again until, exasperated, she snapped, 'Mother, everybody had a neckline lower than mine at Mary Radcliffe's party. I just know that girl we saw round the pool will look twice my age. Didn't you notice the top she was wearing?'

'We don't even know that she was Catrina, you are only surmising, and she looked older than you anyway.'

She wasn't interested, still playing with the neckline of her dress. 'See, if I put this brooch just here it will pull the neckline down on one side. It doesn't matter about the other,' she said eagerly.

'And when you take out the brooch the neckline will be spoilt. Really, Marisa, I wish you would be content to be as you are. I wish I was your age.'

'Would you do all the same things again, Mother? Would you marry Daddy and go to salerooms with Uncle Maurice? Would you let Aunt Mary boss you around and would you go to race meetings instead of that Geraldine McClusky?'

I gasped and sat down weakly on the edge of the bed.

'What do you know about Geraldine McClusky?' I asked

289

nervously.

'Jenny Palmerston said her parents had seen Daddy and her together at the Chester races and I said she was only his secretary and you didn't care for racing. They didn't believe me and they just stood in a corner giggling. I didn't speak to any of them for a week.'

'Oh Marisa, why didn't you tell me?'

'I thought you knew. Beside, what would you have done about it? I hate her, she gives herself such airs and she bosses him about as though she owns him.'

I was aware of my trembling hands and that their palms were sticky with perspiration. The words would not come, and at that moment I felt vulnerable and strangely alone, watching Marisa posture and pose before the mirror as though she expected me to be unconcerned about the intrusion of Geraldine McClusky into our lives.

Satisfied at last she spun round, and seeing my troubled face she said, 'I suppose she's the other woman, isn't she, Mother? Are you upset about it?'

'I don't want you to talk about such things. She's your father's secretary, nothing more, and I won't have you discussing them with any of your friends.'

For a moment she looked at me in pitying silence, then shrugging her shoulders she said, 'Oh all right then, I don't want to talk about them anyway. If you don't care I'm sure I don't.'

All the time I was dressing my mind was on Liam and his mistress. I didn't care about her but I felt outraged that he had been seen with her at places frequented by people we knew. I didn't care for me, but I cared desperately for Marisa. How dared Liam do this to her, and how many people knew about the relationship?

I dressed quickly, not caring too much how I looked, and when Marisa came into my room she said in a surprised voice, 'Why, that's the gown you wore last night and you wouldn't let me wear the blue.'

It didn't matter, I wasn't concerned about me nor would anybody else be concerned. Marisa was looking quite enchanting, and this surely was all that mattered.

Much to Marisa's chagrin we were the first in the restaurant and the first to leave.

'I don't see why we had to come down so early, I wanted to see what people were wearing, particularly the contessa.'

'We shall see them when they come for their coffee.'

'We shall have left by then. Besides, how am I to meet her daughter if we're never in the same place at the same time?'

I was not being fair to Marisa but I had not spent years forgetting the Katie O'Donovan of Heatherlea to have her resurrected now. So, after coffee we went into the hotel foyer where we spent at least ten minutes buying postcards, then I suggested we go into the gardens. Her face was mutinous and in some exasperation I snapped, 'If the contessa really wants you to meet her daughter she will make sure that you do.'

'Well of course she wants us to meet, didn't she say so only this afternoon?'

'This happens often on holiday, Marisa. People say they will visit or write but that's the last you ever hear from them. We don't want the contessa to think we are expecting her to be kind to us just because we are travelling alone.'

She lost some of her boredom when the orchestra came to play in the gardens and we watched tubs of flowers being arranged round an area of the terrace where later on people would dance.

'Are we going to stay and watch the dancing?' she asked petulantly.

'Yes, if you would like to, dear.'

'It doesn't matter, there won't be anybody to dance with anyway.'

'There may be new people who have arrived today.'

She didn't answer. The sound of talk and laughter came to us from the restaurant and I began to feel mean and selfish. We should have been in there instead of sitting out here on our own because I was afraid. Why should I be ashamed that I had once worked as a servant? It had been good honest work, and if I had climbed out of that environment surely I was to be congratulated, not looked down on. That man in the contessa's party was hardly likely to scream from the housetops that we had met in Marsdale where he was a visitor and I a parlourmaid.

Making up my mind very suddenly I said, 'We will go back to the lounge, Marisa. If the contessa wishes her daughter to meet you she will see us there.'

I can't say I wasn't nervous as we sat watching people drift in from the coffee lounge, but tonight people bowed to us and smiled, we were no longer newcomers. At last there was a stir in the sedateness of the room and looking up I saw the contessa with her small procession.

Tonight she was wearing a gown in deep tragic crimson and there were rubies round her neck and in her ears. Instead of the tiara she wore one dark red rose at the side of her face, and the three men were in white dinner jackets instead of sombre black. With them was a young girl, dark and very slender, wearing a long gown in exquisite apricot ninon and with pale peach flowers in her hair. I could not remember having seen this girl round the pool.

Beside me Marisa gasped. 'Oh, Mother, how beautiful they are. This pink thing I'm wearing is so childish.'

'Hush dear, of course it isn't. You must remember that they are Europeans and don't dress like us.'

The contessa caught sight of us and with a bright smile she took hold of her daughter's hand and drew her towards our table.

'So here you are, I looked for you in the restaurant. You had dinner early this evening.'

'Yes, I'm afraid I was hungry. We only had a light lunch across the lake at Bellagio.'

'This is my daughter Catrina, and this is Marisa,' she said, smiling down at her in a friendly fashion.

The two girls smiled at each other and I thought how different the two girls were – Marisa so English fair and Catrina so dark.

'I was hoping I might have your permission for Marisa to go to a party with Catrina at the Rosemar Villa along the lake. This happens all the time when our relatives know we are here. It is Maria's birthday today and they are giving a party for her. Maria is seventeen so there will be older people there, but there will also be many young people the same age as these two.'

Marisa was looking at me with shining eyes.

'Oh Mother, please say yes. I may go, mayn't I?'

'You need have no fear, Mrs Clancy, the girls will be well chaperoned. The chauffeur will take them in the car and bring them back before eleven, and after this evening Marisa will know Catrina's friends and she will be able to go sailing and play tennis with them.'

Marisa was clapping her hands with glee, then doubtfully she said, 'What about my dress? It isn't a ball gown like Catrina's.'

The contessa trilled with laughter. 'You are not going to a ball, Marisa, just a family party. The gown is lovely and you are lovely. All those dark Italian boys will adore your pink and white complexion and golden hair.'

Appeased, she smiled, and I said practically, 'Will you want a light coat or a wrap?'

'The night is very warm,' the contessa said, 'and they will be in the car. Hurry children, the sooner you get there the sooner you can begin to enjoy yourselves.'

They needed no encouragement and we stood watching them hurrying to where the car waited.

The contessa turned to me with a smile. 'You need have no worries on Marisa's behalf, Mrs Clancy. I hope they will be good friends but I know what you are thinking.'

'You do?'

'Yes, you are thinking how sophisticated my daughter seems beside your English rose. Well, perhaps we Continentals are like that, we live behind our frontiers but travel is easy for us, while it is something most Britishers have to discover. Please call me Valeria and I shall call you Kathleen. It is more sociable, and we would like you to join us over a glass of wine.'

'But I don't want to intrude, you have been very kind to Marisa, but there is really no need to take me under your wing as well.'

She trilled with laughter. 'That, I assume, is an English expression and one I haven't heard. We do not in the least object to taking you under our wing and I shall be glad of another woman's company. One grows awfully tired of men's talk.'

I had no alternative but to go with her, but I went in a dream, with trembling limbs and desperately wary eyes. The three men rose to their feet and I was introduced to Stephano the Italian and Nicholas the Canadian, both of whom bowed over my hand and kissed it.

The conversation was informal. How did I like Tremezzo? What did I plan to do whilst there? Had I ever been to Venice which was surely worth a visit?

I answered them to the best of my ability and then they chatted on matters peculiar to men while the contessa and I discussed the fashions in the hotel lounge.

Only once I looked up and found Nicholas watching me with a little smile. He was puzzled by me, I could tell. I was so like the girl he had kissed on the railway platform that day during the war, but I was talking to the contessa about pictures and music, something that servant girl had known nothing about. He was unsure and, because he was unsure, some of my lost confidence returned and I smiled, a smile that seemed to cause him some consternation. I would not be able to pretend indefinitely, but for tonight at least it pleased me that he should have doubts about my identity.

Marisa was having the time of her life. Instead of sulks there were sunny smiles and an incredible new maturity. She demanded casual clothes from the small smart shops in the town and, when I seemed doubtful about their suitability, she merely laughed saying, 'Oh Mother, don't be such a fusspot. All the girls are wearing them.'

Her long slim legs looked even longer in her shorter shorts and the sun bleached her fair hair into strands of gleaming silver, vying delightfully with her tanned skin. The French and Italian boys besieged her with their attentions and it shocked me to see her playing one off against the other with adult dexterity. When I remonstrated with her she merely shrugged, pouting prettily and saying, 'I like André and Pierre best, but all the boys like me because I'm blonde. Mother, I'm having such a good time, I'm so glad that I'm pretty and the boys like me.'

'Flirting with them isn't necessarily going to endear you to the girls, Marisa, you should think about that.'

'Oh I do, but they flirt as well, it's all part of the fun.'

'Well, remember that you are very young and that these boys are older than you. They are also far more sophisticated and a boy's passions are easily aroused.'

'Oh, Mother! Don't fuss so, I can look after myself.'

I tried to remember what I had been like at her age but the comparison was incongruous. I had had none of her opportunities, and memories of Cook's stern commands to leave the boys alone made me wish there was somebody like her to lecture Marisa.

Quite without my knowledge she wrote to Liam to ask if we could extend our holiday beyond the three weeks we had planned, and I was surprised to receive a letter from him enclosing money and his consent.

When I told her she should have consulted me first she tossed her blonde head, saying, 'Surely you want to stay on too? If you went back you'd only spend your time with that Mr Abrahams looking for old furniture.'

I did not spend all my time with Valeria and her friends. There were days when I climbed the hills above the lake, taking a sketch pad and water colours and applying my modest skill in trying to capture the enchanting vista of lake and mountains.

One morning a hand reached out from behind me to take the pad out of my hands and a man's voice said, 'This is remarkably good. I particularly like the way you have captured the pink villa nestling against the hill and the tall cypresses against the sky.'

I blushed furiously as I looked up into Nicholas's face.

'It isn't very good really. I'm only a dabbler but I enjoy what I'm doing.'

'No, really. It has great potential. Are you having lessons?'

'No, I bought the water colours on impulse. It gives me

something to do.'

'You are not seeing much of your daughter, I'm afraid. Are you finding it very lonely?'

'Oh no. All this is very new to me and I like walking.'

'You should see more of Italy while you are here. Venice is not an impossibility, and Milan. Do you enjoy the opera?'

'Very much. I do not hear it often because my husband is not fond of classical music.'

'But he does not object if you visit the opera.'

'No, but it isn't always easy.'

'The opera season is over in Milan for the summer months but you could take a look round the opera house. It is an education, believe me.'

'Perhaps I will do that one day.'

'Why not tomorrow? I have to go into Milan on business, I could leave you to look around the opera house and call back for you. A guide is there to explain things to the uninitiated, and I think you will enjoy the experience.'

'You are very kind, Nicholas, but I am not sure what Marisa is doing tomorrow.'

'I will tell you exactly what she is doing. Tanta Maria is coming to stay for her usual summer vacation and a garden party is planned. My friends will be expected to be there so I am alone tomorrow and I rather think you will be alone also.'

Still I hesitated, and with a smile he urged, 'Come now Katie, surely you can spare one day in the company of an old friend.'

I could feel the hot colour flooding my cheeks and my lips trembled as I murmured, 'You knew all the time.'

'I must confess that at first I wasn't sure. I thought about the young Katie flying up the hillside, but there couldn't be anybody else with that glorious hair and eyes as blue as that lake down there. The last time I saw you was in the station yard and I learned you had married. I take it your husband came back safely and since then you have prospered.'

'We've been very lucky. Liam came in for his uncle's business and I have interests of my own.'

'Why isn't he here with you?'

296

'He doesn't care for foreign travel and Marisa wanted to come abroad.'

'I see.'

He was looking down at me with a half smile, his dark amused eyes narrowed and filled with a speculation I could only guess at, then he surprised me by saying, 'You haven't said you will come with me tomorrow, Katie. I hope you will.'

Still I was doubtful until he said, 'I will wait until this evening. By that time you will know what your daughter intends to do, but I am sure you will find she is in the welcoming party for Tanta Maria.'

'May I let you know later, then?'

'Of course. It is my experience that opportunity doesn't always knock twice, Katie O'Donovan. Your daughter is discovering this now while she is young, but I can assure you the things you and I will discover will have far greater meaning and will afford us greater joy.'

Again I could feel my face blushing furiously and I could not be sure if he was baiting me as he had always done with his impudent grin and his handsome devilish face.

I gathered my paints together so that I didn't have to look at him, and then realized with surprise that he was waiting to walk back to the hotel with me. As we set off down the hillside he asked, 'Do you ever visit the people on Tremayne Hill?'

'Not for some time. Everything is very different now, some of the old houses have been sold, many of the families have died out and I no longer know any of the servants at Heatherlea.'

'What happened to the Carslake family?'

'Colonel Carslake died and Mrs Carslake is living in Cumberland with her sister. The two daughters are married and Mr Ambrose lives away from the area.'

'And Jeffrey?'

'I don't know. The mills are now part of a combine, he is probably managing one of them.'

'You mean you haven't made it your business to find out.'

'Why should I? I was a servant at Heatherlea, I was not part of the family or even a friend.'

'So the stars finally went out, Katie, and the man who was responsible for them is barely remembered.'

'I don't know what you mean.'

'Oh, but I think you do. Whatever did you see in Jeffrey Carslake, Katie, you and Lois Foxland both running whenever he beckoned, and neither of you getting close to him?'

I stopped to stare at him, surprised and not a little angry. 'I didn't go running. I didn't expect him to care for one of his mother's servants.'

'You could and you did. How did you ever get him out of your system long enough to marry somebody else?'

I bit my lip furiously and started to walk away, but uncontrite he followed and fell into step by my side.

'Talk of the past upsets you, doesn't it Katie?'

'I want to forget it. I've made something of my life and I don't need now to think that anybody is better than I am. In the old days it seemed that everybody was better than me, everybody except Polly. Now I'm as knowledgeable as the best of them, I don't have to pretend to be somebody.'

'Oh Katie, you've always been somebody. You're so pretty and have so much spirit. How could you ever exist in that atmosphere of pseudo gentry and false idealism? Seeing you wasting all that made me finally realize why my mother turned her back on it.'

I turned to stare at him and he reached out and took my arm.

'If you walk a little slower and listen without interrupting I'll tell you about it.'

I fell under the spell of his voice with its lazy drawl as he told me about his mother, beautiful, spirited and spoilt. Running away from a wealthy home to marry her father's estate agent who had very little money but a great deal of ambition. They emigrated to Canada where they prospered and when they prospered her father forgave them. Nicholas was made welcome in his grandfather's house and received his education in England, then after the old man died became a constant guest in his uncle's house.

'Is that the uncle you visited on Tremayne Hill?'

'Yes, my uncle is Sir Joshua Tremayne. I was staying with them when war broke out in 1914 but my home is in Canada, where a man is judged by what he is and not by what he has.'

'But you'll always go back to see them in England?'

'Of course. I became the son they never had. And now, Katie, I think that's enough of me. Now that I've told you my story I want to hear yours, right from that moment I deposited you on your aunt's doorstep and all those eyes watched us from behind their lace curtains.'

So I told him about Liam and Maurice, about the Carslakes and Polly, about my aunt and uncle and Frances who had spurned them, and I told him about all the things I wanted for Marisa in a new and alien world. I even told him about my childhood in Ireland and the heroic death of my father which was responsible for sending me to England.

He listened in silence and when the story came to an end he said, 'Are you happy in your marriage, Katie?'

'Happy enough. Liam's a good provider and I am able to provide the things he doesn't consider necessary. We have a nice home and money in the bank. All my ambition is for Marisa.'

'And what do you want for Marisa? A house on Tremayne Hill and a husband like Jeffrey Carslake.'

I spun round in some degree of anger. 'I want her to be able to hold her own with the likes of Jeffrey Carslake. I want her to marry a man who loves her and doesn't look at other women. Surely that's not too much for any mother to ask for.'

There was no mockery in his eyes, but an expression I could not read, and I turned away quickly, afraid of the strange and sharp emotion that filled me. I felt that I was tottering on the edge of a volcano likely to erupt at any moment and that I would be swept into an inferno of towering passions I would be unable to escape from.

'We must hurry,' I said sharply, 'it is almost lunch time.'

By the time we reached the hotel most of the guests were already half-way through their luncheon and we took our places quietly while the contessa merely smiled.

Chapter 28

I was surprised to find Marisa on her bedroom balcony, looking out across the gardens where she must have seen us enter the hotel grounds. She looked sulky, and I wondered if she had quarrelled with her friends.

'Where have you been?' she asked accusingly.

'Walking in the hills and trying to paint a little. Mr Yale found me up there and we walked back together. I'm surprised to find you here. Where are your friends?'

'Oh Tanta Maria is visiting and there's a family party going on.'

'I see. Well, naturally they have to welcome her. It will be nice to have you to myself for a change.'

'They said I could go with them but Catrina said it was always a stuffy party. Tanta Maria is quite old and there will be a lot of older people there, all relatives.'

'In that case you might as well spend the evening with me. I'm not so very old and you can tell me all you've been doing these last few days.'

'Is Mr Yale going to be with Tanta Maria?'

'I don't know, but I shouldn't think so.'

'If we eat early we can walk into Tremezzo.'

'Of course, dear, whatever you like. Now I'm going to take a bath and change for dinner.'

Marisa was being selfish. Over the past few days she hadn't cared in the least how I amused myself, but tonight she didn't want me to chat to Nicholas or anybody else, she wanted me exclusively to herself. One decision however had been made for me. It looked as though I would not be going to Milan the following day.

We dined in a sparsely filled dining room and went to walk leisurely into the town, where we listened to innumerable music boxes and she selected a brightly coloured skirt for herself while I chose a silk scarf for Aunt Martha.

'What do you intend to do tomorrow?' I asked her.

'Heaven knows. I suppose they'll all do what Tanta Maria wants, and André says that will be croquet on the lawn and afternoon tea while they all have to tell her how well they had been doing at school or how rich their parents are becoming.'

'It sounds very boring to me. Would you like to sail down the lake to Como?'

'Well, anything is better than meeting Tanta Maria. Catrina's father has gone back to Rome on business, she says he always escapes if he can.'

'But her mother is there, of course.'

'Yes, the contessa and Stephano. Catrina says they've been lovers for years.'

I stopped dead in the roadway, appalled at the casual way she spoke of the relationship, at the sudden adult assumption that this was natural and normal.

'Really, Marisa, I'm sure that isn't true. Catrina is being too imaginative and you shouldn't listen to her.'

'But it's true. Pierre and André both say so, everybody knows about it.'

'But the conte is charming and they seem a most devoted family.'

'Well they *are*. The contessa was married to the conte when she was sixteen years old and their families arranged the marriage. Besides, he is a lot older than she is and Stephano is very handsome.'

'I don't think the contessa would like to think her daughter was discussing her with her friends.'

'Catrina says it's quite acceptable. Her parents are great friends and Stephano is a family friend also. I told her my father had a mistress who was nothing like as pretty as you and you too had a man friend.'

'Marisa, how *could* you? Maurice Abrahams is my friend and a very good one, he is also my business partner. Geraldine McClusky is your father's secretary, nothing more.'

'Oh, *Mother!*' she snapped, and walked on with her head averted in sulky silence.

We had almost reached the hotel doorway when we heard running footsteps along the drive and then André and Pierre were with us, laughing and cajoling, doing their utmost to persuade Marisa to go sailing with them in the morning.

'There's to be no excitement tomorrow. Tanta Maria is very tired and needs a day to recover from our visit.'

'Does that mean we can all go off together like we did before she arrived?'

'Of course, and tomorrow Father is taking her out to dinner and an orchestral concert at the Villa d'Esti so she wouldn't want us around anyway.'

She looked at me appealingly. 'Do you really want to go to Como, Mother? I'll go with you if you like.'

'I can go to Como alone if I want to, Marisa. You go with your friends.'

She threw her arms around me and hugged me, then with a swift joyful smile she ran off with them in the direction of the music.

I felt suddenly very forlorn. Concerned with her own pleasure, my daughter had little thought for me, but she was very young and I told myself hopefully that the years would bring discretion and thoughtfulness. I decided to go straight to bed, but had been in my room only a few minutes when the phone rang. It was Nicholas.

'Well,' he demanded. 'Have you decided to come to Milan with me or have you better things to do?'

Was it really me saying I would go with him, that I would meet him in the hotel foyer at nine o'clock? I sat down sharply on the edge of the bed, amazed at what I had done.

I tried to get interested in a book until I heard Marisa enter her room then I waited for her to come in to say goodnight, which she always did if it was not too late.

Marisa came in to say goodnight and sat on the edge of my bed, enthusing about her plans for the next day. Almost as an afterthought she said, 'You really didn't mind about Como, did you? We can go some other day when Tanta

Maria has to be entertained.'

'I didn't mind darling. As a matter of fact I have been invited to go to Milan with Mr Yale. He has to go on business and I would like to visit La Scala and see the cathedral.'

For a split second I saw her eyes narrow and become speculative, then her face cleared. 'Will you be gone all day, then?'

'I'm not sure. Perhaps I shouldn't go, dear. If I'm not back for dinner you will be alone.'

'I won't be alone all day, I shall tell them you are in Milan so they'll have to include me in anything they've planned.'

'No, Marisa, that isn't right.'

She waltzed airily across the room. 'Don't fuss, Mother, go to Milan and have a good time. Mr Yale is awfully dishy, isn't he?'

'Is he? I hadn't noticed.'

'Oh Mother, you *are* hopeless. Of course he is, everybody says so.'

'Who is everybody?'

'Well, Catrina and all her friends. Did you know that he got the DSC during the war and had to go to Buckingham Palace to receive it from the King?'

'No, I didn't know.'

'I won't tell anybody you went off with him, and certainly I won't tell Daddy. It serves him right anyway for not coming with us.'

'Darling, it isn't a secret, there's nothing fu ive about my going to Milan.'

'I know, but I shan't tell him away.'

I knew I would remember that day from the first moment I stepped into Nicholas's car, with the warm sun dispelling the early mist where it lay on the surface of the lake. As we drove I sat back to enjoy the opening vista of mountains and lake until before us the spires and domes of Milan filled the horizon.

'I'll take you to the opera house now so that you can pick up a guide and join one of the tours,' he told me. 'I shall be about an hour on my business, then I shall come back here and take you to lunch. We can look at the cathedral together later.'

The time passed too quickly as the guide led my group through the dressing rooms of the great opera house where world-famous singers had sung throughout the years. We looked at scenery and costumes encrusted with jewels, we stood on the great stage looking down at the massive orchestra pit, then at last we stood in the auditorium looking up at velvet-seated boxes where I had no trouble in imagining exquisitely gowned women and elegant men, the flash of jewels and distinguished orders, the colour of many uniforms and the scent of flowers. Then Nicholas was back, taking my arm as we left the theatre.

'Well, what did you think of it?' he asked, smiling a little at my delighted astonishment.

'Oh, it is so marvellous, how I would love to listen to opera here.'

'Yes, it's a pity the theatre is closed. It is a greater pity that we can't go to Verona to see one of the operas in the arena there.'

'But it can't possibly be more wonderful than here,' I objected.

'Well, it's different, but very impressive. The arena is huge and so is the stage. I saw *Aida* there years ago. Can you imagine a stage where they actually had room for chariots and horses? The audience is given tiny wax matches on arrival and, when these are all lit, the scene in the arena is glorious, a half circle of tiny flames, and when the last one goes out that is the signal for the overture to begin.'

'Do their voices carry well in the open air?'

'Oh yes, the acoustics are marvellous. The ancients knew a thing or two about staging masterpieces.'

I wished with all my heart that I could go to Verona but I knew it was impossible and, as if sensing my thoughts, he said, squeezing my arm, 'Some other time, Katie. If you want a thing enough you can make it happen.'

I shook my head. 'I wish I could believe that, but I know it isn't true.'

'You've made a lot of your wishes come true.'

'I know, but there are a lot more that have no chance of coming true.'

'Then I won't ask you what they are, and now I will take you to the most charming restaurant in Milan and one where they serve the best Italian food. You do like Italian food I hope?'

'I haven't had much of it, but I like it. I would have thought the hotel would serve more.'

'Actually, no, they pride themselves on their English cuisine. It dates back to the time when Queen Victoria descended upon them. I know you like Italian wine.'

'Yes, that I do like.'

Nicholas was well known at the restaurant, a charming gay little place with check tablecloths, and great bowls of begonias everywhere. The food was marvellous and we were very gay as we drank our wine.

Towards the end of our meal a wedding party arrived and we were invited to toast the happy couple in champagne before the music started and we joined in the merriment and the dancing.

For the first time in many years I felt young, really young as I waltzed in Nicholas's arms, and looking up into his eyes I was aware of their dark intensity, and behind that maddening amusement something that brought the warm colour into my face.

It was much later when we entered the lofty darkness of the cathedral and I stood in awe before its high altar where memories of my early faith emerged like forbidden spectres.

I saw reproach in the eyes of stained-glass saints, sad betrayal in the face of the madonna and, because I couldn't help myself, I sank to my knees and bowed my head in prayer. All the superstition I had known as a child, all the punishments that had been thundered at me by Father McGinty from his pulpit, emerged anew. Nicholas pulled me gently to my feet, whispering, 'Come into the side chapel, Katie, there is a confirmation service going on there.'

I obeyed in a dream and we were in time to see the procession of children walking with downcast heads. Clad entirely in white, the little girls floated ethereally through the darkened church, followed by dark, solemn-eyed boys, and their families looked on proudly as once my family had looked at me walking down the aisle of that tiny little church nestling in the shelter of the cliff. Tears filled my eyes but I could not have said what I cried for. My lost youth, perhaps, or faded dreams.

I dabbed my eyes impatiently. I could not explain the reason for my tears when I did not know myself, but I made a vow in that great church that we would return home. There was too much danger for me in Italy and my place was at home with Liam, honouring the vows I had made to be a good wife and obey him. Then suddenly we were out in the sunlit square and all around us was warm pulsating life and Nicholas's hand was warm and comforting under my arm.

I was glad that he asked no questions, and soon we were in the car speeding away from Milan.

'Are you anxious to get back to the hotel for dinner?' he asked quietly.

'It doesn't matter. Marisa will be with her friends so I shall be quite alone.'

'In that case we will have dinner in the mountains at a small taverna I have known for many years.'

We dined in the open air where gardens and vineyards climbed the mountain sides, while above us the setting sun tinted the snow-clad peaks with a rosy glow. We dined off tenderly roasted duckling and home-grown vegetables, drank delicious Orvieto and finished with tiny woodland strawberries and clotted cream, and I was hopelessly and gloriously happy.

Nicholas regaled me with stories of his boyhood in distant Canada. He told me of long winter nights and frost-laden mornings when he had skied through the pine forests or down the mountain slopes, and how as a boy he had sped along bubbling turbulent rivers in his canoe. It was a boyhood totally alien from any I had heard of, but it was a boyhood that had fashioned the man with the low timbre to his voice and the devilish charm to his smile.

I forgot Liam, I even forgot Marisa. I wanted that night to go on and on, and later when I heard music being softly played from inside the restaurant I gave myself up to the sheer joy of listening, and watching the pale new moon floating in a deep blue sky.

The doorman was yawning lazily when we entered the hotel. The foyer was empty, and catching sight of the clock I gasped with dismay to discover it was almost two o'clock.

It was then I began to worry. Suppose Marisa had looked in my room for me, suppose she hadn't been with her friends after all?

As if he was aware of my thoughts, Nicholas whispered, 'Take a look in her room, Katie, I'm sure you'll find she's fast asleep.'

She was sleeping peacefully.

Nicholas was standing outside on my balcony and as I closed her door he came back into my room.

In answer to his unspoken question I murmured, 'She's asleep. Thank you, Nicholas, for a heavenly day. I've loved every minute of it.'

'I'm glad. We should go off again together, Katie, some day when Marisa is with her friends.'

'I'd like that, but I feel I shouldn't.'

'I know. I knew it in the church. That upright moral little soul of yours feels it's all wrong, that you should be here when your daughter has time for you, and when she hasn't you should spend it thinking about Liam.'

'Something like that.'

'Katie, you're still young and very lovely. Did nobody ever tell you that life was for living?'

'I'm not so very young any more and I am a married woman.'

'Whose husband hasn't thought fit to accompany her and whose daughter leaves her very much alone.'

He was standing with his hands on my shoulders, and then he was holding me and my arms were around him and

I was kissing him as ardently as he was kissing me.

I felt him lift me off my feet and carry me across the room towards the bed. It was then that sanity came to me and I pushed him away. 'No, Nicholas, no, not here, not with Marisa next door. Please, not here.'

He released me immediately and our eyes met, agonized, imploring. 'If not here, Katie, come to me. For one night of your life don't be afraid to live it.'

He left me abruptly and I lay back on my pillows, my mind in turmoil. How I wanted him, and yet I was sane enough to remember the conventions I had sworn my life to. Fiercely I paced the room, my hands hugging my elbows, tightly and hurting, then I was flinging off my clothes with shaking hands and shrugging my arms into my robe. I caught sight of my white face in the mirror, surrounded by its halo of dark red hair, and I sat down with my head buried in my hands.

Why, oh why didn't Marisa walk into my room? Why wasn't I a stronger, nobler woman? But Marisa's door remained closed and, God help me, I was weak and vulnerable, I was lonely and desperately in love.

I crept like a shadow along the dimly lit corridor and without knocking on Nicholas's door I entered. He was standing at the window looking out into the night and I reached his side without him turning round, then immediately his arms were around me and we clung together, oblivious to anything beyond the moment.

I had been Liam's wife for many years but I had never been made love to as Nicholas made love to me, and I had never given myself so completely, so rapturously or joyously and, when at last our passion was spent, unlike Liam he did not turn away from me to enter his separate world, he held me tenderly like a child, whispering the words of love I had always yearned for but never had.

The first pale light of dawn found us still locked in each other's arms, and then sunlight flooded the room and sanity returned.

I fled like a fugitive. My empty room looked back at me, impersonal and lonely. I was a wraith, an empty thing whose entire being was still with Nicholas, but I made myself bathe and dress, then I escaped into the morning sunshine before life came to the streets.

I walked quickly towards the town, where the shops were still shuttered, and climbed the shallow cobbled steps that led above the town. Canaries sang in their cages outside closed doors and not even a solitary road sweeper came into view. Then suddenly I heard the distant chiming of a bell, then another closer at hand, and almost immediately doors opened and people were pouring out of their doors – men in formal dark suits and women with lace kerchiefs covering their hair, children in summer clothing carrying flowers, and old women in long black dresses.

If they thought it strange to see a visitor they merely smiled shyly and went on their way. I watched them enter the tiny church and when the last one had entered I remained outside, listening to their singing and the priest intoning the Latin prayer I remembered from my childhood.

I had forgotten that today was Sunday.

Back at the hotel there was no sound from Marisa's room. She was still sleeping, but when I opened the doors leading on to her balcony she yawned and opened her eyes.

'Sleepyhead,' I said, going to sit on the edge of her bed.

'What time is it?' she murmured, only half awake.

'Just after seven. You don't need to get up just yet.'

'Gracious, why are you up so early? You're already dressed.'

'I know, I wasn't sleepy.'

She snuggled down in the bedclothes and almost immediately was asleep again.

Memories of the night flooded my being and I longed for Nicholas, I wanted to go to him, I needed him to tell me that the words he had murmured in the night were true, that they had not been figments of my imagination, but I was afraid that the passions of the darkness had evaporated in the calm light of day. Instead I went out into the gardens and sat looking out to where the fishing boats were returning to Tremezzo.

Nicholas found me there, and with that wry smile I had come to love he said, 'I watched you cross the gardens, I called to you but you didn't hear me.'

I didn't answer him, and his hand began carelessly to play with a tendril of my hair lying in the nape of my neck. 'Did you sleep when you went back to your room?' he asked.

'No. I dressed and went into the town. The people were going to church very early and I followed them and stood outside.'

'And being such a sinner you dared not go inside.'

He was taunting me with his slow, easy humour, and when I didn't answer he said gently, 'You're no sinner, Katie, you are a warm loving woman who needs to be loved. Damn the men who have never known how to love you.'

The tears slowly coursed down my cheeks, and with a muttered exclamation he put his arms around me and gathered me into his embrace. He held me gently until the tears had run their course, then just as gently he said, 'I love you, Katie O'Donovan, but I don't know what good it's going to do me.'

'I love you too, Nicholas, but I can't have you. There's Liam and Marisa. But I'll never stop loving you, and nobody can ever take away what I have now.'

'So you are prepared to live the rest of your life on memories?'

'I have to, but I'm not asking you to do the same. You'll meet somebody else to love, somebody you can marry.'

'I want to marry you.'

His face was earnest, his grip on my hands strong and warm, but I steeled my heart against his charm by calling upon the common sense that had upheld me in every crisis in my life.

'Think, Nicholas, if you had loved me years ago when I was a parlourmaid and you were a guest on Tremayne Hill, nothing could have come of it, and nothing can come of it now for different reasons. Love me today and tomorrow and for all the time we are together and then try to forget me as I must try to forget you.'

'It's a snob you are, Katie O'Donovan. Why did I ever fall in love with an Irish baggage who has the makings of Janey Cassidy in her?'

'I have not,' I cried indignantly, then I saw the sadness beneath the banter and I threw my arms around him and held him close.

Chapter 29

Every day was an enchantment, every night an exquisite joy. We walked in the hills and sailed across the lake, we drove into Switzerland and to quaint old villages around the lake, and in the scented darkness of the night we made love until I wanted the time to go on and on endlessly.

Marisa was busy with her friends and showed little interest in how I passed my days until one afternoon when Nicholas and I called at the taverna where we had dined on our way back from Milan.

We were in the garden drinking our wine when we heard laughter and voices from the terrace below us and I saw Marisa standing with her back against an olive tree, wrapped in the close embrace of a boy older than herself.

Suddenly my feet touched the ground and sharply I called out to her, so that they sprang apart and she looked at me with a furiously blushing face.

Abruptly I left Nicholas and walked swiftly towards them. 'Where are the others?' I asked her sharply.

'Oh, they wanted to swim and we didn't feel like it. Giuseppi has borrowed his father's car and we thought it was nicer up here.'

'You told me you were going to Lugano with a party of friends.'

'They changed their minds.'

'I see. Well, why don't you both join us, and we can return to Tremezzo later.'

By this time Nicholas was with us and we walked back to the balcony together. Nicholas ordered fresh orange juice for them but already there was a mutinous look on Marisa's face and the boy's face was flushed with embarrassment. I forced myself to chat normally and Nicholas came to my aid, asking the boy where he lived and how long he was staying in the area. To my surprise he was a local boy and lived permanently in Tremezzo.

Politely he asked, 'Have you enjoyed your holiday, Signora?'

'Very much, Giuseppi, but I'm afraid it is coming to a close.'

'Oh, why is that?'

'Well, Marisa must return to her school. Next year will be a busy time for her.'

Marisa was looking down at the table, her small hands clenched on her lap, and Giuseppi said in a startled voice, 'Marisa is still at school?'

'Why yes, didn't you know?'

Nicholas said quickly, 'English girls seem to go to school until they walk down the aisle, it's one of their quaint customs.'

I looked at him gratefully. I had been about to tell the boy that Marisa was only fifteen, and she would have found it hard to forgive me. Quite evidently he had thought her considerably older.

The conversation was strained for a time, with Marisa taking no part, and then the boy excused himself on the grounds of having promised to return his father's car. Marisa returned with us, staring morosely out of the window, so that Nicholas gave up his attempts to include her in the conversation.

As I left him he pressed my hand gently. 'I'm afraid you are in for trouble, Katie. You are going to have to be very tactful.'

I nodded, and hurried after Marisa who was running along the path towards the hotel. When I reached my bedroom her door was already closed and locked, so I rapped upon it impatiently, calling on her to open it at once and let me in. When she took no notice I went out through the balcony and entered her room that way, to find her sprawled on the bed in an agony of weeping.

I sat beside her until the sobs subsided, then in a calm voice I said, 'Marisa, I am not angry that I found you with

314

Giuseppi, I am angry that you lied to me. Indeed I am wondering how many times you have lied to me during the last few days.'

'I haven't lied to you,' she sobbed, 'they *have* gone sailing, I'm tired of sailing.'

'But who is this boy? You haven't even mentioned him before.'

'They all know him, he lives here.'

'But who is he?'

'He's rich, if that's what you mean; his father owns the fishing fleet.'

'I'm not concerned about whether he's rich or not. How old is he?'

'I don't know.'

'Oh come now, you know very well. I want to know how old he is, Marisa.'

'Nineteen.'

'And you told him you were older, I suppose?'

'Yes, he wouldn't have asked me out if he'd known I was only fifteen.'

'Why should you want him to ask you out? The last time you talked about your friends it was Pierre or André you liked.'

'All the girls like Giuseppi, but it was me he asked out.'

'Are you telling me that is why you went, to score over the other girls?'

'Of course not.'

'Don't you realize you are in danger of losing the girlfriends you have made on this holiday by behaviour of that kind? Catrina and her friends have been very kind to you, they have included you in all their activities and this is how you repay their kindness.'

'It wasn't like that.'

'Then tell me what it was like, I want to know.'

'Giuseppi was Maria's friend but they had a row. She went off with André so I went off with Giuseppi. He said he liked me the best anyway and he'd been waiting to ask me out.'

'Oh, Marisa, and what do you think will happen when

315

you leave here? He'll be back with Maria and they'll laugh together about how easy it was for him to persuade you. Besides you are too young to be going about with a boy of nineteen, and too young to flirt seriously.'

'If I'm too young you're too old.'

'What do you mean by that?'

'You flirt with Nicholas, you're always with him these days, just like Catrina's mother and Stephano.'

I bit back the sharp retort on my lips, and rose to my feet, saying, 'You don't want everybody in the dining room to see you've been crying. There's time to take a bath and change before dinner.'

Dinner was a silent meal and Nicholas merely bowed towards my table when later he entered with Valeria and Stephano. None of Marisa's friends were in the dining room so I could only suppose they were giving her a wide berth. She seemed near to tears and later when the contessa paused at our table Marisa could barely raise a smile.

'I hope you will join us for coffee later,' the contessa said with an encouraging smile.

'Thank you, I would like to but I am not sure how Marisa wishes to spend her evening.'

'Well, the young people have all gone into Lugano. I was surprised to see Marisa in the dining room, I thought she had gone with them.'

So Marisa had lied, and the evidence of her crimson face was proof enough.

'You will be pleased to know that we have tickets for *Aida* at the Roman Arena in Verona, Kathleen. Nicholas said you would like to go but tickets are hard to get and the journey is quite long. Stephan has them for Wednesday.'

'Thank you, contessa, I shall look forward to it.'

With another gracious smile she swept on and I decided at that moment that it was better to ignore Marisa's untruths in case I brought on another storm. She declined the dessert, and complained of a headache.

'I shall go to bed,' she announced. 'You won't want me when you join those people for coffee anyway.'

'Those people have been very kind to us, Marisa.'

316

'I shall be asleep when you come to bed so you needn't come into my room,' she snapped.

'I shall all the same, if it is only to see if your headache is better.'

The contessa looked at me sympathetically when I joined them in the coffee lounge. 'I could see that you were having trouble, Kathleen,' she said gently. 'The young can be very troublesome. Why didn't she go into Lugano with the others? I hope they haven't quarrelled.'

I decided to tell her about Guiseppi.

'Oh dear, Maria and Guiseppi have been close since they were children. Every summer when she is here they have been together, and she won't like Marisa stepping in.'

'She is too young to know what she is doing. I am sure she did not mean to cause trouble.'

'No, perhaps not. Well, I hope she does not interefere with your plans. I will talk to Catrina and ask her to be a little forgiving, ask her friends to be forgiving also. You are not here for very much longer.'

'No. You are very kind.'

'I am also very assertive. I do not want your daughter to interfere with our plans to visit the opera and I do not want Nicholas to lose you too soon. I have not known him so enraptured with a woman before.'

'He is a very attractive man, he has probably loved a great many women.'

'Perhaps, but I do not think so. A man may love many women, but for some men there is perhaps only one woman who can light a lamp in the soul.'

'You think I am that woman?'

'I think it is possible, yes.'

Chapter 30

The enchanted days continued but there was a subtle difference. I felt that Marisa was watching me. If we sat by the pool she was there with her friends but now instead of being at the centre of their activities she was on the outskirts, watching me. If we walked in the hills they found us, and more and more she elected to dine with me and, if she went with the young people, she returned in time to seek me out and go with me to our rooms.

Nicholas made no comment, but we were both aware of the change in the pattern of Marisa's life, though not whether it was beacause she distrusted me or because she was no longer so close to the younger set since her part in Maria's and Giuseppi's quarrel.

'What do I wear for the opera?' I asked Nicholas the day before we were to leave for Verona.

'Oh, the Italians love their opera and always dress up for it. Ask Valeria for details, darling, she'll advise you.'

'How soon must we leave?'

'Early afternoon at the latest, and it will be midday on Thursday before we return.'

'As late as that?'

'I'm afraid so. The opera will start around ten and finish about two, then we have a considerable journey in front of us along roads that are not of the best.'

'I see.'

'You are thinking about Marisa. If you like I'll ask Valeria if she can stay with Catrina at her sister's villa.'

'Oh no, please don't bother. I'll talk to Marisa first to see if she has any suggestions.'

On Tuesday morning before breakfast Marisa complained of feeling ill. She didn't want breakfast and said she had been sick most of the night. Indeed her face was a pasty grey and her palms were damp and sticky. She refused adamantly to have the doctor see her.

'Please, Mother, I'll be fine, just leave me in bed and go off to the opera with the others.'

'I can't go and leave you like this. It's essential that you see the doctor, Marisa.'

'I wish you wouldn't fuss so much.'

By mid morning she was shivering uncontrollably and I informed the others that I would not be able to go to Verona.

'She was perfectly all right yesterday,' Nicholas said. 'I suggest you ignore her protests and call the doctor, Katie.'

I nodded miserably. 'Oh Nicholas, I am so sorry this has happened, I was so looking forward to it but you do see that I can't go, don't you?'

'Yes Katie, I do, but please call that doctor. I'll see you as soon as I get back.'

For a long moment we clung together, then I sat miserably on the balcony watching the big tourer sweep out of the gates and into the road.

The doctor felt her pulse and made notes, looked in her eyes and down her throat, then he shook his head in what I can only describe as a mystified manner. He asked what she had eaten and drunk the day before, then he informed me that it was probably a summer chill and I should keep her in bed, and he prescribed tablets to be taken every six hours.

By this time I had a headache so bad it felt as though bands of steel were tightening around my forehead. From time to time over the years I had suffered from migraine and I decided this was one of those days when I needed to take the tablets my doctor at home had said I must never be without. Before coming to Italy I had placed seven of them in a small silver pill box, and now to my utmost dismay I found only three of them left.

In something like panic I searched the drawers and my toilet things but when I didn't find them I sat down weakly on the edge of my bed, and then white-hot seething anger took possession of me and I wanted to rush into Marisa's room and shake her awake. Then as quickly as it had arisen the anger subsided. Marisa was Liam's daughter, and she had a life to live, a life she believed she was protecting, for I had no doubts that Marisa had swallowed the missing tablets.

She had stopped me going with Nicholas to Verona in a most terrible way. Suppose those tablets had been lethal – she could have died. To reassure myself I fled into her room, but she was sleeping normally and the natural colour was back in her cheeks.

Marisa had punished me for loving Nicholas, but more than that God had punished me. All the terrors and superstitions of my childhood came into my mind now. The figure of Father McGinty was there in the room, his voice thundering, 'Thou shalt not commit adultery', and I was sobbing into my hands, blabbering my confession into the empty space and thanking God that Marisa was not dead.

I was still sobbing when Marisa, yawning sleepily, came slowly into my room. When she saw the tears rolling down my cheeks she ran instantly to my side and fell on her knees with her arms around me.

'What's the matter, Mother? Don't cry please, I'm better, I'm much better.'

'Oh Marisa, why did you do such a terrible thing?'

'I thought you were going away with Nicholas, that you'd never come back.'

'But we were only going to the opera, darling, you knew I would come back.'

'Mother, I want to go home. It's all spoilt, the holiday, everything, I don't even like those people any more.'

'But why, darling? You were so happy with them.'

'They're not like us, Mother, they're so foreign.'

'Well of course they are, but you knew that all the time. The holiday's nearly over anyway.'

'I don't want us to wait that long, I want to go home tomorrow, or the next day for sure. Please, Mother, I want to see Daddy and Aunt Mary and all the other people we know. I hate it here.'

The staff were solicitous about Marisa's health and I was glad to be able to reassure them that she had recovered. The restaurant that night for dinner was only half full, with the contessa and her friends away and the younger people off on some excursion of their own.

Once more the sulky look was back on Marisa's face as she whispered, 'They're all so old, Mother, just like that first day.'

I felt irritated by her. She had been happy enough to leave me to my own devices until she felt threatened, and now I had to drop everything including Nicholas, and return home.

I loved her, but I loved Nicholas too, and I was determined he would find me here when he returned. Fate however played one more trick, and I believed my punishment to be complete. That night I was awakened by my windows slamming, and was appalled to see flashes of fork lightning illuminating the sky while the lake had whipped up into giant waves. Struggling into my robe I fought my way to the edge of the balcony and the sight that met my eyes sent me staggering back into the room. Tiny pleasure craft were being broken up like matchwood and already the promenade was littered with debris from them.

The palm trees along the esplanade bent and tossed as though taking part in some wild primeval dance, and all around the surrounding mountains the thunder rolled. In the cold grey light of morning the rain-lashed promenade was deserted and instead of blinding sunlight the cold crept into the room so that I ran back to my bed, shivering.

At breakfast guests were already talking about their departure and the weather forecast was foul. The sad-faced Italian at the desk informed me that all the mountain passes were closed, and any man venturing out on the roads that day was a fool.

We had been in Italy for almost a month and now Marisa wept and pleaded that we should go home, and at last I was no longer proof against her demands. I went into the writing room and composed my farewell letter to Nicholas, which I handed in at the desk to be given to him on his arrival. In it I thanked him for the joy he had given me and for loving me but I asked him to try to forget me and seek his happiness somewhere else. For my part I would never forget him or stop loving him.

I was sure he would smile at the letter's banality, at the arrogant assumption that he could love me and forget me and love again, but I knew in my heart we had no future together. Then I sent a wire to Liam telling him that we were arriving home the following day and giving him the times of our boat and connecting train, and asking him to meet us at the station.

I was aware of Marisa's searching glances as she kept up a constant stream of chatter throughout our journey, but I was relieved that all traces of her illness had gone. The sea voyage was destined to be a rough one and we sought our cabins immediately we stepped on board. I lay in my narrow bunk, wide-eyed and sleepless, listening to the thunder and the punishing storm, but by the time we reached Dover it had played itself out and a pale watery sun shone out of a washed out sky.

Soon we were in the train speeding northward, and if nothing else brought me to earth it was the sight of the sombre Pennine hills and the drabness of a skyline of mill chimneys.

A thin drizzle was falling at Manchester, and my eyes scanned the station platform looking for Liam's tall figure while Marisa ran ahead of me, her blonde curls flying, and I found a porter for our luggage.

She greeted me at the barrier with a shake of her head. 'He's not here yet, Mother. Suppose he hasn't got your telegram?'

'In that case we shall have to take a taxi. We'll wait just a few more minutes.'

By now the drizzle had become a steady downpour and I began to view Liam's non arrival with some degree of doubt. He could be sulking (I was no stranger to his sulks), he could be ill, or simply unable to meet us because he was otherwise occupied, but he had by this time acquired a considerable workforce, and pressure of business had never prevented Liam from doing the things he wanted to do.

The city looked dark and miserable in the heavy rain and as we stepped from the taxi at our front gate I looked up at the house for some sign of life. It stared back at me, unwelcoming and dejected. The grass needed cutting and the sodden flower heads hung dismally on their stalks. About the entire house was an unlived-in air, and the windows needed cleaning.

The house smelled musty, a mixture of dead flowers and stale food, and I wrinkled up my nose in disgust while trying to avoid Marisa's troubled eyes. In the hall the bowl of roses I had left had strewn their withered petals across the hall table and on to the floor. A small pile of mail had been laid carefully on the corner of the table but there was no sign of the telegram I had sent and I wondered why Mrs Laurie, my daily woman, hadn't made her presence felt, unless she too was away or ill.

A similar scene greeted me in the living room and the dining room. Dead ashes were piled in the grates and on the hearths, and on all the furniture was a fine film of dust. In the kitchen one solitary cup and saucer had been left to drain but in the sink were several dirty plates, and on the window sills the geraniums were wilting.

Marisa had followed me into the kitchen and stood near the door with a frightened, bewildered expression.

'Take your case upstairs and unpack,' I ordered her. 'I'll clean up here and make a fire in the living room before I do anything else.'

'Why hasn't Daddy come to meet us?' she asked in a trembling voice. 'Where is he?'

'I don't know, dear. He doesn't appear to have been home for several days.'

'Shall I go down to the builder's yard to look for him?'

'No. Do as I say, get unpacked. We shall know presently what has happened.'

Still she hesitated, and then in a small trembling voice she said, 'I wish I hadn't written to him, he's angry because I told him we were having such a lovely time.'

'Surely he would want you to have a lovely time.'

323

'Yes, but not you, not with Nicholas.'

'You wrote to your father telling him about Nicholas and me?'

'Yes, I only said you were sailing and walking with him, I didn't tell him about Milan and the opera.'

'Oh Marisa, what a hornet's nest you might have stirred up, and it was very sneaky and disloyal to me.'

Huge tears rolled down her cheeks. 'I didn't mean to be sneaky, Mother, honestly I thought he'd be pleased that we were both having a good time.'

I stared at her, hurt and puzzled. But more, I didn't believe her. Marisa was my daughter and I loved her, but I didn't trust her. Oh surely I wasn't going to be burdened with a daughter as mean and unpredictable as Fanny?

'Mother, I'm sorry,' she was saying, 'I'll never do such a thing again, never.'

'Go and unpack, Marisa, I have work to do.'

She went reluctantly and, weary as I was, I started to clean the house, as though by washing and polishing I could erase the hurt her betrayal had caused me. I made a meal for us both but by this time much of my appetite had gone and Marisa too only picked her food. Somewhat irritated, I snapped, 'Leave it if you don't want it. I'm going to have a bath and go to bed.'

'You mean you're not waiting up for Daddy?'

'I don't know where he is and I don't know if he's coming home. My waiting up for him won't bring him home any sooner.'

She hesitated as I waited for her on the stairs, then with a resigned air she climbed them with me. 'I shan't sleep a wink until I hear him come in,' she said firmly.

'Goodnight darling, I'll see you in the morning,' I replied.

By the time I had had my bath and was ready for bed Marisa was sleeping peacefully, her pretty face calm and untroubled and a tender half smile curving her lips. I thought about Fanny, unconcerned and uncaring after one of her tantrums, and my mother who had made only half-

324

hearted efforts to keep me near her. It seemed to me that this uncaring attitude was a family trait, but one which had passed me by. If anything, I cared far too much.

Chapter 31

For what seemed like hours I lay staring into the darkness with the sound of rain pattering on the windows. I slept at last but was aroused abruptly by the slamming of the front door and the muttered curses from the hall where someone had fallen over my luggage. I snatched up my robe and went out on to the landing, then snapped on all the lights.

Liam stood in the hall blinking owlishly. After a cursory look in my direction he took off his macintosh and shook it briskly.

His face was red and glistening with rain, and as he walked to the stairs I saw that his gait was unsteady.

'So you're back,' he said thickly. 'When?'

'A few hours ago. Didn't you get my telegram?'

'No.'

'Well it isn't here, somebody must have received it.'

'Aunt Mary probably took it.'

'You mean you gave her a key to the house?'

'I told her to call in case there was anything important.'

'The wire was important.'

'Ay well, and it would depend when she picked it up, probably too late for her to be doin' anything about it.'

'Where have you been, Liam?'

His face broke into a grin, and without answering he stumbled into the kitchen. I heard the sound of crockery and the running of the tap, and with my temper rising I ran down and into the kitchen.

'Where have you been, Liam? I've asked you a perfectly civil question.'

'Ay, and now I'll ask you one, where have you been and who with?'

'You know where I've been, with your daughter.'

'Isn't it just as well that I didn't come too? I'd 'ave stuck out like a sore thumb among all them posh folk you've bin mixin' with. What did Marisa call 'er, the contessa, an' all the rest of 'em with their posh villas and their Ferraris. Did ye tell 'em ye were shanty Irish an' married to one?'

I turned away in disgust, aware now of the whisky on his breath and that his hands were trembling, his eyes bleary. Before I was aware of it however he had moved quickly, spinning me round to face him.

'Go on,' he shouted, 'tell me about 'em. Do they get their hands soiled doin' an honest day's work? Foreign gigolos, that's what they are, an' you too besotted to see through 'em.'

'You don't know what you're talking about, Liam. Let me go.'

'You've always fancied yerself, Katie O'Donovan, just like yer father before you. He always thought he was better than anybody else, never drinkin' wi' the lads in the pubs, always up on the headland lookin' at the scenery. It's him that gave you all them high-falutin ideas and don't think I don't know about you an' that young feller in Marsdale.'

'What young fellow in Marsdale?'

'Carslake. Chasin' round after him, if he'd have had yer you wouldn't 'a' looked twice at me.'

'What do you know about Jeffrey Carslake?'

'I went lookin' for you one day an' Polly said you were up on the fell. I saw you together so I set off home, you wouldn't have wanted to see me, that was clear.'

I had no answer for him, but putting all the contempt I had for him in one long look I shook myself free and walked to the stairs. He followed, shouting at the top of his voice.

'You thought I didn't know, didn't ye, Katie? I knew all right, an' who's it been this time, some foreign dago ye picked up with?'

Outraged, I turned upon him with all my quick Irish temper. 'And how about you, Liam Clancy? Don't think I don't know about Geraldine. I don't care what you do, but did it have to be somebody living on your own front doorstep?'

For a moment he was stopped in his tracks, then his eyes narrowed dangerously and he grabbed my arm. 'So you know about Geraldine, do you? Well at least she's not bin as reluctant with 'er favours as mi own wife. You've bin a very expensive housekeeper, Katie O'Donovan, but it's not a housekeeper I'm wantin', it's a woman to share mi bed.'

'Go to her then,' I screamed. 'I'll be glad for you to go to her and you can take your money with you, I don't need it.'

His hands were clutching my arms, his fingers digging into the soft flesh until I could have screamed in agony, and now that he towered over me fear took the place of anger.

His voice was thick with hatred as he shouted at me, 'I knows you don't need it, not wi' Maurice Abrahams only waitin' to step into mi shoes. I wonder if he'll be so eager once I've told 'im what a cold fish ye are.'

I shrank back, my hands straining against his chest, and in as calm a voice as I could muster I pleaded, 'Liam, let me go, you're hurting me.'

My calmness seemed to inflame him more.

'Not half as much as I'm goin' to hurt you. I'll bet you've bin pretty free with yer favours in that exalted society yer've bin livin' in, well let's see if yer any better than Geraldine, let's see what I've bin missin' all these years.'

I fought him, beating my hands upon his hard chest until they were crushed against him, then he picked me up and carried me kicking and screaming into the bedroom. I glimpsed Marisa's terrified face on the landing before he slammed the door shut, then when I still struggled he hit me a stinging blow at the side of my face.

For one agonized moment the room dipped and spun around me, and through the hot searing pain that filled my head his hot bleary eyes looked demonically into mine. I felt his hands tugging and tearing at the delicate lace of my nightgown, then when I screamed again another blow descended on my bruised face, knocking me senseless.

The days that followed were filled with hatred. Loathing for Liam who had violated my aching and bruised body and for

328

Marisa's part in it. Hatred for the house because I must live in it and hatred for Aunt Mary who arrived on the doorstep the following morning, eyeing my bruised and swollen face with narrow inquisitive eyes.

'My, but yer've made a right mess of yer face, Katie. 'Ow did that 'appen?'

'I fell,' I lied quietly.

'What that sore eye wants is 'alf a pound o' beef steak to take the bruisin' out. A don't suppose yer've bothered to do anythin' about it.'

'No.'

'Well it won't get better in a minute, it wants lookin' after. 'Ad a nice oliday then?'

'Yes thank you.'

'I thowt yer wouldn't be back till weekend.'

'We came back early, the weather broke.'

'I can't understand why folk 'ave to go off ter foreign parts. What's wrong wi' the 'oliday resorts in this country, then?'

'Did Liam give you a key, Aunt Mary?'

' 'E did.'

'Then you received the telegram I sent him.'

'I took it down to the yard but there were nobody there except that Geraldine. She said she'd see to it.'

'I see.'

I wanted her to go. My head was throbbing painfully and there was a strange buzzing in my ears which made me afraid that Liam's blow had caused more than bruising to my face.

Instead of going, however, she questioned Marisa about the holiday. Marisa was diplomatic, aware no doubt that she had caused enough mischief. When Aunt Mary finally departed she fussed over me, making tea and insisting that I lie on the couch with the curtains drawn so as not to hurt my eyes. I heard Marisa busy in the other rooms with the vacuum cleaner, and reflected savagely that she was feeling guilty enough to embark on household tasks which she normally did everything in her power to avoid.

I tried valiantly to eat the light meal she served me, but

the boiled egg was underdone and the toast was burnt. When later we heard Liam's key in the door she fled into the kitchen, not wanting to see how I received him.

His face was pale, his eyes like a sad forsaken spaniel's, anxious to be forgiven. Liam had never been able to say he was sorry about anything and today was no exception. He had however brought home a potted yellow begonia, and an enormous cream cake which instantly nauseated me.

Life went on. I cleaned the house and shopped for groceries. I entertained Aunt Mary and Uncle Joel every other Sunday for lunch and I went to the plays given by the pupils of Marisa's school. Liam accompanied me, a thing he had never done in the past, and it gave me grim satisfaction to know he hated every minute of them. I did not ask him to accompany me, it was his decision entirely, but the plays were a punishment for him. Not for Liam the high-flung phraseology of Shakespeare or the even more highbrow productions of Marisa's English mistress. Liam appreciated farce and rumbustious comedy, he liked girlie shows with sequinned dresses, and he tried desperately hard not to fidget. I was always relieved when he quietly nodded off. This was the long uphill task of atonement, and I didn't care. For weeks I hated him, then I discovered that the hatred was punishing me more than it was punishing him.

In the few weeks that followed that terrible night I couldn't bear to look at him, not even when I learned that Geraldine McClusky had left the yard to work for a solicitor in Manchester.

It was Aunt Mary who broke the news to me, and looking at her plump complacent face I wondered if she had known about Geraldine and Liam.

'I had thought that Geraldine was indispensable to the business,' was the only comment I made.

'Why should yer think that?' she snapped. 'There's an older woman at the yard now, very efficient she is too, and she's got a young girl to 'elp 'er.'

I didn't care. If Liam had surrounded himself with the chorus of the Folies Bergères I wouldn't have cared.

It was at one of the school choir concerts that I caused a terrible commotion by fainting in the middle of a spirited rendering of Handel's *Hallelujah Chorus*, and I came round in the headmistress's study surrounded by several members of her staff and the school matron. Liam and Marisa were there also, looking at me with frightened eyes.

The following day Liam insisted I saw the doctor, but there was really no need for it. I knew what was the matter with me. I had been married almost sixteen years and I had a daughter of fifteen, now I was expecting another baby, and whatever its sex I was hating it.

I was thirty-five years old. I didn't want another child with all the upheaval and harassment involved, but already Aunt Mary was fussing round me like an old hen and Aunt Martha was accusing me of stupidity and carelessness. Liam was ridiculously delighted, although it seemed incredible to me that he should feel any delight over a child conceived in lust and anger. I wasn't sure how Marisa felt about the baby, or how she would adapt to sharing.

After that first stupid fainting episode I felt remarkably well. I carried on with my work with Maurice and we went into larger premises. We now employed a small, talented and loyal staff and had embarked upon interior decorating. I was studying for all I was worth on a course dedicated to textile design, and the money was rolling in from wealthy businessmen who had purchased exclusive property in Cheshire or the prettier parts of the lower Pennines in Derbyshire and Lancashire. I was hating the pregnancy which kept me close to home when I felt I ought to be out with Maurice involving myself in improvement schemes.

I was working until seven o'clock on the Friday evening, and the following morning at ten o'clock my son was born in the most uncomplicated manner, and I felt surprisingly strong.

Liam tried to disguise his evident pride while trying abjectly to prove that I was the one he cared about, not the son he had always longed for. Irritably I wished they would all go and leave me alone, but he drooled at the baby asleep in the cot by my bed and his aunt lectured me about leaving

331

a job I didn't need, to stay at home and look after him. I feigned a weariness I didn't feel and scowled at the smiling nurse who raptured about the flowers surrounding me and the basket of fruit which had just been delivered to the hospital from Maurice.

'Aren't you the lucky one,' she enthused. 'And with a foine husband and a beautiful daughter bringin' all these beautiful flowers, and now another gentleman sendin' this fruit.'

'The other gentleman is my business partner,' I felt myself snapping.

'Sure he is, and moity generous he is too. And what moight you be callin' your little son, Mrs Clancy?'

Her Irish accent was strong and I guessed she hadn't been long in England from the old country. It brought back memories of mist-laden mornings, soft summer rain, and gulls wheeling over Horn Head. Now she took the baby out of his cot and placed him beside me.

The last time I had seen him he had been red and wrinkled just after he was born, but now as I held him in my arms I loved him. I loved his dark downy head and the incredibly long dark lashes that swept against his cheeks, and suddenly he opened his wide blue-grey eyes and I found myself devouring his tiny features, delicate and sensitive, and I knew with exquisite certainty that this was not Liam's child. Happiness filled my entire being. In spite of all my sins God had not punished me, instead I had Nicholas's child, all I would ever have of him in the otherwise empty years ahead.

That night when Liam and Marisa came to see me I was kind. I smiled gently at their gifts, and relief glowed in Liam's eyes. On parting Marisa threw her arms around me and said, 'Oh Mother, you've been so strange these last few months, is everything going to be better from now on?'

'Yes darling, I'm sure it is.'

She kissed me again, and then I suffered Liam's embrace before they left me alone with my son.

Chapter 32

Liam wanted the baby to be called Patrick Joel after his father and the uncle who had given him his start in life. I prevaricated. 'Why not Michael after my father and Turlough after my uncle?'

He had no wish to quarrel. He was always wary of me when we didn't agree on anything, and trying to be reasonable, I said, 'Why should we want to call him after anybody? He's an individual, he should have his own name.'

'What do you want to call him, then?'

'I'd like to call him Jeremy.'

'What sort of name is that, one o' them high-falutin English names you've seen in a book?'

'I like the name and it's what I want to call him.'

To my utmost relief Marisa also liked the name and with a shrug Liam capitulated, with the words that he couldn't fight us both.

Neither his protestations nor Aunt Mary's accusations prevented me from returning to the job I loved, but when Aunt Mary saw that it was useless to argue with me she offered to look after Jeremy. Memories of her influence on Marisa made me decline the offer in the gentlest way possible. I told her she was too old to take on a young baby, that she needed to think about herself instead of taking on such a responsibility, and to my utmost surprise I found Liam a willing ally.

'I thought you would have wanted Aunt Mary to look after him,' I said in some surprise.

'She'd ruin the child. In no time at all he'd be thinkin' more of her than he would of us. It's at home you should be stayin' to look after him yourself. Time enough to go back to that job when he's at school. I suppose it's Abrahams that's urgin' you to go back.'

'No it isn't. Maurice hasn't said a word. I want to go back because I need the stimulation the work gives me. I wish you would try to understand, Liam. It's not that we need the money, I just need to do something else besides shop for groceries and clean the house.'

The years passed swifty and Jeremy grew tall. He was a beautiful intelligent child, and one morning I was shaken by Aunt Mary saying, 'I don't know who he takes after, he's not like Liam.'

'Perhaps he's more like me. Marisa has her father's colouring.'

'If he had red hair I reckon 'e'd be a lot like Michael O'Donovan. Yer father was always a good-lookin' lad.'

I had found a very capable woman to look after Jeremy while I was working. Anne had worked as a sister in a hospital until she married, but her husband had developed consumption and died, leaving her a widow only months after their marriage. She hadn't wanted to go back into nursing in a large hospital and my advert for a baby-minder had come at exactly the right moment.

She was competent, with the right degree of sternness, and I paid her well for looking after Jeremy and any work she did in the house. She was honest and trustworthy, and I was experiencing the joys of a newfound freedom.

At first Aunt Mary found fault with her work and Anne complained bitterly that she was round every day, interfering and complaining until I decided to have a few words with her.

She looked at me in hurt surprise.

'I'm only tryin' to 'elp. I don't 'old with all these new-fangled methods o' bringin' up children.'

'Anne is competent and well trained. If you interefere, Aunt Mary, even with the very best intentions, I might lose her. I don't want that to happen.'

Sniffing disdainfully, she snapped, 'If that's 'ow yer feel about it we don't need to come round at all.'

'We are always pleased to see you and Uncle Joel,

whenever you decide to come. I don't want you interfering with the way Anne is caring for Jeremy, that's all.'

She departed in something of a temper and no doubt the entire conversation was reported to her husband at the first opportunity. The following Sunday they came to lunch as usual.'

I was in the office alone several weeks later working on the colour scheme for the master bedroom for one of our customers when there was a knock on the door and my secretary informed me that there was a Mr Earnshaw wanting to see me. I stared at his card for several moments and then my face cleared. Of course, Mr Joseph Earnshaw, Lois Foxland's husband.

He had changed hardly at all, and as he took my hand he smiled down at me with twinkling eyes.

'I can see that you've done very well since you came to my house during the war, Mrs Clancy. I'm very glad.'

'Thank you, Mr Earnshaw.'

'I was recommended to come here by a business friend of mine, but I hadn't expected to see you.'

'I went into partnership with Mr Abrahams several years ago.'

'You've no longer any connections with Clancy's the builders, then?'

'That is my husband's business. I have nothing to do with it.'

'Well, Mrs Clancy, perhaps I should tell you what I would like you to do for me. My wife's illness has progressed as we knew it would. She can no longer walk about the house, not even with the aid of the railings and her sticks. She is even unable to get about in her chair. I'm selling the house, indeed I already have a buyer from Yorkshire. I've bought a smaller place, a newly built property in Cheshire and more or less in the heart of a small village. It needs a bit doing at it, but I thought Lois would see more from the window where she'd feel part of village life.'

'I'm so sorry about your wife, Mr Earnshaw. What had you in mind for the house?'

335

'Well, the drawing room will be her bedroom, and it's on the ground floor to give her a view of the short front garden and the high street, where she'll see people going about their shopping and going to church. So the master bedroom upstairs will have to be the drawing room. I want that house to be perfect. Lois is going to die in it, Mrs Clancy.'

'I would like to see it along with Mr Abrahams.'

'As soon as possible. Tomorrow, if that's convenient.'

I consulted the diary, discovering that Maurice had an appointment late in the afternoon, but Mr Earnshaw said, 'You'll be back in town well in time for that, Mrs Clancy. I take it you'll be driving down.'

'Yes. Shall we say soon after ten?'

'That will suit us very well. You'll see what I mean about her illness, Mrs Clancy, but she's still a lovely woman. Try not to let her see you feel sorry for her, that's all I ask.'

I had been driving my small car for two years and it was decided that I should pick up Maurice at his house in Cheshire the following morning, since it was only a short distance to the village where Mr Earnshaw had bought his new house.

It was an enchanting house. The man who had built it had used his imagination. The rooms were large but oddly shaped, since every one had a curved wall. I loved the large windows and beautiful fireplaces. We were taken into the drawing room last of all and here I looked at Mr Earnshaw in some surprise.

'Lois is still at the manor. I don't want her to see this house till it's finished, but I would like you to visit us with colour schemes and samples of wallpaper and curtains. That way she'll feel she's had a hand in things.'

'Of course, Mr Earnshaw, that can be arranged.'

'How soon will that be, then?'

'I'll hurry things on as fast as I can. I'll start things moving when I get back to the office this afternoon.'

'I'd be grateful if you would, Mrs Clancy. I want her to have some time to spend in this house when it's finished, and quite honestly we don't know just how long she's got.'

My eyes were swimming with tears when I got back into

the car, and I was wiping my eyes while Maurice chatted to him on the doorstep. He looked at me anxiously when he joined me.

'Would you like me to drive, Katie?'

'No. I'm all right now.'

'Poor sad man. It's been terrible for him, watching his wife die by inches each day of their married life.'

'Oh Maurice, she was so beautiful, like a delicate piece of Dresden china. She always reminded me of a chocolate-box kitten, and she dressed so beautifully.'

'Well she obviously has developed great courage. Some people fight adversity, others are defeated by it. Mrs Earnshaw appears to have accepted it.'

I devoted all my time and energies into acquiring colour schemes and patterns to take to the hall as quickly as possible, and was surprised when he invited me to stay over the weekend.

'I don't think I can do that, Mr Earnshaw. I have a small son whose nanny only comes Monday to Friday,' I said hesitantly.

'I was thinking it would be nice company for Lois, she doesn't have many visitors and her old friends are reluctant to come. I don't think they like to see her as she is now and she's just as anxious not to see them.'

When I talked about the situation that evening to Liam he surprised me by saying, 'Couldn't you take the boy with you? I can look after myself for once.'

My eyes flicked over to where Marisa was curled up on the settee leafing through a magazine, oblivious to our talk.

She was nineteen years old, had left school two years before and was now embarked upon a domestic science course at an exclusive college in the centre of the city. I had hoped she would show some interest in my line of work but Liam had quite deliberately steered her mind into other channels by saying it was more essential for a woman to learn skills that would turn her into a good wife and mother – besides, there was enough money coming into the house, she didn't need to find a job.

She had grown up tall and very pretty. She went to

dancing classes and had recently taken up riding, she had an army of friends because she was gay and likeable. Sometimes I wondered if only I saw the petulance under the charm, the waywardness beneath the laughing open face. I liked to think we were good friends, indeed she never failed to come into my bedroom after attending a party so as to tell me who she had danced with and who had brought her home. She brought both her girlfriends and her boyfriends home and I had found the boys likeable and friendly, the girls much like herself.

'What are you doing this coming weekend, Marisa?' I asked.

She looked up with a bright smile. 'Jennie Palmerston has invited me to go with her for the weekend to Keswick, she has an aunt there.'

'If I take Jeremy to the Earnshaw place, your father will be here on his own.'

'Well, that's all right. Daddy can cook eggs and bacon and look after himself. He doesn't need me here, do you, Daddy?'

He smiled at her indulgently. 'Of course not, you go off to Keswick and enjoy yourself. Just the two of you, then?'

She rose gracefully and went to the back of his chair, standing with her arms round his neck.

'Of course. Jennie has the most divine cousins in Keswick, we don't need to take anybody with us.'

'Boys or girls?' Liam persisted.

'Boys, of course. Don't be such an old stick in the mud.'

They laughed together, and I heard her singing happily as she ran upstairs. The expression on Liam's face was fond and smiling, and catching my eye he said complacently, 'She's a fine girl, Katie, we're very lucky in our children.'

'She should find a job, Liam. What is she going to do with her time when she's finished the course?'

'Time to think about that later. It's not necessary for her to work. It's different for the lad, he'll come into a nice little business when he's old enough.'

I stared at him, aware for the first time of the trauma ahead. I did not want Jeremy to go into the building trade, I wanted him to go to the sort of school his real father would have wanted for him, and then I wanted him to do what he was best suited for. I had no doubt that he would not choose to follow Liam into the business.

Now was not the time to argue about it. It would have to be done slowly and diplomatically when Jeremy was older, not now when he was not even of school age.

Mr Earnshaw approved of my taking Jeremy but advised me to travel by train as the roads could be icy at the beginning of December. Liam took us to the station and saw us on the train, smiling, affable and well turned out, which made me suddenly suspicious that he had matters on his mind over the next few days that didn't include his family.

Mr Earnshaw was waiting for us at the tiny country station nearest to his house, and his friendly conversation quickly removed Liam and his devious doings from my mind.

Jeremy sat beside me wide-eyed and curious in the corner of the big car, and I could see that Mr Earnshaw was enchanted by him.

'Didn't you have a young daughter when you worked for me before, Mrs Clancy?' he asked.

'Yes. Marisa is now nineteen.'

'Quite a considerable difference in their ages,' he commented. 'How do they get along?'

'Reasonably well. Marisa has her friends, though, and enjoys a considerable social life.'

Merton Hall seemed unchanged as we approached it through the trees. My eyes scanned the window where Lois had liked to sit, and following their gaze Mr Earnshaw said, 'Lois doesn't sit in the window now, and there is not room for her bed in the alcove. When you see the situation you will understand why I want to move as quickly as possible.'

A woman servant showed us into a charming twin-bedded room overlooking lawns which sloped down to the river, and I busied myself unpacking our small valise. Jeremy yawned, and knowing that he invariably slept for a little in the afternoons I tucked him into bed, and when the servant reappeared I asked her if she would look in on him from time to time.

'Bless ye, yes Ma'am. He might be a bit afraid in a strange bedroom if he wakes up afore ye gets back.'

I thanked her, smiling a little at her warm country voice and accent quite different from the city ones I had been hearing for so long.

Afternoon tea was served to us in the morning room while Mr Earnshaw listened quietly to the plans I had for his new property. At length he smiled, saying, 'I'm no judge of these things, Mrs Clancy, but I'm confident you know what you're doing. We'll let Lois be the judge, shall we? You'll find her brain as alert as always and in spite of her disability she's still interested in pretty clothes and beautiful furniture. She chooses her bedjackets meticulously from catalogues sent up from London, but you have to hold the catalogues for her. She has no strength in her hands.'

Lois's bed was placed as near to the window as possible in the large bedroom overlooking the long drive and the distant view of the moors. She lay propped up by several plump pillows, her transparent hands resting on the coverlet. On the edge of the bed sat a Pekinese dog, who jumped off at our arrival and came bustling up to meet us, tail wagging but barking excitedly at me.

Mr Earnshaw picked him up and deposited him outside the door.

'I'll take him on a turn round the garden while you and Mrs Clancy have a chat,' he said, smiling. 'Take a look at the beautiful patterns she's brought you, Lois, and the designs for the new house.'

She smiled and I was surprised at the still startling beauty of her china-blue eyes and the face which seemed unimpaired by the disease that was killing her.

There seemed nothing of her under the soft bed coverings, and I realized I would have to sit close to her on the bed in order to show the drawings, patterns and catalogues I had brought. Her eyes lit up at the sight of the fabrics and textures, and soon we were animatedly talking about drapes, the colours of the carpets and the walls. She was

340

choosing light fittings and wall lights, bedside lamps and bedroom chairs, and I found myself waxing enthusiastic.

After she had made her selection and I rose to leave, thinking that I had tired her, she said impulsively, 'Would you mind if I called you by your christian name?'

'Of course not. It's Kathleen, but most people call me Katie.'

'I shall call you Kathleen, it's far too pretty to shorten.'

'Very well.'

'And you shall call me Lois. I was so pleased when Joseph said he had found you in partnership with Mr Abrahams. I have been looking forward to seeing you again.'

'I too. Mr Earnshaw asked me to come for the weekend and I have had to bring my little boy with me. He won't bother you in any way.'

'Oh, but I want to be bothered. I want to see him, just so long as he isn't distressed to see me lying here like this.'

'Perhaps I can bring him to see you in the morning?'

'Yes of course, that would be lovely. You will see that I have become steadily more helpless and it is no use fighting against Fate.'

'I think you are very brave, Lois.'

'What else is there? I either make life miserable for everybody else by being resentful and angry or I make the best of it. Joe has been very good to me and I have had the best doctors money could buy. There is nothing else anybody can do and in some strange way I am not unhappy.'

'You will love the new house, Lois. I am trying very hard to get all the work finished before Christmas so that you can move in. You will be part of the village life in a very short space of time.'

She smiled happily. 'Thank you, Kathleen. I have met the vicar of our new parish and he has said if we are in for Christmas he will bring the carol singers to sing outside my window.'

'Then it most certainly will be finished for Christmas.'

As I collected the catalogues and patterns from her bed

we heard a car approaching the house and, frowning a little, she said, 'Oh dear, it seems as though we have company, but Joe didn't tell me we were expecting anyone.'

I smiled down at her. 'I'll go now in case it is somebody to see you. I'm so glad you're pleased with the patterns.'

I moved towards the door, but then it opened and I found myself face to face with Jeffrey Carslake.

In the first few months after I left Heatherlea I had tried to imagine how I would feel if I accidentally met Jeffrey Carslake in the street or on the fells, but always the answer eluded me. Now twenty years on it had happened and I felt exactly nothing.

He smiled, that attractive smile that had charmed me as no other, and with the merest inclination of my head I passed in front of him and out of the door.

He had changed hardly at all in the years between. He was still as tall and graceful as in those remembered moments, his fair hair had silvered at the temples and perhaps there was a world-weary air evident in the tiny lines around his eyes and mouth.

Back in the morning room I sank into a chair, trying to analyse my thoughts. In those far-off days Jeffrey Carslake had been my only God, the one being who had the power to leave me tongue-tied and bring me breathless to his knees. Now he had walked back into my life and it meant nothing. Suppose Nicholas walked back into my life, would I regard him with quite that air of detachment?

Joe Earnshaw came in, smiling somewhat apologetically. 'I'm afraid we have a guest for dinner, Mrs Clancy. He has arrived unexpectedly, a man my wife knew before we married, their families were old friends.'

'That is perfectly all right, Mr Earnshaw.'

'I shall be delighted if you will join us for dinner.'

'Thank you. Your wife wishes to call me Kathleen, I shall be glad for you to call me Kathleen also.'

'What a splendid idea, and far less stuffy. Call me Joe, that is what Lois calls me. Our guest's name is Jeffrey Carslake, by the way. We have dinner around seven. Perhaps you will join us in here for drinks around six-

342

thirty?'

'Thank you. Will Lois be meeting us again this evening?'

'No. By six o'clock she is very weary so I do not disturb her again.'

While the Earnshaws entertained their guest, I walked in the park with Jeremy, exhilarated by the keen wind that swept down from the moors leaving us with rosy cheeks, breathless with laughter as we let ourselves into the house.

The maidservant brought supper for Jeremy: beautifully cooked plaice and vegetables followed by peaches and cream. He had a good appetite and the maidservant smiled with gratification when she took away his empty plate.

I gave him his bath and rubbed him dry with the soft green towels in the bathroom off our bedroom, then I read to him until I saw his eyes close sleepily, and laying the book aside I placed his teddy bear beside him and tucked him in warmly.

I had brought the minimum of clothing for what I had supposed would be a working weekend, but had included a dinner gown should it be needed. I stood in front of the mirror to appraise the finished result.

There had been no sign of recognition in Jeffrey's face, not like Nicholas who had seen the old Katie beneath the sophisticated woman I had become, and now looking in the mirror I could not think that Jeffrey Carslake would connect the two.

He had only seen my dark red hair demurely contained under my white cap or tumbling in wild curls around my shoulders when I walked with him across the fell. Now it was expertly cut and styled and it framed my face in a flattering upswept style, showing my ears in which I had fastened long diamond and pearl earrings.

The folds of my heavy georgette dinner gown fell in graceful lines to the floor and the sapphire blue found an echo in my darkly fringed eyes. It had long tight-fitting sleeves and a neckline that showed off to perfection the three strands of pearls at my throat. It was a slender elegant woman who faced me through the looking glass and, satisfied with my appearance, I went downstairs.

In those old days I had never entered a room when Jeffrey was in it without a feeling of suffocating palpitation. Now my heart beat steadily and it was only when I reached the morning room door that I paused with clenched hands pressing against my breast before I opened the door with my head held high.

The two men rose, and Joe came forward to take my hand.

'This is Kathleen Clancy who has come to assist us with the furnishings for the new property. This is Jeffrey Carslake, Kathleen.'

He shook my hand, then we were sitting round the brightly burning fire and there was a glass of sherry in my hand.

Jeffrey charmed me with the low timbre of his voice, a voice that had once sent me mad with desire. We talked about music and paintings, furniture and foreign shores, then he surprised me by asking, 'Do you ride, Mrs Clancy?'

'Not any more, I'm afraid.'

'That is a pity. I was about to ask if you would like a mount for the next meeting of the hunt.'

I merely smiled, and he went on, 'I take it you live in the area?'

'No I don't. I live on the outskirts of Manchester.'

'I see.'

'Are you still living at your brother's place over at Wilton?' Joe asked him.

'I am, but it is very inconvenient since I have to travel several miles to Marsdale every day. I'm looking around for something nearer the mill.'

'You won't want a large property.'

'Gracious no. Heatherlea was far too large for me but there must be one or two nice little properties going.' He turned his blue-eyed gaze on me. 'Perhaps if I find something that requires renovating you would allow me to call on your expert advice?'

I smiled. How that naive and totally besotted Katie O'Donovan from distant Donegal would have grovelled with pleasure at any indication from him that she might be of use to him. Not so Kathleen Clancy, with a thriving business, money in the bank, and memories of a love that would go with her to the grave.

Dinner was eaten in the large ornate dining room. Candlelight fell on sparkling glass and silver and we were waited on by silent-footed servants who came and went like fleeting shadows. This was Jeffrey's world and he was loving every minute of it. To him it was the old days come back again, but to me it was the old days in reverse. I was no longer one of those fleeting shadows trying desperately hard to catch his eye above the general conversation.

I learned that Jeffrey was staying the night and Joe said, 'I hope Lois will be well enough to see you before you have to leave, Jeffrey.'

'I should have come sooner, but I wasn't sure she would want to see me. My sister said she preferred not to see any of the people she had known when she was well.'

'She has grown steadily worse. If you had called to see her two or three years ago you would have found her propelling herself around the house in her chair. Now she must remain in bed all the time.'

I sensed there was a faint reproach in Joe's words but Jeffrey skated easily over them by saying, 'It is strange how all the crowd from the old days have been affected in some way or another. In those days I think we all believed that life would go on uninterrupted just as it was, but the war altered many things, and as you know cotton is a fluctuating problem. We suffered a great deal after the war, and even now that we are part of a considerable combine nothing is safe and we must keep on condensing to stay alive.'

'All of which would have distressed your father considerably.'

'Gracious, yes. He hated change, he would have lingered on at Heatherlea until it fell to pieces round his head.'

'Who is in the house now?'

Jeffrey smiled deprecatingly. 'Some master grocer with a chain of shops in Lancashire and the West Riding.'

Joe smiled, 'Like me then, a self-made man.'

I was pleased at the swift colour that rose into Jeffrey's cheeks, and he hastened to make apologies. 'My grandfather was a self-made man Joe, there's no disgrace in that, but I wasn't too happy to see Heatherlea going to a man who didn't particularly like the country and only wanted the house because it was a step on the social ladder.'

Joe turned to me, saying, 'I hope we're not boring you, Kathleen. I think you'll understand how hard it is to see beautiful things going to people who don't know their value.'

'I understand, but perhaps one day this man who has bought Heatherlea will have learned values. If not he, then some member of his family, perhaps.'

Jeffrey looked at me with a new awareness. 'Do you know Marsdale at all, Mrs Clancy?'

'I have been there.'

'All the houses on Tremayne Hill are very beautiful, all of them individually designed from the Tremayne house down. It is sad that most of the people who lived there when I was a boy have now sold out because of fluctuating fortunes or death.'

'I often wondered why nobody had taken the trouble to build on Evening Hill,' Joe said. 'Of the two it was the prettier.'

'Oh I agree, but old Farmer Gargrave owns all the land there. We had the utmost trouble when we wanted to hunt over his land. He'll never allow building on the hill.'

'Mmmm, great pity.'

'Well not really, it meant that we were able to look out on lovely scenery instead of modern houses.'

'You don't like modern houses?' I asked.

'Not particularly.'

'Careful, Jeffrey, Mrs Clancy's husband is a builder of modern property.'

'Good modern property, Mrs Clancy?'

'He doesn't concern himself at the moment with housing, he builds mostly offices and industrial property. If he ever decides to build houses he will naturally seek the advice of an architect. He is a very good builder, Mr Carslake.'

Joe laughed heartily. 'I should keep off that subject, Jeffrey, this lady will have an answer for anything you say. Did Lois agree with the designs and patterns you brought for her, Kathleen?'

'Yes, she was delighted with them. I hope she will be well enough to see us in the morning. She said she would like to see Jeremy.'

'If she said that then I'm sure she'll be up to it, and I expect she'll want to see Jeffrey before he leaves.'

Just before eleven I made my excuses, and they both rose as I left the room. As Jeffrey stepped forward to open the door for me our eyes met. I read only admiration in his – admiration, not recollection. It was an aesthetic admiration for a beautiful woman, elegant and intelligent, and remembering Lois's words spoken to me in this house several years before, I thought how that admiration could change if the beauty became marred by illness or length of years.

Chapter 33

I slept fitfully. My mind was tortured by dreams of the past, strangely haunted with visions of my life at Heatherlea. In them I was back once more in that tiny attic, and always pointing the admonishing finger at me were Cook and Mrs Tate. Then there was Polly dropping china on the kitchen floor, and my cousin Frances taunting me that I was a servant and never likely to be anything else.

Jeffrey didn't figure in my dreams, but somewhere in my subconscious I was aware of whispered voices and hurrying feet.

I awoke to the cold grey light of dawn and for a few moments I lay collecting my scattered thoughts and willing the remaining shadows of my dreams to leave me. From the next bed I could hear Jeremy's gentle breathing. It was only seven o'clock, and breakfast was not until nine, so it was too early to get up, yet sleep refused to come back to me. Throwing on my light robe, I walked to the window.

It was a misty December morning, the hills were obscured by a fine drizzle of rain. A flock of rooks came gliding down the sky to settle in the trees that lined the rose garden, and from somewhere in the woods came the gentle cooing of pigeons.

I was wishing I could wake up every morning of my life to the sight of the distant hills shrouded in mist and the silence interspersed by country sounds, but my future lay in other channels and I must not torture my poor heart with impossible dreams.

It felt chilly in the room so, after switching on one bar of the electric heater, I returned to my bed and sat reading for a while. As soon as I heard faint stirrings of life within the house I decided it was time to get up.

I gave Jeremy his breakfast in the bedroom, then I took him downstairs and saw him settled in his chair with a picture book while a young servant girl said she would keep an eye on him.

'He might like you to read to him,' I said, smiling at her.

She looked about sixteen years old and she was pretty, with a fresh country face and clear brown eyes.

'I'm used ter children, Ma'am, I 'as five brothers and sisters all younger ner me.'

'Do you live in the village?'

'I did, now A lives in. Mi mother's glad o' that, it's one less mouth ter feed.'

'What will you do when Mr and Mrs Earnshaw leave here?'

For a moment her face clouded, then with the optimism of youth she said, 'I reckon someat'll turn up, it nearly allus does.'

'What is your name?'

'Mary Dunham, Ma'am.'

'I shall be very grateful if you can keep Jeremy amused until after breakfast, Mary. I promised to take him in to see Mrs Earnshaw.'

'She's not well this mornin', she's bin poorly most o' the night, so p'raps she won't be fit to meet 'im. Cook won't mind mi 'avin' 'im, I'm sure.'

'Thank you, Mary, I'm very grateful.'

So the whisperings and the hurried footsteps had not been a figment of my dreams after all, there had been some sort of activity in the house. I approached the breakfast room with some degree of foreboding. Only Jeffrey was there, helping himself from the long buffet sideboard, and he turned to smile and bid me good morning.

Whatever the problem with Lois, Jeffrey was eating a hearty breakfast and, as I sat opposite him with fruit juice and a slice of toast, he eyed my meagre breakfast with quizzical humour.

'I eat very little breakfast,' I said.

'And the country doesn't seem to have given you an appetite.'

'No, but then I haven't seen very much of it. This has been a working weekend, and apart from a short while in the garden with Jeremy I haven't been outside.'

'It's a typical December morning, I'm afraid. It's a pity you don't ride, we could have taken a canter over the fells.'

I smiled, but my heart said, 'Oh no, Jeffrey Carslake, I've taken my last canter over the fells with you.' Instead I said, 'I hear Mrs Earnshaw hasn't been very well.'

'Oh. I didn't know. I haven't seen Joe this morning but I thought there was something going on during the night. Did he tell you?'

'No. One of the servants told me. Poor lady, she has had more than her share of misfortune.'

'I agree. I remember Lois when she was the prettiest thing.' He laughed a little. 'As a matter of fact there was a time when our families thought we might marry.'

'But you and Lois had other ideas?' I prompted him.

'It would seem so. My mother was more disappointed than anybody else.'

'Parents have no right to plan our lives, but I know that many of them do. I hope when the time comes I will have the good sense to stay out of it.'

'You won't be troubled by such matters for some time, Mrs Clancy. How old is your little boy?'

'I wasn't thinking of my little boy, I have a nineteen-year-old daughter with a will of her own and much of my independent spirit.'

He was eying me with a half smile, a smile that once had the power to turn my knees to water. 'Yes, Mrs Clancy, I can well imagine you have an independent spirit with that lovely red hair and that air of assurance. I doubt if your daughter will get all her own way.'

'Fortunately we are very good friends, even if her father does spoil her.'

'You remind me of a servant my mother had up at Heatherlea. Pretty little thing she was, I've often wondered what became of her. Do you know that girl could ride a horse like a Valkyrie and yet she'd had only a minimum education back in Ireland. Straight from the bog she was, and as pretty as paint.'

I could feel my face burning with resentment. I longed to fling something in his face as he complacently went on with his breakfast, but I clenched my hands under cover of the tablecloth and, waiting until my voice felt calm enough, I said, 'In what way do I remind you of this girl from Ireland?'

He looked up and made a pretence of studying my face. 'It must be your colouring, Mrs Clancy. Of course she was pretty, but it was very rough-hewed. Now what was she called? I remember, Katie, yes Katie.'

'My husband calls me Katie, he has never called me Kathleen.'

'What a pity when Kathleen suits you so much better.'

'I don't really mind.'

I was saved from further talk about my name as Joe Earnshaw came in, wearing a harassed frown. Instantly I said sympathetically, 'I hear Lois was ill during the night. I hope she's feeling better this morning?'

'She's upset because she doesn't feel well enough to see your little boy. But really, Kathleen, it's better for both of them that they don't meet. I got the doctor out to her, but it'll take her a day or two to come round.'

'Is it connected with her illness?'

'Oh no. That will take its natural course, the doctor says she's caught a virus, but heaven knows how. She never goes out of her room, let alone the house.'

'I hope it's nothing I've brought into it. I'm sure Mr Carslake hopes the same.'

'Heavens, yes. I'm leaving during the morning, Joe, perhaps it would be as well if I left without seeing Lois.'

'She wouldn't like that, Jeffrey, she'll be expecting you to say goodbye.'

I heard Joe's answer with grim satisfaction.

Jeffrey would like to leave the house without the distressing sight of meeting Lois again. We would all like to float through life without meeting tragedy or opposition, but few of us enjoyed that blessed benison. He was not a physical coward, he had been brave enough to go to war and face the enemy, but he was not brave enough to face the tragedy of a long, disabling illness.

He was bitter about the loss of family fortunes and a way of life he had believed would go on for ever. He was cynical that money was now in different hands, and he hungered after the old days when men touched their forelocks to him in the street, and women bobbed quaint curtsies as he walked between their looms. Those days had gone for ever, replaced by a frightening world in which he was a stranger.

So much I had gathered in one brief evening and an even briefer morning, and I knew how rightly I had judged when I saw him speak to Lois later that morning.

I had gone in to bid her goodbye and, although I tried not to show it, I was appalled by her face lying back against her pillows, grey and pallid, her eyes ringed by dark circles and her mouth pale and twisted with pain.

Her thin transparent hands plucked at the coverlets, and tears filled my eyes at the sad travesty of her smile.

'I wanted to see your little boy, Kathleen,' she murmured, so softly that I had to bend towards her to hear her.

'I'll bring him again when you are feeling better. He's sorry he can't see you.'

She nodded, and I knew how much it had cost her to say those few words. I sat by her bed, telling her that I would get on with the work on the new house, watching her nod and smile, then the door opened and her husband brought Jeffrey in.

Jeffrey took hold of her thin limp hand and she turned her head painfully to look at him. She smiled, 'Thank you for coming, Jeffrey, it was very kind.'

He bent his head and lightly kissed her cheek.

There was sadness in his face, sadness and regret for something irretrievably lost, but there was also distaste. As he turned away he seemed to shiver delicately and I knew he was glad to be going.

If Lois had been capable of any coherent thoughts at that moment, they must have been that she had indeed been a very fortunate woman when she captured the love of Joseph Earnshaw on that cruise all those years before.

Chapter 34

Liam was not happy to have me working on the Earnshaws'
new house and I couldn't understand his irritation when I
reported progress to him. When at last I remarked on it I
was astounded by his answer.

'I suppose workin' for them you feel ycr back on
Tremayne Hill again workin' for the gentry.'

'What rubbish you do talk, Liam. This isn't in the least
like the work I did on Tremayne Hill and I've never even
connected the two.'

'But you knew her then.'

'I knew who she was, yes, I can't say I knew her.'

'But you do now, so that makes it right. You feel you're
on a level with 'em at last and it's all your own doing, it has
nothin' to do with me.'

'Oh Liam, you're so wrong-headed about my work.
Some husbands would find it in their hearts to be proud of
their wive's accomplishments, but not you, you'd like me to
be dependent on you for every penny coming into this
house.'

'Isn't that the way it should be? How many other women
do you know around here who work like you do?'

'Why don't you ask yourself how many women round
here are capable of working like I do? I don't want to talk
about it because we shall never agree in a million years.'

He sulked, and later slammed out of the house with ill-
disguised bad temper. Marisa came into the kitchen.

'Why is he so cross?'

'He doesn't like me working, and particularly he doesn't
like me working for the Earnshaws. When I first came to
England I worked for a family on Tremayne Hill and Mrs
Earnshaw came regularly to the house.'

353

Her face was puzzled. 'Why should that worry him?'

'I don't know, Marisa, I don't know why he objects to so many things, particularly my work.'

'You love your work, don't you?'

'Yes I do. I need something more in my life than being a housewife.'

'None of my friends' mothers work.'

'Perhaps not. Would you like me to be like them?'

She pondered, a little frown wrinkling her smooth forehead, then with a light-hearted smile she said, 'No, I wouldn't. Our house is nicer than any of theirs and you are far more elegant. Oh, Jenny's mother shops for all the latest fashions but she doesn't pay very much for them, and they don't eat like we do.'

'They don't?'

'No. When they have dinner parties Jenny's mother borrows the silver from people round about, she even asked me to see if you had a decanter or two you could lend them.'

'Yes, and that reminds me, I only got one of them back.'

'That's what I mean, Mother. I'll bet she hopes you've forgotten it.'

'There's a towel over there, Marisa, please help me with the dishes.'

'I hate housework,' she said after a while. 'I hate that domestic science course I'm on, I wish I could come off it.'

'Marisa, it's what you wanted.'

'I know, it was at the time. I think it's awful that we should be expected to make up our minds what we want to do with our lives when we're only just leaving school. None of us really knew, at least none of us except Amelia Gentry who went up to Oxford.'

'And do you know now what you want to do?'

'Yes I do. I want to go to art college and learn about dress designing.'

'You've never mentioned it before.'

'I know. I read in a magazine that there's an awful lot of money to be made if you get with the right fashion house. Besides, if you can design household fabrics and furniture why can't I design clothes?'

'It's not as simple as that, Marisa. How do you know if you have an aptitude for it?'

'Well you didn't know either until you met Mr Abrahams and he helped you. I was good in the art class and I've been doing some drawings in my free time at college. I'll show you if you like.'

Her young face was eager, indeed I had not seen her quite so animated about anything for some considerable time.

'Do you have any drawings here?'

'In my bedroom.'

'Very well then, I'll make coffee and we'll have it in the drawing room. You won't have to object to criticism, Marisa.'

'I won't, Mother, honestly I won't.'

I heard her feet flying upstairs and darting across the landing and by the time I had the coffee in the drawing room she was on the settee with her drawings spread out around her.

I had made up my mind to be honest. I did not want to raise her hopes if her work was inferior. It was not inferior, indeed it was remarkably good, and as I leafed through her sketches I recognized my own flair in the designs, a flair that a good art college would bring out to its full.

She could tell from my face that I was as excited by the designs as she was herself, and after a while I agreed that she was far more suited for this sort of work than she would ever have been in domestic science.

'Will you ask Daddy if I can do something like this?' she coaxed. 'He's always on about my learning how to cook and sew, but there's so much time to do all that, I want this first.'

'Why not finish your domestic science course and then think about this? It hasn't very long to run, so surely you can stick it out for the time that's left.'

'Oh no, Mother, while I'm doing that I could be at the art college getting on with something new.'

'You are going to have terrible trouble with your father if you take up anything as fanciful as dress designing,

Marisa.'

'But you'll tell him won't you, Mother? You'll tell him I have talent, that I've just got to do something with it.'

'I'll tell him when the opportunity is right, and I can't think it'll be tonight. You saw the mood he was in when he slammed out of the house.'

'Oh, he'll be over it by the time he gets home, and the sooner he agrees the sooner I can leave that wretched course and start the new one.'

'I'll see what I can do, darling, I promise.'

I made a special effort with the evening meal, aware that Liam's temper had hardly improved. He sat with a scowl on his face, eating the beautifully cooked food without comment until, exasperated, I snapped, 'Isn't the meal to your liking, Liam?'

He looked up, then muttered, 'The meal's right enough.'

'Then why are you so silent? I thought you'd be in a better temper when you came home.'

'I'm not one for small talk.'

'I know that.'

'Where's the boy then?'

'Across the way at a birthday party, I'm to pick him up after dinner.'

Again there was silence, and I served the sweet course, shaking my head dolefully in Marisa's direction.

Marisa tried to chat to him but met with little success, and when we had finished our coffee she leapt to her feet, saying, 'I'll do the dishes, Mother. You talk to Father.'

Before I could stop her she was piling them on to the tea trolley and I was left alone to look at Liam's doleful face across the polished table.

'That's a turn-up for the book', he remarked, 'she's not usually so anxious to help with the dishes.'

It was the wrong time to talk to him about Marisa, surely she should have recognized that, but she was young and impulsive and with all a young girl's impatience she knew what she wanted, and she wanted it now.

I followed him into the drawing room where he immediately picked up the evening paper and sat with his face buried in it.

I sat listening to the rustle of the paper and the ticking of the clock, the cinders falling into the hearth, and occasionally Liam's snorts of derision of something in the paper. At last, unable to stand it any longer, I said, 'Liam, I want to talk to you about something.'

'I don't want to listen if it's about that house in Cheshire you're working on. I've heard all I want to hear about that.'

'Are you prepared to hear something about your daughter?'

The newspaper rustled, then was laid down. 'What about Marisa?'

'She wants to leave her domestic science course. She doesn't think it's the right vocation for her and neither do I.'

'Oh, and what is the right vocation for her?'

'She wants to design clothes.'

The red angry colour rose into his face and his eyes narrowed ominously.

'You've put her up to this Katie, designin' clothes, designin' furniture, it's all part o' the same thing.'

'It isn't, Liam, and I knew nothing about this ambition until this afternoon. She's been showing me some of her drawings and they're good. It would be wrong to keep her chained to a domestic science course in which she has absolutely no interest when she could be so good doing something else.'

'I'll tell you what's wrong with you, Katie O'Donovan, you've got ideas of grandeur just like yer grandmother. She were always thinkin' she were better than other folk, and didn't mi mother always say you were like her?'

'Your mother never knew me.'

'When I told her I was marryin' you she wrote an' told me to think twice about it.'

'Why didn't you, then?'

'Wasn't mi aunt and uncle dead set on it, an' them givin' mi mi one chance in life? But I remember yer grandmother, that hoity-toity she was wi' folk she thought were nobody.'

Determined not to lose my temper I said reasonably, 'I

357

agree with you, she was like that with my father and me too.'

For a moment he sat staring at me nonplussed, then collecting his thoughts he snapped, 'Well, Marisa's not being like that, she'll carry on with that domestic science course she wanted and I'll 'ear no more talk of her goin' anywhere else. Dress designin' indeed.'

From the hall we heard the banging of several doors and I looked through the window to see Marisa tearing across the garden, her pale hair flying in the wind as she struggled to get her arms into her coat.

'She's been listening,' I said, 'and obviously she's upset.'

'She'll get over it. But that's the last I intend to hear about it in this house.'

'You surely don't think Marisa is going to let the subject drop.'

'She'd better.'

'Even if she hates you for it?'

His eyes wavered and some of the bluster went out of his talk.

'She'll see the sense of it, Katie. Marisa's not like you.'

'She's very like me in a great many things. I've fought you all my married life for the things I believe in, and she will too. If you force her into doing something she hates she'll never forgive you, Liam, and neither will I.'

He was silent with the newspaper in front of his face but he wasn't reading, and after a few minutes he lowered it and looked directly into my eyes.

'I'll talk to her miself. But I'll tell you this, Katie, if you gets your own way about Marisa you won't get your own way with the boy. There'll be no fancy furniture and interior decoratin' for him, 'e'll follow me into the buildin' trade an' you'll keep out of it.'

I didn't speak but I was seething inside. I wanted to shout at him that over my dead body would Jeremy follow him into the building trade, that my son would receive an education and make his own mind up what he wanted to do with his life, but I feared that if he provoked me far enough I would tell him in my anger that Jeremy was not his son.

'Shouldn't you be fetchin' the boy from across the way?' he said.

Silently I rose to my feet and went out of the room.

It was raining as I hurried across the road, holding my umbrella against the wind. I almost collided with Marisa, who was standing on the corner, her hair drenched with rain, the tears vying with the rain on her face, oblivious to the fact that her coat was saturated. Sharply I ordered her to go back home.

'I'm not going home to see him,' she stormed, 'I hate him.'

'I told you it wasn't a good idea to talk to him tonight, Marisa. I've been married to your father long enough to know what he's like. Leave it, there'll be another time to talk to him.'

'I won't go back to that domestic science course, Mother, I just won't.'

'Well, we'll see. It might be a good idea to continue until the end of term and then we'll see about the new one. You can't do much before then.'

Even in the lamplight I saw her eyes open wide with hope, then she hugged me. 'Oh Mother, you really think Daddy will come round, don't you? You will talk to him again.'

'I will, but it'll be in my time. Now run off home and get out of those wet things. If you catch your death of cold you'll not be going anywhere.'

When I came in with Jeremy a few minutes later I found Liam asleep in his chair. Marisa was up in the bathroom washing her hair. I gave Jeremy some hot milk then took him up to bed.

He was soon asleep, and looking down on him I resolved there and then that I would fight Liam every inch of the way for the future of my son.

Strangely enough I did not have to talk to Liam about Marisa's ambitions again because we found an unexpected ally in Aunt Mary when they came for lunch the following Sunday.

There was little conversation at the beginning of the

meal. I busied myself looking after Jeremy and Marisa studiously avoided looking at her father, all of which told Aunt Mary everything was not as it should be. Never averse to stepping in where angels feared to tread, she said brightly, 'Are ye still workin' on that 'ouse in Cheshire, Katie?'

'Not any more, it was finished last week and they'll be moving in tomorrow.'

I saw Liam's lips tighten ominously, a fact that did not escape Aunt Mary, and she went on, 'I don't suppose yer've seen it, 'ave ye, Liam?'

'Why should I see it, haven't I enough to do with mi own business without concerning miself with Katie's?'

Lunch progressed and I served the sweet course.

'Very nice lunch, Katie,' Uncle Joel said, wiping his mouth with his napkin. 'I 'ope you'll be as good a cook as yer mother after yer've finished that fancy course yer on, Marisa.'

Marisa scowled, and quick as lightning Aunt Mary jumped in. 'Yer don't say much about it, Marisa. In my day a girl didn't 'ave to go on any fancy course to learn 'ow to cook an' sew and make a good 'ome for a man, she learned all she needed from 'er mother, an you could do a lot worse than learn fro' yours.'

Marisa's eyes filled with tears, and jumping to her feet she ran out of the room.

'Now what 'ave I said?' Aunt Mary said, astounded.

'You've hit on rather a sore point, Aunt Mary,' I answered. 'Marisa isn't enjoying the course and wants to leave it. She wants to do dress designing.'

'What's that, then?'

'Designing beautiful clothes. Her drawings are good, an art college would help to bring out her talent. I've been lucky, I've been able to take my chance, and I don't want anything less than that for Marisa.'

'Yer've bin lucky cause yer've 'ad that Maurice Abrahams teachin' yer.'

Across the table our eyes met, then as I rose to collect the dishes I said, 'Yes, that's true, he's been one of the best friends I've ever had. I shall always be grateful to Maurice for making so many things possible.'

She bit her lip angrily as I left the room. I found Marisa sitting in the kitchen, her eyes red from weeping.

'Go back into the dining room,' I admonished her, 'and apologize to Aunt Mary. If you behave yourself she's the one person who might be on your side in convincing your father you should come off that course. Show her your drawings, talk to her about what you want to do. She's always taken your part, Marisa, now is the time to be a little clever about things.'

She hovered in the kitchen, unsure if my idea was practical, then she ran out of the room in search of her designs. When I returned to the dining room with the coffee she was kneeling beside Aunt Mary's chair, both of them engrossed with the sketches strewn on the floor.

Liam sat tight-lipped and Uncle Joel looked uncomfortable. Only Jeremy, sitting calmly and grown up at the table, seemed oblivious to the undercurrents.

It was a grey day but it was not too cold, and in the afternoon Uncle Joel accompanied Jeremy and me on our walk in the park. As we watched him running on ahead of us towards the duck pond Uncle Joel said, 'Yer might 'ave trouble wi' Liam over 'im one day, Katie?'

'What do you mean?'

''E'll want 'im to be a builder an' carry on the business, but I reckon yer 'ave other ambitions for 'im.'

'We're talking about the future, Uncle, but I shall want Jeremy to do what *he* wants to do within his capabilities.'

''E's not like Liam, not even like Liam when 'e was a lad. Mary an' me were never blessed wi' a family, an' I watched mi sister's lad grow up thinkin' that one day 'e'd come to us an' learn the trade. 'Is father were a drunken Irishman wi' no ambition an' allus i' some scrap or another. Mi sister never knew when she'd 'ave a week's wage from 'im or good food on't table, but Liam's a good lad, Katie. I'll bet yer've never bin short o' money from 'im, so that yer've bin able ter put yer own earnins away.'

'No, Liam's never kept me short of money, since he came

361

back from the war.'

''E's a lad wi'out much imagination an' 'e thinks yer've flown a bit too high fer im, Katie. Be a bit patient wi' 'im. Underneath, 'e's that proud of yer, Katie, of all of yer.'

I stopped to stare at him. 'But he resents everything I do, Uncle Joel, how can he be proud of me when he's always throwing my work in my face or trying to belittle it?'

'Well, 'e's jealous, isn't 'e? 'E's jealous o' Mr Abrahams because 'e's an educated man an' talks your language, probably because 'e's all the things Liam isn't. Probably Mr Abrahams has had more advantages.'

'Oh, Uncle, that isn't true. Maurice has all the natural cleverness of his race and he's made it work for him. I'm the same. I've had no real education but I've watched and listened and learned. I won't let Liam put me down.'

'Course not, Katie, just give 'im time, that's all I ask.'

'I hope Aunt Mary'll try to persuade him to let Marisa have her chance.'

'I 'ope so too, Katie. Ye know Mary's not a bad woman, she's just too fond of interferin'. It's 'er nature, she thinks she knows best an' there's bin times when she's come between me an' mi folks because I've bin too ready ter listen to 'er.'

I smiled at him gently. 'You have to live with her, Uncle Joel.'

'Ay, that is so, an' there've bin times when I've bitten mi tongue rather than cross 'er. She's cocky an' altogether too forthright fer 'er own good. Puts folks backs up, she does, insists on sayin' 'er piece regardless. It doesn't do, Katie. No, it doesn't allus do.'

'It's too late to alter her now, Uncle.'

'Yer probably right, lass. I'm glad we've 'ad this little talk, it's not often we gets the chance.'

We hurried after Jeremy, who was feeding the ducks with crusts. Watching his beautiful boy's face gay with laughter, I thought sadly about Nicholas. I wondered where he was and what he was doing, and if ever he gave a thought to those ecstatic days in the Italian lakes.

When I thought about them it was as if they had all

happened to some other person and not to me at all, and yet here was Jeremy, warm and alive and laughing, a reproach and a reminder of something irretrievably lost.

Chapter 35

Liam capitulated about Marisa's education, as I knew he would. The next battle in front of me would be Jeremy. When I suggested he went to a private school a little journey from home Liam argued that the school across the way should be good enough for him, and it was ridiculous to spend money on his schooling at such an early age.

I knew that Jeremy was bright and I wanted him to have all the advantages we had never had. There were sulks and tantrums and once again I was accused of trying to be better than I was.

When I complained bitterly to Maurice about my husband's attitude he smiled, saying, 'He resents you, Katie, and he's wary about how to handle you. You've grown away from him, indeed I doubt if you were ever close to him,'

'I should never have married him, Maurice. I liked him but I didn't love him. I thought love would come later with being together, sharing a home and bringing up our children. But we're as far apart now as we were in the beginning.'

'I suppose you're determined to get your own way about Jeremy?'

'Yes, Maurice, I am.'

'Then you should be prepared for a great deal of opposition.'

He was right. Liam and I quarrelled day after day, angry blistering quarrels that left me drained and frustrated and sent Liam into sulks when he spent days without addressing a word to me – until the next quarrel started.

I took Jeremy to the school I had picked out for him and he was given a test to see if he was the right sort of material.

This he passed with flying colours and there and then I wrote out a cheque for his first term.

That night I met the full force of Liam's Irish temper, which sent Marisa scurrying out of the house. Jeremy cowered on the landing, his face as white as chalk. Not since that night when he had dragged me screaming into the bedroom had I seen Liam in such a rage, but this time instead of using the cold contempt which lashed him into a further fury I matched his rage with my own. Eventually he slammed out of the house, vowing never to return, and I heard the car driven at breakneck speed down the short drive, then with a squeal of brakes into the road.

I settled Jeremy into bed, then went downstairs to await events. It was hard to sit calmly watching the fingers of the clock move slowly while my fingers sent the needle in and out of my tapestry work. Marisa came home soon after ten, and I heard her footsteps pause outside the door before she found the courage to open it.

'Where's Daddy?' she asked in a small, timid voice.

'He's gone out, dear. Have you had supper?'

'Yes, I had something at Mary's. Where has he gone to? What time will he be back?'

'Marisa, I don't know. He was in quite a temper when he went out and he said he wasn't coming back. I'll wait up a little longer.'

She stared at me for a few minutes with wide unhappy eyes. 'Don't you care whether or not he comes back, Mother?'

'Well of course I care.'

'Why does Jeremy have to go to that school? I went to the school across the way.'

'I know, dear, but Jeremy is a boy and one day he'll need to keep a wife and children, whereas you'll probably get married and have a man to care for you.'

'Isn't that terribly old-fashioned?'

'Yes, perhaps it is, but it's the way of things.'

'Surely he doesn't need to go away to school to be a builder or a joiner.'

'Perhaps Jeremy won't want to be a builder.'

'Daddy says that's what he's going to be.'

'Your father isn't always right and Jeremy should be consulted, I think.'

'That will mean more quarrels. Why can't you just let him have his own way? After all, he has the business to think about.'

When I remained silent but went on quietly sewing she sidled back into the room. 'I met a friend of Mrs Palmerston's today who asked a lot of questions about us.'

'Oh, what sort of questions?'

'Oh the usual, where we go for holidays, where you buy your clothes. She said she knew you when you first came to live in Marsdale, before you went to work for a family on Tremayne Hill.'

Intrigued, I looked up and found her watching me closely. 'Did she tell you her name?' I asked quietly.

'Mrs Lorimer. Her husband's a solicitor in Marsdale and they live in a big house at the bottom of Tremayne Hill.'

I sat back in my chair, totally dismayed. Cousin Frances. It was as though a spirit from the past had suddenly descended into my life, and resentment made me break off the wool behind the tapestry so savagely that it hurt my fingers.

'Do you know her, Mother?'

'Yes, she's my cousin. Uncle Turlough and Aunt Martha are her parents.'

'I've *never* heard Aunt Martha mention her, and she never mentioned them.'

'She wouldn't.

'Why wouldn't she?'

'I'll tell you about it one day, Marisa, but I don't want you talking to your friends about it. It is family business and nothing to do with anybody.'

'I won't tell them anything, honestly, Mother.'

'Some other time, Marisa. Besides, I'm worried about your father. It's past eleven.'

'Oh, he's probably gone to the club, he's been later than this many times.'

'I know, but not after the sort of quarrel we've had.'

366

'Shall I make coffee?'

I knew that coffee would enable her to prolong our conversation but I had no desire to say more about Frances just now, and I was genuinely worried about Liam. He was in a temper, he would be drinking and he was driving his car. He was not the most careful of drivers and in his state of mind he would be a danger to himself and others on the road.

'I don't want any coffee, Marisa. Go up to bed now and I'll wait up for him a little longer.'

When he had not arrived home by twelve o'clock I went to bed, but I couldn't sleep. I had visions of Liam lying dead in a ditch with his car smashed around him, and when I heard the telephone ringing downstairs I ran to answer it with a wildly beating heart while Marisa watched from half-way up the stairs. It was Uncle Joel.

'Liam's here, Katie. He's gone upstairs to bed but I thowt I'd better ring yer, I knew yer'd be worried about him.'

'Oh yes, thank you Uncle Joel. I was afraid he might have had an accident in his car.'

'Ay, I've towd 'im 'e shouldn't be drivin' it when he's drunk more than was good fer 'im. I take it yer've had a bit of o' bother?'

'Yes. He slammed out in a temper.'

'Well, no doubt Mary'll get it out of 'im in the mornin'. Don't worry, lass, 'e'll 'ave calmed down by then.'

He went straight to the yard from his aunt's house, and it was after six o'clock when he arrived home for his evening meal.

The meal was eaten in comparative silence except when he spoke to Marisa, then as I cleared away the dishes I heard them talking together in the drawing room where I guessed she was showing him her latest drawings. He was not really interested in her prowess but he was making a supreme effort to appear so.

Jeremy sat on the kitchen floor playing with his electric train, and after a few minutes Liam came in and picked up the tea towel, starting to dry the dishes. I made no comment, and after a while he said quietly, 'You got the boy in at the school, then?'

'Yes, Liam. They gave him a test and he passed it quite brilliantly. The headmaster was very impressed.'

A look of pride came over his face. 'Well, why shouldn't he pass? He's a bright boy.'

'Then you don't really mind him going there, Liam?'

'We'll see how he gets on, but I'd like him to have the business one day, Katie.'

'Liam, suppose he wants to be a doctor or take up some profession? Surely you wouldn't stand in his way?'

'What's to happen to the yard, Katie? Mi uncle worked hard for that business an' I've worked a lot harder. I don't want him goin' into any o' that fancy stuff like Maurice Abrahams.'

'I've never even thought about it, Liam. Jeremy is only a little boy, before we start quarrelling about his future can't we wait a while to see what his leanings are?'

'You've got your own way about it, Katie, but I don't want to be shut out. I want to have a hand in his future.'

'Oh Liam, you shall have, I promise. And Liam, please try not to be so resentful about Maurice. He's been a very good friend to me and I can tell you something now that I hadn't meant to tell you until much later. He's made a will including both Jeremy and Marisa.'

'Why should he do that?' he snapped sharply.

'Because he's no children of his own and because he's fond of them. Maurice isn't well, I think the least we could do is invite him round for a meal occasionally. It's a gesture he'd appreciate, Liam.'

Unsure, he prowled round the kitchen, pausing to watch Jeremy playing happily on the floor.

'Liam,' I prompted him, 'please let me invite him this weekend.'

Grudgingly he gave his consent, and I lifted up my face and kissed him swiftly on his cheek. I was surprised at the warm colour that flooded his face, and the sudden look of joy that he was unable to hide.

Long after he had returned to the living room I stood

staring out of the kitchen window, touched by his reaction to my rare show of affection. For years I had exonerated my own behaviour on the grounds that Liam didn't love me and I didn't love him. Now, by that sudden glimpse behind the curtain, I felt unsure and guilty.

Maurice came to lunch the following Sunday and I made a special effort with the meal, having ascertained beforehand what were his favourite dishes.

Liam was affable, plying him with his best port and brandy. Jeremy was on his best behaviour, introducing Maurice to his favourite toys, and Marisa forgot her old antagonism and showed him her sketches, at which he looked with a keen professional eye.

In the afternoon she took Jeremy into the park for his favourite walk to feed the ducks and we dawdled over our coffee, reluctant to move from the warmth of the fire. I watched Maurice staring moodily into the fire and I couldn't prevent myself saying, 'Is something troubling you, Maurice? You've looked so unhappy recently.'

He smiled gently. 'The world's troubling me, Katie. I don't like what I read about or hear on the wireless.'

'What do you mean?'

'I don't like what is happening in Europe. That man Hitler and the Italian Mussolini. If we are not very careful we are heading for war.'

'Oh no, surely not!' I cried. 'I thought those men were only doing their best for their own countries. Why should any of it bother us?'

'Because people who are greedy are never satisfied. Much wants more, and the sin of avarice will spill out over the borders of their own countries until it embraces all of us. Haven't you noticed it in people? How much more terrible it is when it encompasses lands and territories. All my childhood was spent eluding one despot or another, forever moving on, in constant fear, it is surely no wonder that I have become an expert at recognising when the writing is on the wall.'

I looked at Liam uncertainly but he sat gazing into the fire, his expression brooding and watchful.

'Liam,' I said sharply, 'surely *you* don't think there is going to be a war?'

'I don't like the way things are going, all those Hitler Youth marchin' and cheerin', and that man Hitler rantin' and ravin' like a madman.'

I grew silent, thinking about that other war – the queues of grey-faced men and women at the grocers shuffling through the snow with their meagre rations, and the pages and pages of war casualties in the newspapers. I thought about all those young men going gaily to war, and I remembered a girl running across the station yard and a laughing Canadian officer sweeping her into his arms.

Oh no, there couldn't be another war, not now when life was so stable. Poor Maurice had too many bitter memories, it was natural that he should be pessimistic.

He and Liam were chatting about the state of trade, and I took the cups and saucers into the kitchen. I felt restless, and after I had washed them I threw a coat round my shoulders and went out of the house. It was a cool fresh day and I felt the need to walk briskly to the park, but I had only gone a few steps when I saw Aunt Martha and Uncle Turlough.

I waited for them and Uncle Turlough said, 'Were yer goin' out then, Katie? Don't let us keep ye, we'll go right back.'

'I was only taking a walk. Marisa and Jeremy are in the park, I thought I might go to meet them.'

Aunt Martha had been limping along the road and my uncle looked at her with an unspoken question.

'I can't walk as far as the park, Turlough. It's mi arthritis, Kathleen, this weather doesn't suit it at all.'

'Then we'll go back to the house. Liam and Maurice are in the drawing room. Why didn't you let me know you were coming? We could all have had lunch together.'

'We only made up our minds at the last minute. We've got a bit o' news for ye.'

I settled them in the morning room with tea and biscuits,

then sat down to hear their news.

His eyes were twinkling as he started to speak so I could only assume the news was good.

'Our Lucy's finally got 'erself a young man,' he said. 'We'd begun to think she was goin' to be an old maid, she were thirty last birthday.'

'Oh I am so pleased for her, is he a nice young man?'

'He's not much to look at but he's honest and steady and he's got a bit o' money put by that his mother left him. We've known him some years now, 'e's allus called in for the evenin' paper and come round every Saturday to pay for everythin' he's had durin' the week. Him an' his mother lived together an' I allus thought he weren't a marryin' man, but last year the old lady died an' I reckon he's bin a bit lonely on his own. Anyhow him an' our Lucy've struck up a friendship an' they seem right happy together.'

'I'm glad. Does that mean they'll be getting married and moving into his house?'

He and Aunt Martha exchanged glances.

'Well, he works i' cotton, an' cotton's precarious. We thought he could move into the shop, they could manage it between 'em and Martha and me'll look out for a little house somewhere nearby.'

'And what do they say to that arrangement?'

'They're pleased about it. It's a good little shop. It means 'em gettin' up early to see to the papers, but Lucy's used to that an' 'c'll have to get used to it. It's their bread an' butter, Katie, so it's not too much to ask, is it?'

'No indeed. Are they having a large wedding?'

'No, somethin' quiet round about Christmas next year.'

'So far off?'

'Well, we has to look out for somewhere to live. Neither Martha nor me want 'em to start their married life wi' in-laws. We'd like you an' Liam and the children to come to the weddin'. Yer all the family we 'ave, Katie.'

'Well of course we'll come. Where is it to be?'

'At St Michaels. It won't be a long-winded affair coz Alfred isn't Catholic, an' Lucy hasn't asked him to change 'is religion for her.'

'I see.'

'Well, it shouldn't worry you much, Kathleen,' Aunt Martha snapped with some asperity. 'You've never bin a keen church-goer.'

'You don't need to go to church to be a good Christian, Aunt Martha. I don't tell lies, I look after my home and children and I'm unfailingly generous. That's more than can be said for a lot of those men and women who mouth meaningless platitudes Sunday after Sunday and don't exactly practise what they preach.'

Uncle Turlough chortled. 'There ye are, Martha, I told ye ye might get more than yer bargained for if ever ye raised the question o' religion with Katie.'

She bit her lip with exasperation, and determined to have the last word, snapped, 'I suppose Liam attends the church, his Aunt Mary'll see to that.'

'Liam isn't as much under his aunt's thumb as you might think. He does go to church, after all he's friendly with the priest. Don't they play golf together several times a week when the weather's decent?'

Deciding not to pursue that conversation she said, 'I think Lucy'd like Marisa to be 'er bridesmaid.'

'Oh Aunt Martha, Marisa would love that. Will she be the only one?'

'I think so. Lucy's a practical girl and she's not out to spend more than needs be. There'll only be a handful at the weddin' an' she's plannin' all sorts o' changes for the house and shop. She'd rather put 'er money into that then spend it on a fancy weddin'.'

'That's very sensible.'

'Ay, not like our Fanny who had a big affair at the parish church an' a reception at the town hall. Six bridesmaids she 'ad, an' two little 'uns as pages, yer'd a thought she were royalty wi' all them flowers an' that long train she let trail in the dust. Right waste o' money it was, an' no mistake.'

'Did you go to watch it, Aunt Martha?'

Her eyes fell before mine and the rich warm colour flooded her cheeks.

'I wasn't goin' to, but I couldn't stay away. There we

were standin' among the gravestones in the churchyard wi' dark glasses on so nobody could recognize us. She swept along the church path on the arm o' that man she called Father wi' never a look in our direction, and the same when she came out wi' her new 'usband. I cried fer days after that, yer uncle'll tell ye 'ow much it upset me.'

I leaned forward and covered her hands with mine. 'Oh Aunt Martha, I know. I can't help thinking that one day God will punish her for what she's done to you two.'

'She's not bein' punished, they've got a big 'ouse an' 'er 'usband a solicitor in his father's firm, an' a local councillor to boot. I only 'ope her daughter doesn't do to her what she's done to us.'

Liam came into the room, curious to see who I was talking to, and while I went into the kitchen to prepare the evening meal I heard them giving him the news of Lucy's wedding. Maurice came to sit in the kitchen, saying with a wry smile, 'I hope our talk of war didn't upset you, Katie. It was just two men's preoccupation with disaster, like two schoolboys playing with war games.'

'And now you think you can placate me by treating me like a silly little woman who's afraid to know the truth.'

He laughed. 'I could never think of you as a silly little woman, Katie. I've always been able to give you the bad news and know that you'd take it on the chin.'

When Liam arrived home in the middle of the afternoon several days later I sensed in him an excitement which caused me to stop what I was doing and demand to know why he should suddenly appear looking like the cat that had swallowed the canary.

'I've been up at Marsdale this mornin', and who should be in the Royal George havin' his lunch but old Gargrave.'

'Do I know him?'

'Course you know him, Farmer Gargrave who owns that farm on Evenin' Hill an' all the land around it.'

'Well?'

'He's sellin' up and movin' out. Had enough of farmin',

373

he says, an' he wants to go and live with his daughter over at Preston.'

'He said he would never sell that farm or the land.'

'Well he's changed his mind, hasn't he, so I made him an offer for it.'

I sat down weakly on the nearest available chair. 'You made him an offer, Liam! But the farm's more or less decrepit, he never spent any money on it and what would you do with all that land?'

'Build on it, what do you think?'

'Build! But what?'

'Houses. Good houses. Houses fit for the rich to live in and better designed and better built than most o' them on Tremayne Hill.'

I stared at him, unable fully to comprehend what he was telling me, then I collected my scattered wits and said, 'But you build offices and factories, Liam, you've never been interested in building houses.'

'If I can build offices then I can build houses. I'll employ a good architect, and every one of 'em'll be different, no two alike, and the first one to go up'll be ours, right at the top o' the hill, just like the Tremayne house.'

I think at that moment I almost loved him. I was caught by his enthusiasm, my eyes shone with excitement and I started to plan the house on Evening Hill; a house with lawns and stables, a conservatory and the joys of gracious living. 'Do you think he'll accept your offer, Liam?' I asked hopefully.

'Not him, not the first one, but I'm fed up with livin' in the suburbs, I want to get out into the country.'

'So if he doesn't take your offer you'll make him another one?'

'I will. I've set mi heart on it, Katie. We're goin' to live on Evening Hill and the sooner he takes the bait the sooner we can start the building.'

'Marisa likes living in the city, she has friends here. And what about Jeremy's school?'

'There's other schools just as good, and Marisa'll like the idea when she sees what sort o' property's goin' up there.

She'll come to enjoy travellin' to the college by train.'

'What about Aunt Mary and Uncle Joel?'

'We'll think about them later. There's two farm cottages there and they can be made very nice. They're at the bottom of the hill at the top of a cobbled lane, but that shouldn't be any problem. If mi uncle's interested they could have one of 'em and your aunt an' uncle can have the other.'

For the second time in my life I kissed him with enthusiasm and affection, and once more I saw the sudden joy illumine his face.

To my utmost surprise Farmer Gargrave accepted Liam's updated offer and neither Marisa nor Jeremy seemed at all put out by the prospect of moving to the country. Talk of keeping horses thrilled Jeremy, and leaving her friends seemed not to trouble Marisa unduly, particularly when I suggested she would be able to invite them to stay for weekends.

The next few months passed like a single night as we looked at plans for the new house and the others that would be built on the hill. I was given my choice as to the one I wanted and then more than ever before I enjoyed working on designs for the interior as well as furnishings and curtaining. I consulted Maurice all along the line and soon he was as enthusiastic as I was.

I told him about the young Katie O'Donovan with her dreams of living on Evening Hill, but never in my wild imaginings had I expected it would be Liam Clancy who would turn my dream into reality.

At weekends we went to Marsdale to see for ourselves how the work was progressing. We tramped in gumboots over churned-up fields, and once I walked to the top of the fell where I had once sat listening to the low charm of Jeffrey Carslake's voice with stars in my eyes.

In all there were to be six houses built on the hill, with ours erected on the summit, giving the best of views across the town and the surrounding moors.

'Suppose you can't sell the others, what will you do?' I asked Liam anxiously.

'Don't worry your head about that, Katie. I've had more inquiries than I know what to do with.'

'Who are the inquiries from?'

'Oh, local bigwigs and from city folk who want to move out.'

'Liam, why did you suddenly decide you wanted to live in the country?'

'I've been getting fed up with suburbia for a long time, Katie.'

'You never said anything.'

'I know. It was Maurice, if you must know, who made me face up to things.'

'Maurice!'

'Yes. That Sunday when he was on about war. It won't be war like the last one, Katie, it won't be fought solely by the men in the trenches. There'll be bombing of cities, we'll all be in the front line and Manchester won't escape. There's industry here, and the docks. They'll bomb the factories that are makin' things for the war, and we're not stayin' in Manchester to be sittin' ducks.'

'Everybody can't move out of the city, Liam.'

'No, more's the pity, but you'll not have to think like that, Katie. You'll have to think about the children.'

I looked out across the valley to where smoke was curling lazily into the pale blue sky. In the park a brass band was playing and children were bowling their hoops along the paths. Soon church bells would be ringing and church-goers would be scurrying to church while above us the bracken bloomed golden and brittle on the moor and the heather flared purple and blue in great clumps as far as I could see.

'There can't be war, Liam, it isn't possible. Look how peaceful everything is.'

'Wasn't it just like this before the last one? Didn't you sit up there in the sunshine thinkin' it'd go on like that for ever?'

I stared at him, my face bleak with remembrance of those moments on the hill with Jeffrey and then later in the dining room his father's tirades about war and his youngest son's lamentable inadequacies.

Suddenly exasperated, I snapped, 'Oh, Maurice can't get the past out of his head, he thinks it's always going to be like that.'

'You've quoted his common sense often enough to me, Katie. Don't say you're questionin' it now.'

'He's right about so many things, but I'm sure he's wrong about this one. Oh Liam, let us forget about war and build our beautiful house that we're going to be so happy in. Why don't we invite Maurice as our first guest and make him see just how wrong he was about everything?'

'Sometimes I don't know what we're doin' here, Katie. Why should we be worryin' about the English an' their wars? We could be back in Donegal, buildin' houses there.'

'I'm never goin' back to live in Donegal, Liam Clancy, not for a hundred wars. This is where my children were born and they're English even if we're not.'

'I wouldn't like mi old father to hear you, Katie. Now he was a real patriot.'

'Oh, come off it, Liam, I never saw him sober. He never knew two days together what he was, an' your poor mother had to sit waitin' for him to come out of the pub before she had money to put food on the table.'

Chapter 36

My aunt and uncle were delighted to be returning to Marsdale and, because they had given Lucy much of their furniture, the cottage was ideal for what was left. There was one large bedroom, and the other Liam turned into a well-equiped bathroom. There was a nice parlour into which he put a new tiled fireplace, and the nondescript kitchen became a living kitchen, well equipped with cupboards and working tops.

There was a long front garden and a vegetable garden at the back, and I was happy with the way they both enthused about everything they saw.

Not so with Aunt Mary.

'What about my parlour?' she demanded. 'I've bin used to a kitchen, a livin' room and a parlour. What am I goin' ter do with all mi furniture?'

'But you never used your parlour, Aunt Mary, except when the priest came round.'

'Isn't that what parlours are for? Special occasions when yer can entertain yer guests in comfort.'

'But you can do that at the cottage. Why keep one room in the house like a museum, isn't it better to enjoy your best furniture and carpets instead of wrapping them up in tissue paper waiting for visitors?'

'O' course it is, Mary,' Uncle Joel put in. 'That suite's like it was when we were married. It's hardly bin sat on and I reckon it's time we had a bit o' pleasure out of it.'

'And what about mi potted palms an' mi aspidistra?'

'Yer can't build yer life round potted palms an' aspidistras, luv. Yer'll 'ave a nice wide winder sill, an' if they 'ave to come with us I reckon yer'll find room for em.'

She remained unconvinced but there was no way she

would allow us to move away without them moving in the same direction.

Liam grew exasperated with her grumbles and grouses and finally told his uncle the cottage would be put on the market because he couldn't afford to have it standing idle after all the expense he'd put into it.

That message got back to her immediately and we were not surprised when she capitulated a few days later.

We helped in their removal and it took all my patience to persuade her to be ruthless in getting rid of unwanted articles. She had been a hoarder all her life, but now the parish bazaar benefited greatly.

Everything happened so quickly in the spring of 1938. We moved into the new house which I called Innisfree, and I adored it. Built in warm Pennine stone, it stood surrounded by gardens, with well-laid-out lawns on either side of the gentle curving drive. In the stables were a chestnut gelding and stalwart Welsh pony and, during the weekends and the soft spring evenings, Jeremy would ride with me along the old familiar bridle paths that led over the moor towards the pilgrims' cross set high up on the hillside.

Marisa was studying in London having won a scholarship to one of the best design centres in the capital, and now we only saw her during holidays. Liam adored her, and there were times when he seemed somewhat awed by the tall beautiful girl with her pale blonde hair fashionably styled, and her incredible sophistication. She wore her fashionable clothes with an air, and watching her twist him round her finger sometimes made me think that I had never really known how to handle him.

Jeremy was doing well at his new school and we were getting excellent reports on his progress, not all of which delighted Liam, who had not wanted a brilliant son but one who would follow him into the yard.

Now I only accepted work which I could do at home and which Maurice fed to me through his office. He seemed to have aged visibly over the past two years. His hair was now completely silver and he had developed a slight stoop which gave him the air of an intellectual professor. I knew that he was constantly worried about members of his family living in Germany, and occasionally he talked about his fears for their safety.

I deliberately closed my eyes and ears to the far-off rumbling of unrest in Europe. It was all so far away, and weren't we living on an island adequately protected by the finest fleet in the world?

I grew impatient with the men's talk about war. Uncle Turlough and Uncle Joel working in their gardens and shaking their heads across the fence at some disquietening news in the morning paper. Lucy telling me that Alfred couldn't be expected to fight for King and Country when he suffered terribly from asthma, and Liam telling me that two of his builders had volunteered for the army now instead of waiting to be called up.

In that year before we were once more plunged into war I was happier than I had been throughout my married life. Marisa wrote long ecstatic letters about her work and I went up to London to look at the tiny flat she was hoping to share with a friend, and to meet the quite famous dress designer she was working for.

He was charming and effeminate. He raved about my dark auburn hair and my figure, and before we had been in his workroom five minutes he was draping me with georgette and thick duchess satin in glorious shades of jade and emerald. He called me darling with an exaggerated drawl, and flicked ash all over me from an incredibly long cigarette holder. When I seemed a little doubtful about her new employer Marisa collapsed with laughter. 'Oh, Mother, don't be so silly. He's not going to do *me* any harm, is he? Not like some handsome masculine type with ulterior motives.'

People were gay that summer, but it was a desperately brittle gaiety that belonged to the moment and had little to do with stability and the enduring qualities on which most of us had based our lives.

Neville Chamberlain returned from Munich waving a piece of paper that proclaimed that Adolph Hitler had no further territorial claims to make in Europe and promising peace in our time. Why then did nobody believe it?

Instead we had twelve months to prepare for the inevitable, twelve short months to build ships and planes and arm an expeditionary force. Twelve months to send our children away from the large cities into a strange alien world.

It was a cool autumn day when the winds swept down from the moor sending brittle russet leaves scampering across the lawns, and I, clad in my oldest raincoat, in stout shoes and a scarf, was cutting off dead flower heads. I heard the car coming up the hill, but I was not expecting visitors until it stopped at the gate.

I straightened up, shielding my eyes from the sun which hung low in the sky, at first unable to recognize my visitor. I could see that it was a woman, picking her way delicately along the path grown slippery with fallen leaves, but it was only when close that I recognized her.

She had changed considerably from the young girl in her school uniform, wearing her hair in thick pigtails, her plump legs encased in thick black woollen stockings. Now my cousin Frances was dressed in the height of fashion, from her high-heeled court shoes to the neat felt hat on her dyed blonde hair.

'How fortunate to find you in the garden, Kathleen,' she trilled, and a warm smile embraced me. Then before I could answer she looked up at the house in obvious admiration.

'It's absolutely beautiful, I love the Pennine stone and the design of the house. Mrs Palmerstone told me you'd had it architecturally designed, so wise I'm sure, since your husband is only a builder, isn't he?'

I was at a considerable disadvantage in my gardening clothes and I didn't want to be at a disadvantage with this woman I hated.

'Are all the other houses as nice as this one?' she asked.

'I don't know, I only saw them while the building was going on.'

'Can we talk in the house, Kathleen? It is rather cold out here.'

'Very well, I've finished in the garden anyway.'

She followed me across the lawn and I suggested we enter through the conservatory so that I could leave my raincoat and heavy shoes there.

I knew she was looking around her with the utmost interest but we did not converse until we reached the drawing room. I saw her eyes open with obvious admiration at the large, beautifully furnished room, and indicated that she should take a seat before the brightly burning fire, saying, 'I must freshen up, I feel quite windbown.'

'Of course, there's no hurry.'

I did rather more than freshen up. I changed into a fashionable, beautiful gown and attended to my hair and face. Then, wearing heels as high as her own, I returned to the drawing room.

She was standing before the fire looking up at the oil painting above the mantelpiece and turning to face me, she said, 'What beautiful ornaments and paintings you've collected, Kathleen. I suppose you got to know something about such things when you were in service with the Carslakes.'

'I also learned a great deal from my grandmother, even though I didn't exactly get along with her,' I replied, forcing a smile.

'Gracious me, Grandmother Cassidy. I used to hear a lot about her.'

'You remember that, then?'

Her eyes grew wary. 'I remember hearing what a tartar she was, I never met her.'

'You said you wanted to talk to me, Fanny.'

I deliberately used the diminutive form of her name, and saw her flinch slightly.

'Please call me Frances, my husband and all our friends do. I always hated it when my father called my Fanny.'

'Well, my husband calls me Katie and I don't mind in the least. Now perhaps you will tell me why you have come.'

'We're interested in Lyndhurst, that's the last house

before you reach the road.'

'Yes, I know where it is. What do you mean interested?'

'We live in Marsdale, and although our house is extremely nice, I'd like to move into something a little more modern. Those older houses need such a lot of cleaning and it's becoming more and more difficult to get help in the house. The ceilings are far too lofty, not like these, and heating such high rooms is a problem, as you can imagine.'

I was patient, and when I didn't comment she began to look uncomfortable. 'I've always thought this hill far prettier than Tremayne Hill, and of course those houses are so large and cumbersome. My husband quite sees my point, I've finally got him to see that we must move soon even though he likes the house we are living in.'

'Do I take it you wish to buy Lyndhurst?'

'Well of course, if the price is right.'

'I have no idea how much my husband is asking for the house. It *was* sold, but the couple who were buying it have lost a considerable amount of money in cotton and could no longer afford it.'

'Have you any idea how much it will cost?'

'Not off hand, no. I don't know if you are aware that the garden of Lyndhurst borders on the gardens of the two farm labourers' cottages.'

'That won't make any difference at all. We would have high fences put between them and us and that way we wouldn't need to see them.'

'Do you know who lives in one of those cottages?'

'I have no idea. I assumed it would be one of the men who worked on the farm, although they do appear to have been modernized.'

'Your parents live in one of them, and my husband's aunt and uncle live in the other.'

She stared at me, aghast. 'I thought they were living in a newspaper and fancy goods shop with Lucy.'

'Lucy is living there with her husband.'

'Her husband!'

'And daughter.'

'You mean Lucy is married!'

'Of course, so your parents are living just below here in their cottage. Could you face living next door to them?'

'I don't know,' she murmured uncomfortably.

'Well, I couldn't if I'd treated them as shabbily as you have. You've ignored their existence for more than twenty years, why have it any different now?'

'I didn't know they were there.'

'Obviously.'

For a few moments there was silence, then shrugging her shoulders she said, 'Oh well, I suppose we'll just have to give up that idea. There are one or two very nice houses on Tremayne Hill, and of course they are very gracious houses. I know most of the people who live up there. They were always considered to be gentry.'

'It is a long time since gentry lived on Tremayne Hill, Fanny. Apart from Lady Dorothy and Sir Joshua most of them have either died or moved away.'

'Well, we shall certainly look at the house on Tremayne Hill. If we move there we shan't be too near any of you.'

Still she hovered uncomfortably and I felt I was failing lamentably as a hostess, but I could not visualize drinking tea with Fanny as if we were the best of friends, and after a few silent moments she got up to go.

'I've met your daughter at Mary Palmerston's house,' she said stiltedly.

'Yes, I believe so.'

'She's not at all like you.'

'Not in looks, no, she resembles her father far more.'

'You have a boy, don't you?'

'Yes, Jeremy, he's seven.'

'Quite a gap in their ages.'

'Yes.'

'Oh, well, another builder in the family, I suppose.'

'We shall have to wait and see. He's a clever child.'

'My daughter's a clever child too, heaven knows what ambitions she'll have when it comes to work, but my husband doesn't want her to be in a hurry. I'd much rather she stayed at home with me and met the right people. You have a job, don't you?'

'I still work at my old job from time to time. Just being a housewife and chattering over the tea cups has never appealed to me.'

'My dear, you don't know what you've missed.'

'Oh, I assure you I do. A lot of tittle-tattle and gossip I can do without.'

'What is your daughter doing, then?'

'Surely Mrs Palmerston must have told you she is studying dress design in London. Jenny Palmerston and Marisa are very good friends.'

'She may have mentioned it, I must have forgotten.'

By this time we were walking towards the door and it was only when we reached the front step that she turned, saying, 'Well, it's too bad about Lyndhurst but you do see, don't you, Kathleen, I couldn't possibly live there with them next door.'

'If you mean your parents, Fanny, I see very well. Good afternoon.'

The interview had upset me, and when I returned to the drawing room I was trembling. That pretty vapid face still had the power to make me clench my hands in anger, and I resolved that I would say nothing to her parents about the encounter, or to Liam. He might be annoyed that I had turned away a potential customer because he had always maintained that in the case of Fanny and her parents there would be faults on both sides. I only remembered their distress at the way she had abandoned them, and my uncle's loyalty, so that for a long time he would not hear a single word against her.

It was October, a warm golden October, and I stood on the hillside thinking how peaceful it was even though we had been almost a month at war and still the sun shone gloriously in a pale blue sky and smoke curled lazily from cottage chimneys in the tiny village nearby. Above me my horse champed the moorland grass, and below Jeremy galloped his pony across the fell, jumping effortlessly the low stone field walls.

Wood smoke and bracken scented the air, and from above came the steady droning of a tiny plane which left a cloud of vapour across the sky. It was hard to imagine that we were at war when all around me was peace. The newspapers had begun to call it a phony war, without fighting or casualties.

Liam assured me it would all be over by Christmas but Maurice thought differently. 'It hasn't begun yet Katie,' he said, shaking his head sadly. 'There is going to be such a blood bath as the world has never seen.'

'Have you no news of your sister and her family?' I asked him.

'None, and there will be none now. I fear the worst, Katie.'

'But what can they do to them? They haven't done anything wrong.'

'Hitler hates the Jews, one way or another he'll make that hatred felt. I do not think we shall ever meet again.'

'Oh Maurice, you mustn't say that. Don't give up so easily.'

He had smiled the sad slow smile that I had come to know so well, and in the next breath he said, 'How is Liam coping at the yard with most of his young men gone?'

'He's back in overalls, climbing scaffolding. I'm very much afraid it's all going to be like it was last time. There will be no raw materials and only the older men left to carry on. It's the same with you, isn't it Maurice?'

'I'm ready for retirement, Katie. I was thinking about it anyway even if the war hadn't come along.'

'Retirement, Maurice! You!'

'I'm fifty-five, Katie, and I'm tired. I'll carry on for a little while but I think I'm ready to sit back now and act as a consultant. Work will be hard to come by during the war, but after it's over I'd rather like to think Joe will carry on the business. He's a good craftsman and I've been training him for management. He's coming along much better than I expected.'

His manner was entirely calm, even jocular, but I had the oddest sensation that he was not telling me the whole truth, and I looked at him fearfully so that he smiled and put his arm round my shoulders, giving them a small squeeze.

'Don't worry, Katie, I'm really as strong as a horse, but even the strongest horse has to be put out to grass sooner or later.'

In spite of the peace of that warm autumnal afternoon, my mind was plagued with vague uneasy thoughts, and mounting my horse I called Jeremy to my side. His face was flushed and his eyes shone happily. As he grew older, more and more he was reminding me of Nicholas; he had his father's roguish smile and easy charm. He was tall and dark, but his eyes were grey under those same dark incredibly long lashes. There was little of me in Jeremy, and Aunt Mary was sadly disappointed that she discovered nothing of Liam in him either.

There were times recently when I thought about Nicholas and wondered if he was once more in uniform, and I remembered vividly his laughing eyes under the peaked officer's cap and the strength of his arms around me.

Inevitably war changed our world, but in my private life I believed I had reached a state of grace, a peaceful tranquillity that would go on until life itself ended. Then, like a flash of light my complacency was shattered into bits and a new and frightening chasm opened beneath my feet, filling my entire being with doubt and a savage, punishing desire.

In January Marsdale and the surrounding area was stunned by the death of Sir Joshua Tremayne. Flags were flown at half mast on public buildings and in spite of the wartime austerity Sir Joshua's funeral took place in the midst of civic pomp and with many extravagant floral tributes.

I watched Liam covering his dark morning dress with his winter overcoat for it was a cold day with a hint of snow in the air. He was to walk in the procession of town councillors and local dignitaries, and he had spent most of the morning saying I should go with him.

'But I doubt if many of the women will be there,' I

protested.

'Then they should be,' he snapped. 'Out of respect for Lady Dorothy. I've seen her chatting to you at civic balls and you've always said how much ye liked her.'

'I do like her, I just don't want to go to the funeral. I hate funerals.'

'Will you say the same thing about mine, then?'

'Oh Liam, don't be so ridiculous. I might die before you do.'

'Nobody likes funerals, we've got to put up with 'em.'

'I have a cold coming on, it won't do any good standing about in a cold churchyard,' I prevaricated.

'Please yourself, then. I've done all I can to persuade you, I just hope nobody notices your absence, that's all.'

I watched him leave the house after slamming the door behind him, then I started to agonize as I prowled from room to room, my desperation to go warring with the common sense which told me that if I valued my peace of mind I would remain where I was. Desperation was an easy winner, and five minutes later I was running down the drive wearing my trenchcoat and with a black silk scarf covering my hair.

I ran along the pavement where silent women stood with their shopping baskets and men stood hatless in the drizzling rain. A bell tolled dismally from the church tower and I stood on tiptoe in a shop doorway, staring over their heads to see the steady stream of long black limousines pass, headed by the hearse.

They seemed to stretch for miles but after the first few cars had passed I edged my way along the crowded pavements in the direction of the church.

I found a place under one of the giant elms where I could see the funeral party when they emerged from the church. An elderly man joined me, saying, 'It's a sad business. I reckon 'e'll be missed in this town. Allus 'ad the time o' day for ye if 'e met ye on the road an' he were generous to the town. There's a lot o' youngsters fro' round these parts 'as Sir Joshua to thank for their scholarships and their future.'

I agreed, but at the same time I wanted him to go. I was

too excited to speak, and my heart was racing like a mad thing.

We watched the civic party entering the church, with Liam's tall gangling figure standing out above the rest. Rain was dripping from the leaves above us, finding its way down my coat collar.

The beil had stopped and now we could hear singing inside the church. I thought about my father's funeral all those years ago in Donegal and unbidden tears trickled slowly down my cheeks.

It seemed like hours before the church doors opened and the sad procession made its slow way towards the grey granite tomb that had been the last resting place for the Tremayne family for nearly two centuries.

I was not looking at the coffin or the mourners. I had eyes only for one figure, and I found myself shaking like a leaf, suddenly faint so that I shrank back against the tree, asking the snarled bark to give me the courage that seemed to have deserted me.

Nicholas walked with Lady Dorothy and my agonized eyes devoured every inch of his tall uniform-clad figure, hardly glancing at the woman who leaned heavily on his arm.

His white officer's trench coat stood out starkly against the black mourning, and once during the commital his eyes swept over the crowded churchyard. Again I shrank back against the tree but I knew he hadn't seen me. With a sob in my throat I edged away from the crowd and pushed slowly towards the gates. Then I ran as fast as my legs could carry me away from the church and along the empty streets towards the hill.

I was shivering when I let myself into the house. My hair hung in wet strands around my shoulders and rain dripped from my coat hem. I had been a fool to leave the house without an umbrella, but I had been unable to think straight for most of the morning.

By the time Liam arrived home for his lunch I had washed and dried my hair and changed into a warm sweater and tweed skirt. As I faced him across the dining table I could see that he was irritable and I purposely asked no questions. Eventually he snapped, 'There were a few people wantin' to know why you weren't at the church this mornin'. Joe Challenor's wife was there as well as Albert Hardwick's. They both went to speak to Lady Dorothy and her nephew. I told her ladyship you had a bad cold and couldn't get out on such a wet morning.'

'Oh Liam, as if she would care,' I said quietly.

'You wants people round you at such a time, of course she cared.'

'I hope you are not going to keep on about this. You were there, surely that is all that matters?'

There was silence for several minutes, then he mused, 'I wonder what she'll do in that big house at the top o' Tremayne Hill? It's too big for her to live in by herself, it wouldn't surprise me if she gave it to the town as some sort of memorial.'

'What sort of memorial?'

'Well, it's full of expensive paintings and the like, p'raps an art gallery or something like that.'

'There have always been Tremaynes in Marsdale.'

'Well they never had any children and the colonel is Sir Joshua's sister's son so he's not a Tremayne, is he?'

'No.'

'Canadian he is. He'll not want to live in Marsdale.'

'No.'

'I'll bet the old lady moves out, somewhere near the coast, Bournemouth perhaps, or Torquay. One o' those towns where it's warmer an' where the gentry retire to.'

I didn't speak, and warming to his subject he went on, 'She'll be leaving all these matters to her nephew to sort out, so I reckon he'll be kept pretty busy. I hear he's got a month's leave from the War Office.'

'Did you meet him, Liam?'

'We were introduced. He seemed a nice enough feller, but we only had a few words what wi' Iris Challenor pushin' 'erself forward, an' then Mildred Hardwick.'

'Did he tell you he was on leave from the War Office?'

'No, but I did hear it from somewhere. If there's work

390

needed up at Lady Dorothy's I'd like to 'ave a hand in it.'

'Doing what?'

'Well, they'll not want folk tramping round it without some sort of conversion.'

'You're a builder, Liam, I'm sure there will be no constructional work involved.'

'There could be somethin' for you, though, couldn't there, Katie?'

I stared at him in surprise. He had always hated and belittled my work, now he was anxious for me to do something at the Tremayne House. In some exasperation I remarked, 'I didn't realize you were such a snob, Liam. It was rubbish for me to work for the Earnshaws, but it's perfectly respectable to work for the Tremaynes.'

'The Tremaynes are real gentry. If ye can't see that for yourself who am I to tell you?'

I watched him complacently eating his lunch, and was conscious of a certain grim amusement that my husband was trying to inveigle me into a position where I would undoubtedly come into contact with Nicholas and a past I had firmly thrust behind me.

He mused, 'I'll make a few quiet inquiries about what's goin' to happen up there. If Lady Dorothy's leavin', there's no reason why we shouldn't have a hand in things.'

'I'm sure Lady Dorothy will already have made her plans.'

'I suppose ye mean gettin' some London firm up here to convert it? Well, in case you hadn't noticed it, Katie, there's a war on, they'll be glad to get local folk in.'

He was in no mood to be argued with.

A letter from America came that afternoon. I stared at the envelope with its unfamiliar handwriting. Letters from the States had been few over the years, usually at Christmas time and my birthday, penned in my mother's large spindly handwriting, and informing me of my sister's and brother's progress through life.

Eileen was married to a lawyer and living in Boston, and

Terrence was in real estate, also married, with a young family. She appeared to have spent her life between their two homes after Uncle Shamus had died seven years before.

I had the strongest belief that the letter contained bad news, and indeed it did. My mother was dead. The letter came from Eileen. Mother had suffered a slight stroke, followed three days later by a massive one. Her funeral had taken place in Boston, attended by Eileen and Terrence and their families. She regretted that we were all so far away, but she extended an invitation for us to visit her soon, particularly as Europe was once again immersed in a life-and-death struggle.

Those were her words, high-flung and theatrical. For a long time I sat staring out towards the mist-shrouded moor, remembering my mother as I had known her in Ireland, gentle and loving, easily caught up in Father's wild enthusiasms and afraid of her mother's sharp tongue.

I wept silently for Mary O'Donovan and her sweetness, I wept for the courage she had always lacked in her dealings with my grandmother, and I wept for my memories of soft mist-laden mornings and a small, independent, spirited child trudging determinedly through the rain on her way to school.

Later, when I had recovered my composure, I set out with Copper, Jeremy's cocker spaniel, down towards Uncle Turlough's cottage, not in the least surprised to find him on his way up to see me. He carried a similar letter and his face was sad too, and plagued with memories. Together we walked up to the moor. It had stopped raining but the mist was down and the chill dampness invaded our bones but still we walked on, reliving our memories of a past in Donegal, strangly remote.

I told Liam my sad news, passing my sister's letter to him so that he could read it for himself.

Returning it to me, he said, 'Well, that's one funeral you don't have to worry about attending.'

I stared at him, dumbfounded at his insensitivity and without another word marched out of the room.

Chapter 37

I did not speak of my mother's death to Liam again, and if I seemed irritable and unhappy perhaps he believed it was on this score. I had loved my mother and I regretted her death, but the cause of my misery was Nicholas living at the top of Tremayne Hill and my determination not to see him.

Those rapturous days in Italy were part of the past and I had no certainty that he still loved me. For all I knew he could have married, some other woman could fill the empty corners of his life. And how could I even think of jeopardizing my so-called contentment by a meeting with Nicholas?

I hoped and prayed that Liam would have forgotten about involving me in any changes at Tremayne House, but I had reckoned without his persistence.

Several evenings later he took his place at the dining table saying 'Can't the meal wait, Katie? I want to talk to you first.'

'You grumble when it's dried up or overcooked.'

'What I want to talk about is more important than the meal, it concerns Treymayne House.'

I could feel a sudden racing of my heart so that I sat down heavily, the dishes momentarily forgotten, and impatiently Liam pushed them aside while he continued to stare grimly into my eyes.

'It's as I said, Katie, Lady Dorothy's leavin' Tremayne House, she's going to live with her sister in Leamington.'

'How do you know?' Was it really my voice, trembling with anxiety and suddenly faint?

'Everybody in Marsdale knows, I'm surprised you don't.'

'I'm not interested.'

'Then you bloody well should be. For years I've bin listen' to ye talkin' about the fine houses ye've bin workin' in, your paintings and your fine furniture. It's my bet there's never bin a house like this one, and now you don't want to know.'

'I don't think it's any of our business, Liam. Lady Dorothy has her nephew to help her.'

'Ay well, and didn't I meet him only yesterday on the hill? I'll get in before anybody else gets a chance, I thought to miself, so I made it mi business to ask him how the old lady was, and if she was stayin' in the area. I wasn't bein' curious, I was genuinely interested and he knew it. He told me where she was goin' and that the house was to be given to the town.'

'What will the town do with it?'

'It's to be given just as it is, and two of the downstairs rooms are to be made available for private art exhibitions, ye know, local artists and the like. There'll be work needed on it, to turn it into some sort of museum, to arrange things nicely.'

'Oh Liam, you *are* talking nonsense and I'm sure Lady Dorothy's nephew thought so too. That house is so beautiful it doesn't need any help from me. I wouldn't presume to alter a single room, a single painting or piece of glorious furniture.'

His eyes narrowed, snapping dangerously. 'That's where you're wrong, as usual. After Lady Dorothy's taken what she needs the rest'll 'ave to be arranged properly. I told the colonel that mi wife knew about things like that, and I offered your help should it be needed.'

'And what did he say to that?'

'He thanked me, and said he'd be in touch.'

'Oh Liam, he was being polite. He probably thinks you're a busybody and he won't want my help. People like the Tremayne's have got along very well without the help of people like us.'

'Anyway, I gave him our telephone number, so you can expect to hear from him.'

I did not for one single moment expect to hear from

Nicholas Yale.

It was Aunt Mary several days later who informed me that Geraldine McClusky had gone back to working for Liam at the yard.

'I've told 'im to keep 'er in 'er place this time,' she said sharply. 'She got far too big for 'er shoes the last time she worked for 'im.'

I didn't care, but when I mentioned it to Liam he merely said, 'I thought I'd mentioned that Geraldine was back. She's reliable and I can't be after seein' to everything miself.'

I never referred to her again.

Several evenings after our conversation about Tremayne House, the telephone rang. It was around nine o'clock and I had spent the evening writing letters to Marisa and Jeremy. Marisa was a deplorable correspondent but I wrote to her diligently every week, and to Jeremy whose house master made sure that his boys wrote home. I was almost out of the front door on my way to post them when I heard the telephone, and thinking it was Liam, I hurried back to answer. I sat down weakly with my heart lurching painfully as I recognized Nicholas's low familiar drawl.

'This is Nicholas Yale Mrs Clancy, I told your husband I might be telephoning you.'

I couldn't answer him, and his voice prompted gently, 'Katie, is that you?'

'Oh Nicholas, why have you rung? I was hoping you wouldn't.'

'Because you didn't want to hear from me, you don't want to see me?'

'You know I want to see you but there's no point. I don't want to open old wounds, I don't want to suffer when it's over as I suffered last time.'

'I have to see you, Katie. I couldn't believe it was going to be so easy, but now I know where you are I'm not leaving here until I do see you.'

'But I'm still married, Nicholas. Nothing has changed.'

'I do have your husband's urgent permission to see you, Katie.'

'I know, and his presumption is quite terrible. Please don't think too badly of him.'

'I don't. I admire a man who can look after his own interests as long as they don't conflict with anybody else's.'

'They conflict with mine.'

'What have you done with your life since you escaped from Italy as though the hounds of hell were after you?'

I was surprised how quickly he changed the subject, but I answered him as levelly as I knew how. 'I've been building up my business, bringing up my children and trying to be a good wife and mother.'

'Your children, Katie?'

There was surprise in his voice, surprise and something else.

'My daughter and my son.'

His voice was suddenly colder, more circumspect. 'I see. I wasn't aware you had another child.'

I wanted to scream at him that Jeremy was *his* son, but something held me back, some strange primitive dignity that refused to put the responsibility for Jeremy on to anybody except myself. Now his voice was businesslike and entirely unemotional.

'Well Katie, I promised your husband we would discuss the house and he will no doubt expect me to keep that promise. Will you tell him I telephoned you?'

'Yes Nicholas, I will tell him.'

I could not bring myself to mention the call to Liam until he said sourly, 'Did the colonel ever bother to phone you about Tremayne House, Katie?'

'Oh yes, Liam, he did ring about a week ago. I forgot to mention it.'

'You forgot! How could you when you knew I was so set on the thing?'

'Well there's nothing to tell you. He says he was keeping the promise he made to ring me, but obviously nothing can be done about the house yet. These things take time.'

'Did he say so?'

'No, I just assumed so.'

'Well, was anything else said? It seems a rum conversation to me, just to ring up without mentionin' anything about what he wants done.'

'He doesn't want me to do anything, Liam, he never did.'

He stared at me balefully. 'You've handled the conversation wrong, Katie, you should have asked him to get in touch with me. I might have known you'd make a mess of things.'

'Leave it alone, Liam. It's not something I want to do.'

'I don't understand you, Katie O'Donovan. For years you've bin dabblin' in pseudo property that newly rich folk want shapin' into something resemblin' the real thing. And now that ye gets the chance with the real thing you don't want to do it! Well, I'll make mi apologies to Colonel Yale. I'll tell him I'm sorry he had to talk to a woman as didn't know her own mind. No doubt he'll think it's an idiot I've got for a wife.'

'In that case he'll be glad we're taking it no further,' I couldn't resist snapping.

With an angry frown he marched out, his final caustic remark being, 'Well, there's a meeting of the council tonight when the house is being officially turned over to us. I thought you might come along to the cocktail party afterwards but in your frame of mind it's probably best that you stays away.'

I had little faith that Liam would drop the subject, and I had no wish to go to the cocktail party.

Just after eleven I heard a car outside, and was surprised that Liam should be arriving home so early. Functions of this sort could drag on until early morning, and I feared that he was returning in a vile temper to accuse me of spoiling his night.

When I heard men's voices in the hall, however, I looked up with dismay and then there was Liam, all affability, and my heart lurched sickeningly when my eyes met those of his companion, eyes that smiled in a smooth tanned face above impeccable officer's uniform.

'I've brought Colonal Yale home with mi, Katie. I reckon you should talk to him personally.'

Nicholas came and took my hand in his, and Liam

seemed to think it in no way odd that he held it longer than was strictly necessary.

Nicholas's eyes were laughing at me as he said politely, 'We've met before, Mrs Clancy.'

For a quick moment my eyes opened wide, startled, then collecting my thoughts I said, 'Yes, at Tremayne House a long time ago.'

'You were the prettiest girl in that house on that occasion.'

'But not the best dressed,' I was quick to retort.

All this was lost on Liam, who was busy at the drinks cabinet.

Talk at first was general, mostly between Nicholas and Liam, and my racing heart grew calmer until at last Liam turned to me, saying, 'It's like I said, Katie, there will be some work needed at Tremayne House and it's the sort of work you do best.'

Nicholas said, 'My aunt is taking many of her favourite things with her, and the rest will need to be arranged to the best advantage. She has decided that we will need ropes in some places so that visitors can walk round the rooms and see for themselves the beauty of the furnishings without straying in the actual rooms.'

'So that there is a corridor in each room, is that how she visualizes them, Colonel Yale?'

'Exactly. You will have seen this done in other houses opened to the public.'

'I believe two of the downstairs rooms are to be left completely empty?'

'That is how she had decided to leave the house, now the council feel differently. They say it is not necessary for private art exhibitions to be held there, there are facilities at the art gallery and they prefer the entire house to remain more or less as it is.'

'I see.'

'Why don't you come to the house and see for yourself? It would give you a better idea than talking about it.'

'I will talk to my partner Maurice Abrahams about it. I am sure he will be able to spare the time to accompany me, if that is convenient to you.'

'Now what on earth does it have to do with Maurice? He's not well enough to come gallivanting over to Marsdale, and you're quite capable of seeing to things without him,' Liam said testily, and I saw the amusement flicker in Nicholas's eyes.

Blind, oblivious Liam was handing me to Nicholas on a platter.

It was Liam who promised I should go to the house the next day, and when at last I found my hand once more taken in Nicholas's firm grip, I felt that my entire future had been decided in that room and that I was merely a piece of driftwood floating without volition on to some far and distant shore.

Chapter 38

It rained heavily the following morning, and over lunch Liam said, 'I'll drive you up there if you like, but I can't say what time I can pick you up later.'

'I'll drive myself, Liam. If the rain clears I might walk.'

'Don't you be late, mind. I reckon the colonel's not a man to be kept waitin'.'

When I didn't answer he snapped, 'And show a bit of enthusiasm, for heaven's sake, Katie. If Geraldine had anythin' to do with this she'd be fallin' over herself to make an impression.'

'I'm sure she would.'

He stared at me doubtfully. 'Well, it's business, isn't it?'

'Liam, I'm doing what you want, I'm going to the house and I'll do whatever is necessary if I think I'm capable. Can we please talk about something else?'

'I'm worried, Katie. I've never seen you so difficult. Normally you're so enthusiastic about your work I can't shut you up.'

'And you have never been enthusiastic about my work, Liam. Why is this so different?'

'I want to show them down there that mi wife's a capable woman. I know they've bin snidin' at mi all these years because you had your own work and never went to their coffee mornings or their bazaars. You were always too busy, and one or two of 'em asked if I kept you short o' money that you had to go out and work for it.'

'It was none of their business, and I hope you told them so.'

'That I did, but it didn't stop 'em talkin'. I know they thought there was somethin' goin' on between you and Maurice. Can you see how mad it made me?'

'There was never anything between me and Maurice.'

'So you told me and so I told them, but you can't stop folk thinkin' things. Other men's wives stayed at home, mine went all over the place workin' in other folks's houses.'

'Neither your home nor your children suffered, Liam. Surely your friends could see that.'

'They didn't want to see it, Katie. Most of the women were jealous of you anyway, your looks and your clothes.'

'Oh Liam, you never told me any of this. I wish you had.'

'Would it have made any difference, Katie, would you have given anything up?'

'No, Liam, I wouldn't, but I would have been nicer, kinder. I just always blamed you for being so resentful, I thought you were unfair.'

'I wants you to do Tremayne House, Katie, and show all those folk who've been so jealous that you're a cut above the rest of 'em.'

I smiled at him tremulously, thinking how ironic it was that Liam was throwing me into the arms of the man I loved to prove to his friends that I could stand on my own without Maurice, the man who most of them believed had been my lover.

After lunch the rain had cleared, and I decided to walk. It would give me time to think.

At the bottom of Evening Hill I could see that Lyndhurst was occupied. I had never told Liam about my cousin's wish to buy the house, and I had heard that they had moved into one of the houses on the lower slopes of Tremayne Hill. It was not one of the more imposing mansions and, passing, I could see that construction work was being done. I might have known that Fanny would not be satisfied with it in its original state.

Walking up the long drive to Tremayne House I was reminded of that other Katie, with her frilly cap and apron, who had once walked up the drive with a wildly beating heart and a desire to be somebody of importance. Important enough at least to meet Jeffrey Carslake on his own footing. Well, today I was going to meet Sir Jeffrey Tremayne's nephew entirely on his own footing, and with memories of a passion we had shared.

The afternoon was charming. I drank tea with Lady Dorothy and then the three of us toured the house, discussing what I thought was needed to show it off to the best advantage. They were content to leave everything in my hands and I promised to start as soon as Lady Dorothy had moved out.

'My nephew has to get back to London next week so I really want to move before he leaves,' she informed me.

Surprised, I said, 'Oh, so soon? I understood he was on a month's leave.'

At his look of calm amusement, I could have bitten off my tongue, particularly when he said, 'I wonder who gave you that information Mrs Clancy?'

'Oh, it was just something my husband had heard.'

'There will be nobody here to interrupt your work, Mrs Clancy, you will have a clear hand to do exactly what you wish.'

I said my farewell to Lady Dorothy but when we reached the hall, I found Nicholas at the front door wearing his white trench coat and with every intention of walking back with me.

'Oh please, Colonel Yale, you really don't need to walk home with me,' I protested.

'I was going for a walk anyway,' he smiled. 'We may just as well walk together.'

For what seemed like an eternity we walked in silence. Then he took hold of my hand and drew me towards a narrow lane that climbed up to the moor. 'It's too early to go home, Katie. Why don't we walk on towards the fell?'

I had no will of my own. I went with him willingly, blindly, allowing my hand to remain in his, and slowly the years fell away and I was running down this same lane, with Jeffrey watching me from the crest and Nicholas waiting for me at the bottom. As if he could read my thoughts he said, 'You spent hours on these moors, Katie. Do you never come up here and think about them?'

'Sometimes.'

'How long did it take you to forget him?'

'I don't know, I can't remember.'

'Longer, it would seem, that it took you to forget me.'

'What do you mean?'

'I asked your husband how old your son was.'

I didn't answer, but pulled my hand away and walked on alone. Then, at the stile that led on to the moor, I turned to face him.

'I don't want to talk about the past, Nicholas, it's over.'

His face was suddenly cold and I felt shut out. 'Perhaps we should get back, Katie. It is going to rain.'

At the gates of Innisfree he took my hand, saying formally, 'Goodbye, Katie. Do whatever you think necessary at the house. I will see that you are furnished with the name of my aunt's solicitors, the keys of the house and a cheque for the initial cost of materials.'

I was shaken at the suddenness of our parting. I should have taken his hand calmly and dispassionately, but the hurt tears were rolling down my face, and with a little cry I ran for dear life towards the house, as a wounded animal runs to hide in its lair. He came after me, spinning me round to face him, then we were standing with my face buried against his shoulder, his arms around me, his voice murmuring endearments against my hair.

Inside the house he stoked up the fire while I changed into dry clothes. When I entered the drawing room a bright fire was burning and Nicholas sat looking pensively into the flames. He looked up and smiled, and because I couldn't help it I went straight into his arms like a child running home. He started to kiss me, and I responded passionately, but when his hands explored my willing body urgently I came suddenly to my senses. 'No, Nicholas, not here, not in Liam's house.'

'Then where, Katie? I love you, I've got to see you again before I go back.'

'Oh Nicholas, I don't know, anywhere, but not here.'

'Can't you get away for a while, London perhaps? I'll be in London for a few days before I need to return to my regiment.'

'I don't know. Oh Nicholas, I love you and I want you

but none of this is easy. Why are you in this wretched war anyway?'

I tore myself out of his arms and went to the window. It was sheeting down now, making great puddles along the drive and paths, and then he came and put his arms around me again, and sadly I pushed him away.

It was hopeless. This was not Italy where nobody knew us and nobody cared except Marisa.

I went to the sideboard and poured out two glasses of sherry, and again he followed me, but this time he was looking at the portrait of Jeremy which stood on the sideboard. It had been taken the year before at his school and showed him in his school uniform, smiling and debonair, and so achingly like Nicholas that our eyes met in sombre acceptance.

He didn't need to ask, he knew immediately, and drawing me into his embrace he said quietly, 'Why didn't you tell me, Katie?'

'I couldn't, it wasn't possible.'

'And Liam has never suspected?'

'Never.' So I told him about the night Liam raped me in a drunken frenzy which had made it easier to lie about Jeremy, and Liam's pride in the boy and Jeremy's affection for him. Later, when we heard the sound of Liam's car along the drive we were sitting opposite each other calmly drinking sherry and with every evidence of discussing business.

Liam was well satisfied, but under cover of his complacency we stared at each other with a yearning, bewildered dismay.

When Liam insisted on driving Nicholas home, and left us for a few minutes to get the car out of the garage, Nicholas urged, 'I shall only be in London four or five days, Katie. Please promise me you'll try to see me before I leave.'

'I'll try, Nicholas.'

Hastily he scribbled a telephone number on a page torn from his diary, and I stuffed it into my bag before Liam came back.

We shook hands calmly, and I watched them drive away with a composure totally at variance with my racing heart. My resolve was not to go to London. I had to forget him, just as I had resolved to forget him years before. But once again Fate, that strange destroyer of the best-laid schemes, intervened.

Chapter 39

Later in the week I took Maurice to Tremayne House. We wandered through the lovely rooms, and he exclaimed with delight at their treasures. When Nicholas joined us, I found they got along well together, and an entire afternoon passed without any mention of the war though it was close to both their hearts.

As I left the house to join Maurice in the car, Nicholas said, 'Aunt Dorothy and I are leaving the day after tomorrow, Katie. If I do not see you in London we may never meet again.'

I stared at him fearfully, aware of the circumspect grip of his handclasp and the cool impersonal smile with which he sent us both on our way. We were silent on the way back to Innisfree, but once there, Maurice said, 'You're unhappy, Katie. Do you want to talk about it?'

'I don't know what to do, Maurice.'

'You've known Colonel Yale for some time, haven't you?'

'Yes. Almost since I came to live in Marsdale.'

'So long. But I thought Jeffrey Carslake was the man you were in love with in those days.'

'He was, my very first love, Maurice. I met Nicholas again years later and I fell in love with him. The year I took Marisa to Italy.'

'And he with you?'

'Yes. He wants me to go up to London to be with him for a few days. Who knows what this war will do to us?'

'What are you going to do?'

'I don't know, that's the terrible part of it. I want to go to London, I want to be with him every minute of every day until he has to go, but I don't see how it's possible. What excuse can I give to Liam? I have nothing to go to London

406

for.'

'You'll think of something, Katie. Never have I known you not get what you want, if you'd really set your heart on it.'

'That makes me sound mercenary and something of a shrew.'

'No, Katie, I never thought of you like that. Think about your life. You wanted a career and I helped you, then you wanted security, a good business for Liam, a beautiful house and gardens, preferably on Evening Hill, and here it all is, like a fairy tale come true. Now, if I asked you what was the most important thing in your life, the impossible dream, what would it be?'

'I'm not sure.'

'Don't prevaricate with me, Katie. This is Maurice you're talking to, Maurice who has known you and loved you for longer than he cares to remember.'

'I'd want to be with Nicholas. I'll die if I can't be with him.'

'Then I'm quite sure you'll go to London, Katie. Nothing in this world is going to stop you. He's Jeremy's father, isn't he?'

'How did you guess?'

'For years I've looked at Jeremy and wondered how Liam could have fathered such a child. They don't look alike, they have nothing in common, and I marvelled that Liam is too obtuse to see it for himself. Today when I looked at Nicholas I knew for a certainty who Jeremy's father was.'

When I didn't immediately speak he said softly, 'I'm not sitting in judgement on you, Katie. You never pretended to be in love with Liam. He's never been more than a stepladder on your way to the top, and heaven knows you've used each other.'

'I tried to love him, Maurice, I did try. And I *have* made him a good wife and I've been a good mother.'

'That is true, and now you will have to make another decision. Fate has brought you this far, Katie O'Donovan, pray that she doesn't desert you now.'

'I don't believe in Fate, Maurice, only in certainties.'

He smiled and gently kissed my cheek.

'Aren't you coming in for a meal, Maurice?' I said, surprised when he leaned over and opened the door for me but remained in his seat.

'Not today, Katie. Promise to let me know if you are going away for a few days.'

'Oh Maurice, I shan't be. You know I'll be here as usual.'

He merely smiled, his slow maddening smile, and drove away.

Marisa telephoned that night, distraught and tearful.

'Marisa, please speak more slowly, I can't understand a word you're saying.'

'It's Raymond, mother, he's been called up. He's leaving in a few days and the business is closing. We'll have to give up the flat, Mother, I'll have no work and there's none about. There was an air raid two nights ago, it was terrible, all those dead people and their houses in rubble. I'm frightened, but I just can't leave the flat with everything in it.'

'You must come home, darling, of course you can't stay in London. Is Joanna still at the flat?'

'She's going home too, she's talking of joining the Wrens.'

'Marisa, I'll talk to your father as soon as he gets in and I'll try to get up to London tomorrow, if he agrees.'

'Oh, Mother, thank you. Please come. Will you telephone and tell me if Daddy says you can come?'

After I had replaced the receiver I sat staring into space. I could hardly believe that Fate had so readily come to my aid and already I was assuring myself that it couldn't be wrong when everything and everybody conspired to make it happen.

Liam was against it, as I knew he would be.

'You don't have to go to London. Why can't she simply get on a train and come here? Leave the flat, it's a furnished one anyway and she can't have all that much luggage.'

'But of course she has, Liam, she's been living in London for some time. How do we know what she's collected?'

'Something more important than her life?'

'Of course not. I have to telephone her this evening, perhaps you should speak to her.'

Marisa had always been able to convince Liam, more often than not against his better judgement, and this was no exception. Before he went out later in the evening everything was arranged. He would take me to the station the following morning to catch the London train and she would meet me at Euston.

'You can't stay at the flat, there's no room,' he informed me. 'Where will you stay?'

'I don't know Liam, I'll cross that fence when I come to it.'

Later I telephoned Maurice to tell him of my plans and listened uncomfortably to his dry chuckle.

'Didn't I tell you? Fate hasn't deserted you after all.'

'Then pray that she doesn't desert me during these next few days. I love him, Maurice. Is there anything in the world more important, more deserving than love? And Maurice, I've not had too much of it.'

'God bless you, Katie, I'll do as you ask, I'll pray for you.'

I telephoned Nicholas, and hearing the joy in his voice, it seemed to me that indeed Fate had been kind in the most unexpected way, via Liam's daughter.

'Have you somewhere to stay tomorrow night, Katie?' Nicholas asked.

'No, but don't worry about that, I'll find a place as soon as I get there.'

'Katie, London is bursting at the seams, the hotels and guest houses are crowded. You could hunt all day without finding somewhere. Go to number eleven Fitzwilliam Street, I'll telephone the staff to expect you.'

'But where is it, who does it belong to?'

'It's in Mayfair, it belongs to the Tremayne family and I always use it when I'm in London. Katie, do as I say, I'll arrive the day after tomorrow and I'll expect to find you there.'

London had always overwhelmed me by its vastness, but

wartime London was totally unlike what I had imagined. Sandbags covered the bases of monuments and public buildings, uniformed men and women seemed to be hurrying for dear life along the streets and across the parks and I listened to Marisa only haphazardly.

She was pale and I thought her thinner, even though she assured me she was perfectly well. We went first of all to the tiny flat where her flatmate had already filled the hall and most of the living room with suitcases. Marisa's belongings were strewn all over the bedroom.

'You won't be able to stay here, Mother, I hope you'll be able to find some hotel you can stay at.'

'I've got somewhere to stay, I telephoned last night and got a cancellation.'

'Gracious me, that was lucky!?' She made no inquiries and I didn't enlighten her further. It was like Marisa to accept what I told her, providing it needed no effort on her part. While she made sandwiches I attempted to tidy her room, but she stopped me firmly, saying, 'Don't touch anything, Mother, I know where everything is.'

'You can't possibly, this place looks as though a bomb has hit it.'

'Well the bombs missed it, so you can just come into the kitchen and we'll have lunch. I told Raymond I'd be over at the salon after lunch. Poor thing, he's in an absolute blue funk about everything.'

'I can't imagine that Raymond is army material.'

'Pay Corps, Mother. He's awfully good at figures, in fact he's quite a brain, really, even though he is so arty.'

'He's more than arty, Marisa, he's very effeminate.'

'Oh, he makes no bones about that, but he's fit enough. I don't think he'd be the slightest good in a fighting regiment, but he'll get by in the Pay Corps. It's closing the salon that's the most worrying thing. What on earth shall I do back home in Manchester? The bottom's fallen out of the rag trade, so there'll be nothing for me at home.'

'You needn't do anything in a hurry, darling.'

'If I don't they'll call me up.'

'But you're a girl, for heaven's sake.

'That makes no difference. I'll be in the forces or the Land Army before Christmas unless Daddy can fix me up with a job that's protected.'

'Would you mind going into the forces?'

'Not really, but I wouldn't like to be sent to one of those outlandish places like Mary's in. She's somewhere on the Isle of Mull surrounded by mist and Highland cattle. That wouldn't be for me.'

'You haven't asked about your father and Jeremy.'

'There hasn't been time, darling. I know Daddy's okay because I spoke to him on the telephone, and I suppose Jeremy's all right at that school in the country.'

Raymond was pathetically pleased to see us and I began immediately to feel immensely sorry for him. He was emotional, alternating between fits of weeping and hysterical good spirits, and I felt totally unable to cope with his desire for sympathy, often followed by wild extravagant compliments.

After one of these oubursts Marisa said, 'Do shut up, Raymond, my mother doesn't know what to do with you.'

'Your mother's more sympathetic than you are,' he answered, then turning to me he flung his arms about me, saying, 'I hope you're going to stay at my flat tonight. Marisa said you might and I could do with the company.'

'I'm sorry, Raymond, I've managed to find somewhere to stay.'

'Oh but you *can't*,' he wailed. 'I've been looking forward to your visit, and I can't live another single night in that flat on my own.'

'I'm sorry, Raymond.'

'What's the number of your hotel? I'll cancel the room, they'll be glad to let it to somebody else.'

'No, Raymond. Please pull yourself together, I can't stay with you.'

He sat with tears rolling down his face and I stared at him in horror, feeling I had been the cause of his misery. Brusquely Marisa snapped, 'Oh, do stop being so theatrical, Raymond. If you behave like this in the army they'll lynch you.'

'If I have to spend another night in that flat I'll kill myself, the army'll never see me.'

'All right then, you can stay at my flat but you'll have sleep on the floor or in a chair. We'll probably be spending a night in the air raid shelter anyway.'

I returned to Marisa's flat with them, to find most of the suitcases gone and Marisa's friend Joanna perched on the arm of a chair manicuring her nails.

'I've taken the suitcases to the station so I don't have to be bothered with them in the morning,' she explained after greeting me. 'What's he doing here?'

'He's staying here tonight,' Marisa said shortly.

'As well as your mother!'

'I'm not staying here,' I hastened to explain.

In the end none of us stayed in the flat, spending the night huddled like sardines in an air raid shelter at the end of the road. Morning found us struggling back to the flat with our sleeping bags and empty flasks just as the early morning mist swirled about the streets to the welcome sound of the all clear.

My appearance at the address Nicholas had given to me caused no consternation to the urbane butler who opened the door, or to the housekeeper who served me with an impeccably cooked meal, after which I returned to Marisa's flat.

I found her in tears.

'Oh Mother,' she wailed, 'I don't want to stay here another night. I can't stand Raymond going on all the time about his call-up, and I don't want to spend another single night in the air raid shelter.'

'Have you packed your luggage?'

'Yes, all that I'm taking.'

'Well then, why don't you go home? I'll take what you can't manage yourself.'

'But what will you do, aren't you coming with me?'

'Telephone your father to meet you at the station and I'll come home in two or three days when I've had a chance to look at the shops and visit the theatres.'

'But Mother, there's a war on. It isn't safe to stay here.'

412

'It's as safe for me as it is for anybody else. Don't fuss, darling.'

'What will Daddy say if I go home without you?'

'All right then, I'll telephone him myself.'

Liam had never heard such nonsense until I said I wanted to look round the museums – where else was I to get the right ideas for Tremayne House? – and after that it was plain sailing. He promised to meet Marisa's train and I could hardly believe how neatly everything had fallen into place. I told myself sharply that nothing could be so straightforward, that somewhere along the way I would have to pay for what I was doing, but nothing could make me turn aside from the joy of the next few days.

All around us people were grasping at life, aware only too bitterly of how soon it could change. Young lovers and those not so young were living a lifetime in a few brief hours, and every moment of those few days I tried desperately hard to pretend that our time together would go on and on as we walked in the park hand in hand like young lovers in their first dream of love. Young lovers who had time to tease and quarrel, time to dream about the future in a world at peace, while the crisp autumn leaves crunched under our feet, and the bright full moon was the only illumination the night afforded us.

We dined in candlelit restaurants and danced to the haunting love songs of a war-torn world, and through the nights we made love, oblivious of the drone of warplanes over our heads and the weird wailing of the air raid sirens.

Travelling home tearfully after our painful farewell, for the first time I thought of the pitifully few days we had spent. I felt stunned by our arrogant assumption that our luck would hold, that though other people were dying all around us, somehow we would be spared for those few brief ecstatic days. And so we had been spared.

Chapter 40

I spent long hours at Tremayne House. I felt very close to Nicholas there, particularly when I looked at family photographs which Lady Dorothy had left behind, believing that it gave a homely warm look to a house that was to become a museum.

Liam had lost a lot of his interest in the venture. He had made his point to the local dignitaries. His wife was in charge of things, appointed by Lady Dorothy and Colonel Yale, no less, and he became quickly bored when I tried to talk to him about it. Maurice was helpful, but surprised me one afternoon by saying, 'You're going to have to finish this project on your own, Katie. I've been ordered by my doctor to rest for a while, for six months at least.'

'Oh Maurice. Did he say what was wrong?'

'He didn't have to. It's my heart, I've known for years that it wasn't up to scratch.'

'What are you going to do, then?'

'I'm going to stay in a small private nursing home in St Annes. I've heard very good reports of it, and I'm not going to think about the office, the employees or you, my dear, for at least six months, or until my specialist gives me the all clear.'

'You are being very sensible, Maurice. Don't you want me to come and see you?'

'Not a single visit, Katie. Promise me.'

'Very well, Maurice, if that is what you want.'

'Does Colonel Yale intend to come up to see this house when you've finished with it, Katie?'

'Surely he will one day.'

'And what will happen then?'

'I don't know what you mean?'

414

'Will he look at the house and go away, or will he want you to leave with him?'

'Maurice, I don't know. I'm not even thinking that far. I don't really care right now as long as he comes back safe and well.'

'And Liam?'

'I've told you I don't know. Liam doesn't love me like Nicholas loves me.'

'Perhaps not, but he is your husband, Katie.'

'I don't want to think about it now. I'll think about it when I have to make a decision. Something will happen when it has to.'

'Oh Katie, your blind faith in providence hasn't diminished with the years.'

I watched him walk away towards his car, and tears stung my eyes. He looked suddenly so terribly old, an old old man shuffling through the grass with his shoulders stooped, his hair silver white. I raised my hand in answer to his wave and I was appalled at the terrifying conviction that I would never see him again.

Maurice Abrahams did not go into his pleasant little nursing home in St Annes, instead he went into the Manchester Royal Infirmary where he died three weeks later. It was Joe who came to tell us, and I wept bitterly as I stood with Liam and Joe in a strong biting wind at some little distance from the array of dark-clad men at his funeral.

Thanks to Liam's contacts in the local community, Marisa obtained a post teaching art at the local art college, and she seemed happy enough with her small group of mediocre pupils.

She was enjoying herself. I never knew where she acquired her new circle of friends but she constantly filled the house with them and I saw very little of her during the weekends. Most of them rode, so I saw less of Maxton, my horse, and she seemed to have a constant procession of young men calling at the house, most of them in uniform. They appeared for several days, then returned to their units, bases or ports and were not seen again for several months.

Once or twice I found her in tears over the death of one of these boys, but in the main her existence was gay and carefree. Life was for living in the winter of 1942 and Marsdale was thronged with young officers from all over England as well as the Commonwealth.

When I teased her about the constant change in her escorts she merely laughed, saying, 'I'm having such a good time, Mother. I don't want the war to go on for ever, but I don't want it to be over just yet.'

'The war is an abomination, Marisa, it isn't all party-going and enjoying yourself with a stream of eligible young officers.'

'Oh, Mother, I know, and I don't want anybody to be hurt or killed, I just want a little fun. Heaven knows there's enough bad news to make us all feel miserable.'

When I repeated this conversation to Liam he merely grunted and changed the subject.

I was not sure about his relationship with Geraldine McClusky. She remained unmarried and was still working in his office, but if there was anything between them I didn't hear about it. He had learned to be discreet. I never had cause to visit his office, but occasionally when I met Geraldine on the street she would blush and, after murmuring a greeting, hurry past with her head lowered. Once I was with Marisa when we met, and after she had passed Marisa said, 'If I ever see her with Daddy when I'm out with my friends, I shan't know what to do.'

'Why should you see them together?'

'Well, they were often together before. Now that she's back at the yard they could be again.'

'I have no reason to think so, Marisa, and I'd rather you didn't.'

'I don't close my eyes to things like you do, Mother.'

'And I don't believe in looking for scandal where none exists,' I snapped.

In the main, however, I shared a very happy relationship with Marisa, and night after night I looked forward to her coming into my bedroom after some party or other, to tell

416

me if she had enjoyed herself.

One evening she went off blithely on the arm of a young lieutenant whose family lived lower down the hill. They made a handsome couple; he in his new officer's uniform, Marisa wearing a blue lace evening gown, her hair smartly coiffured and wearing my three-strand pearl necklace and dark mink stole.

The boy had been obvious in his admiration for our daughter and he had been charming and pleasant to Liam and myself. After they had gone, however, Liam said, 'They all look alike, those young fellers she brings home.'

'Then it must be the uniform. I thought he was particularly nice.'

'They're all nice, all of 'em wrapped up in her and all of 'em as like as two peas in a pod. No wonder she doesn't know her own mind.'

I laughed at his grumpiness. 'Well, what sort of young man do you want her to choose?'

'I've no preference, as long as he can keep her in comfort without expecting too much from me.'

'Oh Liam, she's not serious yet about any of them. We'll know when she is.'

'They all look mighty glamorous in their uniforms, she could easily make a mistake.'

'Marisa isn't a fool, Liam.'

'Aye well, time'll tell.'

I watched him calmly leafing through the evening paper, a whisky and soda on the table beside his chair, a cigar in his fingers. He had come a long way from the boy with his shock of straw-coloured hair and his long legs and hands he had never quite known what to do with.

The cut of his suit and the crisp whiteness of his shirt were impeccable, and looking at him unemotionally I thought that Liam was a fine upstanding figure of a man, a man some woman would find attractive, might even love. But not me, never me.

He looked up suddenly and found me watching him. 'Anything wrong?' he asked.

'Nothing, Liam, I was just thinking how very smart you

417

were looking, that's all.'

'Aye well, I have to go out later on. I've been invited over to the Briggs's. Margaret's away and we thought we could discuss a few business matters privately over a game of cards.'

'I see.'

I did not miss the warm colour in his usually pallid cheeks, and I knew for a certainty that he had no intention of visiting our neighbours' house at the foot of the hill. I could have staked my life on Liam having an appointment of a far different kind, and I wondered idly if it was with Geraldine or if some other woman had entered his life.

Perhaps I imagined it, or did he smirk a little as I helped him into his overcoat? Perhaps he really did think that I was a fool who had no suspicions about the late nights and absent weekends, but I doubted if he would have been quite so complacent if he had known how little it mattered.

'I'll probably be late home, Katie,' he called out. 'Don't wait up for me.'

We no longer shared a bedroom. For years in the winter Liam had suffered badly from catarrh, keeping us both awake for most of the night, and separate bedrooms had in the end been a joint decision. My bedroom became my sanctuary against boredom and anxiety, anger and grief, and I had furnished it lovingly, beautifully and with the utmost expense.

On this particular night I retired early and lay curled up luxuriously with a book, the radio turned low. The rain pattered dismally against the window. Before putting out the light I drew back the drapes, shivering a little at the wet misery of the night.

For some time before I became drowsy, I lay on my back looking up at the ceiling, watching the reflection of the tree branches weaving and tossing in the wind, and I thought of Marisa dancing in the arms of her young officer, uncaring about the weather.

I was awakened sharply by voices outside in the darkness, and then the sound of a key in the front door, followed by its closing. Propping myself up on one elbow I stared into the darkness then, when there was silence, I switched on the light beside my bed to look at the clock. It was almost two-thirty.

Putting on robe and slippers, I went out on to the landing, calling, 'Marisa, is that you?'

She came into the hall, looking up at me. 'I'm just making some cocoa. Do you want some?'

'Yes, please. It's awfully late, you won't feel like school in the morning. Did you have a good time?'

'Marvellous. I'm coming in to tell you about it.'

She came carrying two cups of cocoa and I settled back against my pillows, aware that there would be no more sleep until she had exhausted her story. Her eyes were shining with excitement and there was a new awareness about her. I had seen Marisa happy before, thrilled with some new boyfriend, some new and happy pastime, but I had never seen this strange new air of tenderness, this diffidence and young insecurity. Marisa had always been so very sure, so ready to take instead of giving.

'Did Peter bring you home?'

She made a little face I couldn't understand. 'Well, he had to didn't he? He was my date for the evening.'

'He seemed very nice, Marisa.'

'Oh, Peter's all right, he's just a friend, that's all.'

I stared at her for a few minutes, watching her sip her cocoa, her thoughts quite evidently on other things. Looking up suddenly and finding my eyes on her, she blushed, then laughing a little she said, 'Oh Mother, I met the most marvellous man tonight. Honestly I never believed those stories of love at first sight but as soon as he entered the ballroom I knew that he was different.'

'What is he then, soldier, sailor, airman? And is there any possibility that he was similarly affected?'

'I can see that you're going to laugh at me.' She pouted prettily.

'No darling, I promise not to laugh at anything you tell me. I know what's it's like to be young and in love.'

Her face dimpled into smiles. 'Well, he's very good-looking, but it wasn't even that. He looked so distinguished,

419

he made all those young officers seem suddenly frightfully immature and ordinary.'

'You mean he's older than they are?'

'Yes, although he doesn't look old. He's simply more worldly and sophisticated.'

'So. He's their commanding officer?'

'No, he isn't even in the war, he manages a cotton mill in the town, so he won't have to go to war at all, he's far too important where he is. He wasn't in uniform, and you know how Daddy's always going on about the girls falling for officers' uniform. Well this man was in evening dress and he made all those uniforms seem terribly ordinary.'

'Where does he live?'

'Years ago he used to live on Tremayne Hill and his family owned about five cotton mills in town. The family are all scattered now but he's bought that darling little house on Pentland Lane. It isn't quite ready yet so he's staying with the Mallinsons until he can move in. Oh Mother, he's so nice. He's tall and fair and he dances divinely, real dancing, not that energetic leaping about, and thank goodness he doesn't talk all the time about the war like all those young officers do.'

'What is his name?'

I didn't need to ask. I had known who he was long before she told me. All the same I felt shaken at hearing his name on my daughter's lips, and when I looked at her happy smiling face my heart was clutched by a desperate fear.

I had made no secret of the fact that I had once worked on the hill as a parlourmaid, but it was a part of my life I wished to forget, a life where I had been put down as being of no account. Marisa had met Cook and Polly as a child and, because she never listened to anything unless it directly concerned herself, any mention of the family itself I felt sure she had forgotten almost as soon as they were spoken of.

Cook no longer lived in the vicinity, and if I wanted to see Polly I had to visit her because she adamantly refused to visit me in what she termed 'such posh surroundings'.

Now, looking at my stricken face, Marisa said, 'Mother,

what is it? You look as though you'd seen a ghost.'

'Perhaps I have darling. I knew Jeffrey Carslake a long time ago.'

'You did? Oh, Mother, was he always so handsome, was he in love with somebody then? I'll bet dozens of girls were in love with him.'

'I don't remember, it was a long time ago. Did he speak to you?'

'Speak to me! Mother, he danced with me, about half a dozen times, and he's invited me to go riding with him one day. He doesn't have a horse now but he can borrow one from the Mallinsons. Mrs Palmer introduced us and he asked me if I was any relation to a Mrs Clancy he had met at the Earnshaws' house. I told him you were my mother.'

I smiled, a twisted smile. It was like Jeffrey Carslake to remember fashionable sophisticated Kathleen Clancy when he had found it so easy to forget Katie O'Donovan.

'You look tired, Mother,' she said suddenly. 'I'll let you get to sleep, and I'll tell you all about everything in the morning.'

'You mean there's more, darling?'

'Oh, Mother, of course there is. What we talked about, how he spends his time, oh, everything.'

She was letting herself out of the door when she turned to say, 'Mrs Lorimer said you would know Jeffrey Carslake, Mother. She told me you would be able to tell me everything about him.'

With another bright smile she was gone.

Mrs Lorimer, my cousin Fanny, had made good use of her time, then. I lay back against the pillows, my mind in a turmoil. There would be no happiness for Marisa in her infatuation with Jeffrey Carslake. He would delight in being seen with her, delight in her youth, her beauty and her vitality, but he would not know how to love her, and I was helpless to do anything about it.

I was still sleepless when I heard Liam's footsteps at five o'clock in the morning.

Suddenly my future seemed clouded with terrifying uncertainties. My daughter was in love with the man who had dominated my young life, my husband was cheating on me yet again, and somewhere in war-torn Europe the man I loved desperately and eternally was in danger.

Chapter 41

In the following weeks I watched Marisa's moods alternate between black despair and ecstatic happiness, and I knew Jeffrey Carslake was the cause.

She no longer brought her young officers to the house, and she spent all her money on sophisticated clothes that were far too old for her. She borrowed Maxton to ride with Jeffrey across the fells when it was convenient for him, and I knew she was desperately anxious for him to take her to the Hunt Ball – she had wheedled a large sum of money out of her father for her dress. Jeffrey went alone to the Hunt Ball, and I lay awake listening to her sobs from the room next to mine.

As a sop he took her to hear the Hallé Orchestra in Manchester, and for that her face was alive with joy. She seldom saw him over the weekends because he spent those at his sister's house in Westmorland, and by this time most of her friends had made plans that did not include her and were reluctant to have her make use of them when Jeffrey was not available. During those weekends she invariably sulked in her room, playing the latest records or curled up in an armchair with a book in her hands, although I knew she wasn't reading. Instead she was staring down at the pages with a frown on her pretty face, her thoughts miles away.

I never mentioned him unless she did, but one day she startled me by saying, 'Mother, isn't it time you asked me to bring Jeffrey here to meet you and Daddy? I'm sure if we invite him next weekend he'll stay on in Marsdale.'

'Does he need an invitation from us to stay on in Marsdale? Isn't the fact that you are here sufficient to make him want to stay?'

'Well, it isn't easy living at the Mallinsons', he feels he's not wanted at the weekends.'

'Surely not, Marisa. The Mallinsons are old friends.'

'I think you and Daddy should meet him.'

'And I don't think your father is ready to meet him yet, Marisa. I doubt if he will approve of your going around with a man older than himself.'

'That's positively archaic, Mother,' she snapped. 'He should be pleased that I've found somebody so cultured and charming, far more cultured than Daddy will ever be.'

'That is hardly a fact likely to endear him to your father.'

'You could talk to Daddy about him, you could help me, but you won't. Why are you so dead set against our friendship and why is it that every time I want to bring him home you put obstacles in the way?'

'Because I think you're infatuated with him, because I think you are too young and can't possibly know your own mind.'

'I do know my own mind, Mother. I love him, I'll always love him, and nothing you can say or do is going to alter that fact.'

'And has Jeffrey Carslake said he loved you, has he asked you to marry him?'

'Not yet, it's far too early. But he will.'

'Like you said, Marisa, it's far too early, and I'd like you to be a little surer before you bring him into this house.'

'You don't want me to marry him, do you? You'd much rather I married one of those young officers.'

I was weary of the same arguments that went on day after day and week after week. When Jeffrey was kind to her she was like an enthusiastic puppy, grateful for his attention, longing to be petted and loved, and I felt more and more helpless.

Just before Christmas the air raids came to Manchester and we stood with a crowd of others high up on the moor watching the city burn, the flames illuminating the sky, the sickening crunch of falling bombs in our ears.

The yard did not suffer a direct hit but sparks were falling in all directions and soon the timber was alight. Liam and his workmen fought for hours to salvage all they could. He was lucky enough to find premises in Marsdale, but at that particular time they were nothing like as convenient.

The builder's yard itself was spacious enough but the tiny office was a disaster – ill lit and with one smoke-blackened fireplace which was hardly adequate to heat the place, and attached to it a tumbledown kitchen containing a single table and one gas jet.

Side by side with Geraldine I worked relentlessly every day in an effort to salvage scorched order books and restore some sort of normality so that Liam could find work for himself and his men. At first we worked in uncomfortable silence, then bit by bit we began to converse until an uneasy friendship developed between us.

That she was in love with Liam I was not left long in doubt. I could not miss the way her eyes followed him from her desk set near one of the windows. She kept him fortified with constant cups of strong tea and, when he came back cold and weary, she piled coal on to the fire. I can see her now standing in the icy kitchen waiting for the kettle to boil, her hands red with chilblains, wearing dark woollen gloves with the fingers cut short, her eyes lighting up at his casual words of praise.

Another thing I learned in those early days was that Liam was not in love with Geraldine. She was an employee, nothing more. So where then did he spend the long nights he was absent from home, and with whom?

One afternoon I found her crying in the kitchen and, perhaps a little unthinking, I said, 'Is it your father, Geraldine?' after which the sobs came from the very core of her misery. I persuaded her to return to the office and sit near the fire, then I set about making tea, lacing it with whisky from the bottle Liam kept in his desk.

'Do you want to talk about it?' I prompted her.

'I couldn't, Mrs Clancy, not to you,' she sobbed.

'It's Liam, isn't it?'

She raised her red hurt eyes to mine. 'How did you know?'

'I've known for a long time, Geraldine. Why are you so

miserable now?'

'Honestly, Mrs Clancy, there's bin nothin' between Liam and me for years, not since I came back to work for him. He's got somebody else now, he's not interested in me any more.'

'But you still love him?'

'That I do, Mrs Clancy. Oh, I knew right from the start that he'd never leave you for me, but that didn't matter. I was quite happy for us to go on just seein' each other whenever it were possible. Now I knows there's somebody else when I sees him goin' off all dressed up.'

'You don't know who it is?'

'I've a good idea. I think it's that Mrs O'Leary, Bridey they call her. Her husband keeps the Bird in Hand pub at the corner of Sansom Street. He goes in sometimes for his lunch, an' a lot o' the men do their drinkin' there. She makes 'em very welcome, she's got a name round there.'

'I see.'

'I'm not really sure, Mrs Clancy, so please don't be sayin' anythin' to Liam, but I 'ave heard rumours and there's not usually smoke without there bein' fire, is there?'

'No, Geraldine, not usually. Geraldine, why do you continue working here? This yard is a long way from your home, and I'm sure you could find work nearer home and with somebody who appreciates you.'

She stared at me in surprise, then shaking her head vigourously she said, 'Oh, Mrs Clancy, I couldn't leave him, 'e does depend on me most of the time and you won't want to stay on here once we've got things right. He'll get fed up with Bridey, or her husband'll put a stop to it one o' these days. Then 'e might come back to me. Oh, I know it sounds awful sayin' all this to you, but Liam's told me ye don't sleep together, that ye haven't been close for years.'

'Liam told you that!'

'Well yes, an' I've allus thought you weren't as much in love with him as I am.'

I felt bemused by her disclosure, then annoyed that Liam should have discussed the state of our married life with her. Then with something approaching my old humour I realized it was natural that he should have whitewashed his actions by telling her he was the misunderstood husband of a wife who didn't love him.

Looking at her in some exasperation, I said, 'I couldn't be a doormat to any man, Geraldine. Liam would respect you more if you moved out of his life.'

'He might respect mi, Mrs Clancy, but he wouldn't give me another thought.'

I shrugged my shoulders philosophically. 'Would you care what he thought if you didn't see him again?'

'I'd care. Any time he crooks his little finger I'll go runnin', an' I'll be no danger to yer marriage, Mrs Clancy, yer can depend on that.'

As I trudged up the hill that evening my mind was obsessed with the complexity of our lives, so I was in no mood to put up with Marisa's chagrin because Jeffrey had not telephoned her after spending a long weekend with friends in Yorkshire.

'He promised, Mother, and I'm not telephoning him,' she stormed.

'Well at least you've got that much sense,' I retorted waspishly.

'It's your fault, Mother. If you'd only invited him here so that he could meet us as a family he'd feel accepted. As it is he thinks I'm just amusing myself at his expense.'

'Oh surely not, not when you go around looking like a dejected spaniel. Jeffrey Carslake is more likely to be bored by such adolescent infatuation than enchanted by it.'

She glared at me out of storm-filled eyes. 'I hate you when you say things like that. You're jealous, that's what you are, jealous because he's nicer than my father and you didn't get him.'

Suddenly sober, I stood stock still listening to her flying footsteps on the stairs followed by the slamming of her bedroom door. Oh surely not, surely that old passion for Jeffrey was as dead and forgotten as those dreary days I had worked in his father's house. That infatuation had been killed slowly and surely over the years, and didn't I love Nicholas now and always?

427

One thing was certain, I had to be sure. I had to know if he had any serious intentions about Marisa, and if he had how much I cared.

From my bedroom that night I heard Liam's and Marisa's voices, and I knew she was telling him about Jeffrey. At times his voice sounded angry, affronted, at others persuasive, and there were times when her voice was raised in anger, at others tearful. Then I heard her running up the stairs and passing my door without coming in to say goodnight.

A few minutes later Liam came into my room and immediately I knew he was bitterly angry. His face was flushed, his eyes cold and vindictive as he hurled his first accusation at me.

'Why didn't you tell mi what she was up to?'

'Up to? I'm not sure what you mean.'

'Oh yes, Madam, you know very well what I mean. She's in love she tells mi, and with Jeffrey Carslake no less. Isn't he the feller you've bin besotted with all these years? Isn't he the chap who's stood between me and you since the day we were married?'

'Don't shout, Liam, I don't want Marisa to hear any of this nonsense.'

'I'll shout if I want in mi own house, and p'raps it's about time she heard this. It might bring her to her senses.'

'It might if it was true, but it isn't. I'd forgotten Jeffrey Carslake's existence till Marisa mentioned she'd met him. I've told her he's far too old for her and I hope she'll have the sense to get over him and forget him.'

'Well you wouldn't want her to wed him, would you, Katie? That's understandable. You wouldn't want your daughter to wed a man who wouldn't wed you.'

'Don't you think I haven't been thankful for that all these years? I did love him when I was a young housemaid at Heatherlea but it was the same sort of infatuation Marisa is suffering from now, and Jeffrey Carslake will no more want to marry her than he wanted to marry me. He won't marry anybody, he isn't capable of that kind of commitment.'

'The reason he wouldn't marry you was because you

were a servant in his mother's house and he won't marry Marisa because she's your daughter. Let's be honest about it.'

'All right, let us be honest. Lois Foxland wasn't a servant and he wouldn't marry her either. I tell you, Liam, Jeffrey Carslake isn't capable of loving a woman enough to ask her to marry him. If ever he does marry it will be some woman who is looking for a presentable escort in their public life and who is willing to keep their private life entirely celibate.'

'You seem mighty sure, Katie.'

'I am sure, Liam.'

'Then why have I thought otherwise all these years? Why have I been so sure about you and him?'

'It was in your imagination. It must have been because Jeffrey Carslake was never my lover. His choice, not mine.'

I was unprepared for the sharp slap his open palm registered on my face and I recoiled with a little cry, staring up at his red face and narrowed, vindictive eyes. His hands gripped my shoulders so tightly I cried out with pain, and a wild unreasonable fear made me hammer my fists against his chest so that he let me go so suddenly I almost fell.

With a voice filled with sarcasm he said, 'Ye needn't worry, Katie, I raped you once but I've nó intention of doin' it again. As the years pass I desire you less and less.'

He strode out of my room, shutting the door with a sharp air of finality, and I sank down on the edge of the bed, rubbing my shoulders where his fingers had left deep dark blotches.

Breakfast was a silent meal, with Marisa's face pale and tearful, and Liam's buried in his newspaper.

Marisa came home early that night, her first words on entering the house being, 'Has Jeffrey telephoned, Mother?'

'No, darling, and I haven't been out.'

'I saw Evelyn Claver in town and she wants us both to go to her engagement party over at Copplethorpe on Saturday.'

'But *you're* going, Marisa. You've neglected your friends

terribly since you met Jeffrey.'

'I won't go if he doesn't come with me.'

'Whether he accompanies you or not you should go. One of these days, Marisa, you are going to need the friends you threw away so lightly when you met him. They are not going to come running back if anything goes wrong between you and Jeffrey Carslake.'

'He doesn't like most of them, Mother. He says they're bourgeois, newly rich.'

'He doesn't like them because he doesn't like to think the money is in different hands these days. He's a fugitive from those days when wealthy cotton manufacturers lived on Tremayne Hill and before all their mills went into massive combines. He likes to have the men touch their caps and the women bob their curtsies to him. He can't come to terms with life as it is now and as it is going to be. It is a resentment that could destroy him, but I don't want it to destroy you.'

'But Mother, they *are* newly rich compared to Jeffrey.'

'And don't you think Jeffrey Carslake's great-grandfather was newly rich when he first put what bit of money he had into cotton? Rags to riches in three generations, that's what they're fond of saying in Lancashire, and I've seen it work the other way. You must go to this party on Saturday, whether he goes with you or not. I insist.'

'I'll telephone him, Mother, I'll try to persuade him,' she said brightly, her face shining with hope.

Her euphoria did not last long. After her telephone call she merely informed me that she was not going to the party. Jeffrey was spending the weekend in Marsdale, so they would probably be going somewhere else on Saturday evening.

'I'll write and apologize,' she said. 'I'll make a very good excuse and I'm sure Evelyn won't mind. Jeffrey wouldn't fit in with that crowd anyway.'

I was furiously angry, with my daughter because she was acting like a doormat, with Jeffrey for his selfish use of her, and with myself for ever having been stupid enough to love him as much as Marisa was loving him now. One thing I was determined to do, and that was stop this friendship before it went any further.

I watched her answering Evelyn's letter that night, and when she didn't have a stamp for it I promised to post it the following day.

'Are you seeing Jeffrey before Saturday?' I asked guilelessly.

'No, Mother. He's going somewhere with the Mallinsons tonight and there's something on at school tomorrow. We've left it until Saturday.'

'What were you planning to do, then?'

'We'll probably ride if it's nice enough, if not we might go into the city to see a show.'

I waited until the night she returned to the school where her students were rehearsing a play, then I telephoned the Mallinsons', asking if I could speak to Mr Carslake.

I was impatient with the stupid fluttering of my heart when I heard his voice, the voice that had once sent me into rhapsodies of joy, and I clenched my hand against my breast, waiting until I was sure my voice betrayed nothing of my anxiety.

'Jeffrey Carslake here,' came his voice.

'Good evening, Mr Carslake, this is Mrs Clancy, Marisa's mother.'

There was a pause, then I was aware of the sudden charm in his voice, the desire to charm me.

'Why, Mrs Clancy, how nice to hear from you, although we did meet some time ago at the Earnshaws', I think.'

'Yes, I remember you, Mr Carslake.'

'Is anything wrong with Marisa?'

'No, except that I feel she should go to her friend's party on Saturday evening. She is missing all their activities at the weekends and unfortunately you are usually away then.'

'I'm not away this coming weekend, Mrs Clancy.'

'No, I believe not, but you don't wish to attend the party, Marisa tells me.'

He laughed, a little self-consciously perhaps. 'They're all such children, Mrs Clancy, they make me feel older than

431

my years. I'm sure you understand.'

'Indeed I do, that is why I am ringing you. I'm sure you will understand why Marisa must go and it is better if she goes alone. She really should keep in touch with her friends, Mr Carslake.'

'Of course, I agree with you. Perhaps we shall meet in the near future, Mrs Clancy.'

'Yes, I'm sure we shall. Does this interfere too much with your plans for the weekend?'

'I shall probably spend Saturday up on the fell if the weather is fine. I am well able to entertain myself, Mrs Clancy.'

We said our goodbyes, and I put the receiver down with a trembling hand. I was not relishing the role I was playing and I knew at the end there would be the breaking of my daughter's heart. Fortunately I knew how quickly the young could heal, particularly Marisa, who had never let anything get her down for too long.

That night she came into my bedroom as usual to report on the progress of the play and as calmly as I could I lied, 'Jeffrey Carslake telephoned, Marisa. Unfortunately he's been called away on business so he won't be able to see you on Saturday after all.'

She sat down heavily on the edge of my bed, her eyes filled with dismay. 'That's rotten,' she said. 'I wish I'd never sent that note back to Evelyn, I could have gone.'

'I didn't post it, darling, I wasn't able to go out.'

She stared at me doubtfully. 'Do you think I should go, Mother?'

'Of course you must go. I shall be furious with you if you don't. Ring up some of your friends and ask if you can travel with them.'

'They might not like it, I haven't seen any of them for months.'

'Then you should eat humble pie and make the first move.'

She nodded unhappily. 'I'll do it tomorrow, Mother. It really is too bad of Jeffrey after he promised.'

I felt wretched. I was gambling with her love for me, our

friendship which had often been precarious. But worse, I was raking over old ashes, exposing emotions which had lain dormant for so long.

I watched Marisa setting out with her friends in a rakish car on Saturday morning, three girls and two boys, and although she had appeared not to be liking the arrangement, by the time they reached the gate I could hear their laughter.

It was fine and sunny, even though there was a cold nip in the air and the rain clouds scudded low over the summit of the moors. Liam had gone to a race meeting at Haydock and I had the house to myself. I went upstairs to dress for my meeting with Jeffrey.

Chapter 42

About an hour later I stood in front of the long mirror in my bedroom making sure that I was looking my best. I was wearing my riding habit, and its severity became me. I was looking at a beautiful elegant woman whose pale magnolia skin was complemented by the sombre black coat, slightly below average height but delicately made and slender as a reed. I picked up my gloves and riding crop and ran lightly down the stairs and out to the stables.

Maxton's feet trod daintly amid the stones of the narrow lane until we reached the stile, and then we were climbing with the sharp wind in our faces, the short moorland grass under his flying hooves and I revelled in the horse's speed, taking the low stone walls with consummate ease. I wanted to be first on the hill, to compose myself and to catch my breath, but I did not have long to wait. And when I caught sight of him riding up the hillside the past came hurtling back to me, and I was a girl again, watching with bated breath and anxious eyes for this man who was the centre of my universe to look up and see me. But this time it was different, I was not Katie O'Donovan hopping impatiently from one foot to the other, but Kathleen Clancy, sitting impassively on my horse, my hands resting lightly on the reins, watching with a mature cynicism and a heart untroubled by flights of love.

At last he looked up and our eyes met. He smiled, and even at that moment with my heart steeled against him, there was no denying the charm of that smile, and I understood how easily it had captured the imagination of my impressionable daughter, captivating her completely as it had once captivated me.

Deliberately I did not move towards him. He came to

me, holding out his hand in greeting, his voice warm with pleasure.

'Why, Mrs Clancy, how delightful to have your company.'

I smiled. 'I remembered that you said you might ride up here today, Mr Carslake. I hoped I might join you.'

For the main part we rode in silence, occasionally pausing to admire the view, and it was only when we reached the rugged crest of Pentland Rise that we stopped our horses and with a sweep of his arm he embraced the vista set before us.

'I always pause here,' he said, 'the view is so magnificent whatever the weather.'

'I agree. It seems years since I took the trouble to come so far.'

'It seems strange that I haven't met you up here before, Mrs Clancy.'

'Not really so strange. We have only been living on Evening Hill about four years, before that we lived nearer the city.'

'In suburbia.'

'Yes.'

'I wonder what made you come out here?'

'My husband heard that the land was for sale and he is a builder. He knew that I had always wanted to live up on the hill, but the farmer had shown no inclination to sell the land.'

'Where are you from originally?'

'You mean before I married or before we lived in suburbia?'

'Before you married?'

'I was born in Ireland, and before I married I lived in the area.'

'How strange that we never met.'

We had dismounted from our horses and because the wind was bitingly cold up on the fell we went to stand in the shadow of the crag that rose in rugged splendour against the winter sky.

'My daughter tells me you have bought one of the

435

cottages in Pentland Lane.'

'Yes. It needs quite a lot doing to it, the previous owner was an old lady who let it run down, but it has great possibilities. Of course it is very small but quite large enough for me. There's a little garden at the front and an apple orchard at the back so I do feel conscious of some space.'

'And you are away a good deal at the weekends, Mr Carslake, so I am sure it is adequate for your needs.'

He smiled. 'I remember Marsdale when it was very different. My family lived on Tremayne Hill and we were a fair-sized family with four boys and two girls. We had horses to ride and a large garden to play in when we were children. Now when I go up there everything is changed. All the old families apart from old Mrs Peers have gone, and even Tremayne House is a museum these days.'

'Yes. Is that very sad for you?'

His face was sad, and he was frowning a little, his eyes reflective, looking inward at the past instead of at the entrancing view of the moors in the splendour of their wintry attire.

'Yes, it's sad, but I mustn't bore you with all this nostalgia, Mrs Clancy. I shouldn't feel sad at all when all those young people are losing their lives in the war.'

'Marisa tells me you do not like her friends. Why is that, Mr Carslake?'

He laughed, a little uncomfortably. 'I don't dislike them, it's just that they are so young we don't have a great deal in common.'

'They are the same age as my daughter.'

'Yes I know. Marisa is different. I'm very fond of her, she's a nice child.'

'My daughter is twenty-seven years old, Mr Carslake, so she is hardly a child. I would like you to be honest with me. How fond are you of Marisa?'

His eyes met mine uncertainly, fearfully, like a cornered animal's.

'I'd like to think we were very good friends. Surely you agree that there can be a friendship between two people if

436

they have many things in common, even if they are a man and a woman.'

For several minutes I didn't answer him. I was thinking of the friendship Maurice Abrahams and I had shared since before Marisa was born, but Maurice had been in love with me. He had been deeply hurt in so many ways, by Liam's high-handed belittling of our friendship, and by my love for Nicholas, and yet I had always been scrupulously honest in my dealings with Maurice. He had always known that the love he had for me had been strictly one-sided, that on my part it had been only affectionate friendship and gratitude.

His eyes were on me, waiting for my answer, and looking up at him I said earnestly, 'It has been my experience that there can be such friendship, but often at a price. You will not fall in love with my daughter, Mr Carslake, but she might fall in love with you.'

'But surely that is something two people have to find out for themselves.'

'We are speaking about uncertainties, about a man and a woman with the same capacity for loving, and finding out by being together if they care enough to commit themselves to a life together. There is no such certainty in the friendship you share with Marisa.'

'Why are you so sure?'

'Because a long time ago, Mr Carslake, I thought I knew you very well and loved you hopelessly, desperately, with all my heart. I hated your father because he was always so quick to disparage you, because you were not his favourite. I hated Lois Foxland when she married Joseph Earnshaw until I realized how little you cared, and then I hated you because I had loved you when my husband went off to war, I bore his daughter loving you. And I hated you for all the long wasted years it took for that love to die and bring the realization that I had been in love with a dream.

'I made a beautiful suit of clothes and fashioned you to fit them, and it didn't ease the pain to know that it wasn't your fault, it was mine.'

He was staring at me in dumbfounded silence, and quietly I reached up and took off my riding hat, allowing it to fall on to the moorland grass, then just as deliberately I took the restraining ribbon off my hair and allowed it to fall around my shoulders in all its russet abandon.

For a few minutes he stared at me in disbelief, and I smiled a little at his astonishment.

'You said that morning at the Earnshaws' house that I reminded you of a girl who once worked in your mother's house, but of course it was unthinkable that Kathleen Clancy could ever have been that girl. Well, take another look. I think you will find Katie O'Donovan, or what is left of her in me.'

He stared at me in stunned silence for several minutes, then taking hold of my hand he murmured, 'Katie, I didn't know, honestly I didn't know.'

'No. I know you didn't, you didn't know because love is something you really don't know very much about. Oh I know, you loved your mother, your family and your way of life, but can you honestly tell me that you have ever really loved any woman, Jeffrey?'

He stood staring down the hillside towards the tarn, dark and forbidding under its pall of purple cloud, then miserably he shook his head. 'No, I never loved a woman enough to want to spend my entire life with her. I thought at first I loved Lois that way, but then I realized I only liked her companionship, I only wanted her friendship.'

'Just like it is with Marisa?'

'Yes.'

'It has cost me a great deal to face you with all this today, Jeffrey, and it isn't over yet. My daughter is going to be very unhappy, until she forgets you, finds consolation in somebody else, or accepts that there is no future for her with you. I shall have to watch that unhappiness eating into her soul, and my husband too will be made unhappy by her. But she will in time get over you if she is given the chance. Please, Jeffrey, will you help me?'

'You don't want us to meet again?'

'I want you to be kind to her, as gentle as you know how without injuring her pride. The young bruise so quickly, but thank God they heal quickly too.'

438

'You're so sure about me, Katie.'

'Yes, I am, but may God forgive me if I'm wrong. Will you forgive me if I'm wrong?'

'Will your daughter forgive you, Katie?'

'That is a chance I have to take and I am relying on your discretion.'

He waited in silence while I tied back my hair, handed my hat back to me, then assisted me on to my horse. Our eyes met but this time his were sombre. 'I remember you riding my horse that day with your red hair flying in the wind, Katie, that is the most unforgettable memory I have of you.'

'Please don't ride back with me now. Goodbye, Jeffrey.'

I held out my hand which he took in his, then after he had released it I turned my horse about and raced down the hillside towards the distant town.

He remembered that afternoon when I had galloped across the moor my long skirts pulled over my knees, holding on to the horse's mane for dear life, my red hair flying in the wind. But he had forgotten that moment when I had thrown myself into his arms, demanding kisses from lips that were unwilling, and love from a heart that did not know how to give it.

Chapter 43

By the time I reached the stables it was sheeting with rain and it took some time to make the horse comfortable before I could grab a raincoat and run across to the house.

I was astounded when the door opened to my touch, as I felt sure I had locked it before leaving the house. The hall was in darkness and I stood there with my ears straining for any sound, my eyes searching the darkened stairs and shadowy landing.

It was then I heard the soft whimpering of the dog behind the closed drawing-room door, and I knew for a certainty that I had left Copper in the kitchen. I was frightened, but the snapping on of every light I could find restored a little of my lost courage and, taking one of Liam's stout walking sticks, I threw open the drawing-room door.

The dog leapt at me, pawing me with delight, making soft ecstatic noises of welcome in his throat. At first I was aware only of the firelight dancing on the walls and ceiling before the lights were switched on and I was staring into Liam's eyes, bloodshot with drink and anger and disgust before he raised his hand and sent me crashing to the floor.

Numb with shock and pain I could only lie there moaning while the spaniel licked my face, then he stood over me, guarding me against my husband with bared fangs and terrifying growls. With a muttered oath Liam reached out for him and, growling and barking, Copper was flung out into the hall to snarl at the closed door.

My shoulder ached where I had fallen against a heavy marble-topped table and I stared dully at a broken vase on the floor, the flowers scattered across the table, the water seeping into the carpet. I reached up to touch the side of my face, burning from Liam's heavy blow, and winced at the sudden spasm of pain that gripped me.

Painfully I struggled to my feet, only to sink trembling into the depths of the nearest chair with the scalding tears rolling down my face, and Liam came to stand over me, glaring down with hot angry eyes.

'You do well to cry, Madam, but by God I could kill you both.'

I stared at him stupidly until the meaning of his words penetrated my dulled senses, then anger took hold of me too, an anger that transcended pain, and I stumbled to my feet, placing the chair between us.

'You are a fool, Liam, if you believe I went to meet Jeffrey Carslake because I love him. I went to ask him to leave Marisa alone.'

'Aye, because you love him, because you couldn't bear to see her happy with him, because you wanted him yourself.'

'It isn't true. I hadn't seen Jeffrey Carslake for years until I met him at the Earnshaws' house, and by that time I'd almost forgotten his existence. I'll admit there was a time when I thought I loved him, but that was years ago when I was too young and foolish to know any different. I asked him not to see Marisa again, and to be kind to her.'

'I don't believe you, nor will Marisa when I tell her the truth.'

'But it is the truth, Liam, and if you tell Marisa anything of this I'll never forgive you. I swear it.'

'She has a right to know. He's goin' to finish with her at your instigation. He's goin' to tell her a load of cock-and-bull stories but he won't tell her the truth, that it's you that's come between 'em. My God, but if I hadn't come back for mi shootin' stick I'd never have seen you settin' out across the fell, so I followed ye. You hadn't gone far when I saw him riding up after you.'

'He wasn't. He didn't know I was there until we met.'

'But you felt pretty sure he'd be there. It's my bet you'd made sure.'

'Oh, Liam, nothing I'm going to say is going to convince you, so you must do as you think fit. Tell Marisa if you must, make her hate me, split this family as surely as if you'd walked out and left us, and then when you see what is left of this sham we call a marriage you'll realize what you've done.'

'What you've done, Katie. It wasn't me settin' out to meet a woman on the fell, a woman I'd been besotted with all mi married life.'

The retort was quick on my lips but instinctively I stifled it before it could find utterance. What was the point of flinging his mistress in his face when I neither knew nor cared who the current one happened to be? But his next utterance swept away all my complacency.

'If this family splits up, Katie O'Donovan, I'll make sure the boy stays with me. Marisa's over twenty-one and can make her own decisions, but you'll not interfere with our son's life like you've interfered with Marisa's.'

I stared at him with agony-filled eyes. He would do that to me, he would take Jeremy and leave me alone, and at that moment deep abiding hatred for him almost made me fling in his face the fact that Jeremy was not his son. But fear, and fear alone, held me back. I could smell the whisky on his breath, see the hard unyielding cruelty in his narrowed eyes and I swallowed my anger and resorted to tears, sinking sobbing on to the carpet with my head buried against the chair, moaning, 'Please Liam, please, you couldn't be so cruel.'

He believed he had won, that I was the defeated penitent wife pleading for the future of her home and children, and the next thing I heard was the slamming of the front door. I sat on the floor until I heard the sound of his car then I rose shakily to my feet, hampered by the dog whimpering beside me.

I did not know what the next few days would bring. Jeffrey would end his friendship with Marisa but I knew I could rely on his discretion and his gentleness. I had no such faith in Liam. Vindictive and unreasonable, he would allow his jealousy to overcome any feeling of compassion. Liam had an Irishman's long inflexible memory for slights and hurts which called out for revenge at any price, revenge without pity, revenge before he began to count the cost.

442

We did not meet again that day and it was after lunch when he returned to the house on Sunday. I did not comment on his absence or ask where he had spent his time, nor did he pass any comment on my bruised face and swollen eye. It was left for Marisa to ask where I had acquired it when she returned home happy and talkative in the early evening.

'Gracious, Mother, what have you done to your face?' was her greeting.

'I fell, darling, and caught my face against a table. It has stopped hurting. Did you have a lovely time?'

'Oh yes, absolutely marvellous. It's not going to be a long engagement so they'll probably be getting married in the summer. I do hope Jeffrey won't be difficult, he's invited to the wedding.'

Liam's eyes met mine across the table, and there was no disguising the grim amusement in their depths.

I never again want to live in the atmosphere that existed during the following days. For the first few days Marisa fretted and fumed that Jeffrey hadn't telephoned, and Liam waited in the wings like a spider, or so it seemed to me.

Instead of telephoning Jeffrey wrote her a short note suggesting dinner in town on Friday evening and for the rest of the week she went about with a bright smile, watched by Liam with a self-satisfied smirk which I longed to eliminate by raking my fingers across it.

I kept myself busy that Friday evening. Liam was out and I retired early, settling down to read in bed, but I was too tense to do anything but lie there, distraught, my thoughts on the past as I relived over and over again my many mistakes.

I heard a car in the drive, then the sudden closing of the door, and I went out on to the landing and called to her, 'Marisa, is that you?'

She was standing in the middle of the hall, bewildered and surrounded by a great loneliness that brought the tears to my eyes, and I had to call to her again before she looked up. Then she too was in tears, racing up the stairs to meet me, dissolving in an ecstasy of weeping on to my shoulder. I pulled her into the bedroom, but it was a long time before I could get any sense out of her, and my heart ached.

At last she looked through her tears, saying pitifully, 'Mother, it's all over, we're not going to see each other any more.'

'What has happened?'

I felt a hypocrite, but I had to know how Jeffrey had ended their friendship and if indeed he had been kind.

'He says he's been giving it a lot of thought,' she muttered between her tears. 'He says he's terribly fond of me but he realizes he's far too old for me. Then he started saying all those rubbishy things like when I'm thirty he'll be over fifty, as though any of that's important.'

'But darling, it is important. A woman should marry a man who can be with her to watch their children grow up. And who knows what younger men you might meet? Your husband could become an invalid while you are still young enough to want gaiety and excitement in your life.'

Roughly she tore herself out of my embrace, snapping, 'Oh, you're as bad as he is. Neither of you seems to realize how much I love him, that I want to spend the rest of my life with him whether he's an invalid or not.'

'Did you say all this to Jeffrey?'

'Yes I did, it needed to be said.'

'And what was his reaction, Marisa?'

'He said he was sorry, that he would have given anything not to have hurt me, but he was too old, too set in his ways, that he'd been a bachelor too long to change. He told me I'd get over him when I met somebody of my own age with the capacity for loving.'

She stared at me out of wide, pain-filled eyes.

'You tried to warn me, Mother, but I wouldn't listen. Oh, I feel so rejected, so worthless.'

'Surely Jeffrey didn't make you feel rejected.'

'No, he looked so sad, so sorry about everything, but I can't help the way I feel. I'll never get over him, never.'

'My dear, I can assure you that you will. I never got

along with Grandmother Cassidy but one of her favourite sayings was "Miss a train at twenty and sure there's another along any minute, miss one at forty an they're few and far between." '

She smiled tremulously. 'Oh, Mother, I'm so miserable. There won't be anybody else for me, ever.'

'Get undressed and go to bed, I'll bring you a warm drink.'

As I prepared it I too wept, for the lost dreams of youth and for all a girl's innocence and trust that life would play fair.

During the next few days, while Marisa went about the house like a pale dejected ghost, Liam said nothing. Yet I felt him watching both of us with the same sort of patience a cat uses when he plays with a mouse, an amused patience which will end only one way – in the death of the mouse.

Aunt Mary was ill, and the following Sunday I filled a shopping basket with fruit and vegetables and set off down the hill. I found her propped up in a chair surrounded by pillows, a fire half-way up the chimney, and by her side a table covered with various bottles of linctus.

'Don't come too near, Katie, I don't want you to catch my cold,' she warned.

'Have you seen the doctor?'

'I don't need a doctor, it's winter and I always has mi bronchitis in winter. Come the better weather and it'll go.'

'I've brought fruit and vegetables. There's a chicken too, so perhaps you'll eat that first.'

'I've no appetite, Katie, but Joel'll enjoy it.'

I went into the kitchen and started to put the things I had brought into the cupboards. Uncle Joel followed me in. 'How's Liam? We haven't seen 'im since we saw 'im climbin' the hill last weekend with a face like thunder. I called to 'im but 'e ignored me an' just went on walkin'.'

'He's all right, Uncle, a bit worried about the business since it moved to Marsdale. The yard's not really big enough and so many of the men are in the forces or on war work.'

'Do ye think 'e's goin' to sell out, Katie?'

'Sell out! Whatever gave you that idea? Liam isn't old enough to retire.'

'Well, like ye said, there's not the same amount o' work now the war's on and it's hard 'avin' ter come back to climbin' scaffoldin'. That's work for younger folk.'

'I haven't heard him complain. I'm sure I would know if he was thinking of selling the business, and he would tell you, he owes it to you to tell you.'

'Oh, young people are not so fond these days o' facing up to their obligations, and Liam's 'ad a lot on 'is mind lately.'

'Well, yes, the loss of the yard was a big blow and this war is going on far too long. How is it all going to end?'

'In the end we'll win, Katie, we 'ave to, but what'll 'appen after it's all over is a different matter. It'll not be the same world for any of us, an' it's my guess it won't be any better.'

Back in the living room Aunt Mary said, 'What's 'e bin sayin' to ye, Katie? Allus mutterin' to 'imself 'e is, 'e thinks 'e knows better than all the admirals and generals put together. On an' on 'e goes, it's a relief when 'im and yer uncle goes out an' Martha and me can 'ave a quiet cup o' tea and talk about somethin' proper.'

Next door at my aunt and uncle's house I met a tirade levelled at Fanny's new property on Tremayne Hill, and her husband's elevation to Barrister at Law, ending with Aunt Martha's 'Every day they passes this 'ouse on their way 'ome,' Aunt Martha complained bitterly, 'and never so much as a look. I don't think mi granddaughter even knows we exist.'

'Stop frettin' about it Martha,' Uncle Turlough advised, 'It's all in the past luv, I came to terms with it years ago.'

'Yer only thinks yer did,' she snapped. 'Yer just as hurt as I am, more so, ye just don't talk about it that's all.'

'But surely when you meet she acknowledges you,' I asked.

'Not if she can help it, and when she does it's a cool smile. We never stop and talk, she never wants to know owt about us, how we're livin', remark 'ow Lucy is. 'She probably doesn't even know Lucy's wed.'

'She knows all right, I told her.'

'You told 'er, Kathleen, when were that?'

'She came to the house to see if they could buy Lyndhurst. I never told Liam she asked for it, but I told her Lucy was married.'

'Did ye tell 'er we were living 'ere?'

'Yes.'

'She wouldn't be so keèn on the 'ouse after that.'

'I don't know. I don't remember, but I didn't want them on the hill. I didn't want Fanny anywhere in the vicinity, and I never see them.'

'You might not, but yer daughter does,' Aunt Martha said sourly.

I stared at her sharply. 'When? When does Marisa see them?'

She became confused, wishing she hadn't spoken, and Turlough said in an effort to cover the lapse, 'Take no notice, Katie, she saw Fanny and Marisa talking one day, in the town.'

I decided not to pursue the subject. I did not stay long after that, I felt I wanted to escape into the cool air of the wet wintry day. As I climbed the hill I felt surrounded by all kinds of betrayal, Liam's and Marisa's. I spent a miserable Sunday evening when Liam went out directly our evening meal was over and Marisa fretted and sulked in her room so that I was glad when Monday came and they were both out of the house.

My grandmother had always maintained that we received premonitions of disaster or tragedy, but I had never had a premonition in my life and this particular Monday was no exception.

By six o'clock neither Liam nor Marisa had arrived home for their evening meal and I sat in the kitchen looking at the clock. The pans bubbled and boiled on top of the stove and although I had turned the oven down I found myself constantly opening the door to reassure myself that all was well.

At last I telephoned the yard, but there was no reply. Then I telephoned the art college, only to be told by a disgruntled caretaker that the pupils and staff had left hours before.

The telephone rang and, frantic with anxiety I almost tripped in my haste to answer it. I was unprepared for Mary Palmerston's voice.

'I thought I should ring you, Kathleen,' she explained. 'Marisa is here. She is terribly upset and asking if she can stay with us for the night. Is something wrong there?'

'No, but Liam isn't home yet. I was getting very anxious about both of them. May I speak to her?'

'Yes of course, I'll get her.'

I waited anxiously for Marisa's voice, but once again it was Mary, saying, 'She won't come to the telephone, Kathleen. I don't know what to make of her.'

'Well, I can't make her come home. Will you please tell her I'm very upset by her behaviour and I want her to come home as soon as possible.'

'I'll tell her. It's probably something and nothing, a lover's tiff or something gone wrong at the school. I'll telephone you in the morning.'

'Thank you Mary. Goodbye.'

I felt sick with worry and in my heart anger against Liam raised its ugly head. I told myself that he was a coward, refusing to face me after he had told Marisa about the part I had played in the ending of her friendship with Jeffrey. It was more than cruel, it was sadistic. By the time I heard his key in the lock my anger had reached enormous proportions.

It was almost midnight, and by this time my nerves were in such a state it was too late for logical thought, too late for sensible and calm behaviour. When he appeared in the room I flew at him, hammering on his chest, the words tumbling over one another until he caught both my hands in an iron grip and held me away from him.

'Are you mad, woman?' he cried. 'What ails you?'

'I hate you, Liam Clancy, you told Marisa and now she's at the Palmerstons', refusing to come home. Oh, how could you be so vile, so contemptible?'

He stared at me, his face red and angry, then flinging me

away from him, he said, 'I told her nothin'. If she's found out she's found out from somebody else.'

'I don't believe you.'

'Please yourself, but she's not stayin' at the Palmerston's, she's comin' home. I'm not having her opening everybody's mouths.'

'It's after midnight, you can't go for her now.'

'Midnight or no midnight, she's coming home,' he snapped, and left the house.

It felt cold in the large room, and shivering with cold and anxiety, I started to stoke up the fire. When I sat back on the rug with the flames leaping and dancing in the grate, the glow from them falling on velvet drapes and polished wood, my eyes looked round the beautiful room with sombre disenchantment.

I had dreamed of this room all my life, I had fought and ached for it, worked and plotted for it. I had got my beautiful house on the summit of Evening Hill and I had furnished it with all the good taste Maurice Abrahams had taught me, and tonight it seemed a dead thing, as much a museum as that other museum on Tremayne Hill. There should be ropes round the rooms where visitors could walk without touching, and I was part of the museum, an empty thing, a doll without a soul.

When I heard the return of Liam's car and voices in the hall I struggled to my feet to meet them.

Marisa came into the room, staring at me with angry, hate-filled eyes, and when I went to take her into my arms she stepped back sharply, saying, 'Don't touch me, don't ever touch me. I hate you.'

'Darling, why? What have I done?'

'You know what you've done, you've come between Jeffrey and me. It's because of you that he isn't going to see me again. You couldn't get me out of the house quick enough, could you? You couldn't bear him to love me instead of you.'

'It isn't true, Marisa, I only wanted what was best for you. Jeffrey was wrong for you, he would never have loved you.'

449

'I hate you, Mother, I'll never forgive you, and as soon as this rotten war's over I'll leave here. I'll never want to see you again.'

'Marisa, I'm your mother. You can't mean it.'

'I do mean it. You'll see.'

She turned, leaving Liam and me staring at each other, and hatred once again filled my entire being. I said sharply, 'I hope you're satisfied, Liam. You've destroyed us as a family.'

Wearily he said, 'Katie, we haven't been a family for years, but I've had no hand in it. Oh, I know I threatened to tell her, but that was in anger and frustration. I wanted to hurt you, but when the anger went I couldn't tell her, I couldn't do that to you, Katie.'

I stared at him sorrowfully, 'Then who, Liam?'

'Why don't you ask him?'

I started in shocked surprise, then after a few minutes I said, 'No, Liam, it wasn't Jeffrey. He isn't capable of love, not the love Marisa wanted, but he wouldn't be so base as to tell her about me. I can't believe it.'

Cynicism filled his eyes. 'You say you don't love him, but you're still protecting him.'

'I don't love him, Liam, I'm telling you the truth. But I won't believe that of him either.'

'Well, we'll never know how she's found out because she'll never tell us. You've excluded him and, although you thought I was base enough to tell her, you know now it wasn't me. You'll have to think about somebody else who hates you enough to have done it.'

After another long hard stare he left me alone with a thought I refused at first to admit. Was this my cousin's revenge for denying Lyndhurst to her? If so, she had repaid me for that action a hundredfold.

Chapter 44

In the days and weeks that followed my only joy was the letters I received from Jeremy telling me of his prowess at games and in the classroom. He wrote lucidly and conversationally and when I passed them across the table for Liam to read he said somewhat grumpily, 'He doesn't take after me. I could never string two words together as you well know.'

'You were never blessed with Jeremy's education, Liam.'

'That's so, and it would have bin wasted on mi. I reckon he takes after you, Katie.'

Between Liam and me there was an uneasy peace, but not so with Marisa. For the first few days after her outburst she ignored me totally until Liam said he would have no sulks and tantrums in his house, that she would be respectful to me and act like an adult instead of a spoilt child. After that she was respectful when her father was present. When he was not she ignored me.

She found friends I didn't know because she never brought them to the house, and one evening I asked if she wouldn't care to invite them home for a meal, but her reply left me shaken and unhappy.

'I'd rather you didn't meet my men friends, Mother. I don't want to lose another one the way I lost Jeffrey Carslake.'

I stared at her with wide, angry eyes, but uncontrite she retreated to her bedroom and that was the last I saw of her that evening.

I was living for Easter and Jeremy's holidays from school. I made plans of what we would do. Unlike Marisa, Jeremy was not difficult to please. He was good at history, and I resolved that we would visit York and Chester, and if the weather was fine there were many old castles and ruined abbeys in the area that I knew he would delight in.

I saw no more of Jeffrey Carslake, but passing Pentland Lane one morning I saw that the cottage windows and door were newly painted and there were curtains at the windows. I felt sure he must have moved into the cottage, but I hurried on with my head down against the wind.

One day I met my cousin Frances in the post office. We merely exchanged distant nods, but I believed her eyes were filled with malice. On that same afternoon I also met Geraldine McClusky hurrying back to the yard after lunch.

'How are you, Geraldine?' I greeted her. 'I hope you got somebody to look at the boiler, it was ridiculous to have no hot water in the place.'

'Oh, it's better now, Mrs Clancy, the men came and put a new boiler in and a new washbasin. We had the chimney swept so the fire burns much better than it did when you were there. I thought you might 'ave called in one day when you were shoppin'.'

'I haven't been anywhere near the yard, Geraldine, but I will call in one day, perhaps when Jeremy is home.'

'That'll be around Easter, won't it?'

'Yes. You decided to stay on in Marsdale, then?'

'Well, yes, for the time bein'. Business isn't good and although I hates the travellin' it's a job I'm used to.'

'And Liam depends on you, Geraldine. He would miss you if you left.'

Her face clouded. 'He'd miss mi in the office, that's all.'

'Oh, Geraldine, you're a very attractive young woman, you should leave Liam and look out for a better job and a man who is free to marry you. Heaven knows there are enough men about needing love and comfort from this ghastly war.'

'It's funny you tryin' to give me good advice, Mrs Clancy, an' I knows your right. He's still friendly with that woman, but I've seen his car outside Mrs Edwards'. Widow she is, lives in Clarkson Street.'

'Oh Geraldine, I had no idea my husband was such a Romeo.'

452

She blushed furiously. 'I shouldn't be telling you all this, but it's not hurtin' you, is it? Otherwise I wouldn't be sayin' a word. I knows Alice Edwards, and suddenly she's smartened 'erself up an' there's new curtains at the windows. If he was my husband I'd mind like the very devil.'

'I shall mind if people are talking about it.'

'And that's the only reason?'

How could I tell this woman that I had no right to mind, that our marriage was a facade with nothing behind it.

'I prefer to ignore it, Geraldine. If the day comes when Liam asks me for his freedom then I shall be made to think about it.'

'He'll never do that, Mrs Clancy. He's like all men, 'e'll want the best o' both worlds.'

The best of both worlds. His beautiful, comfortable home, the exquisitely cooked meals which his daughter ate like a zombie, barely addressing a word to either of us, and his beautiful wife who accompanied him to functions where it was impossible to take his mistress. I was a fool if I didn't think people were gossiping in corners about us, and yet, deplorable as it was, I knew Liam would never ask me for a divorce any more than I would demand one from him.

It was the week before Easter and I went with Aunt Martha into Manchester. She liked to look at the shops but was reluctant to go alone, and she had asked for my help in choosing a new hat. I was back in the house by three o'clock and thinking about the evening meal when there was a ring at the front door. On opening it I was surprised to find two young policemen standing on the doorstep and a police car in the drive. Both of them looked at me solemnly and I was taken aback by the sympathy I read in their eyes.

'Mrs Clancy?' said the one nearest to me.

'Yes.'

'I'm afraid there's been an accident, Mrs Clancy. We have to ask you to come with us to the infirmary.'

'Is it my daughter?' I breathed.

'No Madam, it's your husband.'

'What has happened?'

453

'He's had an accident on a building site. Will you come with us now?'

'Of course, I'll get my coat.'

I felt sick with apprehension as we drove in silence through the busy streets, at first afraid to ask how badly Liam was injured. We had almost reached the infirmary gates when I found the courage to gasp, 'Is my husband badly hurt?'

'We're not sure, Mrs Clancy.'

'Where did it happen?'

'At the building site in Laburnum Grove. You knew he was working there, Mrs Clancy?'

'I'm never very sure where he's working, he moves around a great deal. When did it happen?'

'Around two o'clock. We arrived on the scene minutes later and saw him taken away in the ambulance.'

They accompanied me inside the infirmary and one of them stayed with me while the other went into an office where a nurse sat writing at a desk. For a few moments they spoke together, then she lifted the telephone and spoke into it for a few minutes. Again we waited, then the other door into her office opened and a man wearing a doctor's white coat entered. They spoke together, then the doctor followed by the policeman came to me.

He held out his hand and grasping mine, he said, 'I'm Doctor Rampling, Mrs Clancy. The officer has told you about your husband's accident?'

'Yes. Is my husband badly hurt?'

'I'm sorry, Mrs Clancy, we did all we could, but I have to tell you he died without regaining consciousness. I'm very sorry.'

I stared at him incredulously and one of the officers took my arm and assisted me to a chair. Then I found the nurse at my side with a cup of hot sweet tea.

I couldn't believe it. Only that morning I heard him on the telephone arranging to play golf the following weekend, calling to me as he left the house that he would be late home because of a council meeting. Now he was dead.

When they believed I was ready to face up to it they took

me to the mortuary to identify him, but the Liam I stared at, so white and clinically clean under the stark white sheet, seemed a stranger in my eyes. Then they took me home.

They were so kind, and I found myself feeling sorry for those two boys who would often in their lives have to break sad news to people after accidents of this kind. They asked if I felt able to be left alone, unsure even after I had nodded my head in affirmation, then after stoking up the drawing room fire they left me.

For what seemed hours I sat staring into space, then I went into the kitchen and started mechanically to prepare the evening meal. Once more the doorbell rang, and wiping my hands quickly on my apron I went to answer it. This time it was Uncle Joel, staring at me for confirmation, saying, 'It's in the evenin' paper, Katie. Is he bad?'

'He's dead, Uncle Joel. I'm sorry, I should have called.'

'Nay lass, yer've enough on yer plate wiout thinkin' about us. I don't suppose Marisa knows yet.'

I shook my head. 'Will you stay with me until she comes home? I don't know how I'm going to tell her.'

By this time he was taking off his coat, following me into the kitchen where I went about peeling the vegetables until he said, 'Yer've enough there ter feed a regiment, Katie.'

I stared down at them foolishly, and he came and put his arm around me.

'Leave 'em be, Katie. Come into the parlour, we'll think about food later.'

It seemed incredible that we should be discussing Liam's funeral, talking about flowers and headstones, but it calmed me, made me more ready to face Marisa. But one look at her red and swollen face told me she already knew. Through her tears she told us she had found out from a newspaper.

'Oh darling, what a terrible way to find out,' I murmured.

She glared at me balefully, but I was unprepared for the way she spun round, saying savagely, 'It's convenient for you, isn't it, mother? Now you can have Jeffrey to the house, you won't need to meet him on the moor.'

I stared at her in horror, while Uncle Joel looked from one to the other of us, doubtfully, unsure. Then anger superseded grief and I sprang to my feet and grasped her arm, holding her so tightly that although she struggled she couldn't free herself.

'How dare you speak to me like that, and at such a time? You are talking nonsense and well you know it. Now go to your room and stay there until you can speak to me properly.'

I let her go, and, sobbing with anger and sorrow, she fled upstairs.

Uncle Joel stared at me in amazement. 'Nay, Katie, what was that all about? The girl's upset, she didn't mean anything by it.'

'Oh, Uncle Joel, you don't know the half of it, and right now I can't tell you. There's been so much trouble lately, between Marisa and me, and it's all so cruel, so unnecessary. I don't know how I'm going to bear it now Liam's gone. He stood between us like a bulwark.'

'What does she mean about this Jeffrey comin' to the house?'

'I can't talk about it now, Uncle, she was being ridiculous. But it's something I can only talk about when all this is over.'

'I see.'

He didn't see, how could he? And looking into his puzzled face I took his hand gently, saying, 'Will you stay to eat with us, Uncle Joel?'

'Nay, I must get back now, Katie. Mary'll be anxious to know what's happened. Do you want mi to break the news to yer aunt and uncle?'

'Yes, please. I'll try to get in to see them tomorrow if there's time.'

'Yer uncle'll come up 'ere, lass. If I can be any help ye knows where to find mi. I can't think Liam's gone, but there's bin monny a time I've found 'im in a brown study these last few weeks. Ye can't afford to let yer mind wander when yer up on that scaffoldin', Katie, yer wants all yer wits about yer.'

456

Was there accusation in his voice? I didn't know. In some vague obscure way was he blaming me for Liam's pre-occupation? My quarrel with Marisa perhaps, or was he already mulling over her words about Jeffrey Carslake, looking for reasons and explanations as to why Liam, who had been as sure-footed as a chamois, should suddenly fall to his death?

There was so much to do in the days that followed. I attended the inquest with Uncle Joel, where a verdict of misadventure was brought in, and we went as a family to the requiem Mass that was held for him in the Catholic church. I was surprised to find the church crowded with people who had known and respected him.

On the day of the funeral a pale sun shone over those clustered in the little churchyard, and spring flowers bravely shivered in vases and urns all around us while crocuses thrust their pale yellow and purple heads through the lawns that circled the church.

It seemed to me that I walked like one in a dream as I followed Liam's coffin down the narrow paths towards the open grave, barely aware of Marisa's sobs beside me. I was thinking of Liam as I first remembered him, a tall gangling schoolboy finding all the puddles on his way to school, his satchel slung carelessly over his narrow bony shoulders, his blue eyes peering at me through straight blond hair which he was constantly brushing aside.

Liam striding along the quayside on that wet grey day in Belfast, sitting between his aunt and uncle on the train that was carrying us to Manchester, sulky, like a small boy, a little ashamed that he had left me behind to make my own way. Strangely I was remembering his thin bony wrists under the too-short sleeves, his hands red and chapped from the icy winds, and the too-short trousers that flapped around his thin legs as he strode out of the station yard.

It was those memories that brought the stinging tears into my eyes, sad unimportant things which made me wonder like a lost child if either of us could have lived our lives differently.

Across the open grave Geraldine stood weeping, the tears

457

falling down her face and splashing on to the single red rose she later flung into the open grave. Geraldine had loved Liam. The pity of it was that Liam had never really loved Geraldine and I was afraid to ask myself how much he had loved me.

Chapter 45

I never really knew how much Jeremy loved Liam. He received the news of his death stoically. His lips trembled with emotion but if there were tears they were never shed in my presence. He had all the self-control and maturity a public school gives to a boy and I was so inordinately proud of him.

Aunt Mary sat staring out of the window, watching Jeremy exercising his pony over low stone walls near the house.

'I 'ope yer'll be keepin' the yard on, like yer did durin' the last war, Katie. Yer've got a good 'ead on yer shoulders, yer can 'elp Geraldine in the office an' see that the orders come in. I wants to see the name o' Clancy continuin' in the buildin' trade, an' yer've got ter think o' the boy. It'll be a good business for 'im one day.'

'I'm selling the yard, Aunt Mary.'

'You're what? And what about that lad there? It was 'is father's wish ter keep it goin' for 'im, that was the only reason he didn't sell out when the war came.'

'Aunt Mary, I don't want Jeremy to be a builder, and what's more to the point he doesn't want it either.'

''As 'e said so?'

'Not in so many words, but I have read all the signs. He's interested in veterinary surgery. It's a very difficult subject, with a lot of hard work in front of him. He's young yet, but his school reports are brilliant. Liam saw that for himself. Jeremy's to be given his chance to do what he wants, I'm not going to push him into anything simply to carry on the name.'

''Ow much 'ave yer asked for the yard?'

'Eight thousand pounds.'

'It's worth twice as much.'

'It would be worth four times as much in peacetime, but not now with all the young men away and the orders not coming in because building on a large scale has had to stop. Liam was scraping the barrel, trying to get material to finish orders. He told me himself that after they were done what was left wās negligible.'

'The war won't go on for ever.'

'But there's no sign of it ending yet, Aunt Mary. The Germans have overrun most of Europe and we're sitting here, a beleaguered fortress. Night after night our cities and ports are being bombed and I think it's time we faced up to the fact that for the duration the builder's yard is sterile.'

'Yer didn't say that the last time. Yer fought tooth and nail to save it. Why can't yer do the same this time, if not fer yourself, for yer son?'

'I was young then, Aunt Mary, I had Maurice to help me, and it wasn't the yard that made money even then. Well, both Maurice and Liam have gone and I don't want to fight any more. I have all I will ever need in the way of money, Liam left me well provided for and I have the money I worked for. I know when to give up.'

'What will ye do wi' your eight thousand, then? Allus supposin' yer gets it.'

'I shall have to take less, that is only the asking price. But I shall see you and Uncle Joel right, and the rest is for Marisa.'

'Marisa! What about the boy?'

'He'll be taken care of, Aunt Mary, you needn't worry about Jeremy.'

'He's not a bit like Liam, Katie, I've allus said so, neither in looks nor disposition. Marisa's like 'er father.'

'Yes she is. I'll walk back to the cottage with you after we've had a cup of tea.'

'Aren't we waitin' fer Marisa, then?'

'She's out with friends this evening, I don't know what time she'll be home.'

'She's never once bin down ter see us since 'er father died. I feels a bit 'urt about that, Katie.'

460

'I'll tell her to call, Aunt Mary.'

'I'd rather yer didn't, not if she can't call of 'er own free will. Not when she finds time ter call at that 'ouse on Tremayne Hill.'

'My cousin's house?'

'Aye.'

She was watching me closely but, trying to keep the hurt out of my eyes, I led the way into the morning room saying, 'We'll have tea in here, it's cosier.'

'I suppose yer stayin' on in this 'ouse even though it is too big for yer now.'

'It's a house I love. I think Liam would want us to go on living here.'

' 'E built it fer you, Katie. 'E were like a dog wi' two tails when the farmer sold 'im this land, 'e couldn't wait to get back to tell ye.'

'I know.'

'Does Geraldine know yer aimin' ter sell the yard?'

'I shall tell her, but she'll not be wantin' to stay on now that Liam's gone. She'll want something nearer her home.'

'You knew about 'er an' Liam, didn't yer?'

'It was a long time ago, Aunt Mary?'

'Yer mean 'e stopped it?'

'I only know that they haven't been close for some time.'

'Yer mean 'e found somebody else?'

'I don't know. Why should he find anybody, a married man with a wife and children?'

She flushed and busied herself adding sugar to her tea. 'Well, one 'ears rumours, yer know, yer can't 'elp it when yer visits the shops, and Liam never knew 'ow to keep things to 'imself. I can't say I approved o' some of the women 'e mixed with, that publican's wife fer one.'

'Well, Liam's gone now, Aunt Mary. I think we should forget it.'

'P'raps if yer'd bin nicer to 'im, Katie. But yer 'ad that Maurice Abrahams an' yer changed. Yer climbed above 'im, Katie, an' I reckon 'e felt yer thought yerself too good fer 'im.'

I was standing at the window looking out over the

461

moorland above the house, and there were tears in my eyes when I thought about Maurice, his kindness, his patience and his loyalty. Maurice had understood my ambitions, my desperate desire to rise above my environment, to be somebody – but for all the wrong reasons. Liam had died a solid respected citizen, but he had never tried to be anything other than what he was, consequently he had never understood me. Perhaps Liam had been more honest, setting his sights on the readily attainable instead of crying for the moon.

I looked down at Aunt Mary who had come to stand beside me. She said shrewdly, 'I liked it better in the city, Katie. I'm not one fer moors an' tarns, I likes the shops and the markets. I'd go back tomorrer if Joel'd go.'

'Oh, Aunt Mary, why didn't you insist? Have you been very unhappy since you came to the cottage?

'No. I came to be near Liam, to be part o' your family. But someow it's not a family any more.'

She stared at me sorrowfully, and without hesitation I put my arms around her and held her plump body against mine.

After I dropped Aunt Mary at her cottage I drove into the town. I knew exactly where I was going, it was a decision I had reached while I had been talking to Liam's aunt. Yet as I neared the builder's yard I felt strangely nervous. It was the first time I had entered the yard since Liam's death, but it was deserted, all the men being out on some sort of work, and only the smoke from the office chimney gave some sign of life.

Geraldine looked up from her ledger, her face flushing when she recognized me.

'Why, Mrs Clancy, 'ow nice to see you,' she said a little hesitantly.

'Can we talk over a cup of tea, Geraldine?'

'Yes of course, I'll put the kettle on.'

She pulled up a chair for me, then poked the fire to revive the flames.

I looked round the tiny office. It was clean, the hearth contained a few ashes but the fireplace itself had been black leaded, and the cracked windows had been replaced. I could hear Geraldine bustling round the kitchen with cups and saucers, and in a few minutes she was back carrying a tray.

'The kettle'll soon boil,' she said brightly. ''Ave you bin shoppin' in the area, Mrs Clancy?'

'No, Geraldine, I came specially to see you.'

'To see me!'

'Yes. Do you intend staying on here?'

'No. I want to get back to workin' in Manchester. Most likely as not it'll be war work, in one o' the ministries that 'ave come up here. That's if I'm lucky enough to find something.'

'I'll give you a very good reference. You've worked hard for the yard.'

'Thank you, Mrs Clancy. I'll make the tea.'

She hurried away and when she returned I watched without speaking while she poured the tea.

I could tell she was nervous by the clattering of the cup in the saucer, and the trembling of her hands as she lifted it to her lips.

'I'm selling the yard, Geraldine. The tools, the timber, the goodwill, and I've had one or two tentative inquiries. Most of the workmen will be kept on, and I hope the men coming back from the war can look for their jobs back. I wasn't sure about you.'

'Oh no, Mrs Clancy, I want to get back to the city, but there's many a local girl'll be glad of a job 'ere.'

'I just wanted to be satisfied that you knew about my plans.'

'Isn't your son hopin' to be a builder one day, Mrs Clancy?'

'No, I'm sure he isn't.'

'Don't you think Liam would have been disappointed about that?'

'Possibly, but it has to be what Jeremy wants. Liam is dead, Geraldine.'

Tears filled her eyes and she dashed them away quickly with the back of her hand. 'Oh, I knows that all right, and please don't think I'm meddlin', but Liam used to say 'e was only keepin' goin' for young Jeremy.'

'I think Liam was beginning to see it wasn't what Jeremy wanted. I'd better get back Geraldine. I've left Jeremy out with his pony. He'll be hungry for his meal by the time I get home.'

She nodded, then hurried ahead of me to open the door. 'It was nice of you to call, Mrs Clancy. I'll let ye know when I find somethin' fresh.'

'I mean it about the reference, Geraldine. Please ask me, and please accept this with my gratitude for all you did for Liam and the yard.' I thrust an envelope into her hands, watching her astonishment.

'But what is it, Mrs. Clancy? I've been well paid for all I've done.'

'It's five hundred pounds, Geraldine. Save it or spend it, it's yours.'

'But Mrs Clancy, that's a lot o' money, I can't take all that.'

'Oh yes you can, Geraldine, I want you to have it. Liam would want you to have it.'

I smiled down at her standing doubtfully within the doorway, then giving her arm a little squeeze, I said, 'Let me know about your new job. I'll have a very good reference waiting for you.'

I was surprised to find Marisa sitting in the kitchen helping Jeremy with a jigsaw puzzle that occupied the entire kitchen table. Jeremy smiled, but she merely looked up with her habitual sulky expression.

'I thought you would be late home, Marisa. You said you were seeing your friends.'

'I know, I'm meeting them later.'

'Oh well, it's no trouble to make dinner for three instead of two.'

'I don't want a meal, I'm dining out. I thought you might want to hear my news, that's the reason I came home.'

I looked up brightly. 'Well of course I want to hear your

464

news. What is it darling?'

'I've joined the WAAF, Mother. I'll be going in about a fortnight.' She stared at me defiantly.

I sat down weakly. 'But Marisa, why?'

'I'm fed up with teaching art to kids who don't know a cow from a horse. I want to do something for the war and it seemed like a good idea.'

'But what will you do in the WAAF, what will they find for a girl whose learned fashion designing?'

'They'll think of something. I'm not stupid, I did well at school, and I'm not against learning a new trade.'

'When did you say you would have to go?'

'They said in about two weeks, it could be sooner.'

'I hope the war isn't over before I can join up,' Jeremy said seriously, 'but I shan't want to go into the air force.'

'Whyever not?' Marisa snapped. 'It's the most modern of the lot.'

'Because I'd rather join the army,' Jeremy said firmly, and in that moment I was looking at Nicholas, grey laughing eyes under an officer's peaked cap, a gentle smile around his firm lips.

The world was a savage alien place crashing around my shoulders, but I made myself act normally. Liam had gone, Marisa was going, thank God Jeremy needed me still.

Chapter 46

I was very lonely after Jeremy returned to school after the Easter holidays. I had thought Marisa and I might draw closer together now that she was joining the WAAF, but there seemed little prospect of it. She spent little time in the house now that the days were lengthening, and most evenings she went out armed with a tennis racket or I would hear a light pip from a car driven by some young man I had never met, then I would see her running towards it along the drive. There would be laughter and embraces before she got into the car and it sped off.

Conversation at the dining table was desultory and although she must have been aware that I was lonely, as soon as she had swallowed her food she would excuse herself saying she had letters to write, or something else to occupy her time.

I tried to behave normally, accepting her excuses without question, but one evening after she had appeared particularly morose I could not refrain from saying, 'Will you come with me to Aunt Mary's this evening Marisa? She is constantly complaining that she never sees you these days.'

'I'm sorry, I can't. I'm going back into town to a party.'

'You go to a great many parties, surely your friends won't mind you missing just one of them.'

'*I* would mind, Mother. This party is for one of the boys who is joining his ship tomorrow.

'I see. I'm glad you have a wide circle of friends, Marisa. They are so necessary at your age.'

Her eyes were hard as they looked into mine. 'I haven't found consolation, if that's what you mean. I'm simply on a merry-go-round that isn't going to stop until I do.'

'You are making me very unhappy, Marisa. What I did was for your good, one day I hope you'll see that for yourself.'

'You interfered because you loved him yourself. Daddy told me. He said you were in love with Jeffrey from the day you first saw him, that you were still in love with him when you married.'

'When did he say that?'

'One day when he found me crying in my room.'

I stared at her sorrowfully. It seemed at that moment Liam had reached out beyond the grave to hurt me afresh.

'But it wasn't your father who told you I had spoken to Jeffrey on the moor.'

For a moment her eyes grew sly, amused almost, then with a shrug she said, 'No, that was Frances. She thought I should know.'

'You prefer to believe her rather than me?'

'I only know we don't meet any more. He did what you wanted, Mother, he finished with me.'

'But not as unkindly as you are finishing with me. How long are you going to make me pay? How long are we to go on living together like polite strangers?'

'It can't be that long, I'll be leaving here in just over a week.'

After she had gone out I stood for a long time looking out through the kitchen window. It was a view that had always enchanted me, with the green meadow giving way to the rise of the moor. The evening sun was striking Melston Crag, turning it into a burnished spear, and cropping the short grass Maxton and Jeremy's pony looked the picture of equine contentment. Daffodils bloomed in the flower beds, and the lawns swept away towards the beeches that I had insisted we planted during the first year we occupied the house. They had grown well, but Liam had been no gardener and we had been fortunate in securing Ned, who tramped up from the town three mornings a week. It was from Ned that I heard news of Polly, whose husband was Ned's cousin, and of Cook's death at the end of January.

There had been a time when I had thought to invite Cook

to stay with us but Liam had been against it and I had offered no arguments. Cook was too shrewd, too intuitive, she would analyse us as competently as a vivisectionist might analyse a guinea pig, and Liam had said firmly, 'It's time you put the past away, Katie, instead of rakin' over old ashes.'

Liam had built the house with joy because he believed it would please me as nothing else did, and I had furnished it lovingly as a shrine to my ambition, as the ultimate declaration that I, Kathleen O'Donovan, had arrived. But now, standing alone in the kitchen that had everything, I was only aware of an acute loneliness. I longed to hear Liam's key in the door, Marisa and Jeremy laughing happily over some game or other, and yet that other part of me felt strangely free. Liam wasn't coming home to hide behind his newspaper, to watch me with narrowed distrustful eyes, and soon even Marisa would not be here to make my life miserable.

It was too soon to go to Aunt Mary's, otherwise I would have longer to sit listening to her complaints about Marisa and her reproaches that I took personally because Aunt Mary and Uncle Joel were still living in Marsdale.

I picked up a magazine and settled down in front of the fire, with Copper snoring gently at my feet. The ringing of the doorbell disturbed us, and Copper got to his feet, barking excitedly.

I cautioned him to be silent as I hurried to open the door, then my curiousity turned to amazement to see Jeffrey Carslake standing in the porch, smiling that familiar smile and with his hand outstretched in greeting.

I stepped back so that he could enter, and he said, 'I felt I ought to come, Katie, to tell you how very sorry I was to hear about the death of your husband.'

'Thank you, Jeffrey. Won't you come in?'

He followed me into the drawing room and looked round with kcen appreciation.

'What a charming room,' he said softly. 'It reminds me of Heatherlea.'

I stared at him, then round the room. Had I unconsciously emulated the drawing room at Heatherlea? I had not thought it. Surely this room had been a product of the beauty I had learned from Maurice as well as my own skill in selecting colours and design. I looked at him sharply, but he was staring at a photograph of Marisa and Jeremy taken five or six years previously.

'There is quite a difference in their ages,' he said.

'Yes. May I offer you a drink?'

'Thank you, Katie. A little whisky perhaps.'

I poured myself a small sherry as well, and sat opposite Jeffrey near the fire.

'Do you intend to stay on here, Katie? It's a fair-sized house.'

'I haven't made any plans. It is too soon. I love it here, we all do.'

'Of course. I loved Heatherlea and would have stayed on there for ever, but times change, families dwindle. One has to move with the times.'

'You have moved into your cottage?'

'Yes, several weeks ago. I get by. It isn't exactly what I've been used to but it's convenient and I've managed to find a daily woman who sees to the housework.'

'I'm glad.'

'Do you have servants, Katie?'

'I have a gardener and a daily woman, and a boy who sees to the horses. He wants to be a jockey, so I expect he'll leave us one of these days.'

'How is Marisa?'

'Very well. She's out at a party tonight.'

He smiled, somewhat cynically. 'I didn't think she would wear her heart on her sleeve for very long. The young are very resilient.'

I didn't answer him. I couldn't tell him that Marisa was making my life hell, so I said, 'She's decided to join the WAAF, and is expecting to go in a few days.'

'The glamour of a uniform.'

'Perhaps.'

At first our conversation was stilted and unreal, and then bit by bit my inhibitions faded and he was the old Jeffrey again, the Jeffrey who had talked to me up there on the hillside when I had hugged his confidences to myself as something special. Now once again I was listening to the low charm of his voice, but this time it was in my own drawing room, in the gathering dusk and with the play of firelight falling across the hearth.

He was talking to me of the old days and how much his world had changed. He spoke about his mother with deep affection and his father with hurt pride, and while he talked I was back at Heatherlea, standing with Mrs Tate at the sideboard, ready to pander to whatever whim and request one of them made. I was seeing Milly on that morning she left the house, tearful and miserable, sent away to have her baby in disgrace, and Jeffrey's two sisters, one of them marrying for money, the other for expediency, and Roger with his easy charm and devastating good looks eyeing me roguishly when he thought Mrs Tate was not looking.

Never in a thousand years had I thought to be entertaining Jeffrey in my own drawing room, while he filled my heart and my imagination with talk of a past when all the world was his for the asking and nothing was mine.

He seemed reluctant to leave, and at eleven o'clock I made coffee and sandwiches, watching him attack them appreciatively. I felt utterly helpless when Marisa came into the room. She looked at us with hot angry eyes before she slammed out.

We had both risen to our feet and, looking at me with concern, Jeffrey said, 'She seems very angry, Katie.'

'She is angry. She blames me for the ending of her friendship with you.'

'But that's ridiculous, Katie. I never mentioned your name, it wasn't necessary.'

'I know.'

'Then how can she possibly blame you?'

'She thinks I wanted you myself, that I set out to destroy things between you, and no amount of denial has convinced her otherwise.'

'Then perhaps I should try to convince her, Katie. I was truthful with Marisa, I told her she was too young and I

470

was too old to think about marriage. Perhaps I always was too old, I don't know, anyway none of it had anything to do with you.'

'The damage is done, Jeffrey. Let it alone.'

'But she's your daughter, Katie, you can't allow her to think wrongly of you.'

'Perhaps it would be best if you left now, Jeffrey. I don't really think it would help if you talked to Marisa, she's in no mood to listen to reason.'

He stared down at me anxiously. 'I'm sorry, my dear, I had no idea this would happen. I wish I'd never encouraged her friendship, and believe me that is all it was.'

'I know. Goodbye, Jeffrey.'

I waited until he drove away, then I went directly to Marisa's room. Her suitcase lay on the floor and she was flinging things into it.

For a few minutes I stood near the door watching, before I said, 'What are you doing, Marisa?'

'You can see what I'm doing, I'm leaving here.'

'Where are you going?'

'I don't know. Frances will have me, or the Palmerstons, until I get my papers. God, how I hate you. My father's hardly cold in his grave and Jeffrey's coming to the house. You don't care about either of us, me or Daddy.'

'I didn't ask him to come. He came to offer his condolences, that's all.'

'I don't believe you.'

'Oh Marisa, I'm tired of your tantrums and your insinuations. Believe what you like about Jeffrey Carslake and me but you are not leaving this house to stay with my cousin or with the Palmerstons. You will maintain some dignity instead of opening everybody's mouths about something that doesn't concern them, and you will stay here until you receive your calling up papers. You are my daughter and I love you, but if you hate me as you say you do then it's probably for the best that you are going out of my life. If ever you need me or forgive me I will make sure that you know where to find me. Now unpack that suitcase and for the time that is left to us try to behave in a civilized

471

manner.'

I was trembling when I left her, and for a long time I lay staring up into the darkness, wretched and despairing.

That was the last conversation I had with Marisa. Her papers came three days later and I drove her to the railway station. We did not embrace, we simply stood for several seconds staring at each other, then she picked up her suitcase and got into the train.

I stayed on the platform until it disappeared round the bend, then wearily I went back to the car and drove slowly through the town. I felt bereaved for the second time in weeks.

I had lost my husband and my daughter and I felt singularly alone.

Chapter 47

The days seemed so long in that house on my own. I sold the yard to a local builder for considerably less than I had asked for it, and I gave a sum of money to Uncle Joel and Aunt Mary which they were reluctant to take. I settled what was left on Marisa and, true to my promise, I gave Geraldine McClusky a glowing reference which enabled her to get a position nearer her home with the Air Ministry.

In the early summer Aunt Martha informed me that Frances's daughter had married a young army sergeant, much to her mother's disapproval.

'But why?' I asked.

'You knows our Fanny as well as I do. She was 'opin' for a brigadier at least.'

I laughed. 'Oh Aunt Martha, how do you know?'

'I hears the gossip in the shops and at the market. Nice enough lad they say 'e is, but 'e doesn't suit our Fanny.'

Listening to Aunt Martha's spiteful tirade I marvelled how love could change, how it could be killed, and I hoped I would never suffer such bitterness towards Marisa. I had had only one brief note from her to say she had settled in, and I answered this immediately, informing her how much I had received for the yard and how much I had invested on her behalf. To that letter she made no reply.

The war continued to rage night and day in the skies over our heads, and the papers were filled with tales of bravery and heroism. The Americans had now entered the war and we no longer stood alone, a fact that was heartening to even the most despairing.

It was one of summer's golden days. Three small planes droned overhead and on the hill flowers bloomed in the gardens and the sound of lawnmowers vied with the drone of the planes. It was hard to imagine that war raged around the world that people were dying, suffering invaders across their lands, existing in crumbling cities. Certainly not here on Evening Hill, where as always the birds sang and the air was fragrant with the scent of clover and new-mown grass.

The garden was at its best and I looked out of the window, appreciating the wide sweep of lawns and the tidiness of the drive and hedges. I could see Ned coming in through the gates, shutting them carefully before going to the greenhouse to collect his tools. When he saw me at the window he came over to chat, pushing his cap back from his forehead and scratching it lugubriously.

'Nice day, Mrs Clancy, nice day for air raids.'

'Oh Ned, just when I was thinking how peaceful it all is.'

'It's the lull before the storm, I reckon. Someat's afoot or mi names not Ned Robinson.'

'Well, there's nothing we can do about it, Ned, and it's far too nice to stay indoors.'

'Any news of the lassy, Mrs Clancy?'

'She's settled in, Ned.'

'That's good. It's a funny war we're in. When I were a lad it were the men as went to war. They should let the lassies come 'ome.'

I only smiled, and he walked away shaking his head.

I don't know why the idea suddenly occurred to me, possibly it was when I stood in the hall looking round me and thinking the house was like a museum and just as impersonal. I decided I would visit Tremayne House. It was a pleasant walk and I had not been there once since its completion. Now I felt a strong and urgent desire to go there to try to capture my memory of Nicholas in those gracious rooms. I walked quickly, hoping I would not meet any of my relatives on the hill, and for once I was lucky. As I approached Fanny's house I kept a wary eye open whilst thinking she was the occupant of quite a palatial pile. There was no symmetry about the house, and I deplored the mixing of Tudor and Georgian with a modern extension that owed allegiance to neither. I saw Fanny's husband leave the house and get into a large car. He was a small, portly man, almost dapper. Although I had seen him at several functions in the city, we had never addressed a word to one another.

Soon I was walking through the open gates into the ordered gardens of Tremayne House. Several elderly gardeners were busy weeding the flower beds and mowing the lawns, but they betrayed no interest in me as I walked up to the entrance.

It was quiet in the hall and my footsteps echoed hollowly across the polished floor. Nostalgia swept over me as I thought of that glittering occasion years before when I had served drinks to Sir Joshua's guests. I decided to go into the drawing room which overlooked the formal Italian Garden.

At first I thought the room was deserted until I saw two men looking at a painting that covered most of one wall. They both looked round as I entered the room, then one of them came forward with his hand outstretched.

I recognized him immediately as Councillor Tennant, the chairman of the Library Committee, but I did not know his companion.

'Why Kathleen,' he enthused, 'this is a pleasant surprise. Come to take a look at your handiwork, then?'

'Yes, I thought it was time I came.'

'It's a credit to you. Didn't know you had it in you even when Liam insisted nobody could do it better. This is Mr Byrom, the curator of the museum.'

'It is very quiet, Mr Byrom. Do you find it awfully boring?'

'Not really, Mrs Clancy, I have some cataloguing to do and it gets fairly busy at the weekends. In time we hope to hold piano recitals and musical evenings here but they will have to wait until after the war.'

'Will they be a success do you think?'

'We have to hope so.'

I wasn't sure. None of us had any means of knowing what sort of a world we would find ourselves in after the war, and it might be that the young people coming back to us would ask for something other than musical evenings in stately homes.

'Are you gettin' over Liam's death a bit now, Kathleen?' Councillor Tennant asked. 'I couldn't believe it when I heard. I'd always thought Liam knew what he was doin' up on them buildin' sites, sure-footed as a mountain goat he'd seemed to me. There must 'a' bin somethin' on his mind to make him make a mistake like that.'

When I didn't speak he went on, 'Do ye know, Kathleen, he wouldn't come up here to look at it, not even when he'd bin goin' on for months about you bein' given the chance to sort it all out. He was proud of you, Kathleen, but he was resentful too. I wonder why?'

'That was Liam, Councillor Tennant. He always said he liked things plain and decent and functional. He hated sauces served with food and he hated decorative things, polishes and veneers, gold leaf and lacquer. I too was surprised when he persisted in recommending me for the work here.'

'Well whether or not he liked things plain, Kathleen, it didn't extend to you. I've allus said you were the prettiest woman in Marsdale. Liam didn't know how lucky he was.'

I turned to Mr Byrom in the hope that the councillor would stop talking about Liam. 'Would you hold the concerts in here, Mr Byrom, or in the ballroom?'

'Piano recitals in here, we thought, more ambitious things in the ballroom.'

'What do you think about throwin' the ballroom open for functions like the Hunt Ball and the Police Ball, Kathleen?' the councillor asked.

'I think it would be a mistake. Most of the house is accessible from the ballroom and there could be irreparable damage done if enthusiastic party-goers having too good a time got into those rooms.'

'I agree, Mrs Clancy,' Mr Byrom said, 'those are my sentiments entirely. I have been telling the councillor so and there are other civic halls available in the town for such functions.'

'Aye well, we'll have to think about it,' the councillor said. 'It was an idea to raise a bit o' money, Kathleen, we can allus use that. I was 'opin Colonel Yale would come up to take a look at at the house now that it's looking so nice.'

My heart skipped a beat but I only looked at him inquiringly.

'I managed to speak to him on the telephone last night, but he told me he wouldn't be in London after the twenty-ninth, so there's no hope of him coming north in the near future.'

'But that's tomorrow!' I cried.

'Aye, so it is. I got 'im at the War Office but now 'e's movin' out. It looks as if somethin's movin' at last. Someat's up, all them heavy army vehicles blockin' the roads and the railways crowded. This quiet's gettin' on mi nerves, it isn't natural i' wartime.'

'The lull before the storm,' Mr Byrom volunteered, and I shivered in spite of the warmth of the room and the golden sunlight falling over the richness of velvet and brocade.

'Aye, I'd like to 'ave asked 'im what was on, but I knew he wouldn't 'ave answered that one. I reckon we all know when to keep quiet these days.'

'I'll take a look around the house now,' I said, holding out my hand to each of them in turn, and as a parting gesture the councillor said cheerfully. 'You must call in to see us one of these days, Kathleen. I'll tell Emily to get in touch, perhaps we can make it lunch or a meal in the evening.'

'Thank you, that would be very nice.'

For half an hour I wandered round the house without seeing any of it. I was thinking about Nicholas. For months I had steeled myself not to think of him, even when Liam died, and now memories of him filled my entire being to the exclusion of everything else.

Neither of us had made any attempt to get in touch, it had seemed there would be little point. Now I knew he was in London. At that moment an idea formed and grew, so that by the time I reached home, having run most of the way, it became a certainty.

I would go to London, I would see him once more even if I never saw him again.

Recklessly I changed into something suitable for travel-

ling, asked Ned if he would take Copper for the night, and
before nine o'clock was sitting in the local train heading for
Manchester and the midnight train to London. The
platform was crowded with service men and women but I
had no luggage, and doing my share of pushing and shoving
I was lucky enough to find a seat. The carriage and
compartments were full and I must have seemed incongruous sitting there in my corner seat, wearing a neat grey
flannel suit like a woman visiting the city for a day's
shopping.

There was little conversation. The men seemed weary
and, after a while, the sound of the train speeding through
the night lulled most of them to sleep. Two boys played
cards on top of an upturned grip, and my shoulder
experienced a dull ache as the head of the man sitting next
to me leaned heavily against it. The boy sitting opposite
said, 'Give 'im a shove, luv. Don't let 'im go ter sleep on ye.'

'It's all right, he isn't bothering me.'

Ignoring my remark, however, he leaned across and
pushed the soldier away. When he opened his eyes
grumpily the boy smiled, saying, 'Don't lean on the lady,
Mac, give 'er room ter breathe.'

He smiled at my murmured thanks, then he whispered,
'I can't sleep on trains, never could even though I'm dog
tired. We got no sleep last night.'

'Oh, I'm sorry.'

He grinned. 'I'm gettin' used to it after eighteen months
in the army.'

He was a nice-looking boy with an infectious smile.
Conversation was difficult without appearing curious, and
there were 'Careless Talk' slogans all around us. I ventured
to ask if he was going home on leave, however.

'Wish I was, luv.'

He would have liked to talk to me but the same constraint
held him back and I said, 'Perhaps if you lean back and
close your eyes you might be able to sleep a little.'

'Not a chance, luv. What takes you to London, Ma'am,
are ye sayin' goodbye to somebody?'

'I'm not sure.'

478

'Like as not we'll be arrivin' to the sound of the all clear. Do ye 'ave somebody in the war, Ma'am?'

I nodded, and with a little laugh he pointed to the notice above his head, 'Careless talk costs lives'.

'Yer don't look much like a Nazi spy to me,' he said, 'but we 'ad a talk from the sergeant afore we left Scotland warnin' us not ter get too friendly wi' folks on the train.'

I smiled. 'He's probably right. Spies don't go around advertising their vocation. Is your home in Lancashire?'

'Yorkshire, t'other side o' the Pennines. Ye got the train i' Manchester but I don't think yer comes fro' round there.'

'No, but I've lived in Lancashire for a long long time. I'm Irish, from Donegal.'

'That's Southern Ireland isn't it?'

'Yes, over on the west coast.'

'I reckon ye wished yer'd stayed there. Ireland's not at war wi' Germany.'

'No, not Southern Ireland anyway.'

'Why did ye leave it?'

'I came over here to live with relatives after my father died. I went back just once for my grandmother's funeral but I don't think I shall ever go back again.'

'I didn't think the Irish liked us much.'

'A great many of them don't. I've lived in this country a long time. My children were born here so I've come to think of myself as English.'

He grinned. 'All the same, Ma'am, I doubt if the sergeant'd approve of mi talking to ye, ye bein' Irish like.'

'The Northern Irish are at war.'

'That's so, but you're fro' the south, aren't ye?'

I laughed at his insistence. 'I can see you are determined to make me out to be some sort of Mata Hari.'

We chatted most of the way. I told him about my children and about Liam's untimely death, but when he asked what took me to London I shied away from the truth. Nevertheless the journey passed far quicker than I had believed it would and the train steamed into Euston Station in the light of a chill grey dawn.

I shook hands with my travelling companion and wished

him well. All along the platform men were climbing down from their compartments watched by their officers and sergeants, and the morning was filled with shouted commands. Unhampered by luggage I hurried to the barrier but before I reached it, from behind me came the sound of marching feet.

I waited in the vast hall until they came into view, marching steadily in columns of four, looking neither to right nor left, their heads held high, their shoulders erect, betraying no sign of the weariness that had been so evident on the train journey.

I stood until the sound of their footsteps died away outside the confines of the station, then ignoring the lump in my throat and the dull ache in my heart I went out into the empty street.

A policeman stopped me as I crossed the road, saying, 'The all clear hasn't gone yet, lady. Why have you left the shelter?'

'I haven't been in the shelter, I have just got off the Manchester train.'

'I'd advise you to get off the streets till the siren goes, Ma'am.'

Just at that moment we heard it, mournful and eerie, and as if by magic people were coming out on to the street – grey faces, sad weary people carrying their bedding and baskets. Then, incongruously, there was laughter and good humour, relief too that they had survived another night, another air raid. At that moment I had the strangest feeling that I was looking at a people who were indestructible.

The policeman was kind, directing me to a hotel restaurant where I would be able to get breakfast and freshen up. I was too excited for food but I made myself eat, telling myself that the mere act of eating and drinking would calm me. Any normality in an abnormal world was something to be savoured.

It was over an hour later when I stood outside Nicholas's London home looking up at the long net curtains, wondering if he was asleep or if somewhere in that impersonal house he was preparing to leave. With a thumping heart I lifted the heavy brass knocker and brought it down with a sound that seemed to reverberate throughout the house. I waited expectantly before I lifted it again, then I realized with helpless despair that the house was empty. Nicholas had left.

A milkman clattered his way along the crescent, leaving bottles at every door, but when he reached the iron railings in front of the house where I was standing he passed on, giving me a curious look. Desperation made me run after and question him, but he shook his head. 'I've to leave no milk from now on, lady.'

'When was the last time you left some?'

'Yesterday mornin', an' they've forgotten to put the empty bottles out.'

'They?'

'Yes, lady, the colonel and his batman.'

'I see.'

He looked at me sympathetically. 'Expectin' to catch him before he left, were you?'

'Yes.'

'I'm sorry, love, I don't know when he's coming back.'

He moved away while I looked back at the empty house, which stared back at me, closed and impersonal.

Tears rolled unchecked down my face and I moved on across the square as if in a dream. London was coming to life and I felt that people were staring at me, but it wasn't unusual to see a woman in tears in the aftermath of an air raid.

I have no idea where I intended to walk, somewhere I think in the direction of the park where I could give way to the grief that consumed me. On the way I was jostled and pushed, but oblivious I crossed the roads when the crowd crossed and waited when they waited, until that moment when, oblivious to anything and anybody around me, I stepped out to the sound of shouting voices and the squealing of brakes. Hands pulled me back roughly, I felt my skirt brushed by something heavy, and my handbag was sent clattering to the ground.

I stared in amazement at the red-faced man sitting

glaring at me from the driver's seat of the taxi, but his face was frightened.

'Blimey, lady, if yer must commit suicide don't let it be my cab you chooses.'

At that moment I came to my senses, staring at the crowd that had gathered around me anxiously, and then miraculously I found my eyes staring up into Nicholas's horrified eyes before he took my arm in a firm grip and steered me away. Neither of us spoke until we reached the corner of the street, then he snapped, 'Why do I always find you under somebody's wheels, Katie? What are you doing in London?'

I felt hurt, angry and incredibly stupid and then I saw his mouth twitch at the corner and he was laughing, and in my relief I was laughing too until he put his arms around me and held me close.

'Katie, you haven't answered my question. What are you doing here?'

'I came to see you. Councillor Tennant said you were leaving London, I had to see you.'

'There's not much time, Katie. I'm going back to the house to pick up my things. We'll have to hurry, thanks to you I let the taxi I struggled for go.'

I had to run to keep up with his long strides. Immediately we entered the house I could see his grip and trench coat waiting at the bottom of the stairs. I stared at them helplessly. 'You're going away now?' I asked, stunned.

'Yes, Katie, this very minute. This is all I've come back for.'

I stared at him helplessly, and his face softened and grew tender.

'In spite of you being here, Katie, in spite of the fact that I very desperately want to make love to you, I have to go. Come with me to the station if you like.'

'If I like! Oh Nicholas, there's so much to talk about, and I've come such a long way.'

'I know, darling, and we don't have much time. I have to get to Victoria Katie. We'll have a little time there, enough to get a cup of tea perhaps in some little café where we can

482

talk.'

He snatched up his gear, then opening the door he stood back to allow me to pass out into the street with my head spinning in confusion. He hailed several taxis before one stopped for us, then we were driving across London in silence, but my hand was held securely in his and now and again he looked at me and smiled.

The streets around Victoria were filled with troops, but taking my elbow in his hand he steered me across the street towards a café, saying, 'If we're lucky we might get a cup of tea, here, Katie. It's early, there should be room for us.'

We found a table towards the back and sat facing each other, suddenly grave.

'Have you eaten breakfast?' he asked solicitously.

'Yes.'

'Tea then, Katie, or coffee if you prefer it?'

'Tea, coffee, anything. Oh, I was so hoping we would have a little time together. I had to come, Nicholas. You don't mind?'

'Mind! I'm only sorry we shan't have longer together. What did you tell them at home? How did you manage to get away at all?'

'I'm on my own now, Nicholas. Marisa is in the WAAF, Jeremy is away at school and Liam is dead.'

He stared at me. 'Dead! But how?'

I told him briefly, I didn't want to spend the little time we had in talking about anything beyond ourselves. Covering my hands with his across the table, he said, 'Poor Katie, it's been terrible for you, hasn't it? Tell me about Jeremy, how is he?'

'He's fine, Nicholas, doing well at school, and he's so like you, getting more like you all the time.'

'How did he get on with Liam?'

'Well enough, but Jeremy will never be a builder, Nicholas.'

He smiled. 'And Marisa?'

'Please, Nicholas, I don't want to talk about Marisa or anybody else right now. I don't want to talk about anything except why you are leaving London.'

'I'm leaving for my own peace of mind, Katie. I'm moving out with my regiment, it's as simple as that.'

'But Nicholas, why? You're not a boy any more and you did your share of fighting in the last war. Surely there are enough young men without you having to go.'

At that moment the waitress came to the table and Nicholas gave her our order and we sat in silence while she clattered cups and saucers. From the back of the café a gramophone was playing Glen Miller's 'This is the Story of a Starry Night', and emotion caught at my heart so that I looked away quickly before he saw the treacherous tears in my eyes. When the waitress moved away he said, 'I'm not even sure that I can adequately explain my actions to you, Katie. You would have to be one of us. Call it patriotism if you like but, when you see all those boys waiting at the station who have come from the other side of the world, you might begin to understand, I don't know.'

I was so sure I would not understand. He was my love and I was losing him. At that moment I hated England, I hated the war and all the silly flag-waving and noble sacrifice. I had thought Nicholas was like me, not even English, so why should he be expected to die for a country that wasn't even his? He knew what was passing through my mind, and I watched helplessly as he poured the weak tea.

From time to time he consulted his watch and as soon as we had drunk just one cup of tea he got to his feet and retrieved his trench coat from the stand near the door, then he came back to the table.

'It's time to go, Katie.' he said gently.

Together we walked to the door. The sun had warmed the busy streets and we walked in silence, his arm under my elbow, until we entered the vast hall of the station which was crowded with soldiers, sailors and airmen. Nicholas steered me to where a crowd of soldiers waited near the barrier and I noticed dully that each of them wore across the top of his sleeve the Canadian badge.

He pulled me round to face him, and looking down at me earnestly he said, 'Take a good look at them, Katie. This is for most of them their first view of England. They were born and bred in Canada, they know nothing of English country lanes, soft summer twilights and church spires across the hedgerows. They call this the motherland, but for most of them it was only a dream, something intangible until that September morning when it became a terrifying reality.'

I stared round at them, tall young Gods in khaki uniforms, their faces filled with excitement, imbued with a strange gaiety, speaking with that same low fascinating drawl which had set Nicholas apart from the Englishmen I had met in the Carslake house. Now that same voice was strangely compelling even though he spoke in little more than a whisper.

'They've come from the Pacific coast and the Rockies, the wheatfields of Alberta and the vast unnamed lakes of Ontario, Katie, from great unexplored forests and the silences of the Canadian wilderness, and they've come in answer to a call from this little island they've only heard of in song and story. Some of them were trappers, lumbermen, fishermen from New Brunswick and Newfoundland, sailors on the great St Lawrence river, but not many of them are like me. I went to school in this country. I knew what my parents were talking about when they spoke of home. We had roots here Katie, roots that went deep.'

I stared at him entranced, loving him as I had never in my life loved another human being, and I began to realize for the first time a little of what patriotism was about.

It was not the loud-mouthed boastfulness of Liam's father, brawling in the taverns on a Saturday night, singing the vaunting songs of sedition, or the deep abiding wrath of my grandmother against England, the redcoat bully, the ancient foe, nor the ranting of priests in their pulpits calling for retribution when they should have been asking for forgiveness. It was not the cruel bitterness that nurtured small children so that it grew and festered with the years, it was this need to serve, to stand shoulder to shoulder with the sons and grandsons of the men this tiny island had sent out generations before in search of new utopias.

Perhaps he saw it in my face, that new understanding,

but as the crowd started to move towards the barriers he stood looking down at me with his hands on my shoulders, saying, 'I can't make any promises Katie, it isn't the time for them. I'll love you as long as I live but there's no saying how long that's going to be. If I come through this make sure I'll find you wherever you are, but if you never see me again you'll know it's because I didn't make it.'

For one breathless moment we clung together then he was walking away from me as I had watched him walk away from me years before.

It was over, my dream of love. I caught the midnight train home and sat staring out of the window as it sped through the night, at a dark landscape unlit by street lamps and with only a young crescent moon floating serene and omnipotent above the countryside.

It was midday when I unlocked the front door and wearily I went into the kitchen to make a cup of tea. Without Copper's cheerful greeting the house was as remote and empty as my heart, and the early promise of sunshine had gone, with dark clouds gathering across the fell.

I made myself a hot drink and sat down in the kitchen to drink it, watching the beech leaves tossing in the wind, hearing the sudden pattering of rain against the window panes.

The house stared back at me, impersonal as any museum. There was little to do except sew or read, and I could find no peace of mind in either. Ignoring the rain I snatched a coat and headscarf from the hall cloakroom and went out into the garden and that gentle summer rain peculiar to England. Disregarding it, I climbed the fence beyond the house and walked across the moor until I reached the summit where I could stand looking down upon the town. Smoke drifted up from a dozen mill chimneys, adding to the grey misery of the afternoon. Then, miraculously, as the sun's rays slanted through the clouds above the crags, I saw the rainbow, a perfect thing, its colours shimmering against the dark sky, and a sudden blinding hope filled my heart.

I sat on a low wall of Pennine stone and at that moment I was a child again watching the seabirds wheeling over the wild Donegal coast, listening to my father's soft Irish lilt saying, 'Don't you be cryin' for rainbows, Katie, there'll be another tomorrow, if not here somewhere else. Sure and there's always a rainbow if you knows where to look for it.'

I had looked many times for a rainbow but until this moment I had never been as certain that a rainbow promised hope. As its glorious colours glowed, I sat and watched it with the rain on my face and the wind in my hair.

Slowly it began to fade but I waited until the last faint colour had left the sky, then I turned and walked back across the moor.

By the time I let myself into the house the feeling of euphoria was diminishing, and I was dreading the long night ahead in the lonely house. As I turned to close the front door my eyes lit up to see Ned trudging up the drive, and then Copper was leaping at me with joyful ecstatic sounds in his throat, followed by cheerful barks.

'I thowt yer'd like ter 'ave 'im back, Mrs Clancy. No doubt the house seems a bit empty with the lassy gone and you 'ere on yer own.'

'Yes it does. Thanks, Ned. I hope he hasn't been any trouble.'

'No. Any time yer wants ter go away I'll be glad to 'ave 'im.'

I watched him leave, then closed the door and went into the hall to remove my damp coat. I took Copper into the kitchen to feed him, then from the morning room I heard the insistent ringing of the telephone. I flew to answer, thinking it might be Nicholas ringing from anywhere, but it was Marisa's voice that came to me, a small plaintive voice saying 'Mother, is that you? You're so faint I can hardly hear you.'

'Marisa darling, where are you?'

'I'm at the camp, Mother, I've got a weekend's leave coming up. Can I come home?'

'Well of course you can. Tell me what time and I'll meet the train.'

'I'm getting a lift, Mother, some boy I've met. He's awfully nice, you'll like him I know.'

'Do you want him to stay here?'

'Would you mind?'

'Darling of course not. I'm so glad you're coming home. Are we going to be good friends again just like we always were?'

'Oh yes Mother, I've been pretty horrible, haven't I?'

'We won't talk about it any more. What time will you be home, for lunch or the evening meal?'

Her laughter floated over the telephone. 'Oh Mother, even when you quarrelled with Daddy you were always so concerned about his meals. We'll be there for lunch. I love you Mother.'

As I replaced the receiver my heart lifted and a new confidence brought a song to my lips as I returned to the kitchen. Marisa was coming home and Jeffrey would no longer stand like a dark shadow between us. It was finally over, that long weary enchantment fate had asked me to bear. Somewhere there would be another rainbow with its promise of happiness.